"Tongues are wagg

"Gossip central," he agreed.

"And speaking of wagging tongues," she said, "imagine what people will assume if you come and live in the guesthouse. They'll think we're a couple. I'm not comfortable with that."

"I understand." He looked down at his hands, traced a scar that peeked out from his shirt cuff. "I'm not exactly a blue-ribbon bronco."

"Vito!" She sounded exasperated. "You haven't changed a bit since you had to try on six different shirts for the homecoming dance."

"That was a long time ago. And the truth is, I have changed."

She rolled her eyes. "You're still good-looking, okay? Women don't mind scars." Then she pressed her lips together as her cheeks grew pink.

His heart rate accelerated just a little. Why was she blushing? Did she think he was good-looking?

But of course, she hadn't seen the worst of his scars.

And even if there was a little spark between them, it couldn't go anywhere. Because he was living with a secret he couldn't let her discover.

A HERO'S PROMISE

NEW YORK TIMES **BESTSELLING AUTHOR**

LEE TOBIN McCLAIN

&

USA TODAY **BESTSELLING AUTHOR**

KATHRYN SPRINGER

2 Uplifting Stories

The Soldier's Secret Child and *The Soldier's Newfound Family*

Special thanks and acknowledgment are given to Kathryn Springer for her contribution to the Texas Twins miniseries.

Recycling programs for this product may not exist in your area.

ISBN-13: 978-1-335-43056-4

A Hero's Promise

For questions and comments about the quality of this book, please contact us at CustomerService@Harlequin.com.

Love Inspired
22 Adelaide St. West, 41st Floor
Toronto, Ontario M5H 4E3, Canada
www.LoveInspired.com

Printed in U.S.A.

CONTENTS

Lee Tobin McClain is the *New York Times* bestselling author of emotional small-town romances featuring flawed characters who find healing through friendship, faith and family. Lee grew up in Ohio and now lives in Western Pennsylvania, where she enjoys hiking with her goofy goldendoodle, visiting writer friends and admiring her daughter's mastery of the latest TikTok dances. Learn more about her books at leetobinmcclain.com.

Books by Lee Tobin McClain

Love Inspired

K-9 Companions

Her Easter Prayer

Rescue Haven

The Secret Christmas Child
Child on His Doorstep
Finding a Christmas Home

Redemption Ranch

The Soldier's Redemption
The Twins' Family Christmas
The Nanny's Secret Baby

Rescue River

Engaged to the Single Mom
His Secret Child
Small-Town Nanny
The Soldier and the Single Mom
The Soldier's Secret Child
A Family for Easter

Visit the Author Profile page at LoveInspired.com for more titles.

THE SOLDIER'S SECRET CHILD

Lee Tobin McClain

I will give you a new heart and put a new spirit in you;
I will remove from you your heart of stone
and give you a heart of flesh.

—*Ezekiel* 36:26

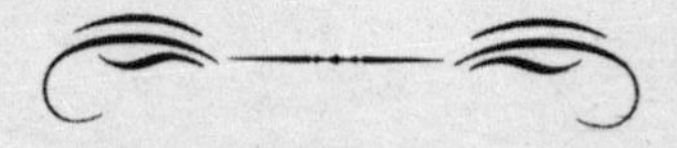

To my daughter, Grace, who shows me every day that families aren't about bloodlines; they're about heart.

Chapter One

Lacey McPherson leaned back, propped her hands on the low white picket fence and surveyed the wedding reception before her with satisfaction. She'd pulled it off.

She'd given her beloved brother and his bride a wedding reception to remember, not letting her own antiromance attitude show. But she had to admit she'd be glad when her half-remodeled guesthouse stopped being a nest for lovebirds.

"Nothing like a spring wedding, eh, Lacey?"

She jumped, startled at the sound of the gruff, familiar voice right behind her. She spun around. "Vito D'Angelo, you scared me!" And then her eyes widened and she gasped. "What happened?"

His warm brown eyes took her back to her teen years. She'd been such a dreamer then, not good at navigating high school drama, and her brother's friend had stepped in more than once to defend her from girls who wanted to gossip or boys who tried to take advantage. She and her brother had welcomed invitations to the D'Angelo family's big, loud Italian dinners.

But now the most noticeable thing about his face wasn't his eyes, but the double scar that ran from his forehead to his jawline. A smaller scar slashed from his lower lip to his chin.

Instinctively she reached out toward his face.

He caught her hand, held it. "I know. I look bad. But you should see the other guy."

His attempt at a joke made her hurt more than it made her laugh. "You don't look bad. It's just…wow, they barely missed your eye." Awkwardly, she tried to hug him with the fence in between.

He broke away and came inside through the open gate. "How're you doing, Lace? At least *you're* still gorgeous, huh? But you're too thin."

"You sound just like your grandma. And you're late for the wedding." Her heart was still racing from the surprise, both of seeing him and of how he looked.

She wanted to find out what had happened. But this wasn't the time or the place.

"Buck won't mind my being late. He looks busy." Vito looked past the wedding guests toward Lacey's brother, laughing and talking in the summer sun, his arm slung around his new bride. "Looks happy, too. Glad he found someone."

A slightly wistful quality in Vito's words made Lacey study her old friend. She hadn't seen him in almost ten years, not since he'd brought his army buddy home on a furlough and Lacey had fallen hard for the handsome stranger who'd quickly become her husband. Back then, after one very stormy conversation, Vito had faded into the background. He'd been in the firestorm that had killed Gerry, had tried to save him and had written to Lacey after Gerry's death. But he'd continued on with another Iraq tour and then another. She'd heard he'd been injured, had undergone a lot of surgery and rehab.

Looking at him now, she saw that he'd filled out from slim to brawny, and his hair curled over his ears, odd for a career military man. "How long are you home?"

"For good. I'm out of the army."

"Out?" She stared. "Why? That was all you ever wanted to do!" She paused. "Just like Gerry."

"I felt awful I didn't make his funeral." He put an arm around her shoulders and tugged her to his side. "Aw, Lace, I'm sorry about all of it."

Her throat tightened and she nodded. Gerry had been dead for a year and a half, but the loss still ached.

A shout went up from the crowd and something came hurtling toward her. Instinctively she put her hands up, but Vito stepped in front of her, catching the missile.

Immediately, he turned and handed it to her.

A bouquet of flowers? Why would someone…

Oh. *The* bouquet. Gina's.

She looked across the crowd at her friend, glowing in her pearl-colored gown. Gina kept encouraging Lacey to date again. Happily in love, she wanted everyone to share in the same kind of joy.

The crowd's noise had quieted, and some of the guests frowned and murmured. Probably because Gina had obviously targeted Lacey, who'd been widowed less than two years ago. One of the older guests shook her head. "Completely inappropriate," she said, loud enough for most of those nearby to hear.

Well, that wouldn't do. Gina was a Californian, relatively new to Ohio and still finding her way through the unspoken rules and rituals of the Midwest. She hadn't meant to do anything wrong.

Lacey forced a laugh and shook the bouquet threateningly at Gina. "You're not going to get away with this, you know," she said, keeping her tone light. "I'm passing it on to…" She looked around. "To my friend Daisy."

"Too late." Daisy waved a finger in front of her face and backed away. "You caught it."

"Actually, Vito caught it," old Gramps Camden said. "Not sure what happens when a man catches the bouquet."

As the crowd went back to general talk, Lacey tried to hand off the bouquet to all the females near her, but they all laughingly refused.

Curious about Vito's reaction, she turned to joke with him, but he was gone.

Later, after Gina and Buck had run out to Buck's shaving-cream-decorated truck, heads down against a hail of birdseed, Lacey gave cleanup instructions to the two high school girls who were helping her with the reception. Then, after making sure that the remaining guests were well fed and happy, she went into the guesthouse. She needed to check on Nonna D'Angelo.

Having Nonna stay here was working out great. The light nursing care she needed was right up Lacey's alley, and she enjoyed the older woman's company. And the extra bit of income Nonna insisted on paying had enabled Lacey to quit her job at the regional hospital. Now that the wedding was over, she could dive into the final stages of readying the guesthouse for its fall opening.

Nonna D'Angelo had mingled during the early part of the reception, but she'd gone inside to rest more than an hour ago. Now Lacey heard the older woman crying and hastened her step, but then a reassuring male voice rumbled and the crying stopped.

Vito.

Of course, he'd come in to see his grandma first thing. He hadn't been home in over a year, and they'd always been close.

She'd just take a quick peek to make sure Nonna wasn't getting overexcited, and then leave them to their reunion.

Slowly, she strolled down the hall to the room she'd made up for Nonna D, keeping her ears open, giving them time. She surveyed the glossy wood floors with satisfaction. The place was coming along. She'd redo this wallpaper sometime, but the faded roses weren't half-bad for now. Gave the place its historical character.

She ran her hand along the long, thin table she'd just bought for the entryway, straightened her favorite, goofy ceramic rooster and a vase of flowers. Mr. Whiskers jumped up onto the table, and Lacey stopped to rub his face and ears, evoking a purr. "Where's the Missus, huh?" she cooed quietly. "Is she hiding?"

Hearing another weepy sniffle from Nonna D, Lacey quickened her step and stopped in the doorway of Nonna's room.

"My beautiful boy," Nonna was saying with a catch in her voice. "You were always the good-looking one."

Vito sat on the edge of the bed, looking distinctly

uncomfortable as Nonna sat up in bed to inspect his cheek and brush his hair back behind his ears.

She felt a quick defensiveness on Vito's behalf. Sure, the scars were noticeable. But to Lacey, they added to his rugged appeal.

Nonna saw her and her weathered face broke into a smile, her eyes sparkling behind large glasses. "There's my sweet girl. Come in and see my boy Vito."

"We talked already, Nonna." Vito was rubbing the back of his neck. "Lacey, I didn't realize you were taking care of my grandma to this extent. I'll take her home tomorrow."

"Oh, no!" Lacey said. "I'm so happy to do it!"

"I can't go home!" Nonna said at the same time.

"Why not?" Vito looked from Nonna to Lacey and back again.

"I need my nursing help," Nonna explained. "Lacey, here, is a wonderful nurse. She's practically saved my life!"

Lacey's cheeks burned. "I'm really a Certified Nursing Assistant, not a nurse," she explained. "And I haven't done anything special, just helped with medications and such." In truth, she knew she'd helped Nonna D'Angelo with the mental side as well as the physical, calming her anxiety and making sure she ate well, arranging some outings and visits so the woman didn't sink into the depression so common among people with her health issues.

"Medications? What's wrong?"

"It's my heart," Nonna started to explain.

Vito had the nerve to chuckle. "Oh, now, Nonna. You've been talking about your heart for twenty years, and you never needed a nurse before."

"Things are different now." The older.woman's chin quivered.

He reached out and patted her arm. "You'll be fine."

Lacey drew in a breath. Should she intervene? Families were sometimes in denial about the seriousness of a beloved relative's health problems, and patients sometimes shielded their families from the truth.

"If you want to move your grandma, that's fine," she said, "but I'd recommend waiting a couple more weeks."

"That's right." Nonna looked relieved. "Lacey needs the money and I need the help."

Vito frowned. "Can we afford this?" He looked down at his grandma and seemed to realize that the woman was getting distressed. "Tell you what, Grandma, Lacey and I will talk about this and figure some things out. I won't leave without saying goodbye."

"All right, dear." She shot a concerned glance at Lacey.

She leaned down in the guise of straightening a pillow for Nonna. "I'll explain everything," she reassured her.

She led the way to the front room, out of earshot from Nonna D'Angelo. Then she turned to Vito, frowning. "You don't think I'm taking advantage of your grandma, do you?"

"No!" He reached for her, but when she took a step back, he crossed his arms instead. "I would never think that, Lacey. I know you. I just don't know if you've thought this through."

She restrained an eye roll. "You always did like to interfere when your help wasn't needed."

"Look, if this is about that talk we had years back..." He waved a dismissive hand. "Let's just forget that."

She knew exactly what he meant. As soon as Vito had found out Gerry had proposed, he'd come storming over to her house and pulled her out onto the front porch to try and talk her out of it. "You were wrong," she said now.

"I wasn't wrong." When she opened her mouth to protest, he held up a hand. "But I was wrong to interfere."

That wasn't exactly what she'd said, but whatever.

"But back to my grandma. I don't know what her insurance is like, but I know it hardly ever covers in-home nursing care. I'm living on limited means and until I get back on my feet—"

"It's handled. It's fine."

He ran a hand through his thick, dark hair. "She's always tended to be a hypochondriac—"

"A heart attack is nothing to take lightly."

"A *heart attack*?" Vito's jaw dropped. "Nonna had a heart attack?"

His surprise was so genuine that her annoyance about what she'd thought was neglect faded away. "About two weeks ago. She didn't tell you?"

"No, she didn't tell me. Do you think I'd have stayed away if I'd known?" His square jaw tightened. "Not a word. How bad was it?"

Lacey spread her hands. "Look, I'm just a CNA. You should definitely talk to her doctor."

"But from what you've seen, give me a guess."

Outside, she could hear people talking quietly. Dishes rattled in the kitchen, the girls cleaning up. She blew out a breath. "It was moderate severity. She had some damage, and there are some restrictions on what she can do. Changes she needs to make."

"What kind of changes?" He thrust his hands in his pockets and paced. "I can't believe she had a heart attack and I didn't know. Why didn't you call me?"

"It's her business what she tells people."

His mouth twisted to one side. "C'mon, Lace."

"I'm serious. Patients have the right to confidentiality. I couldn't breach that. In fact," she said, stricken, "I probably shouldn't have told you even now."

"You're my friend. You can tell me as a friend. Now, what kind of changes? What does she need to do to get back on her feet?"

She perched on the arm of an overstuffed chair. "You can probably guess. It's a lot about diet. She needs to start a gentle exercise program. I have her walking around the block twice a day."

He stared. "Nonna's walking? Like, for exercise?"

"I know, right?" She smiled a little. "It wasn't easy to talk her into it. I make sure we have an interesting destination."

"How did you get so involved?"

She let her forehead sink down into her hand for just a second, then looked back up. Vito. He'd never take her seriously. He'd always been a big brother to her, and he always would be.

He held up a hand. "I'm not questioning it, Lacey. I'm grateful. And I feel awful having been out of the loop, not helping her. I've had lots of personal stuff going on, but that's no excuse."

His words flicked on a switch of interest in her, but she ignored it. "I worked her hall at the hospital, and since she knew me, we talked. She was worried about coming home alone, but she didn't want to bother you, and your brother's far away. I was looking to make a change, anyway, moving toward freelance home care so I could have time to finish renovating this place." She waved an arm toward the unfinished breakfast area, currently walled off with sheets of plastic.

"So you made a deal with her." He still sounded a little skeptical.

"Yes, if that's what you want to call it." She stood, full of restless energy, and paced over to the fireplace, rearranging the collection of colored glass bottles on the mantel. "She's had a lot of anxiety, which is common in people recovering from a heart attack. She's on several new medications, and one of them causes fatigue and dizziness. The social worker was going to insist on having her go to a nursing home for proper care, which she couldn't afford, so this was a good arrangement." She looked over at him, mentally daring him to question her.

He rubbed a hand over the back of his neck. "A nursing home. Wow."

"It wouldn't have suited her."

"For how long? How long do you think she'll need the extra care?"

Lacey shrugged, moved an amber bottle to better catch the sun. "I don't know. Usually people take a couple of months to get back up to speed. And your brother's happy to pay for as long as we need."

Vito's dark eyebrows shot up. "She told him and not me?"

"She said you'd find out soon enough, when you came back home."

"And he's paying for everything?"

"He felt bad, being so far away, and apparently he begged her to let him help. Look, if you want to make a change in her care, I totally understand." It would mess up her own plans, of course; she'd given notice at the hospital only when she had this job to see her through, so if Nonna left, she'd have to apply for a part-time job right away. But Nonna was improving daily. If she had Vito with her, and he could focus on her needs, she'd probably be fine. A lot of her anxiety and depression stemmed from loneliness and fear.

Truth was, Lacey had found the older woman a hedge against her own loneliness, as her brother had gotten more and more involved in his wedding plans.

Now Buck and Gina and their dogs would be living in a little cottage on the other side of town. She'd see them a lot, but it wouldn't be the same as having Buck living here. "Whatever you decide," she said. "For now, we'd better go reassure your grandma, and then I need to attend to the rest of my guests."

Vito followed Lacey back into his grandmother's room, his mind reeling. Nonna had mostly raised him and his brother, Eugene, after their parents' accident, and she was one of the few family members he had left. More to the point, he was one of *her* only family members, and he should have been here for her.

Everyone treated him like he was made of glass, but the fact was, he was perfectly healthy on the inside. His surgeries had been a success, and his hearing loss was corrected with state-of-the-art hearing aids, courtesy of the VA.

He just *looked* bad.

And while the scars that slashed across his face, the

worse ones on his chest, made it even more unlikely that he'd achieve his dream of marriage and a large family, he couldn't blame his bachelorhood entirely on the war. Women had always liked him, yes—as a friend. And nothing but a friend. He lacked the cool charisma that most women seemed to want in a boyfriend or husband.

Entering his grandmother's room, he pulled up a chair for Lacey, and then sat down on the edge of Nonna's bed, carefully, trying not to jolt her out of her light doze. He was newly conscious that she was pale, and thinner than she'd been. A glance around the attractive bedroom revealed a stash of pill bottles he hadn't noticed before.

Nonna's eyes fluttered open and she reached out.

He caught her hand in his. "Hey, how're you feeling?"

She pursed her lips and glared at Lacey. "You told him about my heart."

"Yes, I told him! Of course I told him!" Lacey's voice had a fond but scolding tone. "You should have let him know yourself, Nonna. I thought you had."

He squeezed his grandmother's hand. "Don't you know I would've dropped everything and come?"

Nonna made a disgusted noise. "That's exactly why I didn't tell you. You and your brother have your own lives to lead. And I was able to find a very good arrangement on my own." She smiled at Lacey.

"It *is* a good arrangement, and I'm glad for it." Vito glanced over at Lacey, who had gotten up to pour water into a small vase of flowers.

With its blue-patterned wallpaper, lamp-lit bedside table and a handmade quilt on the bed, the room was cozy. Through the door of the small private bathroom, he glimpsed handicapped-accessible rails and a shower seat.

Yes, this was a good situation for her. "Look, I want to take you back to the house, but we'll wait until you're a little better."

Nonna started to say something, and then broke off, picking restlessly at the blanket.

"I haven't even been over to see the place yet," he continued, making plans as he thought it through. "I just got into town. But I'll check it out, make sure you've got everything you need."

"About that, dear..." Nonna's voice sounded uncharacteristically subdued.

"I hope you don't mind, but I'm planning to live there with you for a while." He smiled. It was true comfort, knowing he could come back to Rescue River anytime and find a welcome, a place to stay and a home-cooked meal.

Lacey nodded approvingly, and for some reason it warmed Vito to see it.

"Neither one of us will be able to live there," Nonna said, her voice small.

Lacey's eyebrows rose in surprise, and he could feel the same expression on his own face. "What do you mean?"

"Now, don't be angry, either of you," she said, grasping his hand, "but I rented out the house."

"You *what?*"

"When did you do that?" Lacey sounded bewildered.

"We signed the papers yesterday when you were out

grocery shopping," Nonna said, looking everywhere but at Vito and Lacey.

"Who'd you rent it to?" If it had just been finalized yesterday, surely everything could be revoked once the situation was explained. Lacey hadn't said anything about cognitive problems, but Nonna *was* in her early eighties. Maybe she wasn't thinking clearly.

Nonna smiled and clasped her hands together. "The most lovely migrant family," she said. "Three children and another on the way, and they're hoping to find a way to settle here. I gave them a good price, and they're going to keep the place up and do some repairs for me."

"Nonna..." Vito didn't know where to begin. He knew that this was the way things worked in his hometown—a lot of bartering, a lot of helping out those in need. "You aren't planning to stay here at the guesthouse indefinitely, right? How long of a lease did you sign?"

"Just a year." She folded her hands on top of her blanket and smiled.

"A year?" Not wanting to yell at his aged grandma, Vito stood and ran his hands through his hair. "Either you're going to have to revoke it, or I'm going to have to find another place for you and me to live." Never mind how he'd afford the rent. Or the fact that he'd named Nonna's house as his permanent residence in all the social services paperwork.

"No, dear. I have it all figured out." She took Lacey's hand in hers, and then reached toward him with her other hand. Once she had ahold of each of them, she smiled from one to the other. "Vito, if Lacey agrees, you can stay here."

No. She wasn't thinking clearly. "Nonna, that's not

going to work. Lacey made this arrangement with you, not with me." And certainly not with the other guest he had in tow. No way could Lacey find out the truth about Charlie.

"But Lacey was thinking of getting another boarder for this period while she's remodeling. It's hard to find the right one, because of all the noise." Lacey started to speak, but Nonna held up a hand. "The noise doesn't bother me. I can just turn down my hearing aid."

Vito knew what was coming and he felt his face heat. "Nonna..."

"Vito's perfect," she said, looking at Lacey, "because he can do the same thing."

Lacey's eyebrows lifted as she looked at him.

No point in trying to hide his less visible disability now. "It's true," he said, brushing back his hair to show his behind-the-ear hearing aids. "But that doesn't mean you have to take us in." In fact, staying here was the last thing that would work for him.

He'd promised Gerry he'd take care of his son, conceived during the affair Gerry had while married to Lacey. And he'd promised to keep Charlie's parentage a secret from Lacey.

He was glad he could help his friend, sinner though Gerry had been. Charlie needed a reliable father figure, and Lacey needed to maintain her illusions about her husband. It would serve no purpose for her to find out the truth now; it would only hurt her.

Lacey frowned. "I *was* looking to take in another boarder. I was thinking of maybe somebody who worked the three-to-eleven shift at the pretzel factory. They could come home and sleep, and they wouldn't be bothered by my working on the house at all hours."

"That makes sense," he said, relieved. "That would be better."

"But the thing is," she said slowly, "I haven't found anyone, even though I've been advertising for a couple of weeks. If you wanted to..."

Anxiety clawed at him from inside. How was he supposed to handle this? He could throttle Gerry for putting him into this situation. "I... There are some complications. I need to give this some thought." He knew he was being cryptic, but he needed time to figure it all out.

Unfortunately, Nonna wasn't one to accept anything cryptic from her grandchildren. "What complications? What's going on?"

Vito stood, then sat back down again. Nonna was going to have to know about Charlie soon enough. Lacey, too, along with everyone else in town. It would seem weirder if he tried to hide it now. "The thing is," he said, "I'm not alone. I have someone with me."

"Girlfriend? Wife?" Lacey sounded extremely curious.

Nonna, on the other hand, looked disappointed. "You would never get married without letting your *nonna* know," she said, reaching up to pinch his cheek, and then pulling her hand back, looking apologetic. It took him a minute to realize that she'd hesitated because of his scars.

"One of my finished rooms is a double," Lacey said thoughtfully. "But I don't know what your...friend... would think of the mess and the noise."

This was going off the rails. "It's not a girlfriend or wife," he said.

"Then who?" Nonna smacked his arm in a way that

reminded him of when he'd been small and misbehaving. "If not a woman, then who?"

Vito drew in a breath. "Actually," he said, "I've recently become certified as a foster parent."

Both women stared at him with wide, surprised eyes.

"So I'd be bringing along my eight-year-old foster son."

He was saved from further explanation by a crash, followed by the sound of shattering glass and running feet.

Chapter Two

Lacey raced out of Nonna's bedroom, leaving Vito to reassure the older woman. A quick scan of the hall revealed the breakage: her ceramic rooster lay in pieces on the floor.

One of the kids, probably; they were all sugared up on wedding cake and running around. She hurried to get a broom and dustpan, not wanting any of the remaining wedding guests to injure themselves. As she dropped the colorful pieces into the trash, she felt a moment's regret.

More important than the untimely demise of her admittedly tacky rooster, she wondered about Vito fostering a child. That, she hadn't expected.

"Miss Lacey!" It was little Mindy, Sam Hinton's daughter. "I saw who did that!"

"Did you? Stay back," she warned as she checked the area for any remaining ceramic pieces.

"Yes," Mindy said, "and he's hiding under the front porch right now!"

Behind her, Lacey heard Vito coming out of Nonna's bedroom, then pausing to talk some more, and a suspicion of who the young criminal might be came over her. "I'll go talk to him," she said. "It wasn't Xavier, was it?"

"No. It was a kid I don't know. Is he going to get in trouble?"

"I don't think so, honey. Not too much trouble, anyway. Why don't you go tell your dad what happened?"

"Yeah! He's gotta know!" As Mindy rushed off to her important task, Lacey walked out of the house and stood on the porch, looking around. The remaining guests were in the side yard, talking and laughing, so no one seemed to notice her.

She went down the steps and around to the side of the house where there was an opening in the latticework; she knew because she'd had to crawl under there when she'd first found Mrs. Whiskers, hiding with a couple of kittens. When she squatted down, she heard a little sniffling sound that touched her heart. Moving aside the branches of a lilac bush, breathing in the sweet fragrance of the fading purple flowers, she spoke into the darkness. "It's okay. I didn't like that rooster much, anyway."

There was silence, and then a stirring, but no voice. From the other side of the yard, she could hear conversations and laughter. But this shaded spot felt private.

"I remember one time I broke my grandma's favorite lamp," she said conversationally, settling into a sitting position on the cool grass. "I ran and hid in an apple tree."

"Did they find you?" a boy's voice asked. Not a familiar voice. Since she knew every kid at the wedding, her suspicion that the culprit was Vito's new foster son increased. "Yes, they found me. My brother told them where I was."

"Did you get in trouble?"

"I sure did." She remembered her grandma's reprimand, her father chiming in, her own teary apology.

"Did they hit you?" the boy asked, his voice low.

The plaintive question squeezed Lacey's heart. "No, I just got scolded a lot. And I had to give my grandma my allowance to help pay for a new lamp."

"I don't get an allowance. Did you..." There was a pause, a sniffle. "Did you have to go live somewhere else after that?"

Lacey's eyes widened as she put it all together. Vito had said he'd *recently* become certified as a foster parent. So this must be a new arrangement. It would make all the sense in the world that a boy who'd just been placed with a new foster father would feel insecure about whether he'd be allowed to stay.

But why had Vito, a single man with issues of his own, taken on this new challenge? "No, I didn't have to go live somewhere else," she said firmly, "and what's more, no kind adult would send a kid away for breaking a silly old lamp. Or a silly old rooster, either."

Branches rustled behind her, and then Vito came around the edge of the bushes. "There you are! What happened? Is everything okay?"

She pointed toward the latticed area where the boy was hiding, giving Vito a meaningful look. "I think the person who *accidentally*—" she emphasized the word "—broke the rooster is worried he'll get sent away."

"What?" Vito's thick dark eyebrows came down as understanding dawned in his eyes. He squatted beside her. "Charlie, is that you? Kids don't get sent away for stuff like that."

There was another shuffling under the porch, and then a head came into view. Messy, light brown hair, a sprinkling of freckles, worried-looking eyes. "But they might get sent away if they were keeping their dad from having a place to live."

Oh. The boy must have heard Vito say he couldn't live here because of having a foster son.

"We'll find a place to live," Vito said. "Come on out."

The boy looked at him steadily and didn't move.

"Charlie! I mean it!"

Lacey put a hand on Vito's arm. "Hey, Charlie," she said softly. "I grew up next door to this guy. I was three years younger and a lot smaller, and I did some annoying things. And he never, ever hit me." She felt Vito's arm tense beneath hers and squeezed. "And he wouldn't hurt you, either. Right, Vito?" She looked over at him.

His mouth twisted. "That's right." He went forward on one knee and held out a hand to the boy. "Come on out. We talked about this. Remember, I look meaner than I really am."

The boy hesitated, then crawled out without taking Vito's hand. Instead, he scuttled over to the other side of Lacey and crouched.

Vito drew in a breath and blew it out. His brow furrowed. "You're going to need to apologize to Miss Lacey, here, and then we'll find out how you can make up for what you did."

The boy wrapped his arms around upraised knees. A tear leaked out and he backhanded it away. "I can't make it up. Don't have any money."

"I might have some chores you could do," Lacey said, easing backward so she wasn't directly between Charlie and Vito. "Especially if you and your foster dad are going to be living here." As soon as she said it, she regretted the words. "Or living nearby," she amended hastily.

She liked Vito, always had. And she adored his grandmother, who clearly wanted her family gathered around her. But Lacey had been planning to have the next few months as a quiet, calm oasis before opening her guesthouse. She still had healing to do.

Having Vito and this boy here wasn't conducive to quiet serenity. On the other hand, young Charlie seemed to have thrown himself on her for protection, and that touched her.

"Can we live here? Really?" The boy jumped up and started hopping from one foot to the next. "'Cause this place is cool! You have a tire swing! And there's a basketball hoop right across the street!"

Vito stood, looking at her quizzically. "The grown-ups will be doing some talking," he said firmly. "For tonight, we're staying out at the motel like we planned. But before we go back there, I want you to apologize."

The boy looked at Lacey, then away, digging the toe of a well-worn sneaker into the dirt. "I'm real sorry I broke your rooster. It was an accident."

She nodded, getting to her feet. "That's all right. I think I can find another one kind of like it."

Her own soft feelings surprised her. Generally, she avoided little ones, especially babies; they were a reminder of all she couldn't have.

But this boy touched her heart. Maybe it was because his reaction to breaking the rooster was so similar to her own reaction when she'd broken the lamp. *Hide. Don't let the grown-ups know, because you never know what disaster will happen when grown-ups get upset.* She'd been fortunate, found by her grandma and father instead of her mom. Come to think of it, her brother had probably gone to them on purpose. He'd wanted her to get in trouble, but not from their volatile mother.

Lacey was beyond all that now, at least she thought so, but she still identified with the feeling of accidentally causing disasters and facing out-of-proportion consequences.

"And the other question you have to answer," Vito said, putting an arm around Charlie's shoulders lightly, ignoring the boy's automatic wince, "is how you got down here when you were supposed to be staying with Valencia."

Lacey moved to stand by Charlie, and her presence seemed to relax him.

"I asked her if we could take a walk," Charlie explained, a defensive tone coming into his voice. "When we came by here, she started talking to the people and I came inside. I just wanted to look around."

"You're not to do things like that without permission." Vito pinched the bridge of his nose. "You have another apology to make, to Valencia. And no dessert after dinner tonight."

The boy's lower lip came out, and Lacey felt the absurd impulse to slip him an extra piece of wedding cake.

An accented voice called from the other side of the yard. "Charlie! Charlie!"

"You run and tell Miss Valencia you're sorry you

didn't stay close to her. And then wait for me on the porch."

As the boy ran toward the babysitter's anxious voice, Lacey looked up at Vito. "In over your head?"

"Totally." He blew out a breath. "What do I know about raising kids?"

"How'd you get into it, anyway?"

"It's complicated." He looked away, then back at her. "Listen, don't feel pressured into having us stay at your guesthouse. I don't expect that, no matter what Nonna says. And you can see that we'd be a handful."

She looked into his warm brown eyes. "I *can* see that. And I honestly don't know if it would work. But what are you going to do if you can't stay here?"

"That's the million-dollar question." He rubbed his chin. "We'll figure something out."

"Let me sleep on it. It's been a crazy day."

"Of course it has, and I'm sorry to add to that." They headed toward the rest of the guests, and he put an arm around her shoulders and squeezed. It was an innocent gesture, a friendly gesture, the same thing he'd done with Charlie.

But for some reason, it disconcerted her now, and she stepped away.

Something flashed in Vito's eyes and he cleared his throat. "Look, tomorrow Charlie has a visit with his birth mom up in Raystown. Let me take you to lunch. We can talk about Nonna and the possibility of Charlie and me staying here. Or more likely, how to break it to Nonna that we *won't* be staying here."

She'd planned to spend the next afternoon cleaning up and recovering from the wedding. "That'll work."

"The Chatterbox? Noon?" His voice was strictly businesslike.

"Where else?" She wondered why he'd gone chilly on her. "I'm looking forward to catching up."

And she was. Sort of.

The next morning, Vito pulled his truck into the parking lot at the Supervised Visitation Center and glanced into the backseat of the extended cab. Yes, a storm was brewing.

"Why do I have to do this?" Charlie mumbled. "Am I going back to live with her?"

"No." He twisted farther around to get more comfortable. "We talked about this. Your mom loves you, but she can't do a good job taking care of you, and you need to have a forever home." He'd practically memorized the words from the foster parenting handbook, and it was a good thing. Because apparently, Charlie needed to hear them a bunch of times.

"Then why do I have to visit? I wanted to play basketball with Xavier, that kid from the wedding yesterday. He said maybe I could come over."

Vito pulled up another memorized phrase and forced cheer into his voice. "It's important for you to have a relationship with your mom. Important for you and for her."

The whole situation was awful for a kid, and Krystal, Charlie's mother, wasn't easy to deal with. She'd neglected Charlie, and worse, exposed him to danger—mostly from her poorly chosen boyfriends—way too many times.

Someone who hurt a kid ought to be in prison, in

Vito's mind, at the very least. But he had to keep reminding himself that Krystal was sick.

"You'll have fun with your mom," he said. "I think you guys are going to go out for lunch in a little while and maybe over to the lake afterward."

"That doesn't sound fun." Charlie crossed his arms and looked out the window, making no move to get out of the car.

Vito looked that way, too, and saw Krystal getting out of the passenger side of a late-model SUV. Maybe things were looking up for her. He'd only met her a few times, but she'd been driving a car noticeably on its last legs.

The SUV roared off, passing them, with a balding, bearded, forty-something guy at the wheel. Vito looked back at Charlie in time to see the boy cringe. "What's wrong, buddy?" he asked. "Do you know that guy?"

Charlie nodded but didn't say anything.

Krystal strolled over to the back stoop of the Center, smoking a cigarette. Vito wished for a similarly easy way to calm his nerves.

He wished he knew how to be a father. He'd only had Charlie full-time for a month, most of which they'd spent in Cleveland, closing down Vito's previous life, getting ready to move home. Charlie had been well and truly welcomed by the Cleveland branch of Vito's family, though everyone had agreed on waiting to tell Nonna about Charlie until the foster care situation was definite. If everything went well, he'd be able to adopt Charlie after another six months and be the boy's permanent, real father.

Learning how to parent well would take a lifetime.

Vito got out of the car. The small, wire-supported

trees around the brand-new building were trying their best, sporting a few green leaves. A robin hopped along the bare ground, poking for worms, and more birds chirped overhead. It was a nice summer day, and Vito was half tempted to get back in the truck and drive away, take Charlie to the lake himself.

But that wasn't the agreement he'd made. He opened the passenger door and Charlie got out. His glance in his mother's direction was urgent and hungry.

Of course. This visit was important. No matter what parents did, kids always wanted to love them.

Vito forced a spring into his step as they approached the building and Krystal. "Hey," he greeted her, and tried the door.

"It's locked, genius." Krystal drew harder on her cigarette. She hadn't glanced at or touched Charlie, who'd stopped a few steps short of the little porch.

Looking at the two of them, Vito's heart about broke. He considered his big, extended family up in Cleveland, the hugs, the cheek pinches, the loud greetings. He had it good, always had. He squatted beside Charlie and cast about for conversation. "Charlie's been doing great," he said to Krystal, not that she'd asked. "Going to sign him up for summer softball."

"Nice for you. I never could afford it." She looked at Charlie then, and her face softened. "Hey, kid. You got tall in the past couple months."

Vito was so close to Charlie that he could sense the boy's urge to run to his mom as well as the fear that pinned him to Vito's side.

The fear worried him.

But Charlie would be safe. This was a supervised visit, if the caseworker ever got here.

"You were Gerry's buddy," Krystal said suddenly. "Did you know about me, or did he just talk about *her*?"

What was Vito supposed to say to that, especially in front of Charlie? The boy needed to think highly of his father, to remember that he'd died a hero's death, not that he'd lived a terribly flawed life. "It's better we focus on now," he said to Krystal, nodding his head sideways, subtly, at Charlie.

She snorted, but dropped the subject, turning away to respond to her buzzing phone.

Focus on now. He needed to take his own advice. Except he had to think about the future and make plans, to consider the possibility of him and Charlie staying with the *her*—Lacey—that Krystal was mad about. Which would be a really rotten idea, now that the ramifications of it all came to him.

He wasn't sure how much Krystal knew about Lacey and Gerry, what kind of promises Gerry might have made to her. From what he'd been able to figure out, Krystal hadn't known that Gerry was married, at least not at first. No wonder she was angry. Problem was, she'd likely pass that anger on to Charlie. She didn't seem like a person who had a very good filter.

And if she talked to Charlie about Lacey, and Charlie was living at Lacey's boardinghouse, the boy could get all mixed up inside.

If Gerry were still alive, Vito would strangle him. The jerk hadn't been married to Lacey for a year before he'd started stepping out on her.

Krystal put her phone away, lit another cigarette and sat down on the edge of the stoop. She beckoned to Charlie. "Come on, sit by me. You scared?"

Charlie hesitated, then walked over and sat gingerly beside her. When she put her arm around him, though, he turned into her and hugged her suddenly and hard, and grief tightened her face.

Vito stepped back to give them some space and covertly studied Krystal. He didn't understand Gerry. The man had had Lacey as a wife—gorgeous, sweet Lacey—and he'd cheated on her with Krystal. Who, admittedly, had a stellar figure and long black hair. She'd probably been beautiful back then. But now the hair was disheveled. Her eyes were heavy-lidded, her skin pitted with some kind of scars. Vito wasn't sure what all she was addicted to, but the drugs had obviously taken their toll.

It looked like she'd stayed sober to visit with Charlie today, knowing she'd have to submit to a drug test. Maybe she'd had to stay clean a couple of days. That would put any addict into a bad mood.

Even before she'd been an addict, Krystal couldn't have compared to Lacey.

A battered subcompact pulled into the parking lot and jolted to a halt, its muffler obviously failing. The driver-side door flew open and the short, curly-haired caseworker got out. After pulling an overstuffed briefcase and a couple of bags from her car, she bustled over to them.

"Sorry I'm late! These Sunday visits are crazy. Maybe we can switch to Mondays or Tuesdays?" She was fumbling for the key as she spoke. "Come on in, guys! Thanks so much, Vito!"

"Charlie." Vito got the boy's attention, held his eyes. "I'll be back at three, okay?"

Relief shone on Charlie's face. He ran to Vito, gave

him a short hug and whispered into his ear: "Come back for sure, okay?"

"You got it, buddy." Vito's voice choked up a little bit.

Charlie let go and looked at Vito. Then his eyes narrowed and he grinned purposefully. "And can we stay at that place instead of the motel?" he whispered. "With the cat and the nice lady?"

Vito knew manipulation when he saw it, but he also knew the boy needed both security and honesty.

"What's he begging for now?" Krystal grinned as she flicked her cigarette butt into the bare soil beside the building. "I recognize that look."

"I'm starting to recognize it, too," Vito said, meeting Krystal's eyes. Some kind of understanding arced between them, and he felt a moment of kinship and sorrow for the woman who'd given birth to Charlie but wouldn't get to raise him.

"Well, can we?" Charlie asked.

"We'll see. No promises." Vito squeezed the boy's shoulder. "You be good, and I'll see you right here at three o'clock."

In reality, he wished he could just sweep the boy up and take him home, and not just to protect him from an awkward day with his mom. Vito wasn't looking forward to the lunch date—no, *not* a date—he was facing in only a few hours. Whatever he and Lacey decided, it was going to make someone unhappy.

Chapter Three

"They left the two of us in charge of the nursery? Are they crazy?" Lacey's friend Susan put her purse up on a shelf and came over to where Lacey stood beside a crib, trying to coax a baby to sleep.

"I'm just glad it's you working with me." Lacey picked up the baby, who'd started to fuss, and swayed gently. "You won't freak out if I freak out."

Working in the church nursery was Lacey's counselor's idea, a way to help Lacey deal with her miscarriage and subsequent infertility. She needed to desensitize herself, find ways to be around babies without getting upset by them, especially if she was going to open a family-friendly guesthouse and make a success of it.

The desensitization had started accidentally, when Gina Patterson had showed up in town earlier this year with her son, Bobby, just ten months old at the time. With nowhere else to turn, she'd spent the early spring at the guesthouse, in the process falling in love with Lacey's brother, Buck. Being around little Bobby had made Lacey miserable at first, but she was learning. More than that, she was motivated; she wanted to serve others and get out of her own pain, build a well-rounded life for herself.

Which included being around babies. "I'm here to work through my issues," she told Susan, "but why are *you* here?"

Susan's tawny skin went pink. "Sam and I decided it would be a good idea for me to get comfortable with babies. I used to be terrified of even touching them, but… I guess I'd better learn."

Something in Susan's tone made Lacey take notice, and she mentally reviewed what Susan had just said. Then she stared at her friend. "Wait a minute. Are you expecting? Already?"

Susan looked down at the floor, and then met Lacey's eyes. "Yeah. We just found out."

Selfish tears sprang to Lacey's eyes as she looked down at the infant she held, feeling its weight in her arms. Something she'd never experience for herself, with her own child. A joy that Susan and many of Lacey's other friends would find effortlessly.

Susan would be a part of the circle of happy young mothers in town. Lacey wouldn't, not ever.

"I'm so sorry to cause you pain. News like this must be hard for you to hear."

Susan's kind words jolted Lacey out of her own self-centered heartache. Finding out you were having a baby was one of the most joyous times of a woman's life. She remembered when the two pink lines had shown up on her own pregnancy test. Remembered her video call to Gerry. She'd shown the test to him, and they'd both cried tears of joy.

Susan deserved to have that joy, too. She shouldn't have to focus on her friend's losses.

Lacey lifted the baby to her shoulder so she could reach out and put an arm around Susan. "It does hurt a little—I'm not going to lie. But what kind of friend would I be not to celebrate with you? I'm thrilled!"

"You're the best, Lace." Susan wrapped her arms around Lacey, the baby in between them, and Lacey let herself cry just a little more. Susan understood. She'd stayed a year at Lacey's guesthouse before the remodeling, the horrible year when Lacey had lost both Gerry and the baby. Susan had been an incredible comfort.

"Anyway," Susan added, "I'm going to need your help to fit in with the perfect mothers of Rescue River. You know I have a knack for saying the wrong thing."

"You'll be fine." And it was true. Susan was outspoken and blunt, but she gave everything she had to the kids she taught at the local elementary school, and people here loved her for it. "How's Sam handling the news?"

"Making a million plans and bossing me around, of course." But Susan smiled as she said it, and for just a moment, Lacey felt even more jealous of the happy-married-woman smile on Susan's face than of the tiny, growing baby in her belly.

"Hey, guys, can I leave Bobby here for a little while?" Lou Ann Miller, who was taking care of Gina's baby while she and Buck enjoyed a honeymoon at the shore, stood at the half door. "I want to go to adult Sunday school, but there's no way he'll sit through our book discussion."

"Sure." Lacey thrust the infant she'd been holding into Susan's arms. "Just hold her head steady. Yeah, like that." She walked over to the door and opened it. "Come on in, Bobby!"

"Laaasss," he said, walking right into her leg and hugging it. "Laaasss."

Lacey's heart warmed, and she reached down to pick Bobby up. "He'll be fine. Take your time," she said to Lou Ann. "Wave bye-bye to Miss Lou Ann, okay?"

Two more toddlers got dropped off, and then a diaper needed changing. Little Emmie Farmingham, who was almost three, twirled to show Lacey and Susan her new summer dress, patterned with garden vegetables and sporting a carrot for a pocket. Then she proceeded to pull the dress off.

Once they'd gotten Emmie dressed again, the infant sleeping and the other two toddlers playing side by side with plastic blocks, Susan and Lacey settled down into the tiny chairs around the low table. "Babies are great, I guess," Susan said doubtfully, "but I have to say, I like bigger kids better. I wish one could just land in my lap at age five, like Mindy did."

"Not me." Lacey looked over at the toddlers, another surge of regret piercing her heart. "I've always loved the little ones."

"I know you have." Susan's voice was gentle. "Hey, want to come over and have lunch with us after this? I think Sam's grilling. You could bring your swimsuit."

"You're sweet." The thought of lounging by Sam and Susan's pool was appealing. And Susan was a great friend; she'd stand by Lacey even as she was going through this huge transition of having a child. She wouldn't abandon Lacey, and that mattered.

Lacey shook her head with real disappointment. "Can't. I'm meeting Vito for lunch."

"Oh, *Vito*." Susan punched her arm, gently. "Is this a date?"

"It's not like that. We're old friends."

Susan ignored her words. "You should see where it leads. He seems like a great guy, from what I saw of him at the end of the reception. Good-looking, too. Even with the scars." Susan's hand flew to her mouth. "I shouldn't say things like that, should I?"

"Probably not." Lacey rolled her eyes at her friend, pretending exasperation. "But it's okay. You can't help but notice his scars. Anyway, we're just going to talk about this crazy idea his grandma dreamed up." She explained how Nonna had unexpectedly rented out her own house, and how Vito was newly a foster father. "Apparently, Vito had no idea that was her plan. He was counting on bringing his foster son, Charlie, to live in Nonna's big house out in the country. I actually got the feeling Nonna had kept it a secret on purpose, to make sure Vito ended up staying at the guesthouse."

"But that would be perfect!" Susan clapped her hands. "Vito could be with his *nonna*, and Charlie could get a sense of family, and they'd be right in town to get, like, reintegrated into the community."

"Yes, but—"

"And you wanted someone else to room in, right? He'd pay rent, which would help with your expenses. He and Charlie could have separate rooms, or those two connecting ones upstairs."

Lacey's response was cut off by the sound of crashing blocks and a wail, and they got busy playing with the babies. The subject of Vito moving into the guesthouse didn't come up again, but Lacey couldn't stop thinking about it.

Susan seemed to think it was a great idea, and Nonna had talked to Lacey over breakfast about how wonderful it would be to have Vito there and to get to know the newest member of the family. Her eyes had sparkled when she said that, and few enough things had brought a sparkle to Nonna's eyes since the heart attack.

There were all kinds of reasons to embrace the idea of Vito and Charlie moving in, but Lacey still felt uneasy about it.

She couldn't begin to articulate why, even to herself.

At lunchtime, Vito stood outside the Chatterbox Café, looking up at the town's outdoor clock, which clearly showed it was only eleven forty-five. He was early. Why had he come so early?

He loosened the itchy collar of his new button-down shirt. He shouldn't have worn a brand-new shirt today, should have at least washed it first, except that he was living out of a suitcase and he'd been rushing to get Charlie ready to go and there hadn't been the chance.

He could have just worn an old, comfortable shirt, but the fact was, he was trying to look good. Which was obviously a losing battle.

It wasn't about Lacey. It was about the fact that he'd probably see other people he knew here at the Chatterbox, and he needed to present a professional image. He had good benefits from the VA—they were paying for his online degree—but a man needed to work, and Vito would be looking for a part-time job just as soon as he'd found a place to live and gotten Charlie settled. Maybe something with kids, since he was looking to become a teacher.

No, it wasn't about Lacey. He'd had some feelings for her once, but he'd turned those off when she'd married, of course. He'd been over her for years.

"Vito!" Lacey approached, a summery yellow dress swirling around her legs, the wind blowing her short hair into messiness.

She looked so beautiful that, for a moment, he couldn't breathe.

He crooked his arm for her to take it, an automatic gesture he'd learned at his *nonna*'s knee. The way a gentleman treated a lady. And then he remembered how she'd stepped away when he'd done the Italian thing and thrown an arm around her yesterday. He put his arm back at his side.

People are disgusted by your scars, he reminded himself. *And she hasn't seen the half of them.*

As they turned toward the café—Vito carefully *not* touching her—he caught a whiff of something lemony and wondered if it was her shampoo, or if she'd worn perfume.

Inside, everything was familiar: the smell of meat loaf and fries, the red vinyl booths and vintage tables trimmed with aluminum, the sight of people he'd known since childhood. Even the counter waitress, Nora Jean, had been here since he was a kid and called a greeting.

"Sit anywhere, you two. Lindy'll wait on you, but I'm coming over to say hello just as soon as these guys give me a break." She waved at her full counter.

Dion Coleman, the police chief, swiveled in his chair and stood to pound Vito on the back. "I'm glad to see your ugly mug," he joked. Which didn't feel awkward, because it was the exact same thing Dion had always said when Vito came home, even before his injuries. "Police business has been slow these past months, but with you home, it's sure to pick up."

Vito shook the man's hand with genuine pleasure.

"I'll see what I can do about knocking down some mailboxes and shooting up signs, just to give you something to do. You're getting soft." He nodded down at Dion's flat belly and then at the grilled chicken salad on the counter in front of him. "Eating too much. Just like a cop."

"You never change." Dion was laughing as he sat back down. "Give me a call, you hear? We have some catching up to do."

Lacey had headed toward one of the few empty booths at the back of the café, and as he followed her it seemed to Vito that conversation stopped, then rose again when he'd passed. He rubbed a hand across his face, feeling the uneven ridges of his scars.

As soon as they sat down, they were mobbed. The young waitress could barely squeeze in to take their order. Everyone, friend or acquaintance, stopped by to say hello. They wanted to know where he was staying, how long he'd be in town, where he was stationed. Explaining that he wasn't in the army anymore felt embarrassing, since he'd always intended it to be his life's work. More embarrassing were the sympathetic nods and arm pats. People felt sorry for him.

But he kept it upbeat and answered questions patiently. Once people knew his story, they'd settle down some. And maybe someone would think of him when a job opening came up, so he made sure to let everyone know he was looking.

After people had drifted back to their tables and they'd managed to eat some of their lunch, Lacey wiped her mouth and smiled at him. "That got a little crazy. Are you wishing we'd gone somewhere else?"

He swallowed his massive bite of cheeseburger and

shook his head. "Best to get it over fast. Let people get a good look."

She took a sip of soda. "You think they all came over to look at your scars?"

"That, and find out the latest news. But mostly to see how bad the damage is, up close and personal." His support group at the VA had warned him about people's reactions, how they might not be able to see anything but his scars at first.

"They're not looking at your scars in a bad way," Lacey said, frowning. "They're grateful for your service."

Of course, that was what most of the people who'd greeted them had said. And they weren't lying. It was just that initial cringe that got to him. He wasn't used to scaring people just by the way he looked.

His friend with severe facial burns had told Vito that you never really got used to it. "Older people do better, but young people like pretty," he'd said. "Makes it a challenge to get a date."

The waitress refilled his coffee cup and headed to a booth across the way. Vito gestured toward her. "You can't tell me someone like that, someone who doesn't know me, isn't disgusted when she first sees me."

Lacey looked at him for a long moment, her brown eyes steady. "Look over there," she said, pointing to a twenty-something man in an up-to-date wheelchair, sitting at a table with an older woman. "That's our waitress's brother," she said. "He served, too."

Vito blinked and looked more closely, seeing how the man's head lolled to one side, held up by a special support. He wore a hoodie and sweats, and as Vito watched, the older woman put a bite of something into his mouth.

"Wounded in service?"

Lacey nodded. "I think he was a Marine."

"Is a Marine," Vito corrected. "And I'm sorry. You're right. I need to get out of my own head. I'm more fortunate than a lot of guys." He met her eyes. "Gerry included, and I'm a jerk to focus on myself."

She shrugged. "We all do that sometimes."

Had Lacey always had this steady maturity? He couldn't help but remember her as a younger girl, pestering him and her brother when they'd wanted to go out and do something fun. And he remembered how flightily she'd fallen for Gerry, swept away by love and unable to listen to anyone's warnings.

Now though, there was real thoughtfulness to her. She was quieter than she'd been, and more assertive.

He liked that. Liked a woman who'd call him on his dumb mistakes.

And he didn't need to be thinking about how much he liked the new Lacey. Best to get to the real reason for their lunch. "So, I was looking into options for Charlie and me," he said. "I talked to the family Nonna rented her house to."

"And? Did you ask if they'd let her out of the contract?"

"I couldn't even bring it up." He lifted his hands, shrugging. "They're thrilled with the house and the price Nonna gave them, and they need the space. And she's pregnant out to here." He held a hand in front of his stomach.

"Well, look who's back in town!" Old Mr. Love from the hardware store, who had to be in his eighties, stopped by their table and patted his shoulder. "I'd recognize that voice anywhere!"

Vito stood and greeted the man, and then looked at the gray-haired woman with him. "Miss Minnie Falcon? Is that you?"

"That's right, young man. You'd better not forget your old Sunday school teacher."

"I couldn't ever forget." He took her hand, gently. Unlike some of the other kids in Sunday school, he'd actually appreciated Miss Minnie's knowledge of the Old and New Testament, and the way she brought the stories to life, infusing them with a sense of biblical history.

Mr. Love was leaning toward Lacey. "I was hoping you'd find romance." His voice, meant to be low, carried clearly to Vito and Miss Minnie. "Now that Buck's out of your hair, it's your turn, young lady." He nodded toward Vito, raising an eyebrow.

"Harold!" Miss Minnie scolded. "Don't make assumptions. Come on. Let's get that corner table before someone else takes it." She patted Vito's arm. "It was nice to see you. Don't be a stranger. We like visitors over at the Senior Towers." She turned and headed across the restaurant at a brisk pace, pushing her wheeled walker.

"When a lady talks, you listen." Mr. Love gave Vito an apologetic shrug as he turned and followed Miss Minnie, putting a hand on her shoulder.

After they were out of earshot, Vito lifted an eyebrow at Lacey. "They're a couple?"

"It's anybody's guess. They both say they're just friends, but tongues are wagging. It *is* Rescue River."

"Gossip central," he agreed, sipping coffee.

"And speaking of wagging tongues," she said, "imagine what people will assume about us if you come and live in the guesthouse. Just like Mr. Love assumed when he saw us together here. They'll think *we're* a couple. And I'm not comfortable with that."

"I understand." He looked down at his hands, traced a scar that peeked out from his shirt cuff. "I'm not exactly a blue-ribbon bronco."

"Vito!" She sounded exasperated. "You haven't changed a bit since you had to try on six different shirts for the homecoming dance."

The memory made him chuckle. He'd gotten her to sit on the porch and judge while he tried on shirt after shirt, running back to his room to change each time she'd nixed his selection.

Little did she know that Buck had begged him to keep her busy while he tried to steal a few kisses from cheerleader Tiffany Townsend, ostensibly at their house for help with homework.

"That was a long time ago," he said now. "And the truth is, I *have* changed."

She rolled her eyes. "You're still good-looking, okay? Women don't mind scars." Then she pressed her lips together as her cheeks grew pink.

His heart rate accelerated, just a little. Why was she blushing? Did *she* think he was good-looking?

But of course, she hadn't seen the worst of his scars.

And even if there *was* a little spark between them, it couldn't go anywhere. Because he was living with a secret he couldn't let her discover.

"Look," she said, and then took a big gulp of soda. "Getting back to the idea of you and Charlie staying at the guesthouse. I'd be willing to consider it, for Nonna's sake, but… I'm trying to build a rich, full life as a single person, see, and I don't want everyone asking me questions or trying to match us up. I'm just getting over being Lacey, the pitiful widow. And now, if I have this good-looking man living in my guesthouse…" A flush crept up her cheeks again and she dropped her head, propping her forehead on her hand. "I'm just digging myself in deeper here, huh?"

She *did* think he was good-looking. All of a sudden, other people's curious stares didn't bother him half as much.

"Can I get you anything else?" The perky waitress was back, looking at Lacey with curiosity. "You okay, Lacey?"

"I need something chocolate," she said, looking up at the waitress but avoiding Vito's eyes.

"Right away! I totally understand!"

Vito didn't get women's obsession with chocolate, but he respected it. He waited until the server had brought Lacey a big slice of chocolate cream pie before blundering forward with their meeting's purpose. "I have an appointment tonight to talk to a woman who might want to rent me a couple of rooms in her farmhouse, out past the dog rescue. And there's the top floor of a house available over in Eastley."

"That's good, I guess." She toyed with the whipped cream on her pie. "But Nonna won't like having you so far away. And Charlie could make more friends in town, right?"

"He really took a shine to the place and to you, it's true."

"And Nonna wants you to live there. She pulled out all the stops at breakfast, trying to talk me into it again."

"She phoned me, too."

Lacey was absently fingering the chain around her

neck, and when he looked more closely, he saw what hung on it.

A man's wedding ring. Undoubtedly Gerry's.

He wasn't worth it, Lace.

A shapely blonde in a tight-fitting dress approached their table. Tiffany Townsend. "Well, Vito D'Angelo. Aren't *you* a sight for sore eyes."

He snorted. "No." And then he thought about what Lacey had said: *Women don't mind scars*. And nobody, even a less-than-favorite classmate like Tiffany, deserved a rude response. He pasted on a smile. "Hey, Tiffany. It's been a long time."

"Where are you hiding yourself these days?" She bent over the table, and Vito leaned back in the booth, trying to look anywhere but down her low-cut dress. "We should get together sometime!" she gushed, putting a hand on his arm.

This was where a suave man would smile and flirt and make a date. But Vito had never been suave. He'd always been the one to console the girls whose boyfriends got caught on Tiffany's well-baited line. Always the friend, happy to take them out for coffee or a milk shake and to listen to them.

Unfortunately for his love life, it hadn't usually gone further than that.

Tiffany was looking at him expectantly. "Where did you say you're staying?"

"I'm not really..." He broke off. Did he really want to get into his personal business with Tiffany?

Lacey cleared her throat, grasped Vito's scarred hand and smiled up at Tiffany. "He's staying at my guesthouse," she said sweetly. "With me."

"Oh." There was a world of meaning in that word,

backed up by Tiffany's raised eyebrows. "Well, then. It was good to see you." She spun on her high heels and walked over to the counter, where she leaned toward Nora Jean and started talking fast and hard.

Vito turned his hand over, palm to palm with Lacey. "Thanks," he said, "but you didn't have to do that."

"Tiffany hasn't changed a bit since high school," Lacey said. "She'd break your heart."

"It's not in the market."

"Mine, either."

They looked at each other and some electrical-like current materialized between them, running from their locked eyes to their intertwined hands.

No, Vito's heart wasn't in the market. He had enough to do to rebuild a life and raise a boy and keep a secret.

But if it *had* been in the market, it would run more toward someone like Lacey than toward someone like Tiffany.

Lacey glanced toward the counter. "Don't look now," she said, "but Tiffany and Nora Jean are staring at us."

"This is how rumors get started." He squeezed her hand a little, then could have kicked himself. Was he flirting? With the one woman he could never, ever get involved with?

"That's true," Lacey said briskly, looking away. "And we've obviously done a good job of starting a rumor today. So..."

"So what?" He squeezed her hand again, let go and thought of living at the guesthouse with Nonna and Charlie.

Charlie could walk to the park, or better yet, ride

a bike. Vito was pretty sure there was one in Nonna's garage that he could fix up.

Vito could see Nonna every day. Do something good for the woman who'd done so much for him.

And he could get back on his feet, start his online classes. Maybe Nonna, as she got better, would watch Charlie for him some, giving him a chance to go out and find a decent job.

Soon enough, Nonna would be well and Charlie would be settled in school and Vito would have some money to spare. At which point he could find them another place to live.

He'd only have to keep his secret for the summer. After that, he and Charlie would live elsewhere and would drift naturally out of Lacey's circle of friends. At that point, it was doubtful that she'd learn about Charlie's parentage; there'd be no reason for it to come up.

How likely was it that Lacey would find out the truth over the summer?

"Maybe you could stay for a while," she said. "I'm opening the guesthouse this fall, officially, but until then, having a long-term guest who didn't mind noise would help out."

"How about a guest who makes noise? Charlie's not a quiet kid."

"I liked him."

"Well, then," Vito said, trying to ignore the feeling that he was making a huge mistake, "if you're seriously making the offer, it looks like you've got yourself a couple of tenants for the summer."

Chapter Four

The next Wednesday afternoon, Lacey looked out the kitchen window as Charlie and Vito brought a last load of boxes in from Vito's pickup. Pop music played loudly—Charlie's choice. She'd heard their good-natured argument earlier. The bang of the front screen door sent Mr. Whiskers flying from his favorite sunning spot on the floor. He disappeared into the basement, where his companion, Mrs. Whiskers, had already retreated.

Some part of Lacey liked the noise and life, but part of her worried. There went her peaceful summer—and Nonna's, too. This might be a really bad idea.

She glanced over at the older woman, relaxing in the rocking chair Lacey had put in a warm, sunny corner beside the stove. Maybe she'd leave the chair there. It gave the room a cozy feel. And Nonna didn't look any too disturbed by the ruckus Vito and Charlie were creating. Her eyes sparkled with more interest than she'd shown in the previous couple of weeks.

"I'd better get busy with dinner." Lacey opened the refrigerator door and studied the contents.

"I used to be such a good cook," Nonna commented. "Nowadays, I just don't have the energy."

"You will again." Lacey pulled mushrooms, sweet peppers and broccoli from the fridge. "You'd better. I don't think I could face the future without your lasagna in it."

"I could teach you to make it."

Lacey chuckled. "I'm really not much of a cook. And besides, we need to work on healthy meals. Maybe we can figure out a way to make some heart-healthy lasagna one of these days."

As she measured out brown rice and started it cooking, she looked over to see Nonna's frown. "What's wrong?"

"What are you making?"

"Stir-fried veggies on brown rice. It'll be good." Truthfully, it was one of Lacey's few staples, a quick, healthy meal she often whipped up for herself after work.

"No meat?" Nonna sounded scandalized. "You can't serve a meal to men without meat. At least a little, for flavor."

Lacey stopped in the middle of chopping the broccoli into small florets. "I'm cooking for men?"

"Aren't you fixing dinner for Vito and Charlie, too?" Nonna's eyebrows lifted.

"We didn't talk about sharing meals." Out the window, she saw Vito close the truck cab and wipe his forehead with the back of his hand before picking up one of the street side boxes to carry in. "They *are* working up a sweat out there, but where would I put them?" She nodded toward the small wooden table against the wall, where she and Nonna had been taking their meals. Once again, she sensed their quiet, relaxing summer dissolving away.

At the same time, Nonna was an extrovert, so maybe having more people around would suit her. As for Lacey, she needed to get used to having people in the house, to ease into hosting a bed-and-breakfast gradually, rather than waiting until she had a houseful of paying guests to feed in her big dining room. And who better than good old Vito?

"There's always room for more around a happy home's table," Nonna said, rocking.

"I guess we *could* move it out from the wall."

Vito walked by carrying a double stack of boxes, and Lacey hurried to the kitchen door. "Are you okay with that? Do you need help?" Though from the way his biceps stretched the sleeves of his white T-shirt, he was most definitely okay.

"There's nothing wrong with me below the neck." He sounded uncharacteristically irritable. "I can carry a couple of boxes."

Where had *that* come from? She lifted her hands and took a step back. "Fine with me," she said sharply.

From above them on the stairs, Charlie crowed, "Ooo-eee, a fight!"

Vito ignored him and stomped up the stairs, still carrying both boxes.

"You come in here, son." Nonna stood behind Lacey, beckoning to Charlie.

Lacey bit her lip. She didn't want Nonna to overexert herself. And being from an earlier generation, she might have unreasonable expectations of how a kid like Charlie would behave.

But Nonna was whispering to Charlie, and they both laughed, and then he helped her back to her rocking chair. That was good.

Lacey went back to her cutting board, looked at the stack of veggies and reluctantly acknowledged to herself that Nonna was probably right. If she could even get a red-blooded man and an eight-year-old boy to eat stir-fry, the least she could do was put some beef in it. She rummaged through her refrigerator and found a pack of round steak, already cut into strips. Lazy woman's meat. She drizzled oil into the wok, let it heat a minute, and then dumped in the beef strips.

"Hey, Lace." It was Vito's deep voice, coming from the kitchen doorway. "C'mere a minute."

She glanced around. The rice was cooking, Nonna and Charlie were still talking quietly and the beef was barely starting to brown. She wiped her hands on a kitchen towel. "What's up?" she asked as she crossed the kitchen toward him. "You're not going to bite my head off again, are you?"

"No." He beckoned her toward the front room, where they could talk without the others hearing. "Look, I'm sorry I snapped. Charlie's been a handful and…" He trailed off and rubbed the back of his neck.

"And what?"

"And… I hate being treated like there's something wrong with me. I'm still plenty strong."

"I noticed." But she remembered a similar feeling herself, after her miscarriage; people had tiptoed around her, offering to carry her groceries and help her to a seat in church. When really, she'd been just fine physically. "I'm sorry, too, then. I know how annoying it is to be treated like an invalid."

"So we're good?" He put an arm around her.

It was a gesture as natural as breathing to Vito as

well as to the rest of his Italian family. She'd always liked that about them.

But now, something felt different about Vito's warm arm around her shoulders. Maybe it was that he was so much bigger and brawnier than he'd been as a younger man.

Disconcerted, she hunched her shoulders and stepped away.

Some emotion flickered in his eyes and was gone, so quickly she wasn't sure she'd seen it.

"Hi!" Charlie came out of the kitchen, smiling innocently. He sidestepped toward Nonna's room.

"Where you headed, buddy?" Vito asked.

"Lacey, dear," Nonna called from the kitchen. "I'd like to rest up a little before dinner."

"I'm glad she called me." Lacey heard herself talking a little faster than usual, heard a breathless sound in her own voice. "I try to walk with her, because I have so many area rugs and the house can be a bit of an obstacle course. But of course, she likes to be independent." Why was she blathering like she was nervous, around Vito?

"I'll help her." Vito went into the kitchen and Lacey trailed behind. "Come on, Nonna, I'll walk with you. Smells good," he added, glancing over to where the beef sizzled on the stove.

It *did* smell good, and the praise from Vito warmed her. She added in sliced mushrooms and onions.

For a moment, all she could hear was the slight sizzle of the food on the stove and the tick of the big kitchen clock on the wall. Peace and quiet. Maybe this was going to work out okay.

The quiet didn't last long. From Nonna's room, she

could hear Charlie talking, telling some story. Vito's deeper voice chimed in. His comfortable, familiar laugh tickled her nerve endings in a most peculiar way. Then she heard his heavy step on the stairs. No doubt he was going up to do a little more unpacking while Charlie was occupied. Vito was a hard worker.

And just why was she so conscious of him? What was wrong with her?

She walked over to the sink and picked up the photo she kept on a built-in wooden shelf beside it. Gerry, in uniform, arriving home on one of his furloughs. Someone had snapped a photo of her hugging him, her hair, longer then, flying out behind her, joy in every muscle of her body.

She clasped the picture close to her chest. *That* was reality.

Reassured, she moved out the table and located some chairs for Charlie and Vito, almost wishing Buck hadn't taken her bigger kitchen table with him when he'd moved. She checked on the dinner. Just about done. She found grapes and peaches to put in a nice bowl, both a centerpiece and a healthy dessert.

"What's going on here?" She heard Vito's voice from Nonna's room a little later. He must have come back downstairs. She hadn't even noticed. Good.

Charlie's voice rose, then Nonna's. It sounded like an argument, and Lacey's patient shouldn't be arguing. She wiped her hands and hurried to check on Nonna.

When she looked into the room, both Nonna and Charlie had identical guilty expressions. And identical white smudges on their faces. Beside Nonna was a box from the bakery that someone had brought over yesterday. Cannoli.

"Dessert before dinner, Charlie?" Vito was shaking his head. "You know that's not allowed."

"Nonna!" Lacey scolded. "Rich, heavy pastries aren't on your diet. You know the doctor's worried about your blood sugar."

"She told me where they were and asked me to get them for her," Charlie protested. "And you told me I was supposed to treat older people with respect."

Vito blew out a sigh. "You just need to check with me first, buddy. And Nonna, you've got to stick to your eating plan. It's for your health!"

"What's life without cannoli?" Nonna said plaintively. "Do I have to give up all my treats?"

Vito knelt beside his grandmother. "I think you can have a few planned treats. But sneaking cannoli before dinner means you won't have an appetite for the healthy stuff."

"I didn't anyway," Nonna muttered.

"Me, either." Charlie went to stand beside Nonna on the other side. Obviously, he'd made a new friend in Nonna, and that was all to the good for both of them—as long as it didn't lead to Nonna falling off the diet bandwagon.

It was up to Lacey to be firm, so she marched over and picked up the bakery box. "Whatever you men don't eat for dessert is getting donated tonight," she said firmly. "Obviously, it's too much of a temptation to have things like this in the house."

An acrid smell tickled her nose.

"What's that burning?" Vito asked at the same moment.

"Dinner!" Lacey wailed and rushed into the kitchen, where smoke poured from the rice pan. In the wok, the beef and vegetables had shrunk down and appeared to be permanently attached to the wok's surface.

All her work to make dinner nice and healthy, gone to waste.

She turned off the burners and stared at the ruined food, tears gathering in her eyes. In her head she could hear her mother's criticism of the cookies she'd baked: *you'll never be much of a chef, will you?*

She remembered Gerry shoving away his dinner plate the first night they'd come back from their honeymoon, saying he wasn't hungry.

Nonna was calling questions from her room and Charlie shouted back: "Lacey burned up dinner!"

The acrid smoke stung her eyes, and then the smoke detector went off with an earsplitting series of beeps.

This was not the serene life she had been looking for. She was a failure as a cook.

She burst into tears.

Vito coughed from the smoke and winced from the alarm's relentless beeping. He turned down the volume on his hearing aids and moved toward Lacey, his arms lifting automatically to comfort her with a hug.

She clung on to him for one precious second, then let go and looked around like she didn't know what to do next.

He needed to take charge. He shut off the smoke detectors, one after the other. Then he opened all the windows in the kitchen, gulping in big breaths of fresh air.

Lacey flopped down at the kitchen table, wiping tears. He beckoned to Charlie. "Run and tell Nonna everything's fine, but dinner will be a little late." As Charlie left the room, Vito scraped the ruined food into the garbage and filled the two pans halfway with soapy water. They'd need some serious scrubbing later.

Lacey was sniffling now, blowing her nose and wiping her eyes.

He leaned back against the counter and studied her. "How come this got you so upset? You're not a crier."

She laughed. "I am, these days. And I'm also a loser in the kitchen, in case you didn't notice. My mom always told me that, and Gerry concurred."

"Gerry?" That was a surprise. The man had eaten enough MREs in the military that he should have been grateful for any home cooking, however simple.

She pushed herself to her feet. "What'll we eat now? Nonna needs dinner. We all do. I guess, maybe, pizza? But that's not the healthiest choice for your grandma."

"Do you have canned tomatoes?" Vito asked her. "Onions? Garlic? Pasta?"

She nodded and blew her nose again. "I think so."

"Great. You sit down and I'll give you stuff to chop. I'm going to make a spaghetti sauce." He might not know what words to say to comfort her, but he could definitely cook her a meal.

"Spaghetti!" Charlie yelled, pumping his fist as he ran into the kitchen.

"That's right." Vito stepped in front of the racing boy. "And you, young man, are going to do some chores. Starting with taking out this garbage."

Charlie started to protest, but Vito just pointed at the garbage can. Charlie yanked out the bag and stomped out of the house with it.

Lacey chopped and Vito opened cans of tomatoes and set the sauce to cooking. As the onions sizzled in olive oil, the day's tension rolled off him. When Charlie came back in, he had Gramps Camden, a weathered-looking, gray-haired man, with him.

Lacey gave the older man a hug, then turned to Vito. "You remember Gramps Camden, don't you?"

Vito stood and greeted the older man, who'd been a part of the community as long as he could remember.

"Wanted to pay a visit," he said in his trademark grouchy way. "See what you've got going on over here."

"You'll stay for dinner, won't you?" Lacey asked.

"Twist my arm," the old man said. "Cooking's good over at the Senior Towers, but nothing beats home-made."

Lacey asked Charlie to take a couple of bills out to the mailbox, and he went happily enough.

A knock came on the back screen door, and there was Gina, the woman Lacey's brother, Buck, had married, holding a toddler by the hand. "Hey, Lace, are you in there?"

"C'mon in." Lacey got up and opened the door for the woman, a rueful smile on her face. "Welcome to the zoo."

"Hey," Gina greeted Vito and Gramps Camden, and then turned to Lacey, holding the little boy by his shoulders as he attempted to toddle away. "Can you watch Bobby for ten or fifteen minutes? I have to run over to the Senior Towers to check out a few facts."

Vito's curiosity must have shown on his face, because she explained. "I'm doing some research on the town and the guesthouse. This place was a stop on the Underground Railroad and has a really amazing history."

"Laaaaas," the little boy said, walking into Lacey's outstretched arms.

"Hey, how's my sweet boy?" Lacey wrapped the child in a giant hug, and then stood, lifting him to perch on her hip. Her bad mood was apparently gone. "Look, Bobby, this is Vito. And this is Mr. Camden. Can you say hi?"

Bobby buried his face in Lacey's neck.

"Taking off," Gina said, and hurried out the back door.

Lacey cuddled the little boy close, nuzzling his neck, and then brought him to the window. "Look at the birdies," she said, pointing toward a feeder outside the window where a couple of goldfinches fluttered.

"Birdie," Bobby agreed.

"You're a natural," Vito said, meaning it. Lacey looked right at home with a child in her arms, and the picture made a longing rise in him. He wanted a baby. More than one.

And Lacey probably needed to have another baby. It would help her get over the pain of her devastating miscarriage.

Lacey set the table, having Bobby bring napkins along to help, letting him place them haphazardly on the table and chairs.

Vito tasted the sauce and frowned. "It needs something."

"I have basil growing outside. At least, I *think* it's still alive. Want some?"

"Fresh basil? For sure."

"Come on, Bobby." She helped the little boy maneuver across the kitchen and through the back door.

Could Vito be blamed for looking out the window to see where her herbs were planted? After all, he might do more cooking here. He was enjoying it.

And once he looked, and saw her kneeling in the golden late-afternoon sunlight, pointing and talking with Bobby, he found it hard to look away.

"Take a picture, it lasts longer," Gramps muttered. "Do I have to chaperone everyone around here?"

Vito blinked and went back to his cooking, but the image of Lacey, the curve of her neck, soft hair blowing in the breeze, stayed with him.

Who was he to think romantically about someone so beautiful, so perfect?

Half an hour later, they were about to sit down to a not-bad-looking dinner when Gina tapped on the back door.

"Mama!" Bobby cried and toddled toward the door.

She opened the door, scooped up her son and gave him a big loud kiss.

"You'll stay for dinner, won't you?" Lacey asked Gina.

"Oh…no. I would but… I need to get home." Her cheeks went pink and Vito put it together. She was a new bride, must have just gotten back from a brief honeymoon. She wanted to get home to her new husband.

Envy tugged at Vito's heart. Would he ever have a wife who was eager to return to him, or would he always remain just the best friend?

Dinner was fun. Nonna insisted they put on some Italian opera music—"the most romantic music on earth!"—and then got into a good-natured argument with Gramps Camden, who insisted that Frank Sinatra sang the best love songs. Her eyes sparkled with pleasure as everyone talked and joked and ate. Charlie enjoyed the company, too. Both of them would benefit from being part of a bigger family, Vito realized. He would, as well.

He just didn't know how to make it happen. But at least for the summer, it was something they could enjoy here at Lacey's. He would talk to her about having meals together as often as possible, splitting grocery bills and sharing cooking duties.

When he stood to clear the dishes, Lacey put a hand on his arm. "It's okay, Vito. You cooked, so I'll clean up."

"It's a lot," he protested, trying not to notice the delicate feel of her hand.

"I have an excellent helper," she said, letting go of Vito and patting Charlie's arm. "Right?"

"Sure," the boy said with surprising good cheer.

Of course. Lacey had that effect on every male of the species. Her charm wasn't meant specially for him.

"You can walk me back over to the Towers," Gramps said unexpectedly to Vito, so after a few minutes of parting conversation, the two of them headed down to the street. The Towers were almost next door to Lacey's guesthouse, and Gramps seemed plenty strong to get there on his own, but maybe he just wanted the company. Fine with Vito. He needed to get away from pretty Lacey, get some fresh air.

"How you handling those scars?" Gramps asked abruptly.

Vito felt the heat rise up his neck and was glad for the darkness and the cool breeze. "Apart from terrifying women and children, no big deal."

Gramps chuckled. "It's what's on the inside that counts. Any woman worth her salt will know that. The kid over there seems like he gets it, too."

It was true; the few occasions Charlie still cringed away from Vito had more to do with leftover fears related to his mother's boyfriends than with Vito's looks.

They were almost to the front door of the Towers now, and Vito was ready to say goodbye when Gramps stopped and turned toward him. "Just what are your intentions toward Lacey?"

Vito pulled back to stare at the older man. "Intentions?"

"That's right. Some of us over at the Towers got to talking. Wondered whether you and she had more than a landlord-tenant friendship."

"Hey, hey now." Vito held up a hand. "Nobody needs to be gossiping about Lacey. She's had enough trouble in her life already."

Gramps propped a hand on the railing beside the door. "Don't you think we know that? For that matter, you have, too. The both of you have— What is it young folks call it?"

"Baggage," Vito said. "And we may be young compared to…some people, but we're not so young we need to be told what to do."

Gramps snorted. "Think you know everything, do you?"

"No. Not everything. Not much. But I do know my love life's my business, just as Lacey's love life is hers."

"Give it some thought before you mingle them together, that's all. I'd hate to see either Lacey or that boy hurt."

"I'd hate to see that, too." Vito lifted an eyebrow. "We done here?"

"We're done," Gramps said, "but have a care how you spend the rest of your evening over there."

And even though he found the warning annoying, Vito figured it was probably a wise one.

Chapter Five

When Vito walked back into the guesthouse, he heard dishes clattering in the kitchen. Lacey. Like a magnet, she drew him.

And maybe Gramps knew just what he was talking about. Being careful was the goal Vito needed to shoot for. A vulnerable woman and a vulnerable child were both somewhat under his protection, and Gramps didn't know the half of how any relationship between Lacey and Vito could cause damage to both of them.

He'd expected to see Charlie in the kitchen, but when he got there Lacey was alone, squatting to put away a pan.

"Hey," he said softly, not wanting to startle her. "Where's Charlie?"

She stood and turned toward him. "I told him he could watch TV. He was a good helper, but apparently, it's time for one of his favorite shows."

"Oh, right." Vito should go. He should go right upstairs, right now.

But in the soft lamplight, he couldn't look away from her.

She was looking at him, too, her eyes wide and confused.

He took a step toward her.

Leaning against the counter with one hip, she picked up a framed photo from the counter, studied it for a few seconds, and then placed it carefully on the shelf beside the sink.

"What's that?" He walked over but stopped a good three feet away from her. A safe distance.

She picked it back up and held it out for him to see. "It was Gerry's second time home on furlough. I'd missed him so much that when he came off the plane, I broke away from the other wives and ran screaming to hug him. Somebody caught it on film."

Vito studied the picture of Lacey and his friend, and his heart hurt. They *did* look happy, thrilled to see each other. "Could've been in the newspaper. Good picture."

"It was in the *Plain Dealer*," she said, smiling shyly. "That embarrassed Gerry. Me, too, a little. Everyone kept coming up to us to say they'd seen it."

"Gerry didn't like that, huh?" Vito felt sick inside, because he knew why.

Gerry had already been involved with Krystal at that point. Maybe she'd even been pregnant with Charlie. He thought about asking Lacey the year, and then didn't. He didn't even want to know.

How awkward for Gerry that his girlfriend might see his loving wife hugging on him.

Gerry had been such a jerk.

"He was everything I ever wanted," Lacey said dreamily, studying the picture. "Sometimes I don't think I'll ever get over him."

"Right. Look, I'd better go check on Charlie and

catch some sleep myself." He turned and walked out of the room. An abrupt departure might be a little rude, but it was better than staying there, listening to her express her adoration of a man who'd not been worth one ounce of it. Better than blurting out something that would destroy that idealized image she had of Gerry.

Don't speak ill of the dead. It was a common maxim, and valid.

Was he making a huge mistake to stay here, even though that was what Nonna and Charlie both wanted?

He scrubbed a hand across his face and headed up the stairs. He needed to focus on his professional goals and forget about his personal desire to have a wife and a large family. He needed to make sure that personal desire didn't settle on Lacey, like Gramps seemed to worry it would.

He and Charlie were living in the home of the one woman he could never, ever be involved with. He'd promised Gerry at the moment of his death, and that meant something. It meant a lot. The sooner he got that straight in his head, the better.

On Friday, Lacey strolled along the sidewalk with Vito and Charlie and tried to shake the odd feeling that they were a family, doing errands together. It was a strange thought, especially given that her goal was to get her guesthouse up and running so that she could dive into her self-sufficient, single-woman life and make it good.

She just needed to keep in mind the purpose of this trip: to create a cozy room at the guesthouse for any child who came to stay for a night or a weekend.

It was only midafternoon, but with the arrival of

summer, a lot of people seemed to be taking off work early on Fridays. A group of women clustered outside of the Chatterbox Café, talking. A young couple pushed their baby in a stroller. Several people she knew vaguely from the Senior Towers were taking their afternoon walk, and outside Chez la Ferme, Rescue River's only fancy restaurant, Sam Hinton stood with sleeves rolled up, talking to another man in a suit, smiling like he'd just tied up a deal.

"You're sure you don't mind focusing on Charlie's room right now?" Vito asked as Charlie ran ahead to examine a heavily chromed motorcycle in front of the Chatterbox. "It's not the project you were planning on, I'm sure."

"It's not, but it's a good change of plans. Having a room or two decorated for kids will only add to the guesthouse's appeal. And that little room off the big one is perfect for that."

"And you're being kind. Charlie's been in a mood, so maybe this will help." They reached Love's Hardware, and Vito held the door for her, then called for Charlie to come join them.

The front of the store was crowded with summer merchandise, garden tools and stacked bags of mulch and grass seed. A faint, pungent smell attested to the fertilizer and weed killer in stock. Farther back, bins of nails and screws and bolts occupied one wall while pipes and sinks and bathtubs dominated the other. Overhead, modern light fixtures, price tags hanging, intermixed with old-fashioned signs advertising long-gone brands of household appliances. The soft sound of R & B played in the background.

A string of small bells chimed on the door as it

closed behind them, and the store's owner, Mr. Love, came forward immediately, one weathered brown hand extended, subtly guiding him through the store aisle. His vision wasn't the best, but he still managed his hardware store almost entirely on his own.

"Hey, Mr. Love, it's Lacey. And you remember Vito D'Angelo, right?"

"I sure do, sure do. Glad to see you folks on such a fine day." Mr. Love fumbled for their hands, and then clasped each in a friendly greeting.

"And this is his foster son, Charlie."

"Say hello," Vito prompted the boy, urging him forward.

Charlie scowled as if he might refuse. But as he looked up at Mr. Love, he seemed impressed by the man's age and courtly dignity. "Hi, it's nice to meet you," he said, holding out his hand to shake in a surprising display of good manners.

After Lacey had explained their mission, Mr. Love led them over to the paint section, where Charlie's momentary sweetness vanished. "I want this blue," he said, selecting a bold cobalt paint chip and holding it out as if the decision was made.

Lacey bit her lip. She'd told Charlie he could help pick out the color, but she and her future guests were the ones who'd have to live with it. "How about something a little lighter, Charlie? It's an old-fashioned house, and this is a pretty modern color." She offered up a sample card featuring various shades of blue. "I was thinking of something in this range."

"That's boring. I want this one."

"It's Lacey's decision, buddy," Vito said, putting a

firm hand on Charlie's shoulder. "We're guests in her house, and she's nice to let you choose the color blue."

Charlie's lower lip stuck out a mile.

"Let's look at the cobalt in shades," Lacey suggested. "We could have that color, just a little lighter. Do you like this one?" She pointed at a shade halfway down the sample card.

"That one's okay." Charlie pointed at one toward the end, almost as bright as his original pick.

"Charlie. Lacey has the last word."

Lacey bent to see Charlie's downcast face. "I promise I'll take your ideas into consideration."

"Fine." Charlie gave Lacey a dirty look.

"Come on, let's go see the power tools," Vito suggested. "Guy stuff," he added, winking at Lacey.

Immediately, her distress about Charlie's attitude faded as her heart gave a funny little twist.

"I have to let my granddaughter mix the paint or she gets mad at me," Mr. Love said to Lacey. In a lower voice, he added, "I can't see the colors too well, but if you'd like, I can ask her to add in a little more white to whatever shade the boy picked."

"That would be fantastic," Lacey said gratefully. "Thank you."

"Don't you worry about young Charlie," Mr. Love said, patting her arm. "Kids usually come around."

That was true, and besides, Charlie wasn't her problem to worry about. But there was no point in explaining that to Mr. Love, so she let it go.

On the way home, they walked by a group of slightly older boys playing basketball in the park, and Charlie wanted to join in.

"No, buddy," Vito said. "We're painting today."

"I don't wanna paint! I wanna play outside!"

That made sense to Lacey, but Vito shook his head. "You can run ahead and play basketball outside the guesthouse for a while."

"That's no fun, playing by myself." But Charlie took off ahead of them, staying in sight, but kicking stones in an obvious display of bad temper.

Vito blew out a sigh. "Sure wish there was a manual on how to parent," he said.

"I think you're doing great," she said, reassuring him. "What's Charlie's background, anyway? Was it difficult?"

Vito looked away, then back at her. "Yeah. His mom's an addict. She loves him, but not as much as she loves to get high."

Poor Charlie. "What about his dad?"

Vito looked away again and didn't answer.

A sudden, surprising thought came into Lacey's head: was Charlie *Vito's* biological son?

But no. If Vito had fathered a child, he wouldn't deny it and pretend to just be the foster dad.

"His dad's passed," Vito said finally. "And Mom keeps getting involved with men who rough her up. It happened to Charlie a few times, too, which is why he originally went into foster care. His mom wasn't able to make a change, so Charlie's free for adoption. I hope we'll have that finalized within a few months."

"That's great, Vito." Even as she said it, she wondered how and why he'd gotten involved in foster care. It was so good of him, but not something most single men in their early thirties would consider. "Why did—"

"Charlie learned a rough style of play in some of

his old neighborhoods," Vito interrupted quickly, almost as if he wanted to avoid her questions. "And he doesn't have the best social skills. If he's going to play basketball in the park, I need to be there to supervise."

"You could stay with him now. You don't have to help me paint his room."

"Thanks, but no. It's only right that we help. And besides," he said, flashing her a smile, "it's what I want to do."

So they spent the afternoon painting as a team. Sun poured through the open windows, and birds sang outside. Stroking the brush, and then the roller, across the walls, soothed Lacey's heart. Again, more strongly this time, she got that weird feeling of being a family with Vito.

He was good around the house. He could fix things, he could paint, he could cook. And he liked to do those things with her.

Unlike Gerry, who'd always begged off family chores.

Charlie burst into the room, planted his feet wide and crossed his arms. He looked around the half-painted room, his lip curling. "That's not the color I wanted."

Something about his stance and his expression looked oddly familiar to Lacey, but she couldn't put her finger on what it was.

"The second coat'll make it brighter, buddy," Vito said. "Why don't you stay in here and I'll teach you to paint with the roller?"

"No way. That's boring." Charlie turned to stomp out and landed a foot directly in the tray of paint. When he saw what he'd done, he ran out of the room, tracking paint the whole way.

Vito leaped up and hurried after him, while Lacey raced to wipe up the paint before it dried on the hardwood floors, chuckling a little to herself. With Vito and Charlie around, there would never be a dull moment.

"Oh, man, I'm sorry," Vito said as he returned to see her scrubbing at a last footprint. "Charlie's in timeout in the kitchen, since I can't exactly send him to his room, and he'll be back up in a few minutes to help. Neatly. To make up for this mess."

"It's okay. It's part of having a kid."

Vito sighed. "I guess it is, but I wasn't ready for it. I never know if I'm doing the right thing or not."

"You're doing a good job. Really good." She smiled up at him.

"Thanks. I don't feel so sure."

Just like the other night, their eyes caught and held for a beat too long.

Charlie burst into the room in sock feet and stood, hands on hips. "I'm here, but I ain't apologizing and I ain't helping." He lifted his chin and glared at Vito as if daring him to exert his authority as a father.

Vito opened his mouth to speak, but Lacey's heart went out to the hurting little boy, and she held up a hand. "Let me talk to him," she said, and walked over to Charlie. "It's been a rough day, hasn't it? But that paint came right off and it won't be a problem."

"So?"

In every stiff line of his body she read a need for a mother's comfort. "Hey," she said, putting an arm around him, "I'm glad you're here and I think this is going to be a great room for you. You can help decorate it."

For a second Charlie relaxed against her, but then he went stiff again and stepped away, his face red. "That's what you said about the paint, and then I got this baby color!" He waved a hand at the nearest wall.

"Oh, honey—"

"Don't call me that! Only my real mom can call me that!"

"Charlie…" Vito said in a warning voice, approaching the two of them.

"She doesn't have any kids! She's not a mom, so why is she acting like one?"

The words rang in Lacey's ears.

It was true. She wasn't a mom, and Charlie, with a child's insight, had seen right into the dream inside her head. On some barely conscious level she'd been pretending that Charlie was her child and Vito was her husband, and it had to stop.

Slowly, she backed away from Charlie just as Vito reached him.

"I want you to apologize to Miss Lacey," Vito said firmly.

"I'm not apologizing!" Tears ran down Charlie's reddened face, but he ignored them, frowning fiercely and thrusting his chest out.

"Charlie." Vito put a hand on the boy's shoulder.

"Don't you touch me! You're not my real dad. And you're ugly, too!" Charlie ran from the room.

Vito's hand went to his scarred face for just a moment, and then he followed Charlie.

Even in the middle of her own hurt feelings, Lacey wanted to comfort him, to tell him he *wasn't* ugly.

But that was exactly the problem. She wasn't the mom of the family. She wasn't the wife.

She never would play that role, and she needed to stop pretending and accept the truth.

Chapter Six

"Let's see if we can scare up a basketball game at the park," Vito said to Charlie the next day after lunch.

"Yeah!" Charlie dropped his handheld game and jumped up.

Vito laughed. He was still getting used to the time frame of an eight-year-old. "In ten minutes, okay? I have to clean up our dishes and make a phone call."

Vito had planned to spend Saturday setting up Charlie's room and looking for jobs online. But Charlie's behavior the previous day had changed his mind. Vito was no expert, but it seemed to him that Charlie needed structure, and chores, and attention. So they'd spent the morning weeding the gardens around the guesthouse, and with a little prodding Charlie had worked hard. He'd even taken a glass of lemonade to Lacey, who was sanding woodwork in the breakfast room, and Vito had heard her talk cheerfully to Charlie, which was a relief. Apparently, she wasn't holding a grudge against Charlie for yesterday's behavior.

So, amends made, Vito and Charlie half walked, half jogged to the park together, bouncing a basketball.

Lawn mowers and weed eaters roared, filling the air with the pungent fragrance of vegetation, and several people called greetings from flower beds and front yards. Things weren't much different than when Vito himself had been eight, growing up here.

The call he'd made had been to Troy Hinton, an old acquaintance whose son, Xavier, was just Charlie's age. Troy and Xavier met them by the basketball courts at the park, and immediately, the boys ran out onto the blacktop to play. Vito and Troy sat down on a bench to watch.

Xavier played well for an eight-year-old, making a few baskets, dribbling without too much traveling. Charlie, though, was on fire, making well more than half of the shots he took. Paternal pride warmed Vito's chest. He'd make sure Charlie tried out for the school team as soon as he got to sixth grade.

"That's a good thing you're doing, fostering him," Troy said, nodding toward Charlie. "He seems like he's settling in fine."

That reminded Vito of yesterday, and he shook his head. "A few bumps in the road."

"Yeah?" Troy bent down to flick a piece of dirt off his leg.

"I think he misses his mom. He sees her once a week, but that's hard on a kid."

"Any chance of her getting him back?"

Vito shook his head. "No. Supervised visits is all."

"Gotcha." Troy was watching the two boys play.

Even at eight, Charlie used his elbows and threw a few too many shoves.

"Charlie!" Vito called.

When Charlie looked over, Vito just shook his head. Charlie's mouth twisted, and then he nodded.

"We talked about sportsmanship this morning. I don't know why he thinks he can play street ball here, in the park."

Troy chuckled. "It's a process. And Xavier's holding his own." Indeed, the boy did some fancy footwork and stole the ball from Charlie.

Which was impressive, considering Xavier's background. "How's his health?"

"Almost two years cancer-free."

"That's great." Although Vito had been overseas, he'd heard from Nonna about the careworn single mom who'd come to town to work at Troy's dog rescue, bringing her son who was struggling with leukemia. Now Troy and Angelica were married, with another child, and it was great to know that Xavier was healthy and strong.

"He's doing so well that we can't keep up with him in the summer. So we've got him in a weekday program here at the park. Six hours a day, lots of activity. Charlie should join."

"Well…" Vito thought about it. "That's tempting, but Charlie has a few issues."

"People who run it are good with issues. And you should also bring him to the Kennel Kids." Troy explained the program for at-risk boys, helping once a week at the dog rescue farm Troy operated.

Vito had to thank God for how things were working out here in Rescue River. It was a great place to raise kids. "Sounds perfect, if you've got a space for him."

"Might have one for you, too. I could use a little help."

"Oh, so that's how it is," Vito joked, but truthfully, he was glad to be asked. Vito liked dogs, and Troy. And most of all, he wanted to do positive things for Charlie, and with him. "Sure thing. I can help out."

The boys came running over, panting, and grabbed water bottles to chug.

"You guys should come play!" Charlie said, looking from Vito to Troy.

"Aw, Dad's too tired." Xavier bounced the basketball hard so it went back up higher than his head.

"Who says?" Troy got to his feet and grinned at Vito. "Hintons against D'Angelos, what do you say?"

"I'm not a D'Angelo," Charlie protested.

"But you're going to be, pretty soon." Vito stood, too, and ruffled Charlie's hair. "Meanwhile, let's show these Hintons how it's done."

After an hour of play that left them all breathless and sweating, Troy and Xavier invited Charlie to come out to the farm for a few hours, and Vito agreed. It was good for Charlie to make friends.

But that left Vito with a hole in his day. He'd finished the preliminary work for his online courses, and the term didn't start for another week. Nonna was spending the day visiting at the Senior Towers.

He thought of Troy Hinton, married, raising two kids, the town veterinarian and dog rescue owner, volunteering with the Kennel Kids. What was Vito contributing by comparison? And Troy had a big property to handle, a place for kids to run, while Vito was living in two rooms.

He walked through the park, feeling uncharacteristically blue. There was a soccer game going on, a coed team of kids a little younger than Charlie, and

Vito stopped to watch. The game wasn't too serious. Parents chatted with each other in the bleachers while coaches hollered instructions, mostly encouraging rather than overly competitive. Nearby, a family with a new baby sat on a blanket, cheering on their kids who were playing while cuddling with toddlers who looked like twins.

Vito wanted that. Wanted a family, a large family. It was in his blood.

Suddenly, someone tapped his shoulder, and he turned to see Lacey and another woman, pretty, dark-haired, with Asian features.

"Hi!" the dark-haired woman said, holding out a hand. "I'm Susan Hinton. I've heard a lot about you."

What did that mean? He shook Susan's hand and shot a glance at Lacey. Her cheeks were pink. What had she been telling Susan?

"Vito D'Angelo," he supplied, since Lacey seemed to be tongue-tied. "It's a pleasure. Are you related to Troy?"

"Sure am. I'm married to his brother, Sam."

"I know Sam. Sorry to have missed the wedding." He'd been invited, but he'd been in the thick of his surgery at that point.

"Mindy could score," Lacey said, gesturing toward the soccer game. She looked like a teenager, dressed in cutoffs and a soft blue T-shirt. Her short blond hair lifted and tossed in the breeze, and Vito liked that she didn't glue it down with hair spray.

He felt an urge to brush back a strand that had fallen into her eyes, but that would be completely inappropriate. They weren't that kind of friends.

"C'mon, Mindy, go for it!" Susan yelled, and the

little girl in question kicked the ball hard, making a goal. “Good job!”

“Susan’s a teacher,” Lacey said when the hubbub had died down. “She might have some good ideas about your career change.”

“You’re switching over to teaching?” Susan asked. “What age of kids?”

“I like the little ones,” Vito admitted. “Seems like elementary teachers make a big difference.”

“And we need more men in the profession,” Susan said promptly. “Are you planning to stay local?”

“If I can find work.”

Susan opened her mouth as if she were going to ask another question, but a shout interrupted her. Mindy, the child who’d scored a goal, ran over, accompanied by two little girls about the same age. “Did you see, Mama, did you see?”

“I saw.” Susan hugged the little girl close. “You’re getting better every day.”

Vito was watching the pair, so it took a minute for him to become aware that the other two girls were staring up at him.

“What happened to the side of your face?” one of them asked.

“He looks *mean*,” said the other little girl.

The remarks shouldn’t have stung—he’d known that was how kids would feel, hadn’t he?—but they did, anyway.

“Cheyenne! Shelby!” Susan spun and squatted right in front of the other two girls. “You know it’s not polite to make personal remarks about someone’s appearance.”

“I’m sorry, Miss Hayashi,” one of them said right away.

"It's Mrs. Hinton, dummy," the other said. "Don't you know she got married?"

Susan put a hand on each girl's shoulder. "First of all, it's more important to be... Do you remember what?"

"More important to be polite than right," the two and little Mindy chorused.

"And furthermore, Shelby," Susan said sternly, "this gentleman got those injuries serving our country, and you *will* show him the respect he deserves."

Vito didn't know which felt worse: being told how bad he looked by a second-gradeish little girl, or being defended by a woman approximately half his size. "Hey, it's okay," he said, squatting down, too, making sure his better half was turned toward the girls. "It can be a surprise to see somebody who looks different."

Mindy shoved in front of him. "I'm *glad* he looks different. Different is cool." She reached up and unhooked something from her back and then started fumbling with her arm.

"Don't take it off! Don't take it off!" the other two girls screamed, sounding more excited than upset.

At which point Vito realized that Mindy had a prosthetic arm, which she seemed set on removing.

Other kids ran in their direction, no doubt attracted by the screams. Vito stood and glanced at Lacey, who gave him a palms up that clearly said she had no idea how to handle the situation.

"Mindy!" Susan's voice was stern, all teacher. "Don't you dare take off that arm. You know the rules."

Mindy's forehead wrinkled, and she and Susan glared at each other. Then, slowly, Mindy twisted something back into place and let go of her prosthetic.

"I just wanted to show them that everybody's different, and that's okay," she said sulkily.

Susan knelt and hugged her. "That was a very kind impulse. Now, why don't you girls get back on the field? I think the second half is starting."

Vito took a step back. "Hey, it was nice meeting you," he said to Susan.

"Vito—" Lacey sounded worried.

"Got to go. See you later." What he really needed to do was to be alone. Today's little scene had hammered the truth home to him: he couldn't work with kids in person. His appearance would create a ruckus that would interfere with their learning.

The trouble was he liked kids. And interacting with them through a computer screen just didn't have the same appeal.

Lacey looked from where Susan was ushering the little girls back into the soccer game, toward the path where Vito was walking away, shoulders slumped.

"I'm headed home," she called to Susan, and then took off after Vito. She couldn't stand what she'd just seen.

He was walking fast enough that she was out of breath by the time she got within earshot. "Vito, wait!"

He turned around to wait for her.

"Where are you going? Are you okay?" she asked breathlessly.

"I'm going for a walk, and I'm fine." His words were uncharacteristically clipped.

"Mind if I come?" She started walking beside him, sure of her welcome. After all, this was Vito. He was always glad to see her.

"Actually..." He walked slowly, glanced over at her. "Look, I'm not fit company. Go on back and hang out with Susan."

She gave him a mock glare. "No way! You hung out with me plenty when I wasn't fit company. I'm just returning the favor to an old friend."

He started to say something, then closed his mouth, and mortification sent heat up Lacey's neck. She was being intrusive. It was one of her flaws, according to Gerry, and she half expected Vito to bite her head off.

But he didn't speak and his face wasn't angry. They walked quietly for a few minutes, past the high school. The fragrance of new-mown grass tickled Lacey's nose. From somewhere, she smelled meat grilling, a summer barbecue.

"Where are you headed?" she repeated, because he hadn't answered. "Can I tag along?" Then she worried she'd pushed too far.

"I'm going to the river. To think." He gave her shoulders a quick squeeze. "And sure, you can come. Sorry to be such a bear."

So she followed him down a little path between the grasses and trees and they emerged on the riverbank. As if by agreement, they both stopped, looking at the sunlight glinting off the water, hearing the wind rustle through the weeping willow trees overhead.

"I'm sorry that happened back there," she said. "That must be hard to deal with, especially..." She trailed off.

"Especially what?"

"Especially when you were always so handsome."

He laughed, shaking his head at the same time. "Oh, Lace. My biggest fan."

She had been, too. In fact, as a younger teen, she'd dreamed of a day when she'd be older, with clear skin and actual curves, and Vito would ask her out. A visceral memory flashed into her mind: lying on the floor of her bedroom, feet propped up on a footstool and CD player blasting out a sad love song, which in her fourteen-year-old brain she'd applied to herself and Vito's lost love.

"You were the best looking of all the guys in your class," she said. "Everyone said so."

He didn't deny it, exactly, but he waved a dismissive hand. "A lot of good it did me. I could barely get a date."

That had to be an exaggeration; she remembered plenty of girls noticing him. But it was true, he hadn't dated as much as you'd expect of a boy with his looks. "You were too nice. You weren't a player."

He laughed. "That's true, I never got that down." They turned and strolled along the river's grassy bank. "Now I look mean, like the little girl said. Maybe I should cultivate a mean persona to match. I'd get all the girls."

"As if that's going to happen." Lacey couldn't imagine Vito being mean. It just wasn't in his nature. "Is that what you want, Vito? All the girls?"

He gave her a look she couldn't read. "Not all. But I'd like to get married, start a family, and I'm not getting any younger."

"Is that why you're adopting Charlie?"

He lifted a shoulder and looked away. "That's part of it."

"As far as getting married," she said, "you could have any woman you wanted."

A muscle contracted in his scarred cheek. "Don't, Lace."

"Don't what?" She stumbled on a root and he automatically caught her arm, steadied her.

"Don't lie to me. If I couldn't get the girls before, I'm not going to get them now."

"I'm not lying. You have a..." She paused, considering how to say it. "You have a rugged appeal."

"Is that so?" He looked over at her, his expression skeptical.

For some reason, her face heated, and she lifted it to cool in the breeze from the river. She focused on the birdcalls and blue sky, visible through a network of green leaves, while she tried to get her bearings.

When she looked back at him, he was still watching her. "Think of Tiffany Townsend," she said, trying to sound offhand. "She was all over you."

He rolled his eyes, just a little, making her remember him as a teen. "Tiffany Townsend isn't what I want."

"What do you want?"

Instead of answering, he walked a few paces to the right and lifted a streamer of honeysuckle growing against a thick strand of trees. Beyond it was a cave-like depression in a natural rock wall. "Wonder if kids are still carving their names in here?"

She laughed. "Lover's Cave. I'd forgotten about it." She followed him inside, the temperature dropping a good few degrees, making a chill rise up on her arms.

Vito pinched off a vine of honeysuckle flowers, inhaled their scent, and then tucked them into Lacey's hair. "For a lovely lady."

Wow. Why wasn't Vito married by now? He was

chivalrous, a natural romantic. Who *wouldn't* want to be with a man like that?

Inside the small enclosure, she turned to him, then stepped back, feeling overwhelmed by the closeness. *Make conversation; this is awkward.* "Did you ever kiss a girl in here?"

He laughed outright. "My *nonna* taught me better than to kiss and tell. Why? Were you kissed in here?"

"No." She remembered bringing Gerry down to the river, showing him the sights of her younger days. She'd hoped to finally get a kiss in Lover's Cave, but he hadn't wanted to follow her inside. Romantic gestures weren't his thing, but that was okay. He'd loved her; she was sure of that.

"What was wrong with the boys in your grade? Why didn't you get kissed here?"

"Guys didn't like my type." She turned away, catching a whiff of honeysuckle.

He touched her face, making her look at him. "What type is that?"

"Shy. Backward."

"Are you still?"

Lacey's heart was pounding. "I… I might be."

His fingers still rested on her cheek, featherlight. "Don't be nervous. It's just me."

A hysterical giggle bubbled up inside her, along with a warm, melty breathlessness. She couldn't look away from him.

He cupped her face with both hands. Oh, wow, was he really going to kiss her? Her heart was about to fly out of her chest and she blurted out the first nervous thought she had. "You never answered my question."

"What was it? I'm getting distracted." He smiled a little, but his eyes were intense, serious.

He was *incredibly* attractive, scars and all.

"I asked you," she said breathlessly, "what *do* you want, if you don't want someone like Tiffany?"

"I want..." He paused, looked out through the veil of honeysuckle vines and let his hands fall away from her face. Breathed in, breathed out, audibly, and then eased out of the cave, holding the honeysuckle curtain for her, but careful not to touch her. "I want what I can't have."

Suddenly chilled, Lacey rubbed her bare arms, looking away from him. Whatever Vito wanted, it was obviously not her.

Chapter Seven

"Come on, Nonna, let's go sit on the porch." Vito was walking his grandmother out of the kitchen after dinner. Nonna hadn't eaten much of it despite his and Charlie's cajoling. Vito wished Lacey had stayed to eat with them, but she'd had something else urgent to do.

Most likely, urgently avoiding *him*. And rightly so. He was avoiding her, too, and kicking himself for that little romantic interlude in Lover's Cave.

"I'm a little tired for the porch, dear." Nonna held tightly on to his arm.

She sounded depressed, something Lacey had mentioned was common in patients recovering from a heart attack. Activity and socializing were part of the solution, so Vito pressed on. "But you've been in your room all day. A talk and a little air will do you good."

"Well..." She paused. "Will you sit with me?"

"Nothing I'd rather do." He kissed her soft cheek, noticing the fragrance of lavender that always clung to her, and his heart tightened with love.

He and Nonna walked slowly down the guesthouse hall. She still clung to his arm, and when they got to the bench beside the door, she stopped. "I'll just…rest here a minute. Could you get me another glass of that iced tea? I'm so thirsty."

"Sure." He settled her on the bench and went back to the kitchen to pour iced tea, looking out into the driveway to see if, by chance, Lacey had come in without his noticing. He'd feel better if she were here. Only because Nonna wasn't feeling well.

When he reached the guesthouse door with the tea, he saw that Nonna was already out on the porch. "Charlie helped me out," she said, gesturing to where the boy was shooting hoops across the street. "He's a good boy."

He set their tea on the table between the rocking chairs and sat down. The evening air was warm, but the humidity was down and the light breeze made for comfortable porch-sitting. In fact, several people were outside down the block, in front of the Senior Towers. A young couple walked by pushing a stroller, talking rapidly in Spanish. Marilyn Smith strolled past the basketball hoop with her Saint Bernard, and Charlie and his friend stopped playing to pet it and ask her excited questions.

Evening in a small town. He loved it here.

"Tell me about your course work, dear," Nonna said. "Is it going well?"

"Just finished a couple of modules today. It's interesting material."

"And you like taking a class on the computer?"

He shrugged. "Honestly, I'd rather be in a classroom where I could talk and listen, but we don't have a college here, and this is the easiest, cheapest option."

"That's just what Lou Ann Miller says. She's almost done with her degree. At her age!"

They chatted on about Vito's courses and Lou Ann and other people they knew in common, greeted a few neighbors walking by.

After a while, Vito noticed that Nonna had gotten quiet, and he looked over to see her eyes blinking closed. In the slanting evening sunlight, her skin looked wrinkled like thin cloth, and her coloring wasn't as robust as he'd have liked to see.

Lacey's little car drove into the driveway. She pulled behind the guesthouse, and moments later the back screen door slammed. Normally, she'd have come in by the front porch, stopping to pull a couple of weeds from the flower bed and say hello to Nonna. So she was still avoiding him, obviously, but at least she was home in case Nonna needed her.

Nonna started awake and looked around as if she was confused. "Tell me about your courses, dear," she said.

"We just talked about that." Vito studied her. "Are you feeling okay? Do you want to go inside?"

"I'm fine. I meant your job hunt. Tell me about your job hunt." She smiled reassuringly, looking like her old self.

"I keep seeing jobs that look interesting, but they're all in person." He paused, then added, "I want an online job."

As usual, Nonna read his mind. "You can't hide forever," she said, patting his hand.

"You're right, and I'm a coward for wanting to hide behind the computer. Except...would you want your kids to have a scary teacher?"

"I'd want them to have a smart, caring teacher. And besides, once people get to know you, they forget about those little scars. I have."

It was what Lacey had said, too. It was what Troy had said. It was even what his friends in the VA support group said. He didn't know why he was having such a hard time getting over his scarred face.

And okay, he was bummed for a number of reasons. If things had been different, if Charlie hadn't needed a home and if he hadn't been so scarred, then maybe he and Lacey could have made a go of things. She'd seemed a little interested, for a minute there.

But things weren't different, and he needed to focus on the here and now, and on those who needed him. He glanced over at Nonna.

She was slumped over in her chair at an odd angle, her eyes closed.

"Nonna!" He leaped up and tried a gentle shake of her shoulders that failed to wake her. "Charlie, come here!" he called over his shoulder.

He lifted his grandmother from the chair and carried her to the door just as Charlie arrived and opened it for him. "Is she okay?" Charlie asked.

"Not yet. Get Lacey, now!" Vito carried Nonna into her bedroom and set her gently on the bed. He should never have encouraged her to go out on the porch. On the other hand, what if she'd fainted in her room, alone? What had brought this on? Up until tonight she'd seemed to be improving daily.

Lacey burst into the room, stethoscope in hand, and bent over the bed, studying Nonna. "What happened?"

"She wasn't feeling well, and then she passed out."

Lacey took her pulse and listened. "It's rapid but..."

She stopped, listened again. "It's settling a bit." She opened Nonna's bedside drawer and pulled out a pen-like device, a test strip, and some kind of a meter. "I'm going to test her blood sugar."

Charlie hovered in the door of the room as Lacey pricked Nonna's finger, and Vito debated sending him away. But he and Nonna were developing a nice friendship, and Charlie deserved to be included in what was going on.

Nonna's eyes fluttered open. She was breathing fast, like she'd run a race.

Vito's throat constricted, looking at her. She was fragile. Why hadn't he realized how fragile she was?

Lacey frowned at the test strip, left the room and returned with a hypodermic needle. "Little pinch," she said to Nonna as she extracted clear liquid from a small bottle and injected her arm. "Your blood sugar is through the roof. What happened? It hasn't been this high in weeks!"

There was a snuffling sound from the doorway; Charlie was crying. Vito held out an arm, and Charlie ran and pressed beside him, looking at Nonna with open worry.

Lacey propped Nonna up and sat on the bed, holding her hand. "Are you feeling better? You passed out."

"Was it the cake?" Charlie blurted out.

Vito's head spun to look at the boy at the same time Lacey's did. "What cake?" they asked in unison.

Charlie pressed his lips together and looked at Nonna, whose expression was guilty.

"I… I gave him money…" Nonna broke off and leaned back against the pillow, her eyes closing.

"What happened?" Vito set Charlie in front of him,

put his hands on the boy's shoulders and studied him sternly. "Tell the truth."

"She gave me money and asked me to get her cake from the bakery. I didn't know what to do! I wanted her to have a treat. She said it would be our secret. And she gave me the rest of the money so I could get something, too." Charlie was crying openly now. "I'm sorry! I didn't know it would hurt her.'"

Vito shook his head and patted the boy's shoulder, not sure whether to comfort or punish him. "Remember, you're supposed to come ask me, not just go do something another adult tells you to do. Even if it's Nonna."

"Is she going to be okay?"

"She'll be okay." Lacey gave Charlie's hand a quick squeeze. "But your dad's right. Don't ever bring her something to eat again without asking one of us."

Even in the midst of his worries, Vito noticed that Lacey had automatically called him Charlie's dad. He liked the sound of that.

But he was second-guessing himself for bringing Charlie to live here at all. The kid was eight. He didn't know how to properly assist in the care of a very sick elderly woman, and he didn't have an idea of consequences.

Nonna said something, her voice weak, and Lacey put a hand on Charlie's arm. "Let's listen to Nonna."

"I…told him…to do it. Not his fault." She offered up a guilty smile that was a shadow of her usual bright one.

"Nonna! This is serious. We're going to have to take you to the emergency room to get you checked out."

"Oh, no," Nonna said as Charlie broke into fresh tears. "I just want to rest."

Lacey bit her lip and looked at Vito. "I might be able to talk Dr. Griffin into coming over to take a look at her," she said. "It would be exhausting for her to go to the ER, and I *think* she's going to be okay once her sugar comes down, but I'm not qualified to judge."

"If you could do that, I'd be very grateful." He knew that old Dr. Griffin lived right down the street.

"Okay. Charlie, would you like to come help me get the doctor?"

Charlie nodded, sniffling.

"Could you run upstairs and get my purse out of my bedroom?"

"Sure!" Charlie ran.

Vito was grateful. Lacey had every reason to be angry at the boy, but she was instead helping him to feel better by giving him a job. But that was how she was: forgiving, mature, wise beyond her years.

"Doc owes me a favor," Lacey said quietly to Vito. "I'm sure he'll come, if he's home. Just sit with her until we get back. It'll only be five minutes."

He nodded, gently stroking Nonna's arm, and Lacey and Charlie went out the door.

Beside Nonna's bed was a photo of him and his brother as children. She'd taken them in and raised them after their parents' accident, putting aside her bridge games and bus trips to rejoin the world of PTA meetings and kids' sporting events. And she'd done it with such good cheer that he'd never, until recently, understood the burden it must have been to her.

Now it was time for him to return the favor. To make sure that she was getting the very best care she could.

Which meant that later tonight if, God willing, Nonna was okay, Vito needed to have a very serious talk with Lacey.

After ushering Doc Griffin out the door with profuse thanks, Lacey walked back into the guesthouse as Vito emerged from Nonna's room, gently closing her door behind him.

"She's already asleep," he said. "She's exhausted, but she said to tell you again that she's sorry."

Lacey shook her head and paced the hall. "I'm the one who should be sorry. I should have been keeping closer track of her food."

"She's an adult," Vito said. "She made a choice." But something in his voice told her he didn't completely believe what he was saying, and what he said next confirmed it. "If you have a minute, could we talk?"

"Of course." She gestured for him to come into the front sitting room as her heart sank.

She'd been avoiding him hard all week, since that crazy moment in Lover's Cave. She'd thought he was going to kiss her, and she was sure that expectation had shone on her face. But instead of doing it, he'd gently pushed her away from him.

He was too kind to give her a real rejection, but even his careful one had made her feel like a loser.

He stood in the middle of the room, looking more masculine than ever amidst the delicate Victorian furnishings, and she realized he was waiting for her to sit down first. Who had those kind of manners these days?

Vito, that was who. And she was starting to care for him more than she should. Even though he didn't return the feelings, and nothing would come of it, she felt guilty. What would Gerry think if he knew that she was looking at his best friend in a way she'd once reserved for him?

Or, if the truth be told, in a different way but with the same end game? Because there weren't two men in the world more different than Vito and Gerry. And while Gerry's confidence and swagger had swept her away when she was young, Vito's warm and caring style appealed to her now.

He was still standing, waiting, so she sank down onto the chesterfield and pulled her feet up under her, leaving Vito to take the matching chair. It was a little small for him. Good. Maybe this conversation would be brief.

He cleared his throat. "I was wondering if you've been avoiding me."

Lacey felt her eyebrows shoot up, and against her will, heat rose into her cheeks. "Avoiding you?"

He nodded patiently. "After what happened last weekend. You know, at Lover's Cave."

She blew out a breath. She'd hoped to avoid that topic, but here he was bringing it out into the open to deal with. "I, um..." She wanted to lie, but couldn't bring herself to do it. "Maybe a little," she admitted.

"I thought so." He leaned forward, elbows on knees, and held her gaze. "You don't have to worry about a repeat. And you don't have to stay away from your own house to keep me at bay."

Keep *him* at bay? But of course, chivalrous to the core, Vito would put it like that. Make it seem like she was the one rejecting him, when in point of fact, it had been the other way around.

She swallowed and tore her eyes away from his. And for the life of her, she couldn't think of what to say.

How could she respond when she didn't even know what she felt, herself? When these feelings about Vito tugged at her loyalty to Gerry, even making her question some of her husband's behaviors? When Vito didn't seem to share her attraction at all?

"The thing is," he said, "I'm worried about Nonna's care. If Charlie and I are keeping you from focusing on that, then we should move out."

"She wouldn't like that."

"But if you hadn't come home tonight, and known just what to do, and given her that injection, something much worse could have happened, right?"

Miserably, Lacey twisted her hands together, staring at the floor. "I'm really sorry. I can see why you think I've been neglectful."

"That's not it. I don't think you and she ever had an arrangement where you had to be here with her 24/7. Did you?"

"No." Honesty compelled her to add, "But part of the appeal of living here was that she'd have me around a lot while I remodeled. Which I usually am. It's just been a week of running errands instead of remodeling."

He nodded. "I've been too focused on my own stuff, too, and apparently, it's given Nonna and Charlie too much time to get into trouble together."

"Does Charlie understand that he's not to do that anymore?"

"Yes. He was pretty upset when he saw Nonna passed out. He's grown very fond of her." He looked into her eyes again. "And of you. You've been very kind to him."

"He's a good kid."

He nodded. "So, this arrangement is working out well for Nonna, and well for Charlie. It's just you and me who need to manage our…interactions."

If he could be up front and honest, so could she. "I won't need to avoid you if you're serious about no repeat of that. I… I'm not over Gerry, you see." She fingered the necklace where she wore his wedding ring. "I know it's been over a year, which some people say is enough time, but it's not. He was everything to me."

A shadow crossed Vito's face, and for the first time she realized that he didn't talk much about Gerry. She wondered why. They'd been close comrades, right? Close enough for Gerry to come home with Vito on leave from the army. "You know what he was like," she persisted. "What a great guy he was."

Vito nodded once. "I know what he was like."

"So you can see why…well, why it's hard to get over him. He'll always be my hero."

A muscle worked in Vito's scarred face. "I understand. And believe me, the last thing I want is to displace that feeling in you. So please, stay and care for Nonna and don't worry about Charlie and me."

He stood and walked quickly out of the room.

And Lacey stared after him, wondering why it seemed that he was leaving a lot unsaid.

Chapter Eight

Vito was deep into finishing a research paper on the educator John Dewey when Charlie barged into his room. "Nonna's bored," he announced.

"Bored?" Vito came slowly back to twenty-first-century Ohio. "You're bored?"

"Well, yeah," Charlie said thoughtfully, "a little. But I came to tell you that *Nonna* is bored."

That brought Vito to full attention. "Did she ask you to get her sweets again?"

"No." Charlie shook his head vigorously. "She wouldn't. But she wants me to play a card game called Briscola, and it's too hard. And she wants me to watch TV with her, only I don't like her shows."

"I'll go spend some time with her." Vito ruffled Charlie's hair. "You probably want to go outside and ride that bike, don't you?" He'd fixed up an old one for Charlie over the weekend.

"Yeah," Charlie said, looking relieved that Vito understood. "Can I?"

"Let's see who's outside. If you stay on this block and be careful of cars, it's okay."

After he'd walked out with Charlie and made sure there were several parents in yards up and down the street, keeping an eye on the kids, Vito went back inside and headed toward Nonna's room. He'd stayed up late working on his research paper and spent most of the day on it, as well, and he felt like the letters on the computer monitor were still bouncing in front of his eyes. But it was all good. He was finding all the teaching theories extraordinarily interesting and it made him certain he'd done the right thing, enrolling in school.

Distracted, he tapped on the edge of Nonna's open door and walked in before realizing that Lacey was there, sitting beside Nonna, both of them engrossed in a television show.

A week had passed since Nonna's health scare and their talk, and they were settling into a routine in which Lacey spent more time at home. A routine that most emphatically did *not* include strolls to Lover's Cave. In fact, it barely included being in the same room together.

Lacey glanced up, saw him and looked away.

Nonna clicked off the television. "I can't believe he picked the blonde. I'm very disappointed in that young man."

"Well, she *was* the prettiest," Lacey said, laughing. "But you're right. I don't see the relationship lasting very long."

"Hey, Nonna." Vito bent over to kiss his grandmother's cheek, conscious that it was the first time he'd seen her that day. He'd been neglectful, working on this paper. He'd do better tomorrow.

The silver lining was that Lacey was spending more time with Nonna, staying home more. He'd heard her up at all hours, working on the renovations. Now, he realized guiltily that one reason she might be staying up late was that Nonna was needing her companionship during the day. Which was partly her job, but also partly his responsibility.

Lacey stood up. "I should go get some stuff done." It was clearly an excuse to get away from Vito.

Perversely, that made him want her to stay.

Apparently, Nonna felt the same. "Could you wait just a minute, dear? There's something I want to talk to you two about."

"O-kaaay." She sat down again with obvious reluctance.

Vito focused on his grandmother. "Charlie says you're bored, Nonna."

"Oh, my, bored doesn't begin to describe it." She patted Lacey's hand. "Although it's not for this one's lack of trying."

"I can't hang out as much as I'd like," Lacey said apologetically. "I've got to finish the renovations before the end of the summer, and there's so much to do. But I was thinking, maybe you're well enough to do more of the activities over at the Senior Towers."

"That's a great idea," Vito said, relieved. "Don't they have a bridge group?"

"Yes, and a drop-in lunch program, as well." Lacey smiled at Nonna. "You'd definitely get more exciting lunch choices over there than you get when I fix lunch. And it would get you walking more, which would be great for your health."

"How does that sound, Nonna?"

She shrugged. "Good, I guess," she said. "But..." She trailed off, plucking at the edge of her blanket.

"But what?"

She looked up. "I need a project."

"Like what, a craft project?"

"No, I want to start something new. With people."

That made sense; Nonna wasn't a sit-home-and-knit type of person, or at least, she hadn't been. "Like when you started your baking club that burned everything? Or that barbershop quartet, back when we were kids?" Vito smiled, remembering the off-key singing that had emanated from the big old house's front room when the ladies came to practice. Both groups had been disasters, but entertaining for all involved. Everyone wanted to join in Nonna's projects because she was so much fun as a person.

It made all the sense in the world that she would want to do something like that again.

"Do you have any ideas of what you might want to do?" Lacey asked her.

"Well..." She smiled winningly.

Vito shook his head. "Nonna, when you get that look on your face, I get very afraid."

"What's the idea?" Lacey sounded amused.

Nonna pushed herself up, looking livelier than she'd been the past week. "All right, I'll tell you. You know the show we were just watching?"

"*Bachelor Matches*, sure," Lacey said. "But what's that got to do with you having a project?"

Nonna clasped her hands together and swung her legs to the side of her bed. "I want to start a new matchmaker service in Rescue River."

"What?" Vito's jaw about dropped. "Why?"

"I don't think—" Lacey began.

"You remember the stories from the old country," Nonna interrupted, gripping Vito's hand. "My Tia Bianca, she was a *paraninfo*. Known for matchmaking throughout our village and beyond. She continued until she died at ninety-seven, and the whole region came to her funeral."

Vito nodded, frowning. He did remember the stories, but he wondered what was behind this.

"I need to start with some test clients," she continued, "and because of all you two have done for me, you can have the honor. For free!"

"Oh, Nonna, no," Lacey said. "I don't think this is a good idea. I don't want you to overexert yourself."

"She's right." Vito moved to sit beside his grandmother. The last thing he needed was Nonna trying to match him up with some unsuspecting woman who would be horrified by his scars.

"If I don't do this, then what do I have to live for?" Nonna's chin trembled. "Why do I even get up in the morning? Of what use am I to the world?" She buried her face in thin, blue-veined hands, her shoulders shaking.

Vito looked over at Lacey and saw his own concern mirrored on her face.

"Nonna, you have so much to live for!" she said.

"So many people who love you," Vito added, putting an arm around her shoulders.

"But none of it *means* anything!" she said, her face still buried in her hands.

Tears. Vito couldn't handle a woman's tears. "Oh, well, Nonna, if it's that important to you…"

"I could maybe see it if you get someone else involved to help you," Lacey said. "Someone sensible like Lou Ann Miller or Miss Minnie Falcon."

Nonna lifted her head, her teary face transformed by a huge smile. "Yes, they can help, both of them!"

"Good," Lacey said. "And not too much at once. Don't get carried away."

"It'll be just the two of you to start. Now, Vito. What do you want in a woman?"

Vito blinked. How had she recovered from her tears so quickly? Had he missed something?

Or had Nonna been hoodwinking them?

"Could you get me a tablet of paper, dear?" Nonna said to Lacey. "I don't want to miss a word."

"Here you go," Lacey said, handing Nonna a legal pad and a pencil. "And now I've got to get to sanding woodwork."

"Oh, stay, dear. I want to talk to you, too."

Lacey laughed. "Don't you think these interviews should be private?" She spun and walked toward the door.

Vito watched her go, thinking of Nonna's question. The truth was, he wanted someone like Lacey. But because of the secret he had promised to keep, he could never, ever have her.

The next Saturday, Lacey climbed out of her car at A Dog's Last Chance, Troy Hinton's animal rescue farm. As she stretched her arms high, she felt like a weight was gone from her shoulders.

Grasses blew in the soft breeze and looking off to the fenced area by the barn, she could see one dog's shiny black fur, another's mottled brown and white coat. Beside her, the creek rushed, a soothing sound, and red-winged blackbirds perched on the fence.

It was good to get away from the guesthouse. Good to do something for others.

Good to get away from Vito and the constant tension of trying to avoid him.

He'd been in her thoughts so much lately, and in a confusing way. He was so hardworking—up late most nights at his computer, making steady progress toward finishing his degree. He spent time with Charlie every evening, getting involved in the life of the town, even lending a hand with the youth soccer team when one of the coaches had a family emergency.

And he was so patient with Nonna, whose matchmaking service was going full speed ahead, obviously giving the woman something fun to do, but in the process, making Lacey uncomfortable.

A shiny new SUV pulled up beside her car, and Lacey was surprised to see her friend Susan getting out. "Nice car!" she said, remembering the rusty subcompact that Susan had driven when she'd lived for a year at the unrenovated guesthouse.

Susan made a face. "Sam. Just because we're expecting, he thinks we need to have a huge vehicle. I had to talk him down from a full-size van."

"How are you feeling?" Lacey could now ask the question without even a twinge of pain, and that told her she was moving forward, getting over her miscarriage and ready to celebrate other people's happiness.

"I'm feeling great, but Sam treats me like I'm made of glass." Susan rolled her eyes. "He didn't want me to come today. He's afraid one of the big dogs will knock me down. Like I haven't done this eighty thousand times before. And like a stumble would hurt the baby!"

"He loves you."

"He does." Susan's eyes softened. "And he's a control freak. But speaking of men...how's Vito?"

Lacey shrugged. "He's fine. Seems busy."

"You don't see much of him?"

"Well, since he's staying at the guesthouse, of course I see him. But we keep to ourselves."

"By choice, or would you like to see more of him?"

Lacey met her friend's perceptive eyes and looked away. "It's by choice. He makes me nervous."

"Nervous? Why?"

Lacey shrugged. "I don't know. He's so…"

"Big? Manly?"

Lacey laughed and shook her head a little. "Something like that. Come on, you've got to show me the ropes before all the kids arrive."

Susan was a longtime volunteer at the Kennel Kids, and she'd talked Lacey into getting involved. Lacey's therapist thought it was a good idea, too—a way to be involved with others and kids, not necessarily babies but with people. Making a difference.

"Speaking of Vito…" Susan said as they approached the barn where the sound of dogs barking was more audible.

Or at least, that was what Lacey thought her friend had said. "What?" she called over a new wave of barking.

"He's here. Vito." Susan gestured toward the barn, where Vito and Charlie stood talking to Troy Hinton, who ran the place and the Kennel Kids.

Lacey swallowed. What was he doing here?

Just then, he turned around and saw her. "What are you doing here?" he asked, sounding surprised.

"My question, too." They both looked at each other, and Lacey saw in Vito's eyes the same ambivalence she felt herself.

Susan nudged her. "I'm gonna go get set up. Come over when you're ready. No rush."

"Charlie's doing Kennel Kids," Vito explained.

Relief washed over Lacey, along with something like disappointment. "Oh. So you're just dropping him off?"

"I'm…actually staying to help. Unless that's a problem?"

She lifted her hands, palms out. "No! No, it's fine."

Across the barn, Troy Hinton was hoisting a dog crate to his shoulder. "If anyone has a free hand, we could use your help here," he called.

Lacey moved forward at the same time Vito did, and they jostled each other. And then bounced apart like two rubber balls. "Sorry!" they both said simultaneously, and Vito stepped back to let her go ahead.

Lacey blushed as she hurried toward Troy. She started to lift a crate.

"Vito, could you help her with that?" Troy nodded her direction. "It's a heavy one."

So she and Vito took ends of the crate and followed Troy.

"Put it down there. We like to have a few crates out here for the dogs to get away from the kids. It's a tough gig for them. Could you two bring one more so I can get started with these kids?"

"Sure." Vito headed back, and then turned to see if she was coming.

She followed reluctantly. Why had she and Vito ended up together? Why wasn't it Susan over here with her?

"Hey, look, why don't you go ahead and help Susan?" Vito said, apparently reading her mind. "I can get that last crate."

"No, it's okay. I'll help you. It's too heavy."

Vito gave her a look. "I'm every bit as strong as I used to be, even if I do have a few injuries."

"I know that!" Then, ashamed of her exasperated tone, she followed him into the barn and took the bull by the horns. "I'm sorry if this is awkward, Vito. I wish it wasn't."

"You don't want to be around me?"

"It's not that. I just..." More seriously, she was worried he didn't want to be around her.

"Hey, D'Angelo, c'mon! We don't have all day here!" Troy sounded impatient.

Lacey flinched and stole a glance at Vito. That kind of thing had always made Gerry livid; he'd hated to be corrected. It was a guy thing.

Except, to her surprise, Vito laughed. "That's rich, coming from you, Hinton." And then he hustled over to the crate. "Guess we'd better get a move on."

She hurried to help him, wondering as she did what it meant that Vito hadn't gotten angry.

Had Gerry been unusually touchy?

She went to the crate and lifted the other side, breathing in the good smells—hay and animals. And maybe it was the thought of hay, but her necklace felt itchy on her neck.

"Dad!" Charlie ran over, his whole face lit up in a smile. "Can I get a dog? Mr. Hinton said they need homes." He jogged alongside them as they carried out the large crate.

Vito went still, looking at Charlie, then at Lacey. "It's the first time he called me 'Dad,'" he whispered.

Lacey wanted to hug both of them, but her hands were full, so she settled for a *"Wow"* mouthed across the crate as they continued carrying it out.

"Hey, Lacey," Charlie added, coming up beside her,

obviously unaware of the emotions he'd evoked. "Want me to help with that? That's no job for a girl."

Lacey chuckled. "Girls can do a lot of jobs, including moving things. But yes, if you'd like to, you can take that corner." She winked meaningfully at Vito, warning him to slow down.

He gave a subtle nod, and something arced between them. It was nice to be able to communicate without words sometimes.

After they'd put the crate down, Charlie grinned at her. "*You* wouldn't mind having a dog around, would you, Miss Lacey?"

He was way too cute with that grin. She couldn't resist ruffling his hair. "I won't answer that on the grounds that it might incriminate me with your dad," she said, "but confidentially... I do like dogs."

"See, Dad?"

"Way to throw me under the bus," Vito complained, but there was a smile in his voice.

"Can we get one?"

Vito held up a hand. "That's not a decision we're going to make today."

Charlie looked like he wanted to whine, but shouts from a couple of newly arrived boys distracted him and he ran off. Vito watched him go, shaking his head. "It's hard for me to deny him anything."

A man Lacey knew vaguely emerged from the barn with two pit bulls on leads. As he approached the boys, Charlie took several steps back in obvious fear.

The man clearly noticed. "Hey, Troy," he called, "we have some new Kennel Kids here today. You want to give the bully breeds talk?"

She and Vito drifted over and listened while Troy

explained that it was all in how the pit bull was raised, how some were taught to fight while others were raised in a gentle environment, how one always had to be careful in approaching a dog like this.

Troy's words triggered a thought. Charlie had apparently been raised in a rough environment, and he, too, acted out sometimes; he needed to be approached with care. But with love—the kind of love that Vito was so unselfishly offering him—he was starting, even now, to grow into his potential and to become the person God had made him to be.

She watched as one of the smaller pit bulls, a white female named Gracie, was brought out and went from boy to boy. The group started dissolving, some of the boys playing with puppies, others learning to clean kennels, others helping to leash and train dogs. Charlie knelt, and the white pit bull approached him slowly, cautiously.

"Hold out your hand so she can sniff it," Vito encouraged, and after a moment's hesitation, Charlie did.

Watching Vito, she saw someone so much more than the handsome older boy who'd protected her from school bullies when she was younger. He was fatherly now, a man, a hero. He accepted what had happened to him and ran with it, growing into a person of value.

But then again, the seed of the man he'd become had been present in the kind, handsome boy next door.

"Lacey!" Susan gave her a light punch on the shoulder, and she started and turned to her friend. "I've been trying to get your attention forever." She looked where Lacey was looking, and then a slow smile broke out across her face. "Are you *sure* you don't have feelings?"

"No! It's just Vito."

"Somehow, I'm not convinced."

"No way! The truth is, I keep thinking about Gerry."

One of the other volunteers turned. "Gerry McPherson? Boy, that guy was a piece of work."

Lacey cocked her head to one side, feeling her smile slip a little.

"What does *that* mean?" Susan asked, her voice protective.

Lacey looked at the other volunteer, and suddenly, she didn't want to hear what he was going to say.

And then Vito stepped up beside her. "Gerry McPherson was my friend and Lacey's husband." He put an arm around her, a tense arm. "And he died serving our country." His chin lifted a little and he gave the man a level stare.

The other guy raised his hands. "Hey, didn't mean anything." He turned and walked rapidly away.

Susan gave Lacey a curious look and went over to help one of the younger Kennel Kids, who was having trouble unhooking a black Lab's leash.

"Thanks." Lacey sidestepped away from Vito so she could see him better, and immediately he let his arm drop from her shoulders.

A chill ran over her where his arm had been.

What had the man meant, that Gerry was a piece of work?

She didn't want to face the tiny sliver of doubt that had pierced her.

A couple of hours later, Vito stood up from repairing a broken crate and was startled to find himself surrounded: Susan on one side and Troy's wife, Angelica, on the other.

"So, Vito," Angelica said, "what's going on between you and Lacey?"

"Not one thing. Why?"

"Oh, just wondering." The two women sat down beside him, each working on one of the broken crates.

He wasn't lying about nothing going on, at least not in a guy sense; there wasn't anything of the dating variety going on, that was for sure. On the other hand, there was a lot going on emotionally, every time he saw Lacey.

Man, that had been a close one with that stupid guy almost revealing something bad about Gerry. Lacey had looked so shocked and stricken that he hadn't been able to handle it.

She for sure still believed the best about Gerry. And that was good. He'd always remain a hero in her eyes.

And Gerry *had* definitely had a heroic side. In battle, there wasn't another man in the world Vito would've trusted more. They'd saved each other's skins more than once.

But the home front—specifically, women—had been Gerry's downfall. Something rotten in the way he was raised, or maybe the fact that he'd been so handsome and suave. Too many women had flocked to him, and Gerry hadn't ever been taught how to treat women with respect. To him, a woman who threw herself at him was fair game.

Any woman was fair game. Lacey definitely hadn't thrown herself at him; she wouldn't have known how. But she'd gotten swept away and before Vito could turn around and warn her, she'd gone and fallen for Gerry.

Vito had tried to talk her out of it, but that had been

a miserable failure. Once someone was that far gone, you couldn't bring her back.

At that point, the only thing he could do was to insist that if Gerry wanted Lacey, he needed to marry her, not just use her and throw her away.

It had just about killed him to do it, because by that time, he'd thought Lacey was something pretty special himself. Talking his friend into marrying her was like cutting off his own arm. He'd had to admit, just to himself, that he'd been waiting for Lacey to get old enough that he could honorably ask her out.

Gerry had beaten him to it, had gotten in there and stolen her heart.

And he'd treated her despicably.

And now Vito was in a position of hiding Gerry's wrongdoing from the woman he still, if the truth be told, carried a torch for.

"Earth to Vito," Angelica teased, and he snapped back into the here and now. "You *sure* there's nothing going on?"

"I'm sure," he said heavily. "And there never will be anything going on."

Chapter Nine

The next Friday, Vito heard a high-pitched shout from Nonna's room. "Vito! Lacey!"

He scrambled up from the computer and down the stairs on Lacey's heels. "What's wrong, Nonna?" she was asking as they both entered Nonna's room.

"Are you okay?" he asked his grandmother, who was sitting at the small writing desk looking perfectly fine. In fact, her color was better than he'd ever seen it.

Lacey put a hand on Nonna's shoulder. "You scared us. What's going on?"

"It's my first success," the older woman said. "I found you both dates for tonight!"

Vito had to restrain himself from rolling his eyes. Just what he needed, a blind date.

"Tonight?" Lacey sounded just as distressed as Vito felt. "I… I have plans."

Nonna's eyes sparkled behind her glasses. "The same plans you've had for the past three Friday nights, young lady? A date with a paint can?"

Lacey smiled ruefully. "Actually…yes."

Nonna rubbed her hands together. "I hope you both

have some dressy clothes. You'll need to be ready at six o'clock."

Vito groaned inwardly. The last thing he wanted was to put on a suit. "Why dressy? This is Rescue River."

"You both have reservations with your dates at Chez la Ferme."

"No way!" Vito said.

"That's not how you do a blind date, Nonna." Lacey's forehead creased. "For one thing, it's really expensive."

"You get coffee first," Vito added. And then he processed what Lacey had said and looked over at her. How would she know? Was she doing online dating?

He found her looking back at him with a similar question in her eyes, and he felt himself flushing. The truth was, he *had* put his profile up on a Christian dating site a couple of times. And he'd gotten no results worth pursuing, which he attributed to women being turned off by his ugly mug. Or his lack of wealth.

"What if we don't like them, Nonna? Then we're stuck spending hours together." Lacey sank down onto the edge of Nonna's bed, facing them both.

"Whereas with coffee," Vito added, "you can escape after half an hour."

"You're taking a negative attitude," Nonna said. "Why do you think you'll want to escape?"

Vito looked at Lacey, and she looked back at him, and they both laughed. And then he narrowed his eyes at her. So she *had* online dated. But when?

Nonna steepled her hands and stared down at the floor. "I'm sorry," she said. "Do you want me to cancel the whole thing?" Her tone was desolate.

Vito looked at her bowed head and slumped shoulders and his heart melted. "No, Nonna, it's okay. I'm game. But just this once."

"Me, too," Lacey said with a sigh. "Who's my date?"

Nonna smiled gleefully up at them. "It's a surprise! You won't know until you get to the restaurant."

"Wait," Vito said. "We're *both* at Chez la Ferme tonight? Why there?"

"It's the only nice place in town. I'm so excited for you. You're going to have a wonderful time."

There was no trace of her former sadness, and Vito studied her narrowly. He had the feeling he'd just been manipulated.

"Be ready at six. You're meeting your dates at six thirty."

As they walked out, Vito couldn't help shaking his head. That Nonna. She really was a matchmaker, and she was also someone to whom he, at least, couldn't say no.

At five minutes before six, Vito came out of his room at the guesthouse. He'd driven Charlie over to a new friend's house, and as a result, he'd had to get ready quickly. Not that it mattered. Less time to spend in this necktie that felt like it was strangling him.

He needed to work on his attitude, he knew that. Maybe Nonna's matchmaking was God's way of finding him a partner, someone who'd help him fulfill his dream of building a loving family. Lacey wasn't the only woman in the world, despite what his heart said.

Halfway down the stairs, he caught his breath.

There was Lacey in a sleeveless blue dress that highlighted her figure and her coloring. She stood in front of an ornamental mirror, attempting to fasten a necklace.

Breathe. She's not for you.

He walked slowly the rest of the way down the stairs, watching her struggle with the small clasp. "Need some help?"

"Oh! Um, sure." She held out the ends of the necklace, her back to him, bowing her head.

Her neck looked slender and vulnerable. Her short hair brushed his fingers, soft and light as bird feathers.

He could smell her sweet, spicy perfume.

Breathe.

He fumbled a little with the tiny clasp, dropped one end, had to start over. "Sorry. Big fingers." But that wasn't really the problem. He knew how to fasten a necklace; he'd been doing it for his women friends forever.

Why did it feel so different with Lacey?

Why was he going slowly on purpose, trying to extend the moment, to stay close to her?

He finished and stepped back quickly, forbidding his hands to linger on her shoulders. "Whoever you're meeting tonight is going to be very happy."

She turned toward him, a smile curving her lips as she gave him an undisguised once-over. "Your date will be, too."

He laughed a little, shook his head. "My date is going to be in for a surprise, but not such a pleasant one."

"You look good, Vito." She reached up and, with one finger, touched his face. The bad side of it. "Except that there's a little shaving cream…right…here."

Their eyes met and her touch lingered on his face.

That soft, small finger, touching a place no one had ever touched, except in a medical capacity, made him suck in a breath. "It's hard to shave with…this." He gestured toward the ridged, scarred side of his face.

She let her hand open to cup his cheek. "I'm sure."

The moment lingered. He felt like he couldn't look away from Lacey's steady, light brown eyes.

Until Nonna opened her door and clapped her hands. From her room came strains of opera music. "Don't you both look gorgeous!"

Vito took a step backward and Lacey let her hand fall to her side.

"We clean up okay," he said, clearing his throat, trying to keep his cool. "How are we going to know our dates?"

"It's all set up at the restaurant."

Vito bit back a sigh and slid his hands into his pockets. "You're not going to tell us who, are you?"

"And spoil the anticipation? Of course not. That's just one of the things that will be unique about my matchmaking service. Now, you two had better get going."

That brought up another angle he hadn't considered. "Would it be awkward if we walked together to dates with other people?" he asked Lacey. "Or would you rather drive, with those heels?" *Which look spectacular*, he thought but didn't say.

"They're wedges—they're fine." Her cheeks were a little pinker than usual. "Um, sure, we can walk."

So they strolled together through the downtown of Rescue River, all dressed up. The evening air was warm, and shouts from the park indicated that families were enjoying the evening. Vito leaned just a little closer to Lacey to catch another whiff of her perfume, wishing with all his heart that he could spend this evening with her, as her date.

His thoughts toward his old friend Gerry, who'd made him promise to keep Charlie's parentage a secret, were becoming more uncharitable by the minute. The man had been a hero and a friend, and Vito mourned the loss of him, but he couldn't deny resenting the promise that stood like a wall between him and the woman he was coming to care for more each day.

"Who do you think our dates are?" she asked, looking up at him with laughter in her eyes. "Will it be people we know or complete strangers?"

"Bound to be people we know. It's Rescue River. And Nonna knows the same people we do." He actually hoped it was someone who knew what he looked like, just to spare himself the awkward moment that often happened when people met him for the first time.

They approached Chez la Ferme to discover a small crowd of people waiting outside. "Looks like they're backed up. Hope Nonna really did make a reservation."

"Or not." Lacey made a wry face. "I do have that paint can waiting for me at home."

He chuckled. She wasn't any more into this whole game than he was. "Look, there's Daisy."

"And Dion." Vito lifted an eyebrow. Were the police chief and the social worker officially admitting they were a couple? Because being together at Chez la Ferme pretty much guaranteed that they'd be perceived that way.

"Hey!" Lacey hugged both of them, first Daisy, then Dion. "Long wait?"

"Not if you let them know you're here." Dion

punched Vito's arm lightly. "Get with the program, my brother."

So Vito walked in to the hostess stand and gave his name.

"Oh, yes, Mr. D'Angelo. We've been expecting you." The hostess gave him a broad smile. "Your table will be ready in just a few minutes."

Obviously, she was in on Nonna's secret.

Almost as soon as he'd exited the restaurant, while he was still walking toward his friends, the hostess came behind him. "Dion Coleman?" she called. "And Lacey McPherson?"

A slow smile crossed Dion's face. "Oh, your grandma," he said to Vito, shaking his head. And then he crooked his arm for Lacey. "Shall we?"

Lacey's eyebrows lifted as she looked up at the police chief. "Well, okay, then." She took his arm and the two of them turned toward the restaurant.

Vito's stomach seemed to drop to his toes as he watched the pair. He couldn't help noticing the details: the large squared-off college ring that glinted against Dion's dark skin, the expensive cut of his suit, the suave way he put a hand on the small of Lacey's back to guide her inside.

They were good-looking enough that several people in the crowd turned to watch. Or maybe the raised eyebrows were because Dion was linked with Daisy in the town's collective, gossipy mind.

Vito had known he couldn't be with Lacey himself, on account of Charlie. He'd almost—not quite, but almost—accepted that.

What he hadn't anticipated was how seeing Lacey with someone else would feel like a punch in the stomach.

And he should have known, because it had happened before, with Gerry. This exact same feeling: *You're not going to get her. She's going to choose someone else. And you're going to have to stand there and be a man about it. Do the right thing.*

Speaking of doing the right thing, he was being rude to Daisy, standing there watching Lacey and Dion disappear inside the restaurant like a hungry dog, tongue hanging out.

He schooled his expression before he turned to Daisy. Was that a similar look on her face?

That brought him out of himself. He couldn't have Lacey, and it was wrong to think she should save herself for him, that she shouldn't find happiness with someone else. Dion was a good man, respected by everyone in town.

And now, he needed to go through with the evening's plans as if he didn't feel gutshot. He didn't know Daisy well, but he assumed that if Dion was set up with Lacey, Daisy was probably set up with him. He turned to her. "Any chance you're here for a blind date, too? Set up by my grandma?"

"Yeah." She nodded. She didn't look enthusiastic.

He soldiered on, as he'd been trained to do. "Well, you didn't get the prize," he said, "but you'll get a good dinner. I think I'm your date."

"Oh. Okay." She didn't sound thrilled, but not horrified, either. "What do you mean, not the prize?"

He gestured vaguely toward the scarred side of his face. "Only a doting grandma could love this mug."

She didn't deny the ugliness of his scars, but she shrugged them away. "Most women care more about what's inside. Whereas men..." She trailed off, and then glanced down at her own curvy body. "I'm not the prize, either, compared to her." She gestured toward the door through which Dion and Lacey had disappeared.

It was true. Vito didn't find Daisy as attractive as he found Lacey. But then, he didn't find *any* woman that attractive. For better or worse, his heart had attached itself to Lacey, and he was realizing more every minute that his wasn't the kind of heart that could easily change directions. Still, Daisy—blonde, vivacious and with a killer smile—was something of a showstopper herself. And he wasn't going to be rude to her. "You *are* a prize. Anyone with any sense would wonder how someone like me got to go out with a knockout like you. I'm honored to be your date."

The crowd by the door was thinning out, and a bench opened up. "Want to sit down?"

So they sat, and talked about her work in social services, and his desire to become a teacher. She was a good conversationalist, easy to talk to. He found himself confessing his worries about scaring kids, his desire to work with them in person, and his pretty-sure decision to go with online teaching. When the hostess called them to go inside, she had to do it several times, apparently, from her expression when she came out to get them.

As they followed her into the restaurant, replete with stained glass and low lighting and good smells of bread and prime rib, they kept talking.

"Don't do online teaching if your heart is in the real classroom," she urged him as they crossed the restaurant behind the maître d'. "Kids respond to the whole person, not just how you look. I used to worry about them teasing me about my weight, but they're completely fine with it."

"As are most men," he assured her. "Women think we all like stick-skinny women, but that's not the case. You're beautiful."

"Your table, sir." The maître d' gestured, and Vito held Daisy's chair for her.

Only then did he realize that Dion and Lacey were just around a small corner from them, probably within earshot of most things they would say.

Not only that, but the two of them were leaning toward each other, sharing an appetizer and appearing to have a marvelous time.

Chapter Ten

Lacey looked at the handsome man across the table from her and tried to ignore Vito and Daisy being seated practically right behind them.

Unfortunately, she couldn't ignore what she'd heard. "You're a beautiful woman," Vito had said to Daisy.

Which was true, and she didn't begrudge Daisy the praise, but the way it stung alerted her to something she hadn't quite realized before: she wanted Vito for herself.

"Hey," Dion said. "What's going on?"

She shrugged and toyed with her water glass.

"All of a sudden you're not comfortable," he said. "Is it something I said?"

"No! No, you're fine. What were we talking about?" She laughed nervously. "I'm sorry, I'm a little intimidated."

His forehead creased. "Intimidated? Why?"

"You're kind of known for your wisdom," she said, "not to mention that you're the police chief."

"Which is all a nice way of saying I'm an old man,"

he said, "who's fortunate to be out with a fine-looking young woman."

The words were gallant, but Lacey could tell Dion wasn't interested in her in *that* way. Rather than feeling insulted, she felt relieved and suddenly more comfortable. This was a little awkward, especially with Vito and Daisy so close, but at least she knew she wasn't misleading Dion.

"I'm the fortunate one," she said. "I might pick your brain about some Bible stuff. You're said to know everything there is to know."

"Who says that?"

"Angelica's husband, Troy. He thinks you're the font of all wisdom. And my brother's a fan, too."

"Don't you be thinking I'm perfect," he warned. "Nobody's perfect. Nobody's even close, right? That's what the good book says."

"See, you're making my point for me, quoting scripture at the drop of a hat." She frowned. "Anyway, of course, you're right. But I've spent my whole life trying to be good. Trying to be perfect."

"We all try," he said, "and that's not bad."

She did her best to ignore the rumble of Vito's voice behind her, but it played along her nerve endings like an instrument. She forced it away, forced herself to talk with Dion about her brother, with whom he'd had a good deal of official contact until Buck had dried out and they'd become friends. She forced herself to rave over the delicious, beautifully presented food: Dion's prime rib, her own organic grilled salmon.

"That was great," she said when they'd pushed away their plates.

"Yes, it was," he said, "but let me ask you something. Are you in this matchmaking thing for real?"

She looked at him and slowly shook her head. "Not really. I'm just doing it for Nonna. You?" She only asked the question to be polite, because she was pretty sure of the answer. "I always heard you were with Daisy."

"Everyone thinks that," he said, smoothly changing the subject. "You're a newish widow. It makes sense you're not ready to do a lot of dating."

"Yeah. I… I really loved my husband."

Dion didn't say, "He was a good guy." That would normally be the remark you made, wouldn't it? But instead, he said, "That's obvious. Gerry was blessed to have you. But—" he raised a finger and pinned her with a steady gaze "—at some point, you're going to have to move on. You're too young of a woman to give up on life."

She wasn't going to tell him about her infertility. Instead, she turned the tables. "Do you take your own advice?"

Dion cocked his head to one side, smiling at her. "Touché. I've been on my own a lot longer than you have, and I should probably be letting go of some baggage by now."

She wanted to ask him about his past, but the way his face closed when he mentioned it told her she shouldn't. "Moving on isn't as easy as it sounds, is it?"

"No," he said. "But let your feelings lead and you'll be fine. Your feelings and your heart. And most of all, the Lord."

Well, if she were to let her feelings lead… Involuntarily, she glanced over at Vito and then back at Dion.

"I'm ashamed to say that I haven't spent much time consulting the Lord about this," she admitted.

The server took their plates away and promised to be right back with the dessert tray. "There's no time like the present," Dion said, "to take it to the Lord. Want to?"

So she let him take her hand in his, closed her eyes, listened to Dion's quiet words and said a few herself. Asked for forgiveness that she'd neglected to seek God's guidance in her feelings. Asked Him to lead her in the right direction.

When they were finished, she felt cleansed.

"And now," Dion said, "if we can get their attention, do you think we should move our table together with our friends for dessert?"

"I, um, I don't know if Nonna would approve."

"Nonna's not here, is she? Hey, Vito." Dion caught his attention and made the suggestion, and the servers rushed to help, assuring them it was no problem.

Once they were all sitting together, there was a slightly awkward silence, broken by the approach of the dessert tray. The waiter began to describe the offerings.

Lacey looked over at Daisy. "I need chocolate. Now. You?"

"I agree."

After a restless night, Vito woke Charlie up early, figuring they'd grab breakfast and go burn off some energy on the basketball court. But even before they reached the main floor of the guesthouse, delicious smells of cinnamon and bread wafted toward them.

Could Lacey be up baking cinnamon rolls?

But when they walked into the kitchen, there was Nonna in her Kiss the Cook apron, bending over to check on something in the oven and looking like her old self.

At the table was Miss Minnie Falcon, matriarch of the Senior Towers and former Sunday school teacher to almost every child in Rescue River. Next to her was Lou Ann Miller, stirring sugar into a cup of coffee.

"You're looking good, Nonna," he said, walking over to the stove and giving his grandmother a kiss.

"And that smells good!" Charlie came over as Nonna removed the pan from the oven. "Can I have some?"

"Five minutes, *cùcciolo.*" She patted Charlie's shoulder, smiling.

Vito felt a great weight lifting off him, a weight he hadn't known he was carrying. Nonna was going to be okay. Suddenly he could see it and feel it and believe it. Not only that, but she'd called Charlie by the same affectionate name she used to use on Vito and his brother. That, more than anything, meant Charlie was becoming part of their family. He swallowed against a sudden tightness in his throat and walked over to greet the ladies at the table.

As good as her word, Nonna brought a steaming loaf of cinnamon bread, along with small cups of butter and jam, and placed them in the middle of the table.

"Italian breakfast like the old days." Vito put an arm around Nonna, still feeling a little misty-eyed.

Charlie's hand froze in the act of grabbing a piece of the bread. "Why is it brown?" he asked.

"Because I used the healthy flour. It tastes just as good, so eat up."

Charlie grabbed a piece, slathered it with butter and

jam and took a huge bite before anyone else had even secured a piece. "It's good, Nonna," he said, his mouth full of food.

Vito leaned close to Charlie's ear. "Good table manners will get you more food," he whispered.

Charlie raised his eyebrows. "What'd I do?"

"Don't talk with your mouth full." They'd cover the grabby behavior later. First things first.

Miss Minnie put a clawlike hand on Vito's arm. "I understand you were our first matchmaking client," she said.

"Yes, tell us all about it." Lou Ann Miller raised a slice of bread to her nose and inhaled, closing her eyes. "Fabulous, dear. You've outdone yourself."

As Nonna beamed, the door from the backyard opened and Lacey breezed in. She wore a red-and-white-checkered shirt and cutoff shorts and she looked as carefree as she had at twelve.

And he was a goner.

"That smells amazing, Nonna D'Angelo," she said, approaching the table. "And look, whole grains! I'm impressed."

"Hey, Miss Lacey, you're not wearing your necklace."

Lacey's hand flew to her throat. "Oh, wow, I'll run up and get it before I eat."

"Want me to get it for you?" The words were out of Vito's mouth before he realized that he didn't, in fact, want to get her the necklace. Didn't want her to wear Gerry's wedding ring around her neck anymore.

"Oh, it's okay. I'll get it." She half walked, half skipped out of the kitchen.

"My Vito." Nonna pinched his cheek—the second

time someone had touched his scars in the past two days. "Always too nice for your own good."

"That's right," Miss Minnie said unexpectedly. "Being kind isn't all there is to life. Take a stand!"

"What are you ladies talking about?"

Lou Ann Miller glanced over at Charlie, who'd grabbed his handheld game and was immersed in it, still chewing on a huge mouthful of bread. She turned back to Vito. "Your love life is what we're talking about."

Vito looked from Lou Ann to his grandmother to Miss Minnie. "Seriously? Is that what I'm doing wrong? Being kind and nice?" But of course, they didn't know about his Charlie deception, which wasn't nice at all.

"Tell us about last night," Nonna said instead of answering his question. She removed her apron and sat down at the table and looked up at him expectantly.

"It was...fine. Daisy is great."

"And you don't want to date her."

"Well, of course he doesn't. For one thing, she's attached to Dion Coleman at the hip."

"And then there's the fact that Vito's affections are elsewhere."

"That's obvious. The question is what can we do about it?"

The three women's conversation was spinning out of control. "Nobody needs to do anything about it," he protested. "I can handle my own life."

The only good thing was that Charlie wasn't listening; he was just eating bread and playing with his game.

Lacey came back into the room and Vito didn't

know whether to be glad or sorry. He got busy cleaning up the breakfast dishes and washing mixing bowls and bread pans.

"How was your date with Dion?" Lou Ann asked her.

Vito couldn't help tuning his ears to hear what she would say. They'd all ended the evening together, on a friendly note and laughing about various people's efforts to play matchmaker over the years, but Vito still had a sinking feeling he couldn't compete with Dion, suave and good-looking and successful.

And he *couldn't* compete, he reminded himself. He couldn't have Lacey, because telling her the truth would destroy her world. Destroy her image of the husband whose ring she wore around her neck.

"It was great," she said easily. "He's a lot less intimidating on a date than when he's being the police chief. Mmmm, this bread is good."

Vito glanced over to see three gray heads turn toward Lacey. "So," Nonna said, "do you like Dion?"

"She means *like* like," Charlie supplied, his mouth full. "Like a boyfriend."

It seemed like everyone in the room—except Charlie—was holding their breath.

"No, I don't think so." Lacey seemed unconscious of how much interest her words were generating. "And I don't think he likes me that way, either, but I'm glad to get to know him better as a friend. He's a good guy and a wonderful Christian."

Vito let out a breath and his tight shoulders relaxed. He grabbed a dish towel and started drying cutlery with great energy.

"I'm not really ready to date," she continued, fingering her necklace. "I'm afraid you're going to have to find some other clients."

There was a little commotion outside the door, and then it opened, framing Buck, Gina and little Bobby, who toddled across the room toward Lacey. "Laasss," he crowed reverently, crashing into her leg and hanging on.

"Hi, honey!" She lifted him onto her lap and tickled his stomach, making him laugh.

She looked beautiful with a baby.

She would look beautiful with *his* baby.

Man, he had it bad and he had to stop.

"Mind if the dogs come in, Lace?" Buck asked.

She glanced down at Mr. Whiskers. "Run while you can, buddy," she said, and then beckoned for Gina to let the dogs in.

Immediately, Crater, a large black mutt with a deep scar on his back, galloped in. At his heels was a small white mop of a dog, barking joyously.

Charlie threw himself out of the chair and started rolling and roughhousing with them.

Vito looked at the ladies to see if they found the ruckus disturbing, but they were watching and laughing. Bobby struggled out of Lacey's lap and toddled fearlessly into the fray.

Buck and Gina came over to the table and talked above the kids and dogs, and all the noise created a dull roar Vito couldn't really follow, given his hearing loss. His aids worked well with individual conversations, but big noisy groups were still a challenge.

He was wiping down counters when Charlie came over and tugged at his arm. He bent down to hear what the boy had to say.

"Can we get a dog now, Dad?"

That had been predictable. "Of these two, which kind do you like?"

"Can we get two?"

"No!"

"Then, I like the big one. Can we get one like that? With cool scars?"

The phrasing made Vito lift an eyebrow. Cool scars, huh? That scars could be cool was a new concept to him. "We'll start thinking about it more seriously," he promised.

Given how strong his feelings for Lacey had become, he had some serious thinking of his own to do, as well.

When there was a knock on the front door, Lacey hurried to answer it, relieved to escape the busy kitchen and the probing questions of Nonna D'Angelo, Miss Minnie and Lou Ann. Not to mention Vito's thoughtful eyes.

It was Daisy. "Hey, I was walking by, and I thought I'd take the chance that you were here. Do you have a minute?"

"Um, sure." She and Daisy knew each other, but they weren't drop-in friends. She came out on the porch and gestured toward a rocking chair, tucking her feet under herself in the porch swing. "What's up?"

"I just wanted to make sure we're okay about last night."

Lacey forced a laugh. "We were clearly all victims of the grandma matchmaking brigade. What happened isn't your fault or mine, or any of ours."

"And it was fun in the end, right?"

"Sure." As she thought back, she realized that it *had* been fun, sitting and laughing with Vito and Daisy and Dion. Except for that nagging anxiety at the pit of her stomach.

Daisy was watching her, eyes narrowed. "But…" she prompted.

Lacey shrugged. "Nothing."

"It's not nothing. I *knew* something was bugging you last night. What's going on?"

"Nothing's going on." She paused. "If you're worried about whether I like Dion, I do, but not as a boyfriend."

Daisy waved a hand. "I know. I could tell. And it's not my business, anyway. I *wish* Dion would meet someone."

Lacey lifted an eyebrow, but didn't comment. She couldn't tell if Daisy meant it or not.

"And I'm not interested in Vito that way, either."

Lacey tried to school her facial expression, but she couldn't help feeling happy. "I…wasn't sure."

"I mean, he's great," Daisy said, "but I'm pretty sure he only has eyes for you."

Lacey had thought she couldn't get any more joyous, but an extra wave of it washed over her at Daisy's words. "You really think so?"

Daisy nodded. "I sat and had dinner with him, and he was great, he really was. So nice and flattering and kind. But he couldn't stop himself from looking over at you guys every time you and Dion laughed."

A breathless feeling took Lacey over then. Maybe this—her and Vito—could really happen. Maybe it would. "Do you think it's wrong for me to think about another man, so soon after losing Gerry? As a social worker, I mean?"

Daisy studied her thoughtfully. "It's been over a year, right?"

She nodded.

"And what have you done to get over the loss?"

"Well..." Lacey thought about it. "I've had counseling, with a psychologist and with Pastor Ricky. And with some of my friends, too, unofficially. I'm doing desensitizing things about kids, because...did you know I lost a baby, too?" She was amazed that she could say the words openly now, with only an ache instead of a sharp, horrific pain.

Daisy nodded. "I heard, and I'm sorry for your loss. That must have been terribly hard to deal with."

"Well...yeah. The worst. And I never thought I'd heal, but Buck, and little Bobby, and the church... Lots of people have helped me, and life goes on."

The door flew open and Charlie emerged. He threw his arms around Lacey and said into her ear: "I think Dad's getting me a dog!" Then he ran down the stairs and across the street to the basketball hoop where a couple of neighborhood kids were playing.

Lacey looked after him and blinked. "That came out of nowhere. I thought he didn't like me."

"If you seem to pose a threat to his relationship with Vito, he may act out. On the other hand, he might very well need a mother figure." Daisy leaned back in the chair, rocking gently.

"A mother figure?" Lacey laughed. "Why would he think of me that way? I'm not even dating his dad."

"Yet. Charlie may see something that the two of you won't yet acknowledge."

Heat suffused Lacey's cheeks and she didn't know how to respond. Because the truth was, she was interested in dating Vito. After last night, watching him with Daisy, she was sure of it.

There was a fumbling sound at the door and Miss Minnie Falcon made her way out, struggling a little with her rolling walker. Both Lacey and Daisy jumped up to help her.

"Would you like to sit a spell on your old porch?" Lacey asked. She'd bought the house from Miss Minnie two years ago when it had become too much for her to handle, and she tried to encourage the older woman to maintain her connection. It made Miss Minnie happy, and as her brother's wife, Gina, had discovered, Miss Minnie and the house itself were full of stories. Besides, Lacey enjoyed the sharp-tongued woman's company.

"Thank you, dear. I wouldn't mind."

Lacey made sure Miss Minnie was settled comfortably while Daisy folded her walker and put it against the porch railing.

"It got a little too noisy in that kitchen. I like children, but in controlled circumstances."

"I hear you," Daisy said. "It's probably just as well I don't have children." Then Daisy's eyes went round and she looked at Lacey apologetically. "I'm sorry. I guess this is a sensitive topic for you."

"Kind of," Lacey said. Then, to her own surprise, she added, "Especially since I can't have kids."

"Never?" Daisy's eyes widened, and she reached out to give Lacey's hand a quick squeeze.

"That's what they say." She lowered her head, and then looked from one woman to the other. "Please don't tell anyone, okay? I… I'm still getting used to it. And it's not common knowledge."

"It shouldn't be," Miss Minnie said, her voice a little sharp. "Young people share far too much about themselves these days. Some things are simply private."

Daisy laughed. "I take it you're not baring your soul on social media, Miss Minnie?"

"My, no." The older woman turned back toward Lacey. "There are other ways to nurture children, besides bearing them."

Lacey opened her mouth to disagree, and then realized she was wrong. Miss Minnie knew what she was talking about from personal experience. "You taught Sunday school for almost all the kids in Rescue River, so I guess you're right. That's one way."

"And you're sure getting close with Charlie, from the looks of things," Daisy said. "Kids need all kinds of people in their lives to grow up right. Not just their parents." She turned to Miss Minnie. "Did you ever regret not having kids?"

Lacey flinched a little. That was definitely a personal question. Daisy was the type to ask them, but Miss Minnie was the type to offer a sharp reply.

"Not that it's commonly known, but of course I did," the older woman said. "That's the reason I taught Sunday school all those years. If you don't have a family, you have to do a little more figuring to build a good life for yourself."

"You may not have much family, but I hear you do have a boyfriend," Daisy said slyly.

Lacey smiled, remembering what she'd seen at the Chatterbox. "Mr. Love, right?"

"You young people and your gossip tire me out. I

need to get back home." But a faint blush colored Miss Minnie's cheeks.

"We're sorry." Lacey stood to help the woman to her feet. "We don't mean to tease. It's just nice to see..." She paused to clarify her own thoughts. "It's nice to see a single person having a fun, active social life."

"That's right," Daisy contributed, picking up Miss Minnie's walker. "We single ladies have to stick together. And what's more, it's crazy that any time you're friends with a man, people start linking you up romantically."

Lacey and Miss Minnie glanced at each other as they made their way down the steps. Was Daisy talking about Dion? Was she or wasn't she involved with him?

After they'd walked Miss Minnie back to the Senior Towers, they stopped on the sidewalk to talk before parting ways.

"You going to the fireworks tonight?" Lacey asked.

"Yeah, I love the Fourth of July. You?"

Lacey shrugged. "I'll probably watch them from the front porch, with Nonna."

"And Vito?"

"Stop trying to match-make," Lacey scolded. "You heard what Miss Minnie said. We all share too much about our personal lives." But even saying that felt hypocritical, because the thought of Vito, of watching fireworks under the stars together, made a delicious excitement fill her chest. "I'm sure he and Charlie will watch the fireworks, one way or another."

"Then I'm sure you'll enjoy plenty of fireworks," Daisy teased.

"Hey, now!" She watched the woman—who was

maybe going to become a closer friend—wave and stroll down the street.

A fluttery excitement filled her. Maybe it *would* be a night to remember.

Or maybe not. She herself was starting to feel like a relationship with Vito might be possible. But she wasn't sure how he felt. With Vito, it always seemed to be one step forward, one step back.

Chapter Eleven

On Monday afternoon, Vito was tempted to turn down his hearing aids as he drove home from the dog rescue with Charlie and his new dog going crazy in the back. Had he just made a big mistake? What was Lacey going to think of this new, and very loud, guest?

At a stop sign, he looked back to check on them. Wolfie, the new white husky mix, stood eager in the giant crate Troy had lent them, bungee-corded in place in the bed of the pickup. Charlie was turned around as far as his seat belt would allow, poking at the dog through the open back window, talking nonsense to it, turning back toward Vito to shout "look at him, *look* at him." The disbelieving thrill in his voice and his eyes melted Vito's heart.

Whatever the challenges, he thanked God that he could do this for Charlie.

When they pulled into the guesthouse driveway, Lacey was outside on her knees, weeding the narrow flower garden that fronted the house. Dressed in old jeans and gardening gloves, she looked up and smiled, brushing blond bangs out of her eyes with the back of her hand.

Vito felt an unbelievable warmth just looking at her.

They'd finally relaxed around each other, watching the fireworks together, eating Nonna's new, healthy concoctions, hanging around the house. Homey, domestic stuff. It was dangerous territory, but he couldn't resist reveling in it for a little while, at least.

He stopped the truck, and Charlie jumped out. "Miss Lacey, Miss Lacey, come see my new dog!"

She stood easily and pressed her hands to the small of her back, smiling, then headed toward the vehicle where Vito was opening the back hatch. "I can't wait to meet him!"

Vito opened the hatch and the crate, and Wolfie bounded out. He leaped up on Lacey, his paws almost to her shoulders, nearly knocking her down. Then he ran through the yard in circles, barking, his big feet tearing at Lacey's flowers. Finally, he approached Charlie in a play bow, his blue eyes dancing, his mouth open in a laughing pant.

"Sorry, sorry!" Vito ran to hook the new leash on to Wolfie's collar, but the dog darted away.

Charlie tackled the dog, and the two of them rolled on the ground together like a couple of puppies, while Vito struggled to find the ring on the dog's collar to hook on the leash.

Finally, he attached the leash and put the looped end in Charlie's hand. "Hold on to him!" he told Charlie, and then stepped back beside Lacey to watch the pair. "I'm sorry about your garden. I'll fix it. He's a little excited."

"So what happened to the concept of a small dog?" she asked drily.

Vito inhaled the scent of wild roses that seemed to come from Lacey's hair. "I know. I'm sorry. I should have called to make sure a bigger dog was okay. It's just… We were playing with a bunch of the dogs, and it was as if they chose each other."

"He was the one, Lacey! Isn't he cool?" Charlie rose to his knees as the dog bounded around him in circles, barking.

A smile tugged at the corner of Lacey's mouth, and in that moment, Vito saw her tenderness for Charlie and fell a little bit more in love with her.

"Well…we did have Crater here, and he was as big as…what's this guy's name?"

"Wolfie!" Charlie shouted, pouncing on the dog again.

"Hold tight to that leash while I get his stuff out," Vito warned, and then turned back to the truck and started unloading dog food and dishes. Rather than an expensive dog bed, they'd stopped by the Goodwill store; a big blanket would do for the dog to sleep on.

He was carrying it all up to the porch when Nonna came out.

"What have we here?" she asked, smiling.

"It's Charlie's new dog." Vito looked over in time to see the dog pull out of Charlie's grip and head for the porch.

Before Vito could do anything, Lacey dived for the leash and held on. The dog actually pulled her for a couple of feet before she was able to stop it. "Sit, Wolfie!" she commanded, but the dog just cocked his head at her, his mouth open in what looked like a laugh.

Lacey sat up cross-legged and held the leash firmly. "Nonna, this dog's a little crazy. Make sure you're sitting down when he's around, and wear long pants until he settles down." To Vito she added, "He's strong and he's got big claws. He could knock Nonna down in a second, and those claws could scratch her up pretty bad."

"He knocked me down," Charlie said, almost proudly. "And he scratched me, too." He held up an arm. Even from this distance, Vito could see the thin line of blood.

They'd definitely start training Wolfie today.

"Why was Wolfie at the shelter?" he heard Lacey ask Charlie. "He looks like a purebred, and he acts like a puppy."

"He's two years old, and the people who had him said he was un, un…" He looked up at Vito.

"Unmanageable?" Lacey asked drily.

"That's it!"

Lacey rolled her eyes at Vito, looking exactly like she had as a teenager.

He put down the supplies and spread his hands. "I know. I know, and I'm sorry. It was just something in his eyes."

"Wolfie's, or Charlie's?"

"Both. Charlie fell in love with Wolfie as soon as he saw him, for whatever reason." He noticed the "I found a home" placard they'd gotten at the shelter. "Supposedly, we have two weeks to test everything out. If he doesn't work for us, we can choose another dog."

"And two other families tried him and he didn't work out, so he was really sad," Charlie said. "I hope we can keep him. We can keep him, can't we, Dad?"

Vito blew out a breath. "We're going to do our best to give him a good home. With love and attention and discipline, he should settle down."

"Like me," Charlie said offhandedly, and went to hug Wolfie. "Don't worry, guy. Dad let *me* stay."

Lacey's hand flew to her mouth and Vito felt his throat tighten. They glanced at each other, and it was as if they agreed without words: this *had* to work.

His phone buzzed in his pocket, and seeing that the dog was safely under Lacey's control, he pulled it out for a quick look.

He didn't recognize the number, but it was local. "Hey, I'd better take this just in case it's about a job," he said to Lacey. "Can you..." He waved a hand at Charlie, the new dog and Nonna.

"Got it," she said instantly. "Come on, Charlie. Let's see if we can teach him how to walk nicely on a leash."

The fact that she had his back so readily and without complaint made Vito's heart swell with gratitude. He clicked on the call.

"Vito D'Angelo? This is Sandra Sutherland, head of the school district's summer programs. You interviewed with one of my people last week."

"That's right." He sank down onto the porch step to focus. "What's up?"

"I'd like to talk to you about a job opening for this summer, with a possibility of extending into fall. How are you with special needs boys? Older, say from eight to sixteen?"

Without even thinking about it, he laughed. "That's getting to be my specialty." He looked down the street at Charlie.

She went on to detail the job of Vito's dreams: part-time for now, sports centered, mentoring and counseling a small group four mornings per week. "We thought you'd be perfect for it."

"Can I ask why?"

She spoke slowly, thoughtfully. "Your background as a veteran, your leadership experience and the fact that you're familiar with the foster care system all play into it. And..." She hesitated.

Why would she sound so uncomfortable? Even as he thought of the question, Vito's hand went to his face and he knew the answer. "Do some of the kids have physical disabilities? Visible ones?"

"That's it," she said, sounding relieved. "We actually have two boys, siblings, who were in a terrible house fire. They lost their mother, and they have some disfiguring burns. They've been acting out, even within the small group, so when Marnie came to me and said she had a good interview with you, and she mentioned your scars..."

Vito blew out a breath and looked skyward. Was this what God was doing? He'd never thought his scarred face would be an asset.

"Look, if you're interested and available, we could set up a time to talk. Sooner rather than later, though. Their current group leader just quit."

He couldn't help chuckling again. Between Charlie, and Wolfie the dog, and these boys, it looked like he was headed toward a career in rehab. "I'm free later today," he said, and they set up a time.

He clicked his phone off and just sat a minute, thinking.

He wanted a career in education, with children. But with his looks, he'd figured he couldn't do anything but online teaching. Now, come to find out, there was a perfect job within reach—partly *because* of how he looked.

Special ed. Physical limitations. He hadn't thought about it before, but he was definitely strong enough to lift kids in and out of wheelchairs. At the VA, he'd gotten to know guys with all kinds of disabilities. And with his own very visible scars, the students would know instantly that he understood.

Father God, You work in mysterious ways.

His heart beating faster, he looked down the street and saw Lacey and Charlie coming back toward the house, laughing, trying to manage the unruly Wolfie. He stood up and headed toward them. He wanted nothing more than to tell Lacey the good news.

A job, Charlie, and maybe Lacey. Everything he wanted was within reach. Under one condition: he had to figure out a way to tell Lacey the truth about Charlie.

Lacey looked up from trying to contain Wolfie's enthusiasm and saw Vito walking toward them, face alight with some kind of excitement. The call he'd gotten must have been good news.

"Dad! Dad!" Charlie bounced toward Vito, leaving Lacey to try to hold Wolfie back with both hands as he lunged after the boy he seemed to know already was his.

Vito ruffled Charlie's hair. "How's it going? We better help Lacey, huh?"

They came toward her and Vito took hold of the out-of-control dog's leash. "We need to figure out how to work off some of his energy," he said.

"That's what me and Lacey were trying to do! Only,

he's so crazy and he doesn't know how to walk on a leash and he ran after a squirrel and we almost couldn't hold on!"

"He's excited, buddy. We'd better let him run in the yard at the guesthouse, if that's okay with Lacey."

"Good idea," she said. "He was about to yank my arm off!"

Once they'd gotten him inside the fence, they all ran and played with him. It didn't take long to discover that the fence had a broken section; Charlie and Lacey ran after the dog and brought him back while Vito did a makeshift fix. After Wolfie's energy finally started to calm, Vito and Lacey sat down on a bench together while Charlie lay beside the dog, holding tightly to his leash.

"So, finally I can ask. What had you looking so excited after that phone call?"

Vito's face lit up. "I might have a job."

As he told her about the offer, Lacey nodded. It sounded perfect for someone as nurturing—and strong—as Vito.

"I'm going to have to set up some doggie day care for Wolfie, I think, and Charlie has his park program, so we'll be out of your hair a little more if this all works out."

She tilted her head to one side, studying him. "You're the least self-centered guy I know."

He looked blank. "What do you mean?"

"Most men would be crowing and bragging about getting a job, but you're all about how to take care of your responsibilities and how it'll affect other people. That's…refreshing."

His eyes narrowed. "You sound like you've had some experience with another type of guy."

She looked at the ground, nodding, feeling guilty. Lately she'd been having some realizations that were altering her view of her marriage, and it wasn't at all comfortable.

"Gerry?"

She hesitated a moment. But she could tell Vito, couldn't she? "Yes. I hate to say it, but he tended to think of himself first. When the time came to reenlist, he didn't even ask me—he just did it and bragged about it. And I was pregnant!"

"You're kidding. That wasn't right. You deserved better." He touched her chin, forcing her to look at him. "You deserve the very best."

She met his warm brown eyes and her heart beat faster. She didn't know about deserving the very best, but she had the feeling that being with Vito would *be* the very best. Maybe even, in some ways, better than being with Gerry. It was a disloyal thought that made her look away from Vito, but that lingered in her mind long into the night.

Two days later, Vito set out lawn chairs at the lake and pulled a picnic lunch—courtesy of the Chatterbox Café—out of the back of the pickup.

It was his way of making it up to Lacey for all the hassles of having a giant new dog in her guesthouse. He'd talked her into taking the day off with them—his last day off for a while, as his new job started tomorrow.

"I wish we could've brought Wolfie," Charlie said, his face pouty as he reluctantly helped unload the picnic basket. Since Monday, he and the dog had been inseparable.

"This is a good way to test out the doggie day care where he's going to spend mornings. And Lacey needs a break."

Charlie made a face, and Vito sighed. The boy and Lacey had been getting along great, but when he was in a bad mood, he tended to take it out on everyone. He hadn't wanted to come to the lake because it meant being separated from Wolfie. And probably because Vito's new job started tomorrow. Even though it wouldn't mean much of an adjustment for Charlie, even though he liked his summer parks program, anything new was tough on a kid who'd had too many changes and losses in his young life.

"I'll take over if you want to check out the water," Lacey said to Charlie, coming over to the table. "Man, it's hot! I'm coming in as soon as we get our stuff set up."

She was wearing a perfectly modest black one-piece and cutoff denim shorts. With her blond hair and sun-kissed, rosy face, the combination was striking.

Very striking.

"Hey, Charlie!" came a boy's shout from the beach area.

"Xavier's here!" Charlie's bad mood dissipated instantly. "Cool!" Without asking permission, he ran down toward the water.

"Stay in the shallow part," Vito called after him. He waved to Xavier's mom, Angelica, who was sitting with several other women right at the dividing line between grass and sand. He pointed at Charlie and she nodded, indicating she'd keep an eye on him.

"Can he swim?" Lacey asked.

"Not real well. His old life wasn't conducive to swimming lessons."

She spread a red-and-white plastic tablecloth on the splintery picnic table and anchored it with mustard, ketchup and pickle bottles. "Speaking of his other life, how are his visits with his mom going?"

"Okay, when she shows up sober." She and Charlie had had two supervised visits since the first Sunday one. One of the other planned visits she'd canceled, and once, she'd shown up high, causing the social worker to nix her seeing Charlie. "Whether the visit works out or not, he gets upset. Tuesdays are rough."

"Well, let's make his Wednesday better." She flashed a brilliant smile at him as she set out a big container of lemonade. "Man, I'm hot. I'm going to go say hi to Angelica and dip in the water."

"I'll probably be down." Vito wiped his forehead on his T-shirt sleeve.

Before Iraq, he'd have whipped off his shirt and jumped in the water in a heartbeat. Now, though, he hesitated.

For one thing, he'd have to take out his hearing aids. And while he could still hear some, especially if a person spoke clearly and was close by, he couldn't keep up with conversations, especially when there was a lot of background noise.

Add to that the dark, raised scars that slashed across his chest and back, ugly reminders of the plate glass window that had exploded beside him that last violent day in Kabul. He'd taken the brunt of the glass in his chest, with a few choice gashes in his face and back.

Outside of a hospital, the only person who'd ever

seen the scars on his torso was Charlie, and he'd recoiled the first time Vito had taken off his shirt in his presence.

To have a whole beach full of people do the same might be more than Vito could handle.

It wasn't that he was vain, but he hadn't yet gotten used to turning people off, scaring kids. And mostly, he couldn't stand for perfect, gorgeous Lacey to see how he looked without his shirt.

Hearing young, angry voices shouting down at the water, Vito abandoned his load of beach towels and headed toward where Charlie and Xavier seemed to be in a standoff.

"It's not *fair*." Charlie clenched a fist and got into fighting position.

"Charlie!" Vito shouted, speeding up to a run.

"Take that!" Xavier let out a banshee scream and brought his foot up in an ineffectual martial arts kick, at the same moment that Charlie tried to punch him.

Somehow, both boys ended up on the ground, which seemed to end the disagreement.

Vito reached the boys. "Hey, Charlie, you know hitting doesn't solve any problems."

Angelica came over, not looking too concerned. "Xavier. You know you're not to practice karate on your friends. You need to apologize."

"You, too, Charlie."

Identical sulky lower lips came out.

Identical mumbles of "Sorry."

Then Xavier's face brightened. "C'mon, let's get in the lake!" he yelled, and both boys scrambled to their feet and ran to the water as if nothing had happened between them.

Getting in the lake sounded really refreshing. "Sorry about that," Vito said to Angelica. "I didn't see how it started, but I'll speak to Charlie."

"Don't worry about it. These things happen with boys, and they don't last but a minute." She smiled at him. "How's Wolfie working out?"

"He's a handful," Vito said, chuckling. "Bet Troy's glad to have him off his hands."

"There's a sucker born every minute," she teased. "Actually, he's a great dog. He just needed to find the right home." She nodded toward the other women. "Come on over and say hi."

The sight of Lacey, hair slicked back, perched on the end of someone's beach chair, was all the magnet he needed. He went over and greeted Gina and a woman named Sidney. They had their chairs circled around three babies, and as he watched, little Bobby held out his arms to Lacey and she lifted him up. "Such a big boy!" she said, nuzzling his bare stomach and blowing a raspberry on it, making the toddler laugh wildly.

Vito's heart seemed to pause, then pound. Lacey looked incredible with little Bobby, like she was born to be a mother. And suddenly, Vito wished with all his heart that she could be the mother of all the children he wanted to have.

If only he could tell her the truth about Charlie, cutting away the huge secret between them, he could let her know how he felt and see if there was any chance she'd be interested in him. But telling the truth would destroy her happy illusions about her husband and her marriage. Not to mention the impact the truth would have on Charlie, if he could even understand it.

And Vito didn't take promises lightly, especially deathbed promises.

The trouble was, he was having a hard time imagining a future without Lacey in it. Somehow, in these weeks of living at the guesthouse, she'd become integral to his life and his happiness.

"Dad! Come in the water!" Charlie and Xavier were throwing a beach ball back and forth.

"You should get in." Lacey smiled up at him. "The water feels great."

The sun beat down and he was sweating hard now, partly from the heat of the day and partly from the warmth he felt inside, being here with Lacey.

"Let's take the babies down to dip their feet in the water," Angelica suggested. The other women agreed, and soon they were all at the water's edge, wading.

"You're not worried about getting burned, are you?" Lacey asked him. "You're dark skinned. But I have some sunscreen back at the car if you need it."

"Why d'you have your shirt on, Dad?" Charlie asked, crashing into Vito as he leaped to catch the ball.

Vito's face heated, and to avoid answering, he splashed Charlie. That led to a huge splash fight and Vito was able to cool off some, even though he didn't dunk to get his shirt entirely wet. It was white, and his scars would show through.

When they got hungry, they headed back up to the picnic tables and Vito grilled hot dogs. The women and babies had declined to join them, but Xavier had come over to get a hot dog. It was fun and relaxing, just the kind of day he'd hoped they could have, a gift to Charlie and to Lacey, too.

"You nervous about starting your job tomorrow?" Lacey asked as they ate.

"A little," he admitted. "It's definitely going to be a challenge. I expect some testing."

"You'll handle it well," she reassured him. "You're great with kids."

Charlie grabbed the ketchup and squirted it on his hot dog. The bottle made a raspberry sound which Charlie immediately imitated, laughing.

"Let me do it!" Xavier cried, grabbing for the ketchup. As he tried to tug it from Charlie's hand, he accidentally squeezed the bottle. Ketchup sprayed around the table, painting a line across Charlie, Lacey and Vito's chests.

"That's enough!" Vito plucked the squirt bottle from Xavier's hand and set it at the other end of the table, away from the boys.

"I'm sorry," Xavier said, looking serious and a little frightened as he surveyed the damage.

"It looks like blood!" Charlie said. He and Xavier looked at each other. Charlie made another raspberry sound, and both boys burst out laughing.

Vito rolled his eyes. "Sorry," he said as he handed napkins to Lacey, and dabbed at the mess on his own shirt.

She shrugged and met his eyes, her own twinkling, and he was struck again with how great she was. She didn't get bent out of shape about boys and their antics. What a partner she'd be.

"This isn't coming off, and it stinks," she announced, gesturing to the ketchup on her shirt. "I'm getting in the water. And I bet I can beat you two boys." She jumped up from the picnic table and took off.

Immediately, the boys followed her, laughing and yelling.

Vito watched from the picnic table, alone and sweating in a now-even-smellier T-shirt. More than one male head turned to watch Lacey's progress. With her short hair and petite figure, laughing with the boys, she looked like a kid. But if you took a second look—as several guys were doing—she was all woman.

He dearly wanted to take his shirt off and follow her into the water. To be an easy, relaxed part of things. A partner she could be proud of.

He let his head drop into his hands, closed his eyes and prayed for insight and help. Insight to understand what to do, and help to do the right thing. Not just now, in regards to his ultimately silly shirt dilemma, but overall, in regards to his promise.

The smell of warm ketchup got to him, though, and he lifted his head again without any answers.

Except a memory from his time rehabbing at the VA: had *he* ever lost esteem for someone because they had scars?

And the answer was glaringly obvious: of course not. He respected the way they'd gotten them, and he looked beyond.

Charlie and the other kids might not be mature enough to do that, but Lacey? Of all people, she was one of the least superficial he knew.

On the other hand, he wasn't just interested in gaining her respect. He wanted more. He wanted her to be drawn to him physically, as he was to her.

And why was he so obsessed with what Lacey thought of him, when their relationship couldn't go anywhere?

Like a slap in the face, it hit him: he was in love with her.

Not just a crush, a remnant of high school attraction.

Full-fledged, grown-up *love.*

Wow.

He just sat and tried to wrap his mind around that concept for a while, until the boys got out of the water and started throwing a football and Lacey came back toward the table.

"Hey, lazy," she said, grabbing his hand and tugging it. "The water feels great. Come get in!"

He let her pull him up and she laughed and let go of his hand, walking toward the water with a flirtatious smile over her shoulder.

All of a sudden, he didn't want to be the good friend anymore. For once, he wanted to follow his instincts and desires, to be the main man. To try and see whether his scars were really the turnoff he feared they'd be.

He pulled off his T-shirt, removed his hearing aids and located their case, all the while psyching himself up for an encounter in some ways more terrifying than heading into battle.

Chapter Twelve

Lacey's cheeks heated as she headed down toward the lake. Had she been too forward? What was she thinking, insisting that Vito come swimming?

She glanced over her shoulder to see if he was following her. When she saw him fiddling with his ear, her hand flew to her mouth.

She usually didn't even remember that he wore hearing aids. But of course, he couldn't wear them into the water.

Was that why he'd been reluctant to come in?

She glanced again. Or was it the scar that slashed across his back, dark and very visible?

Pushing him had been a mistake. He was such a good sport he'd come if begged, but she hoped she hadn't caused him to do something he didn't want to do.

Kids shouted as they ran and splashed in the shallow part of the lake. As she walked by a group of teen girls, she inhaled the fragrance of coconut oil, something every dermatologist in the world would blanch at. Some things never changed.

She just hoped the kids and teens would be tactful about Vito's scars.

She waded into the lake, waist deep, then looked back to see whether he was following. And sucked in her breath.

The front of his chest, which she hadn't seen before, was crisscrossed with scars. Long ones and short ones, visible even with his dark Italian skin.

Their eyes met, and Vito's steps faltered a little.

Should she say something? Walk back toward him? Tell him his battle scars didn't affect her feelings toward him, except maybe to warm her heart that he'd sacrificed for his country?

But instinct told her to treat him just as she always had. Meaning, how they'd all acted at the lake as kids, since they hadn't been here together since.

He'd reached the water's edge now, and she grinned in invitation and flicked water at him with her hand. "Scared?" she taunted.

"A little." There seemed to be a double meaning in his words. "But I can play scared." He took a few steps toward her. Suddenly, he dived underwater. A few seconds later, she felt a hand wrap around her ankle, and then she was under, giggling into the green water.

She surfaced, shaking her wet hair out of her eyes. Hooked a toe around Vito's ankle and pushed hard.

He toppled backward and came up, grinning and holding up his hands. "Truce! Peace!"

Their playfulness attracted Xavier and Charlie, who came splashing toward them. "Dad, gross—put a shirt on!" Charlie yelled loud enough for the whole beach to hear.

And apparently, despite his hearing impairment, Vito could make out the words, too.

Around them, a few kids and teens stared openly at Vito. One boy, a little older than Charlie and Xavier, said something that made the nearby kids laugh.

A flush crawled up Vito's face. "I never claimed to be a beauty queen," he said to Charlie with a half smile.

He was handling it well, but she ached for him. He'd earned those scars defending his country, and she honored him for it.

Xavier studied him thoughtfully. "Kids used to tease me for being bald, when I had cancer. Mom said to ignore them."

Vito didn't respond.

Charlie went up and tugged his arm. "Hey! Are your hearing aids out?"

Vito looked down at Charlie. "What?"

"Can't he hear?" Xavier asked.

This was getting to be a little much, and Lacey decided to intervene. "Have you boys ever heard of chicken fights?"

Neither had, so she knelt in the water and told Xavier to climb up on her shoulders. "Get on your dad's shoulders, Charlie," she said, deliberately speaking loudly. "The game is, try to knock each other off."

"Get down, Dad!" Charlie yelled into Vito's ear.

Vito grinned at her, kneeled and took Charlie onto his powerful shoulders. When he stood, he and Charlie towered over Xavier and Lacey.

"Come on, Xavier. We may be short, but we're fast," she said, and went in low.

They splashed and played for a while, with both boys getting thoroughly and repeatedly dunked. Lacey's shoulders ached from carrying a heavy, wiggling boy, but she didn't mind. The water was cool and she hadn't laughed so hard in a long time.

Most of the rest of the swimmers drifted away, except for a few kids who talked their parents into participating.

Best of all, nobody was talking about hearing problems or scars.

Finally, Angelica called the boys to come and rest, and when she offered up watermelon as an enticement, they splashed their way to shore.

"Do you want to go get some?" Vito asked.

She shook her head. "I'm not hungry."

"Swim out to the dock?"

"Sure, and I'll beat you!" Lacey plunged her face into the water and started swimming fast.

It felt good. She seemed to have some extra energy saved up, a shaky excitement that made her want to move.

She was starting to feel such a mix of things for Vito. Admiration. Desire to protect. Caring.

Maybe even love.

She shoved that thought away and swam faster. She couldn't be falling in love with Vito, could she? Vito, her old friend and high school crush. Vito, the guy who'd always been around, always ready to lend an ear or a smile or a hand with whatever you were working on, be it figuring out algebra problems or speaking up against bullies or healing a broken heart.

Was he spending time with her now just to help her get over Gerry? It seemed like, in his eyes, she'd been seeing something more.

She reached the dock at the same moment he did, but touched it first. "I won!" she crowed into his ear.

"You did." He grinned at her as he hoisted himself out onto the wooden platform.

She found the ladder and climbed up, narrowing her eyes at him. "Wait a minute. Did you try your hardest?"

"Let's just say the D'Angelos are swimmers. And gentlemen."

"You *did* let me win!"

He didn't admit to it, but he flashed a grin that took her breath away. Standing above her dripping wet, his teeth flashing against dark skin, his eyes laughing, he looked like a hero from some ancient, epic tale.

She couldn't seem to move. She just knelt there transfixed, halfway up the ladder, staring up at him.

He extended his hand toward her. "Come aboard, milady," he said, and helped her to the dock.

She needed the help. She couldn't seem to catch her breath.

They lay side by side, faces toward the blue sky, the sun warming their wet bodies. Beside them, a little railing shielded them from those on the beach, though their shouts were still audible. Lacey was exquisitely conscious of Vito, the warmth of his arm close to hers, the even sound of his breathing.

She couldn't understand what was going on inside her. This was Vito, her old neighbor, comfortable and safe. Vito, who'd always seemed out of reach because he was older.

Yet he was someone else, too, someone new. The things he'd been through had forged him into a man of strength and valor, a man she couldn't help but admire. It was starting to seem like she both wanted and needed him in her life.

"Do you remember coming out here as kids?" he asked unexpectedly.

"Sure." She watched a cloud laze across the sky, and then turned so she could speak into his ear. "Buck and I came with Dad pretty often when we were little."

"How come your mom never came? Was she…sick, even back then?"

"I don't know. She never wanted to do family things. Always busy with her dreams and plans, I guess."

Vito didn't answer, but he reached over and patted her hand, warm on the dock beside her.

"I don't know when she started with the pills." Lacey followed the swooping path of a dark bird, thinking about it. "I think she was okay when I was real small, but then she just started going in her bedroom and shutting the door." As she said it, she got a visceral memory of standing outside the closed door, hand raised to knock. She'd tried not to do it, knowing that Mom didn't like to be disturbed, but she hadn't been able to stop herself from knocking, then pounding on the door.

Where had Buck and her father been? Why had she been there alone for so long, with just her mother?

"If I had a kid," she said, still speaking into his ear to help him hear her, "I just hope I'd have more sense than to leave her to fend for herself like Mom did to me."

"You would. You're great with Charlie."

His automatic, assured response touched her. "Thanks, Vito."

"It's not about having the sense, it's about heart," he said with a shrug. "And heart, you've got."

His words surprised tears into her eyes. "I appreciate that."

He propped himself on one elbow to look at her, shading the sun. He was all she could see. "I can't say enough about you, Lacey. You were always sweet, and likable, and cute..."

She snorted. "Cute like a little brat, you mean."

He cocked his head to one side. "No, not exactly. I found you...appealing, as you grew up."

"You *did*?"

"Uh-huh." He reached out and brushed back a strand of her hair.

"Why didn't you ever, you know, ask me out?"

His eyebrows drew together. "You were three years younger! That wouldn't have been right."

She laughed up at him. "You're such a Boy Scout."

His eyes narrowed. "If you could read my mind, you'd know that's far from true."

"Then, or now?"

"What do you mean?"

"Are you talking about what was in your mind then, or now?" Something, some magnetic force field, drew her to reach toward his chest, the thick, luxuriant mat of hair sliced through by scars.

He caught her hand, held it still. "Don't."

"Why not?"

Shaking his head, he continued to hold her gaze.

"Because of this?" She tugged her hand away from him and traced the air above one of the multiple fault lines on his chest. Almost, but not quite, touching it.

He sucked in a breath, his eyes still pinning her. "Do you have any idea of what you're doing?"

"What am I doing?"

He caught her chin in his hand and let his thumb brush across her lower lip.

She drew in a sharp breath, staring at him. Every nerve felt alive, every sense awake.

"You have no idea how long I've wanted to do this." He leaned closer, studying her face as if trying to read her thoughts, her mood, her feelings.

"Do what?" she asked, hearing the breathy sound of her voice.

"This." He slid his hand to the back of her head and pressed his lips to hers.

The next Saturday, Vito's head was still spinning.

Kissing Lacey had been the sweetest and most promising moment of his life. Now he just had to figure out what was next.

He'd been busy with his new job for the past couple of days, and Lacey had been taking up the slack, spending extra time with Nonna and Charlie. She hadn't said anything about their kiss, but she'd given him some secret smiles that burned right into his soul.

He had to talk to her, and soon. But this morning, to give her privacy and time to get some detailed renovation work done, he'd taken Nonna and Charlie out for breakfast at the Chatterbox.

Now, seeing Charlie wave to a friend, hearing Nonna's happy conversation with a woman at a neighboring table, he felt full to the brim. His new life in Rescue River was working out, and he had a lot to be thankful for.

"Hey, Dad," Charlie said. "Am I still seeing Mom on Tuesday, now that you're working?"

"Yes. I'll drive you, and then we're going to see if the social worker can bring you home. If she can't, I can take off early." He'd explained his commitment to Charlie's schedule during his job interview, and his new employer was willing to be flexible.

"Mom said maybe she could drive me, only there's a lady she doesn't like in Rescue River."

"That's nice of her to offer, but your mom isn't allowed to transport..." All of a sudden Vito processed what Charlie had said and his heart skipped a beat. "Did she say anything about the lady?" he asked, carefully keeping his voice even.

"I think it was because of my dad. My other dad," Charlie clarified around a mouthful of pancakes. "Hey, Rafael asked if I could go to the park and play basketball, and they're leaving now. Can I?"

"Um, let me talk to his mom." His thoughts spinning, Vito slid out of the booth and made arrangements with Rafael's mother, forcing himself to focus. Charlie's social skills were improving rapidly enough that he felt okay about letting the boy go play some ball without him—after a stern warning about sportsmanship and manners.

Once that was settled, he paid the check and escorted Nonna out of the restaurant.

As they walked slowly toward the guesthouse, Vito wondered what Krystal had said to Charlie. If she was talking that openly about the past—what did it mean?

He took Nonna's arm when the sidewalk got bumpy. Quite possibly, it meant the whole truth could come out soon.

The woman in Rescue River whom Krystal had told Charlie she didn't like—and who was connected to Charlie's other dad—could be no one else but Lacey.

But Krystal didn't know Lacey, did she? Was there a chance she'd say enough that Charlie would put it all together?

He looked over at Nonna. "What if there were something you needed to tell the truth about, only you'd made a promise not to?"

"Ah, difficult," she said, looking at him with sharp, curious brown eyes.

Clearly she was waiting for him to say more, but he didn't. If he was going to tell the truth, it had to start with Lacey. So he focused on watching a couple strapping twin babies into a double stroller.

A pang of envy swept through him. He wanted what they seemed to have. A happy, uncomplicated relationship of raising children together.

"Have you prayed about this problem?" Nonna asked.

Had he prayed? He nodded slowly. He'd sent up some urgent, brief pleas to God, for sure.

"And listened to the response?"

He blew out a breath. "Not really. I guess I need to."

They reached the guesthouse in time to see Lacey hauling a big load of trash to the curb, struggling a little. Vito jogged over and took the boxes out of her hands, earning a smile.

Lacey went to Nonna. "Are you going around the block another time? I can walk with you if Vito's got things to do." Lacey didn't look at him, but her cheeks were pink and he didn't think it was just the exertion.

There had been a tentative, sweet promise in their interactions since their kiss earlier this week.

Nonna put a hand on Lacey's arm and another on Vito's. "I've had enough for now. Why don't you two walk?" She gave Vito a meaningful look, and when Lacey turned away, she mouthed *"Tell her!"*

How had Nonna guessed that his secret had to do with Lacey?

Was he supposed to tell her *now*?

As soon as they'd gotten Nonna settled on the porch with her latest large-print library book, Vito and Lacey headed out, strolling toward the park. Behind them, Wolfie barked a request to go along.

"Should we go back and get him?" Lacey asked, clearly unaware of Vito's inner turmoil. "He's about to break through the fence again."

"Not this time. I put another nail in it yesterday."

"Thanks. I'll have to get somebody to do a real repair soon." Lacey lifted her face to the sun. "I've been inside all morning, painting woodwork. The fresh air smells good."

"I'm glad you could come." He wanted to put his arm around her. He wanted to build a family with her! But the wretched secret stood between them.

Should loyalty outweigh love? He pondered the question, watching a jogger and his golden Lab loping across the park.

"We haven't had a chance to talk since you started your new job," Lacey said. "How'd it go, really? Did the kids give you a hard time?"

The cowardly side of him was grateful for the distraction. This was territory he could handle. "It went well. The kids are a challenge, for sure, but I liked working with them."

"And your scars didn't make one bit of difference, did they?" She was smiling smugly, obviously sure she was right.

And she *was* right. "The kids made a couple of comments, but it was no big deal. I didn't overreact and the whole discussion just went away." He hesitated, then added, "You've helped me feel okay with how I look, especially because of…of how you responded to me the other day, at the lake."

She stared down at the sidewalk, but the corner of her mouth curved up in a smile.

He needed to tell her the truth about Charlie. He was going to tell her.

"I admire your being able to handle a big group of kids like that," she murmured, so quietly he had to lean down to hear her.

Thinking about how he could break the truth gently, he gave a distracted answer to her comment. "I like big groups of kids. In fact, that's my dream—to have enough kids of my own to form a baseball team."

He was about to add "with you" when she stopped still. The smile was gone from her face.

"You know what," she said, "I just realized I left something cooking on the stove. I need to run back and get it. You keep walking, okay? I don't want to interrupt your morning exercise."

She turned and hurried back toward the guesthouse.

Vito looked after her, puzzled by her abrupt departure. His *morning exercise*? And he was surprised to learn she had something cooking when she'd been painting woodwork.

He'd been about to tell her the truth. Was that God, letting him know it wasn't the right time yet?

And if so, why had Lacey suddenly started acting so weird?

Chapter Thirteen

Numb from Vito's comment about wanting a large family, Lacey stirred canned soup on the stove and tried not to think.

If she didn't think, maybe it wouldn't hurt so much that she could never, ever give Vito what he wanted.

"Miss Lacey! Miss Lacey!" Charlie barged through the screen door, letting it bang behind him. He threw his arms around her. "Guess how many baskets I made today in one-on-one?"

She clung to him for a minute, relishing the feel of sweaty boy, and then resolutely untangled herself from his arms and stepped back. Charlie was getting way too close to her, given that she'd just learned she and Vito should never, *could* never, be a couple.

"Maybe you and Dad can come watch me play," he continued, unaware of her turmoil. "And Dad said sometime we could go see a real live Cavaliers game, all three of us!"

There is no "us."

She needed to be truthful. That was kinder in the long run.

Wolfie whined at the back door and Lacey let him in, figuring the dog could comfort Charlie in the face of what she was about to say. "I don't think that's going to happen," she said, crossing her arms, deliberately keeping her distance. "You and your dad are going to move out soon, and then we won't all see so much of each other."

Charlie visibly deflated, sinking down to put his arms around Wolfie's neck. "But I don't want to move."

How quickly he accepted the truth of what she said, and her heart broke for this child who'd seen too much change and loss. She didn't know much about Charlie's background, but she knew his mom wasn't reliable enough to raise him. That had to hurt him right at the core.

And it meant he shouldn't get overly close to Lacey, because she was just going to be another loss. "You and your dad are going to be a forever family," she said, resisting the urge to hug him. "But that's not going to happen here." She forced herself to add, "It's not going to happen with me."

He looked at her with wide, sad eyes and she felt like she'd kicked a puppy. And even if her words had been for Charlie's own good, she hated that she was hurting him.

"Later," he said, then turned and straightened his shoulders. "Come on, Wolfie." And then both dog and boy ran up the stairs.

Tears rose in Lacey's eyes, and one spilled over and ran down her cheek. She wanted to call him back, to hug him and tell him that yes, they'd still be close, and yes, they could do things together in the future.

But that would just prolong the pain. Vito needed

someone who could give him and Charlie a family, and he *would* find someone.

And that someone wouldn't be her.

Automatically, for comfort, she felt for her necklace. But she wasn't wearing it. After kissing Vito, she'd decided that it was time to remove it. Time to stop focusing on Gerry, and start focusing on life ahead.

She'd been wrong.

She turned off the soup, for which she had no appetite, and trudged up the stairs. Went into her room, opened her old jewelry box and pulled the chain back out.

She'd thought she was going to make new memories with Vito and Charlie, but she was going to have to stick with the old memories. Of Gerry and the child she'd lost. Memories that didn't seem like nearly enough to build a life on now that she'd tasted what love and family could mean at Vito's side.

But Vito wanted a big family. He'd be wonderful with a big family, and she wasn't going to deny him that.

The chain and ring settling around her neck felt heavy in a way they never had before.

Suddenly bereft of energy, she closed her bedroom door, pulled the shades and lay down in the semidarkness, too tired and miserable even to pray.

Saturday afternoon, Vito arrived at the church food distribution late and out of sorts.

Lacey had been scheduled to volunteer, too, he was sure of it; she'd come out onto the porch, car keys in hand.

But when she'd realized that he and Charlie were

planning to go, she'd turned abruptly and gone back inside, shutting her door with a decisive click.

Not only that, but Charlie was on his worst behavior. After Lacey's defection he'd refused to go and, when Vito had insisted, he'd let loose with a tantrum that had surely roused the neighborhood. Now he wore a sneer better befitting a teenage delinquent than an eight-year-old boy.

"Hey, Charlie's here!" Angelica waved from where she and Troy were sorting out boxes of doughnuts and pastries. "C'mon, the Kennel Kids scored the best place on the line. We get to give out the desserts, and eat whatever's left over!"

Charlie scowled, but he walked down to the end of the line where several other boys from the group stood joking and roughhousing. Troy and Angelica seemed to have them under control, though, and Xavier greeted Charlie enthusiastically.

Relieved, Vito scouted around for a role that didn't involve a lot of chitchat. He wasn't in the mood today. As the line of food bank patrons entered the church's fellowship hall and picked up boxes to fill, Vito started carrying crates of produce from the loading dock at the back of the building to resupply those on the front lines.

He tried to distract himself from his gloomy thoughts by focusing on the scent of sun-ripened tomatoes and bundles of green onions, but it didn't work. He kept going back to Lacey's pale, strained face, to the definitive click of her door closing.

Had their new connectedness been an illusion? Had she had second thoughts about pursuing a relationship with someone who had disabilities and a challenging child to raise?

Was there some way she could have found out the truth about Charlie?

But they'd walked together this morning, and she'd been perfectly fine, seeming interested in him, his job, their conversation.

"Hey, Vito!" The father of the migrant family who was renting Nonna's house—was his name Vasquez?—took the empty crate Vito handed him and started filling it with bundles of kale. "Thanks for working today."

"Thank *you*." Vito tried for a good humor he didn't feel. "I'm impressed that you're helping, as busy as you must be with the new baby."

"The bambino has not arrived yet, and my wife, she is very uncomfortable." The man worked deftly as he spoke, lining up the bundles for maximum space in the box. "She cannot work now, so I will have to join the food line this month. But at least I can help others, too."

"Good plan." Vito took the crate from Mr. Vasquez and reminded himself that his weren't the worst problems in the world. Some families struggled to scrape together enough food to eat.

He walked back toward the line, focusing on the friendly chatter between helpers and recipients. Interesting that the line between the two sometimes blurred, as with Mr. Vasquez.

He'd just put the crate down when a highly irate voice sounded behind him. "Vito! I need to talk to you!"

It was Susan Hinton, and she tugged him over toward a quiet corner of the fellowship hall. "What did you say to Lacey?"

"What do you mean?"

Susan's hands were on her hips. "She's been doing

so well, but when I stopped by the guesthouse to pick her up for volunteering, she looked awful. Said she couldn't come, and when I asked her if she was sick, if she needed anything, she said no and went back in her room. She *never* misses."

Vito lifted his hands, palms up. "I could ask you the same question. She's backed off from me, just today, and I don't know why."

Susan's eyes narrowed. "Since when? What went on?"

"I have no idea."

She actually smacked him on the arm. "Come on. Don't be a typical guy. What did you say to her?"

"I don't know." He leaned against a stack of boxes, trying to recreate the scene of their walk this morning in his mind. "I was talking about my new job. And not just because I was going on and on about myself. She wanted to know. She was fine one minute, and then boom, she lit out of there like I'd insulted her best friend."

"What, exactly, did you say?" Susan leaned back, crossing her arms over her chest. "And I'm not just being nosy. Lacey's had a lot happen to her, and she went through a pretty bad depression. I'd hate to see her sink back into that."

"Me, too." He frowned, thinking. "I was talking about working with the kids, and she said she didn't know how I could handle working with that many. I told her I love kids, want to have a passel of them myself someday, and it was about then that she seemed to back off. Was that...do you think I somehow offended her?"

Susan threw her hands up and snorted with disgust.

"Vito!" Several people turned to look at them, and she tugged him closer and lowered her voice. "Look, I don't know that it's my place to tell you this, but Lacey *can't* have kids."

That hit him like a blow to deflect, news that had to be wrong. "But...she got pregnant with Gerry, right?"

She looked from one side to the other, making sure they weren't overheard. "When she miscarried, there was some damage. She's infertile now, and that's been really, really hard for her to deal with."

Pain sliced through him just as if it were he, himself, who couldn't have kids. Lacey would be such a great mom. Sometimes, life just wasn't fair.

"And so when you said..." Susan trailed off.

Understanding broke through. "Did she back off because I said I wanted a lot of kids?"

"I don't know. She's the type who'd sacrifice her own desires so other people would get what they wanted."

"Wait a minute, I'm confused. What *are* her own desires?"

"She really likes you, Vito, if you haven't wrecked it. Talk to her. That is, unless her infertility means you aren't interested in her, like some ancient king who only likes women so he can get a son."

Vito lifted his hands, palms up. "Whoa. That's not me. Not at all." His mind was reeling, but this was something he could maybe fix. "Look, I have to go. Can you tell them... Do you think they can handle the rest without..."

"Go." Susan actually shoved him toward the door. "The line's short today and it's almost done."

"Thanks. Thanks, Susan. Let me get Charlie, and I'm outta here."

Despite the sad news he'd learned about Lacey, hope was rising in him. If she cared for him so much that she'd sacrifice her own desires so he could have kids… But didn't she see that what he wanted was her? Kids came into families in all kinds of ways. Just look at Charlie.

The boy wasn't with the rest of the Kennel Kids. "He said he needed to talk to you," Angelica said. "Didn't he come over?"

"No…" Vito turned and scanned the room. "I'll find him. Thanks."

Alongside his excitement about possibly working things out with Lacey, self-blame pushed at him. He'd been paying so much attention to Susan's story that he'd forgotten to keep an eye on Charlie.

Finally, he thought to talk to the other Kennel Kids. "He said he was outta here, going home," one of the younger ones finally volunteered.

"Thanks." Vito blew out a breath, quickly left the church and walked the three blocks to the guesthouse at record speed. He'd told Charlie he had to stay and help the whole time. What did this new wave of defiance mean?

Nonna was at the front gate, headed out for lunch with Lou Ann Miller. "Did you see Charlie come in?" Vito asked.

"No, but I've been getting ready. I wouldn't have heard him if he went right upstairs. Is anything wrong?"

"Everything's fine. He's just in trouble."

"Don't be too hard on him, dear." Nonna patted

Vito's arm, and then the two women headed down the sidewalk.

He trotted up the stairs. Noticed the door to Lacey's room was still closed. Was she in there?

He *really* wanted to talk to her, but he had to deal with Charlie's disobedience first. He pounded on the door to Charlie's room, and when there was no answer, flung it open.

The lecture he'd been about to give died on his lips.

The room was empty. Not just empty of people, but empty of stuff. Charlie's stuff.

He opened the closet door. There was a hamper of dirty clothes, but the clean ones were gone. As was Charlie's suitcase.

His heart pounding, he ran out onto the landing. "Charlie! Charlie!"

No answer, but Lacey's door opened. "What's wrong?"

He looked from window to window, searching the yard on both sides of the guesthouse, but they were quiet, empty.

"Vito? What's going on?"

"Have you seen Charlie?"

"Not since you guys left for the church. Where is he?"

"That," Vito said grimly, "is the million-dollar question. I think he's run away."

Chapter Fourteen

Vito continued searching even as he explained the situation to Lacey, trying to stay calm.

"I just can't believe he'd run away. He's so happy here, and with you." Lacey walked into Charlie's room. She opened the closet door, and then squatted to look under the bed—all places Vito had already checked.

Vito strode into his adjoining room. He flung open the closet door and checked it top to bottom. "I never thought of him running, either, but he's not here. And his suitcase is gone." Quickly and methodically, he searched the rest of his room. News stories of all the bad things that could happen to kids played through his head, one after another.

A thought struck him and he went back to the window, lifted the screen and leaned out. He gave a whistle, and Wolfie trotted over to that side of the yard, panting, looking up expectantly.

"It's okay, boy," he said, and shut the window. Surely Charlie wouldn't have left without his beloved dog.

When he looked back into the room, Lacey was at

Charlie's little desk, rifling through papers and magazines and empty potato chip bags.

"I'd better call Dion." He had his phone out to punch in the police chief's number when Lacey cried out softly.

"Look at this. Is this his handwriting?"

Vito took the torn piece of notebook paper from her and scanned it quickly, his heart sinking with every word he read.

I thot I cud have a mom and dad. I need a mom. Take care of Wofie.

And he'd signed it, "Love, Charlie."

Vito's heart seemed to stop in his chest.

"What does it mean?" Lacey clutched her arms around herself. "'I need a mom.' And who did he think would be his mom? Was it…was it me?"

"Maybe." He caught Lacey's eye, held it. "Believe me when I say I didn't try to plant that idea. But right now I'm more worried about where he's headed."

"Could he have gone to his mom?"

"That's what I'm afraid of." He turned toward the door. "I can't even imagine how upset he was, to leave without Wolfie."

"But you said she's an addict…"

"She is, and she isn't very selective about her boyfriends. I've got to find him." He headed down the stairs.

She followed behind. "Where does she live? Where has he been meeting her?"

"He's been meeting her at a center in Raystown. But

she actually lives in Barnsdale. Way too far to walk, and he knows that."

Lacey grabbed his arm, stopping him. "There's a bus that goes to Barnsdale. We were talking one day, Charlie and Nonna and me, and we looked over the bus route together. He was sounding out the words, and when he came to Barnsdale, he said that's where he used to live."

Vito groaned. "I have a feeling that's exactly what he did. Is the bus stop still at the front of Cramer's Drugstore?"

She nodded. "Let's go. Maybe we can catch him before he gets the bus. I don't even know the schedule anymore, but the bus can't run very often."

They each grabbed phones, wallets and keys and rushed out to Vito's car. As they climbed in, Wolfie howled his distress at being left behind.

"Let's drive slow and watch. He could be headed back home. I doubt a bus driver would even take a kid as young as Charlie."

"I don't know. He can be pretty smart about figuring out ways to do things and making up stories."

They were at the drugstore in minutes, and Lacey got out of the car and rushed in before Vito even had a chance to park. By the time he got inside, seconds later, she was in heated conversation with a teenage clerk.

"Why didn't anyone stop him?" she was lamenting. "A little boy, alone?"

"Kids eight and over can ride unaccompanied." The young woman shrugged. "He had the right paperwork, looked like. The driver always checks."

Vito's heart sank. Charlie was perfectly capable of

talking an adult into filling out a form for him. "How long ago did the bus leave?"

The teenager looked at the wall behind her, taking what seemed like an extremely long time to skim over a schedule. "Must've been about…an hour ago?"

He and Lacey looked at each other. "Let's go," she said.

As they reached the truck, the ramifications of what might be in front of them rushed into Vito's mind. Krystal, Lacey, Charlie. All together. "Lace…you might not want to go along. Someone should stay back at the guesthouse, in case he comes back."

"I'll call Lou Ann on the way and ask her and Nonna to go back."

"It's not safe—"

"*Charlie's* not safe. And you need backup."

He pulled out of the parking lot and headed toward Barnsdale. "I need backup I don't have to worry about. You can only come if you stay in the truck and be ready to call the police if needed. That's it, Lacey. I don't want you tangling with Krystal and her boyfriends, or whoever else is crashing at her place."

"Fine."

As they drove in silence, Vito's mind hopscotched from topic to topic. How would Charlie get from the bus stop to his house on the poorer side of town? Should he explain the whole situation about Charlie and Krystal and Gerry so that Lacey could be prepared? Why had Charlie run away, really?

He heard a small sound from the seat beside him. When he glanced over, he saw Lacey brushing her forefinger under her eye. "What's wrong?"

"I think I know why Charlie ran away," she said with a hitch in her voice. "I think it's my fault."

"How could it be your fault?" He kept his eyes on the rural road before him, pushing the speed limit.

"Because I told him we couldn't keep doing things together." She fumbled in her purse, found a tissue and blew her nose. "I told him we couldn't be a family."

Whoa. "How did you get into that conversation? When?"

"Just this morning." She paused, took a breath. "He came in from basketball, talking about all the things we three were going to do together, and I thought… I thought he'd better not expect that. So I just…told him it wasn't happening."

"Why?"

"Because it can't." He could barely hear her voice, low and hoarse.

He risked taking a hand off the steering wheel and gave her arm a quick squeeze. "We have to talk. Susan told me some stuff."

"What stuff?" She shifted to face him, sounding uneasy.

A passing road sign told Vito they were halfway to Barnsdale. "Look, I'm sorry if this is none of my business, but apparently Susan thought I should know about your infertility."

She drew in a little gasp, her hand rising to her mouth.

There was probably a tactful way to have this conversation, but he didn't know it, not now. "I'm sorry, hon. That's got to be tough, maybe the toughest thing for a woman."

She didn't say anything, and when he glanced over,

her lips were pressed tightly together and her body rigid.

"But there are all kinds of ways to be a parent. It's not just biological. I mean, look at me and Charlie."

She didn't answer, and they rode without talking into Barnsdale, passing the automobile factory on one side of the road and a couple of small machine shops on the other.

He tried again. "When all this is over, when we find Charlie and get him home safe, I want to have more of a conversation about this. Okay?"

She nodded, reached over and squeezed his arm. "We'll find him."

Vito pulled onto the street where Krystal had been renting a place, the last address he had for her. Dingy cottages and overgrown yards lined both sides of the street. "This isn't going to be pleasant. Remember, I want you to stay in the car."

"I know. I'm ready to call the cops." She looked around uneasily.

He stopped the truck in front of Krystal's place. "And Lace…"

"What?"

He hooked an arm around her neck, pulled her to him and gave her a fast, hard kiss. Then he pulled back to look into her eyes. "Remember, whatever happens, I want this with you." He got out of the truck before he could say too much.

There was a bang as the screen door flew open and back on broken hinges, slamming into the front of the house.

"Hey, what's going on, my man Vito!" Krystal came

out on the front stoop, started down the concrete steps, and then grabbed the railing and sat down abruptly.

A man appeared in the doorway behind her, the same one Vito had seen driving the SUV. The balding, bearded one who'd made Charlie cringe.

Vito strode up the narrow walkway. "Is Charlie here?"

"Yeah, he's here." Krystal held up a can of beer like she was making a toast. "Decided he'd rather live with his good old mom after all."

Relief that he'd found Charlie warred with worry about the situation the boy had gotten himself into. "I'd like to talk to him."

The bearded man came out onto the stoop, his face unfriendly. "What's your business here?"

"Just looking for my son." Vito visually searched the place, glancing around the weedy yard, up at the little house's windows.

A curtain moved in one. Was it Charlie?

"You been stepping out on me?" The man nudged Krystal with his knee, none too gently.

"Aw, cut it out, Manny."

"You've got it wrong." Vito kept his voice calm, because he could tell that the man was volatile. "I'm just an acquaintance of Krystal's. Taking care of her son."

"You the daddy?" Manny asked.

Behind him, Vito heard the window of his truck being lowered. Lacey.

"I'm not his dad yet, but I'm going to adopt him. Let's just get him down here and I'll be on my way."

"Maybe I don't like the way you look." Manny shoved past Krystal and came down the steps. "Maybe I want you to leave right now."

Vito automatically straightened up, his fists clenching. He wanted to punch the jerk, but for Charlie's sake he couldn't. He needed to stay calm and keep things peaceful. "I'd be glad to leave you people to your own business as soon as I have Charlie."

Then everything happened at once.

Manny drew back a fist, but Krystal rushed up and grabbed it. Manny shook her off and shoved her back, roughly, causing her to fall back onto the steps. At the same moment Charlie came running out of the house. He crashed into his mother, who reached out reflexively to grab him.

Manny, unaware what was going on behind him, threw a punch that Vito dodged, but landed a second one on Vito's shoulder, knocking him back.

Behind him, the truck door opened. "Charlie!" Lacey cried. "Over here!"

Manny advanced on Vito, and with no time to regret the violence, Vito threw a one-two punch, connecting with Manny's ribs and then the side of his throat. Manny fell to the ground, gasping for air.

Vito spun to help Charlie just in time to see the boy extract himself from his mother's grip and run to Lacey. She was turning to usher him into the truck when Krystal spoke up.

"Hey!" she called, her voice slurred but plenty loud. "Wait a minute. I know who you are!"

Vito's heart skipped a beat and he ran toward Lacey and Charlie, intent on getting them into the truck so they didn't find out the truth this way.

Her heart pumping, her adrenaline high, Lacey ushered Charlie into the backseat. Then she turned to see where Vito was. She'd drive Charlie away herself if she needed to, even if it meant temporarily leaving Vito behind. He could fend for himself better than Charlie could.

Vito was approaching the truck at a run, so Lacey went around to get in the passenger's seat.

The dark-haired woman, Charlie's mother, reached the truck just as Lacey opened the passenger door. "I know who you are," she said, her tone angry.

Vito came back around from the driver's side. "Come on, Krystal, we'll talk another time. When you're sober."

"I'm sober enough to recognize *her*."

Lacey studied the woman. "How do you know me? I don't think I've met you."

"Krystal—" Vito started.

She held up a hand and interrupted him, still glaring at Lacey. "*You're* the woman who stole my man away."

That was so far from anything Lacey expected that she could only stare at Krystal.

"Hey, now," Vito said, "this can wait. Charlie doesn't need to hear this."

Lacey stepped away from the truck door. Before she could close it in an effort to block Charlie's hearing them, Krystal slammed it shut.

Someone clicked the locks. Vito.

She looked past Vito to Krystal, filled with a sinking feeling she didn't understand. "How do you know me?"

"Guy named Gerry McPherson sound familiar?"

"Ye-e-e-s," Lacey said slowly. "He was my husband."

"Well, he was *my* fiancé. And the father of my child."

"The father of your…"

"Him." Krystal pointed toward the backseat. "Charlie."

Lacey looked at Vito, who should be denying what this madwoman said, but Vito's face was a stone.

The edges of her world started to crumble. "Gerry was Charlie's father?"

"That's right. I gave him more than you ever did."

The words stabbed her, but she ignored the pain. She had to explain to the woman how wrong she was. "But Charlie's eight. I was married to Gerry when…" She stared at Krystal.

Krystal threw up her hands. "You didn't even know, did you?"

Slowly Lacey shook her head. What she was hearing couldn't possibly be right.

"Yeah, he was seeing me on the side. At first, I didn't know about you, either." The anger was draining out of the woman's voice. "When I figured out that he was married, I tried to break it off, but he said your marriage was on the rocks and he was leaving. It was only when I saw that photo in the paper that I realized he'd been lying. You two were hugging each other like lovebirds, all happy." She shook her head, her expression bitter. "He wasn't worth the time I put into him."

"At least you got… Charlie." She heard the choked sound of her own voice as if from a distance.

Gerry had been cheating on her?

Could it be true?

She cleared her throat. "How long were you seeing him?"

"Couple of years. He didn't come around as much after Charlie was born. To be fair, he was overseas a lot after that."

"Don't be fair to him!" Lacey snapped. "Did he see you when he came home, too?"

"Yeah. Some. Not much." Something like compassion had crept into Krystal's voice. "Charlie doesn't remember him."

Lacey sagged back against the truck, unable to process what she was hearing.

Gerry had been unfaithful during the whole course of their marriage.

He'd conceived a son with this woman in front of her.

He'd met the son and seen the woman when he came home on leave.

And she'd known none of it.

She put her hands over her face, trying to block it out, trying to preserve the memory of the husband she'd adored, of the happy marriage she'd thought she had.

Vito cleared his throat.

The sound brought a whole new betrayal into focus, and she dropped her hands away from her eyes and turned to stare at him. "You knew."

Slowly, he nodded.

"You knew, and you stayed in my house, brought Gerry's son into my house, and you didn't tell me."

"Cold, Vito," Krystal said.

"Lacey, I wanted to tell you. Started to, so many times. But I promised Gerry I wouldn't."

Krystal snorted. "Yeah, well, we all made promises, didn't we? And look how much good that did."

Lacey stared from Krystal to Vito, trying to process it all.

Vito was still talking. "I promised that I'd take care

of Charlie and look out for you, too. He knew how much it would hurt you..."

"Oh, that's rich," Krystal said.

Lacey just stared and shook her head. He'd kept the truth from her so as not to *hurt* her? At Gerry's behest?

There was a sound from inside the truck, and she turned to see Charlie knocking on the window and mouthing words, his face anxious.

Lacey just stared at him, the boy she'd come to care for so much. The boy whose eyebrows arched high and dark, just like Gerry's had.

He was Gerry's son.

Gerry *had* a son. She herself had had so much trouble conceiving, and when she'd finally gotten pregnant, it had been too late: Gerry had been killed, and she had lost the baby.

Charlie was rattling the truck door now, and Vito and Krystal were arguing about something, but the words blurred into a mishmash she couldn't understand.

It was all too much. She had to get out of here.

She spun away and started walking down the road, faster and faster until she was nearly at a run.

Chapter Fifteen

For a few seconds, Vito was paralyzed, watching Lacey disappear down the street.

Charlie's rattling of the door and the sounds of Krystal's voice speaking to Manny, who was waking up, snapped him out of it.

He needed to go after Lacey. He needed to reassure and help Charlie. And he probably needed to make sure Krystal was okay, too.

The confusion of prioritizing made his military training kick in. *Secure those closest and most vulnerable.*

He opened the truck door and leaned in toward Charlie. "Listen, we're going to talk this through and figure it all out."

Charlie slumped. "Am I in trouble?"

"Yes, you're in trouble, but everyone gets in trouble. It's okay." He knew what Charlie would ask next, and he held up a hand to forestall it. "You're not getting sent away. You're still going to be my son and you can still see your mom every week."

"What about Miss Lacey?"

Vito blew out a breath. No dishonesty. That was what had gotten him in trouble in the first place. "I just don't know, Charlie. She's pretty mad at me right now."

"How come?"

"Grown-up business. We'll talk about it later." He stood, patted Charlie's shoulder, and then reached in and gave the boy a hug. "Sit tight. I've got to check on your mom and then we'll go make sure Lacey is safe."

He shut Charlie's door gently, and then walked a few steps toward Krystal. "You going to be okay?" he asked, nodding toward Manny. "I can call the cops for you."

"I got this," she said. "Go after her."

He took her word for it and drove out in the direction Lacey had gone, scanning the road. It was late afternoon and clouds were rolling in, thick and ominous. He had to get her before this storm started—or, given the neighborhood, something worse happened. "Help me watch for Lacey," he told Charlie.

A moment later, Charlie leaned forward in the seat and pointed. "Is that her?"

He could see her yellow shirt. She was desperately waving down a truck. No. She wouldn't get in a stranger's vehicle. Would she?

Did she want to avoid him that badly?

The truck stopped. The passenger door opened, and Lacey climbed in.

Vito hit the gas. "Do you know anyone who drives a blue pickup?" It seemed to have writing on the side, but Vito couldn't read it.

His stomach was lurching. If something happened to Lacey…

He got behind the truck, which was traveling at a

normal rate of speed, and was relieved to see it was headed toward Rescue River, rather than away. Maybe she'd known the person and was getting a safe ride. But he still followed, just to be sure.

His head was still spinning from the way it had all gone down. Lacey had found out the truth about Gerry in the worst possible way.

Why hadn't he told her before? The betrayal in her eyes had just about killed him.

How awful for her to find out about her adored, war hero husband from his lover, screaming jealously at her.

And normally, she'd have turned to him for comfort. But instead, she'd looked at him as the betrayer, and rightly so.

Except he'd promised Gerry he wouldn't tell.

He tried to think of how it could've worked out differently. What all he'd done wrong. He shouldn't have made the promise. He shouldn't have moved in with Lacey. But that had been for Nonna…

There was a sniffle from the seat behind him, and Vito pulled his attention away from his thoughts and to Charlie. "Hey, buddy. What's the matter?"

"I thought Mom would want me," Charlie said in a subdued voice. "But when I got to her house, she told me to go away because Manny would get mad. And then Manny saw me."

"Did he hurt you?" Vito would kill the man if he had.

"No, but he made Mom shut me in the bedroom. And they said I couldn't come out. And they were gonna call you, but then they started fighting and kind of forgot about me."

"You can't do that, buddy. You can't run away. And

you can't live with your mom." As he spoke, he was watching the truck in front of him, relieved to see it taking the exit that led to the guesthouse.

"I know." Charlie's voice was subdued.

"We're gonna figure this out, talk about it." Vito reached over and ruffled Charlie's hair. "Right now, though, we've got to check on Lacey."

He followed the truck, and when it pulled up in front of Lacey's place, he pulled up behind it.

"Do I have to stay in the truck again?" Charlie's voice was quiet.

"No, buddy, but you have to let me talk a little bit to Lacey. Grown-up business. Go see Wolfie. Okay? Take him out and walk him down the street, but stay where you can see me. We'll go inside in just a minute."

"Good, because I'm hungry."

They both got out of the truck, and Vito watched to make sure Charlie was safely out of earshot. He turned in time to see a dark-haired man walking beside Lacey toward the front door.

Jealousy burned inside him. He didn't want anyone else walking with Lacey. Especially not some tall, buff, thirty-ish guy with no scars and, probably, no baggage.

He followed them up the steps. "Lacey, I need to talk to you."

She ignored him and turned to the dark-haired man. "Thank you for the ride."

"Would you like me to stay?" the man asked in a courteous voice with just a trace of a Spanish accent.

She glanced toward Vito without meeting his eyes. "Maybe for a few minutes, if you don't mind. I just need to talk to…my other boarder, without him bothering me, and make a couple of arrangements."

"It's no problem." He sat down in the porch chair Vito had begun to consider his own.

Lacey turned to go inside.

Vito started to follow. "Lacey—"

"The lady prefers that you don't come in," the other man said, standing up to block Vito as Lacey continued on inside.

Vito stopped, lifted an eyebrow, wondered if he was going to have to fight again that day.

"She's an old friend, and she told me on the way home that she doesn't want you around. Not my business why." The man shrugged. "Sorry, man."

Vito sat down heavily on the front steps. He could smell someone barbecuing for Saturday dinner. He and Lacey had done the same just last week.

Before everything had fallen apart.

Charlie came back into the yard, tugging Wolfie. He started up the steps. "Let's go in. I'm starving."

"Can't. Not yet."

"Why not?"

"Lacey is… She doesn't want us to come in just yet, but we can in a little while."

Charlie's lower lip began to stick out. "I want to go to my own room."

Except it wasn't his own room. "Just a little while, buddy."

The dark-haired man stood and went down to his truck. He came back with a sandwich encased in plastic wrap and an apple. "Here," he said to Charlie. "It's good. Turkey and cheese."

"Thanks!" Charlie grabbed the sandwich and started unwrapping it.

"That's your lunch, man," Vito protested.

"I have kids. I understand." He sat back down in the same porch chair.

"Hey, you don't have to wait around. I won't bother her."

"I said I'd wait," the man said quietly. "No offense."

So they sat in silence while Charlie scarfed down the sandwich, and then played in the yard with Wolfie. It was another forty-five minutes before Lacey came out the door.

"Thanks, Eduardo," she said, still not looking at Vito. "I'm sorry to keep you from your work. I'm fine now."

"You're sure?"

"I'm sure."

They both watched as Eduardo trotted down the steps and swung into his truck. Charlie came over, holding Wolfie tight on his leash, in control for once. "Hi, Miss Lacey," he said uncertainly.

She knelt in front of him, giving Wolfie a quick head rub, and then turning her full attention to Charlie. "I need to talk to you about something serious," she said. "Can you listen?"

He nodded, eyes wide.

"I like you a lot," she said. "I'm really sorry it didn't work out for me and your dad, but that's not your fault."

Charlie swallowed hard, and Vito did the same.

"You always have a safe home with your dad. That isn't changing. You don't run away from him anymore, okay?"

"Okay." Charlie's voice was low.

"And because I really like you, this is hard, but…you and your dad are going to need to move out."

Charlie looked down at the floor, nodded and turned

away, nuzzling his face in Wolfie's fur. Wolfie, seeming to understand the boy's sadness, whined a little and licked Charlie's face.

Vito felt like he'd been punched in the stomach, hard.

Lacey stood and faced him. "Vito, I've made arrangements for Nonna to stay at the Senior Towers. They have a room open for her for however long she needs, and they can help her move in tomorrow. I have a call in to a friend of mine, a nurse, who'll check on her every day."

"You didn't have to—"

"Let me finish." She held up a hand. "You're going to have to find another place for you and Charlie to stay. I'm going away for a few days, and I want you out when I get back." Her voice was cold and distant.

She didn't wait for an answer, but turned and walked into the house, letting the door bang behind her.

Vito's shoulders slumped and he felt like collapsing down onto the porch and burying his head in his hands.

She was really, truly rejecting him. He loved her, and he'd lost her. Despair clutched his stomach with strong, cold fingers.

But he had a son to care for.

He swallowed the lump in his throat and straightened his shoulders. Looked out across the lawn.

There was Charlie's basketball. They couldn't forget that.

He walked down the steps, heavily, to pick it up.

"We gonna play, Dad?" Charlie asked eagerly.

"No, son." Vito carried the basketball up the stairs, not even bouncing it. "We're going to have to start packing, and I have to start looking for a new place for us to live."

He went to the front door, held it open for Charlie, and then followed the boy inside.

He felt utterly broken. And the only reason he was standing upright, trying to be strong, was because Nonna and Charlie depended on him.

It was Lacey's fifth day at the Ohio Rural Retreat Center, and she was finding some small measure of peace.

She'd cried so much that her eyes felt permanently swollen. She'd prayed almost continually. She'd sought counsel with the center's spiritual advisors.

She knew now that she needed to put her faith in God, not men.

She knew she wasn't healed yet, not even close.

The thought of Fiona Farmingham coming to visit with her today was terrifying. It wasn't that she didn't like Fiona; she barely knew her. And she had Fiona to thank for the idea of coming here. When she'd blurted out a piece of an explanation to Eduardo in that horrible truck ride home—"my husband wasn't who I thought he was"—Eduardo had urged her to get in touch with Fiona, who'd had something similar happen to her. And then he'd gone further and called Fiona, who'd texted her the address of the retreat center where she'd stayed when her world had fallen apart.

There was a knock on the door of her small, monk-like cell. "Your visitor is here," came the quiet, soothing voice of the retreat receptionist.

Trying not to show her reluctance, Lacey went out to the reception area and greeted Fiona with a handshake, then an awkward hug.

"Would you like to walk?" Fiona asked. "When I was here, I always liked the trail around the pond."

"Um, sure." She hoped Fiona didn't plan to stay long, that she wouldn't say anything to burst the fragile, peaceful bubble Lacey had built around herself.

But it couldn't last forever, of course. She was going to have to get back to renovating the guesthouse. To rebuilding her life in Rescue River as a strong single woman.

That had been her goal all along. When and why had she let that fade? But she knew the answer: it was when Vito and Charlie had come. Ever so gradually, they'd slipped into her heart so that now, having lost them, she didn't feel strong. She felt weak and vulnerable and raw.

"Thanks for agreeing to a visit," Fiona said as they walked toward the center's small pond, separated from the main building by a stand of trees. "I just felt really led to talk to you. And if your nights have been anything like mine were, you're not sleeping well, so I figured an early morning visit would be okay."

"I appreciate it," Lacey lied politely. "Where are your kids?"

"With the nanny," Fiona said, sounding apologetic. It was no secret that she was quite wealthy after her scandalous divorce settlement, but she didn't flaunt her money; in fact, people said she didn't like mentioning it.

A red-winged blackbird, perched on a cattail at the pond's edge, let out its trademark "okalee, okalee" before taking flight, bright red and yellow wing patches flashing in the early morning sun. "This is an amazing place," Lacey said, meaning it. "Thank you for telling me about it."

"Of course. How are you doing?" The question wasn't a surface platitude, but a real inquiry.

"I'm…managing, but barely," Lacey admitted.

"That's normal," Fiona said matter-of-factly. "When I found out my husband had a whole other family, it took a year to even start to feel normal again."

Her blunt words reached Lacey in a way the retreat counselors' soothing tones hadn't. Fiona had been there, had experienced the loss and humiliation Lacey was going through. "Did you ever feel like it might have been a dream, like you were going to wake up any minute and none of it would be true?"

Fiona nodded. "All the time. And then you keep on realizing, no, it's true, my life wasn't at all like what it seemed to be."

"Exactly. It's like my memories were stolen. The happiness I had with Gerry was all a huge lie."

"Well." Fiona reached out to run her fingers alongside the reeds that rimmed the pond. "I don't know if it was all a lie. My therapist said that men who lead double lives can really believe they love both women. Or in my case, both families."

Lacey inhaled the rich, damp-earth fragrance of the wetlands. "I don't know how you stood it, with four kids to watch out for. I'm barely managing with just myself."

"You do what you have to do. For me, the betrayal was the worst part. It messed with my whole image of myself as a woman, like I wasn't enough."

Lacey looked over at Fiona, tall, with long, wavy red hair and an hourglass figure. *She* had felt like she wasn't enough? "Did you get over that?"

Fiona shook her head. "You will, I'm sure, but I didn't. I've got my hands full with my kids and starting a business. Even if I felt like I could trust a man again—which I don't—I wouldn't have time for it."

"I hear you. My guesthouse is yelling for me to get back to renovations."

They walked in companionable silence for a few minutes. Green-headed mallards flew down and landed on the pond, skidding along. Overhead, the sky turned a brighter blue.

"I just wonder if everyone in town knew but me," Lacey burst out finally.

"I wondered the same thing, and I found out as soon as the truth started getting publicized. People *did* know, and they rushed to tell me how they'd suspected, or what they'd heard." She sighed. "That was bad enough, but when my kids started getting teased and bullied, I'd had it. I had to leave. It's why I moved to Rescue River."

"Oh, how awful for you *and* your kids!" Lacey felt almost ashamed for being upset about her own situation. Fiona, with her four kids suffering, had it so much worse.

"It was awful, but things are better now. Much better. What happened with your husband? How did you find out?"

So Lacey explained the whole situation. "And then Vito, he brought Gerry's child into my home! He was living there all along, knowing that secret."

"Ouch."

The sun was rising higher, and Lacey slipped off her sweatshirt and tied it around her waist. "He was an old friend, but he lied to me."

"Did he actively lie? He seems like a really nice guy, but you never know."

Lacey thought back. "No, he never actively lied. I think the subject of Charlie's dad might have come up once, but he told me Charlie's father had died. And that he was Vito's war buddy. All of which was technically true. But—" she lifted her hands, palms up "—why did he come to live in the guesthouse—with my husband's son—when he had to know how much the truth would hurt me? And then we..." Tears rose to her eyes and she blinked them back. "We started getting close. I thought he cared for me." She almost choked on her words.

Fiona put an arm around her, giving her a quick shoulder-hug. "That sounds so hurtful. But do you think he did it on purpose, to be mean?"

Unbidden, an image of Vito's kind face swam before Lacey's teary eyes. She thought back over the time when he'd decided to stay at the guesthouse. "Nooooo," she said slowly. "He was actually reluctant to stay, and only agreed because his grandma was so keen on it."

"So he didn't exactly come knocking on your door, looking for a place to live."

"No. But he should have told me the truth!"

"He should have." Fiona hesitated. "That's a pretty hard thing to tell."

"I guess." Lacey didn't want to look at Vito's side, not yet. She was still too angry at him.

"And the thing is, were you perfect? That's what my counselor made me look at, in my situation. Were there any mistakes you made, in your marriage?"

"I was stupid," Lacey said bitterly.

"Well...yeah. You kind of were."

Lacey blinked, surprised. Not many people would speak that bluntly to someone who wasn't an old friend.

"We weren't wise as serpents, were we?" Fiona stared off into the distance. "Neither of us. And people suffered because of it."

Lacey had never thought of it that way. She'd focused on how she was an innocent victim, not on how she'd had a responsibility to be wise as well as gentle and kind.

And yes, people had suffered. She thought of Charlie's hurt face when she'd told him she wouldn't be doing things with Vito anymore. It was a big part of why he'd run away.

Kicking him and Vito out on the street… Making Nonna move to the Towers… Yeah. "I've made a lot of people miserable, dragged them down with me."

They were coming to the end of the loop around the pond. "Don't beat yourself up. That's not what I mean at all. I'm really sorry for what happened to you. It's just…we're all a mix, right? Nobody's perfect. Not your husband, not you. And not Vito, either."

"True."

They walked quietly for a few more minutes, and when they reached the parking lot, Fiona stopped. "I've got to get back to the kids. But I just want you to know, there's life after this. You can come back, live well. Keep on praying, and I'll pray for you, too."

They hugged, for real this time. "Thanks for coming to see me," Lacey said. "It helped. A lot."

And as she waved, and then headed back inside, she felt better. Not healed, but better. And it was a good thing, because tomorrow she had to go back to town, hold her head high and probably encounter Vito and Charlie.

Chapter Sixteen

A week later, Vito parked in front of the Senior Towers and headed inside. He'd been so busy with Charlie and his job that he hadn't visited his grandmother for the past couple of days, and he felt guilty.

That wasn't the reason for the heaviness in his soul, though. *That* came from his unresolved issues with Lacey. Even now, if he looked down the street, he could see her on the porch of her guesthouse, talking and laughing with a couple of visitors.

He hoped to catch her eye, but she didn't even glance his way.

He trudged inside the Senior Towers, trying to look at the bright side. Charlie was doing well; Vito had explained the whole situation to his social worker, and a couple of sessions with her, Vito, and Charlie had helped the boy to understand as much of the truth as an eight-year-old needed to know. They'd talked over running away, and Charlie had promised to make a phone call to his social worker if he ever felt like doing it again.

They'd found half of a double to rent on the edge

of town, with a huge fenced yard and a dog-friendly neighbor in the other half of the house. So that was another good thing.

His course work was going well, and his new job even better. He loved working with the at-risk boys, and already his supervisor had talked with him about a possible full-time opening once he had his degree.

The scars weren't really an issue, in the job or otherwise. In fact, he felt almost foolish about how much he'd let them get in his way when he'd first returned to Rescue River. Now if a newcomer stared or a kid made a comment, he could let it roll off him, knowing that to most people, it was what was inside that mattered.

Lacey had helped him see that first. He owed her a debt of gratitude, but it was one he couldn't pay. To approach her again, after what he'd done, would be an insult to her.

He straightened his shoulders and ordered himself to focus on what he could do, not on what he couldn't. He'd go spend time with Nonna, help her feel better and recover from the move.

He walked into the Senior Towers and crossed the lobby. He was about to push the button on the elevator when he distinguished Nonna's voice, and he turned to see her emerging from the exercise room in the midst of a crowd of women. She wore hot pink sweats and a T-shirt that said… He squinted and read the words, Vintage Workout Queen.

She walked to him and gave him a strong hug. "My Vito! Come on. Sit down here in the lobby. I can spare a few minutes before I meet with my business partners."

Vito blinked. "Business partners?"

"Yes, Lou Ann and Minnie. The matchmaking business is taking off. Now, tell me what's new with you, and you know what I mean."

He tried to deflect the conversation to his work, and to Charlie, but Nonna saw right through it.

"I'm glad those things are going well, but what about Lacey? Have you mended that fence yet?"

He shook his head. "No, and I don't think it's going to get mended. Some things just can't be fixed." Nonna didn't know the details of what had happened between them, didn't know about Charlie's parentage, but she knew something serious had split them apart.

"Bella? Are you ready?" It was Lou Ann Miller, and it took Vito a minute to realize she was talking to Nonna. He'd almost forgotten his grandmother had a first name. "Oh, hello, Vito."

"Go rouse Minnie," Nonna instructed the other woman. "We have to do a quick consultation with our first client, Vito, here, before we start working on our business plan."

That was the *last* thing he needed. "Nonna… I was really just coming to check on you, not to talk about my own troubles. How are you feeling?"

She waved a hand. "I'm fine. Better every day, and these ladies—" she waved toward Lou Ann and Minnie, now both coming down the hall, talking busily "—they keep me in the loop. Lou Ann knows about all the news outside the Towers, and Minnie knows what's going on inside. I love it here!"

Vito felt a pang. He wasn't really needed by his grandma, not anymore. Nonna was making a new life for herself.

The other two women reached the cozy corner where Nonna and Vito sat, and Lou Ann pulled up chairs for both of them, leaving Vito surrounded and without an escape route.

Immediately, Nonna launched an explanation. "Vito, here, is estranged from the woman he most loves, because of some kind of fight. He thinks the relationship is doomed."

"Do you still have feelings for her?" Lou Ann demanded.

He was torn between telling the three interfering woman to go jump in the lake and embracing them for taking his troubles seriously. He chose the latter. "I still have feelings. But I did something that hurt her terribly."

"Did you apologize?" Miss Minnie asked.

"Yes, of course. But she kicked me out of the guesthouse, and she isn't speaking to me."

"Why did you do it?" Lou Ann asked.

He shrugged helplessly. "Loyalty, I guess. Loyalty to an old friend."

"Loyalty is an important value," Miss Minnie said. "But love…remember your Bible, Vito. The greatest of these is Love."

It was true. He saw that now, too late.

"So he's just backing away. Out of politeness!" Nonna leaned forward and pinched his cheek. "My Vito. Always the best friend. Always so nice."

"Too nice," Miss Minnie declared.

Lou Ann Miller looked thoughtful. "If you give up on her, maybe you just don't care enough. Why, I know a couple right here in Rescue River who had to keep huge secrets from each other. But they pushed through their problems. Now they're happily married."

Happily married. If there was any possibility at all of that for him and Lacey…

"The choice is yours," Nonna said. *"Coraggio, ragazzo mio."*

Lacey was what he wanted most in the world. Could he risk another try, a heartfelt apology, a grand gesture that might sway her back in his direction?

What did he have to lose?

Nonna seemed to see the decision on his face. "If you need any help," she said, "we're here for you."

He stood and kissed her cheek. "I will most definitely take you up on that."

From a high-backed chair that faced away from their corner, Gramps Camden stood and pointed a finger at Vito. "For once, the ladies are right. Being polite doesn't get a man much of anything."

As the ladies scolded Gramps for eavesdropping, Vito waved and headed for the door, feeling more energy with each step he took.

He had some serious planning to do.

A week later, Lacey hugged Nonna at the door to the Senior Towers, glad to feel that the older woman was gaining weight and strength. "Don't worry," she said. "I'll take you to the party next week. Are you sure you don't want me to walk you upstairs?"

"I'm fine. And I'm sorry I got the date wrong. Maybe I'm losing my marbles." Nonna shrugged.

"It's all right. I enjoyed spending some time with you." Truthfully, the excursion had filled a gap in Lacey's week. Even though she'd tried to rebuild her life, to spend time with girlfriends and focus on her work, she still found herself lonely.

Still found herself missing Vito and Charlie.

Nonna reached up and straightened Lacey's collar, plucked a stray hair off her shoulders. "Do you know what we always said in Italy? *Si apra all'amore.* Be open to love."

"Um, sure." Maybe Nonna *was* getting a little confused, because that remark had been apropos of nothing.

She drove the half block to the guesthouse and parked in the driveway, taking her time. She didn't want to go inside an empty house. Without Charlie roughhousing and Wolfie barking, without Vito's deep voice, the place felt empty.

But delaying wouldn't solve her problem. She clasped the cross she'd hung around her neck, in place of the wedding ring she'd worn before. It was a reminder: she could do all things through Christ.

Including survive loneliness.

She climbed out of the car and walked slowly toward the front entrance, checking her flower beds, which were doing great. Looked reflexively at the broken fence. She really needed to…

She stopped. Looked again.

The makeshift fix they'd done weeks ago, when Wolfie had escaped, wasn't there. Instead, the fence was repaired.

She knelt down, awkward in her dress and heels, and examined it. The two broken pickets had been replaced with new ones, painted white. Only when you were very close could you see that the paint was a little brighter on the new pickets.

She frowned. Who would have repaired her fence?

Wondering, she walked toward the front of the house. As she rounded the corner, she heard music.

Opera music. *Italian* opera music.

What had Nonna called it? *The most romantic music on earth.*

What in the world?

The wonderful smell of Italian food—lasagna?—wafted through the air.

As she climbed the front steps, she saw something pink.

Her heart pounding, she reached the top of the steps. A trail of rose petals led her across the porch to a table set for two, topped with a white tablecloth.

She stared at the centerpiece, and tears rose to her eyes.

A ceramic rooster, exactly like the one Charlie had broken the day she'd met him.

No longer could she doubt who was responsible for what she was seeing.

She turned toward the front door. At the same moment, Vito emerged through it, a bowl of salad in one hand and a tray of pasta in the other. He wore dress trousers, a white dress shirt and an apron. Focused on balancing both dishes, he didn't notice her at first, but when he did, a strange expression crossed his face.

"Lacey," he said his voice intent. "Wait." He turned and carefully put down the two items on a side table.

Then he undid his apron and took it off, his eyes never leaving hers.

"How did you..." She broke off.

Walking slowly across the porch, he stood before her, not touching her. "I trespassed. Nonna gave me her key."

"Nonna…" She cocked her head to one side and reviewed the afternoon. Nonna's sudden invitation to a party, her insisting that Lacey dress up, the realization that it was the wrong date… "She was in on this. And you fixed my fence."

"For a good cause."

"What do you mean?"

He walked around her and pulled out a chair. "Explaining will take a minute. Would you like to sit down?"

She hesitated, feeling a little railroaded, but curious, too. "Oka-a-a-ay."

He poured iced tea, the raspberry flavor she always ordered at the Chatterbox, looking for all the world like a handsome Italian waiter. But then he pulled a chair to face her and sat down, close enough that their knees almost touched. Almost, but not quite. "The good cause is…an apology. Lacey, I am so sorry for what I did to you. There's no excuse for dishonesty."

She wanted to forgive him instantly. The music, the tea, the rose petals, the mended fence, the ceramic rooster—all of it created a romantic little world. But she couldn't just succumb to it. She needed to be as wise as a serpent, not just gentle as a dove. Not just go with her heart. "I would like to hear why you did what you did. I wasn't in a condition to listen before."

He drew in a breath and nodded. "Of course. You deserve that." Still, he seemed reluctant to speak.

"I can take it, Vito! Whatever happened, it's probably better than what I've been imagining."

"Right." He reached for her, then pulled his hand back. "It was only in the last couple of months of Gerry's life that I found out he'd been unfaithful to you."

The word stung, even though she knew it was true. "How did you find out?"

"He was burning letters," he explained. "Building a fire was dangerous over there, so I went to stop him. He said he had just a few more to burn, and he was turning over a new leaf. I still had to stop him—I was his commanding officer by then—and I happened to see a…suggestive card. It didn't look like something you'd send, so I asked him about it."

The thought of another woman sending racy cards to her husband made Lacey's face hot with anger and humiliation. Was that what Gerry had wanted in a woman? Hadn't her tame, loving letters been enough?

Vito was watching her face, and he reached out and wrapped his hand around her clenched fist. "He was *burning* it, Lace. He'd had a couple of risky encounters that had made him think about his life, and he wanted to get a fresh start."

"Either that, or he was afraid of getting caught."

"No, I think he was sincere. He really did love you. He just wasn't used to…" Vito seemed to cast about for the right word. "To monogamy, I guess. That's why I regret introducing you two."

"That's why you tried to warn me about him. You knew what he was like."

Vito nodded. "But you were in love, and I hoped marriage would change him. And it did. It just took a while. When you let him know you were expecting a baby, it made him want to change his ways, be a better husband and father."

"He already had a child!"

"Yeah." Vito sighed. "I found out about that at the very end. You sure you want to hear?"

"Tell me."

"Okay." He looked out toward the street, his shoulders unconsciously straightening into military posture. "Three of us were cut off from the others, and both Gerry and Luiz were hit and bleeding pretty bad. When Luiz died and Gerry realized the medics might not get there in time for him, either, he told me about Charlie. He asked me to take care of Charlie if Krystal couldn't. And he asked me to look out for you, and to keep you in the dark about who Charlie was, because he thought it would kill you to know. Before I could make him see it wasn't possible to do all those things together, he was gone."

Lacey just sat, trying to process what Vito was saying.

"I tried to save him, Lace. And I tried to do what he asked, though I didn't succeed very well." He sighed. "I thought things were okay for Charlie and Krystal. I thought it might be best for you if I stayed away. But then I got injured, and there was the rehab, and then everything hit the fan with Krystal and I found out Charlie was about to be put into the system… Well, first things first, I thought. Charlie is a kid."

"Of course." Lacey stared down at the porch floor. "It was my own fault I was so foolish, marrying Gerry. I was vulnerable to anyone."

"I was foolish, too, but I've learned. I've learned that honesty and…and *love*…trump loyalty to a bad cause."

She froze, not daring to look at him. "Love?"

He squeezed her hand, then reached up to brush a finger across her cheek. When he spoke, his voice was serious. "I love you, Lacey. I… Maybe I always have, kind of, but now it's grown-up and serious and forever."

Cautiously she looked at him through her eyelashes, not wanting to let her joy and terror show. She drew in a breath. "I have an apology to make, too. I was wrong to kick you and Charlie out. I was angry at Gerry, really, and at myself, and I took it out on you."

"Understandable."

"Is Charlie okay?"

He nodded. "We've had a few sessions with his social worker to talk it all through. She helped me understand how much to tell Charlie. Right now, he knows that his dad was a hero, but made some mistakes. That he felt ashamed he wasn't married to Charlie's mom. And that none of it is Charlie's fault. That seems like about as much as he can take in, right now."

"That's good." She bit her lip. "I shouldn't have taken out my hurt on you, and especially on an innocent child."

"For whatever you did wrong, I forgive you."

"And I forgive you."

They looked at each other. "Are we good?" he asked.

"We're good." She felt a strange breathlessness as he stood and pulled her gently to her feet.

And into his arms.

Being held by him, seeing and believing how much he cared, soothed some deep place inside her that wanted to be cared for and loved.

His hand rubbed slow circles on her back. "I hated being at odds," he said, and she felt the rumble of his voice against her cheek. "I want to be your friend. At *least* your friend. I want to be more."

She pulled away enough that she could look up at his face. "What kind of more?" she murmured in a husky tone that didn't even sound like her.

"This kind." He leaned down and pressed his lips to hers.

After a long while he lifted his head, sniffing the air, and then pulled away.

Lacey smelled it at the same time he did. "Something's burning!"

They ran inside and Vito pulled a scorched cake from the oven. "Oh, man, it was chocolate, too!"

She burst out laughing.

And then they were both laughing, and crying, and hugging each other, and kissing a little more. "It was so awful being apart from you. I never want that to happen again," he said.

"I don't, either." She pulled back. "But Vito. That nice meal is getting cold."

He laughed. "It'll warm up just fine. Come here."

He was right, of course. She stepped forward into his arms. "I love you," she said.

Epilogue

One Year Later

"I predicted this as soon as I saw you catch that bouquet," Susan Hinton said, looking around the guest-house lawn with satisfaction.

"You couldn't have!" Lacey laughed. "Vito wasn't even back yet."

"I saw him come up behind you and I knew."

Gina, Lacey's sister-in-law, came over to where Lacey and Susan sat, under the party tent they'd put up against a summer shower. "Vito and Buck are exchanging fatherhood tips with Sam."

Lacey craned her neck and saw Sam Hinton, holding three-month-old Sam Jr. as if he were made of glass. Buck squatted to wipe the cake from little Bobby's face. And Vito was bending down to speak to Charlie, who looked adorably grown-up in his junior tux.

Lacey felt fully recovered from the devastating news about Gerry being Charlie's father. There even seemed to be a strange rightness in her helping Vito to raise Gerry's child.

Nonna approached Vito and took his arm, pulling him toward Lacey. She seemed years younger than she had after her heart attack; indeed, she was helping to teach heart attack recovery classes at the Senior Towers and was so happily enmeshed in the social circles there that she'd decided to live at the towers full-time.

"I need to talk to the bride and groom," Nonna said as she reached Lacey and her friends. "Alone."

Vito lifted an eyebrow and reached to pull Lacey from her reclining position. The very touch of his hand gave her goose bumps. They'd spent glorious time together during the past year, getting to know each other as the adults they were now. Vito had finished his online studies and student teaching, and had the offer of a job for the fall. Meanwhile, he'd been working with Lacey at the guesthouse, which had become so successful that she'd had to hire help—help that would now manage the place while she and Vito honeymooned.

The thought of their honeymoon on a South Carolina beach made Lacey's skin warm. She couldn't even regret that they could only manage a long weekend, with the guesthouse to run and Charlie to parent. She was so, so ready to begin married life with Vito.

"I'm afraid I've been interfering again," Nonna said, a twinkle in her eye.

"Nonna! What now?" Vito's tone was indulgent.

"You have that look on your face," Lacey added. "What have you been up to?"

Nonna looked from Vito to Lacey and bit her lip. "First, I have a confession to make." She hesitated, then added, "My interfering has been going on for a while."

"What do you mean? The matchmaking date?" Lacey had suspected for some time that Nonna had arranged for her and Vito to go out with Daisy and Dion, knowing it would push them into acknowledging their feelings for each other.

Nonna patted Lacey's arm as if she were a bright student. "Yes, the whole matchmaking service was a scheme to get the two of you together. Of course, it's grown beyond that." Lou Ann and Miss Minnie had become Nonna's first lieutenants, matching up the singles of Rescue River.

"I'm just wondering when you three ladies will do some matchmaking on each other," Vito said. He didn't sound particularly surprised about Nonna's interference, either.

"Oh, no!" Nonna looked shocked. "We're having far too much fun to weigh ourselves down with cranky old men."

That made Lacey burst out laughing. "You're incorrigible."

"Well, and it didn't begin with the matchmaking service, either."

"What else?" Vito put on a mock-serious tone. "Tell us everything."

"I…well, I may have arranged for Lacey to take care of me, and my home to be unavailable, when I found out you were coming home, dear." She looked up through her glasses at Vito, her face tender. "You're going to be a wonderful husband, but I was afraid you'd be my age before you figured it out. When I ended up on Lacey's floor at the hospital, and heard about her history, and saw how lovely she'd grown up to be… well, I may have done a little scheming."

"Nonna D'Angelo!" Indignation warred with laughter in Lacey's heart. Laughter won on this glorious day.

"I have a way to make it up to you," Nonna said hastily. "You both know I came into a small inheritance when my cousin Paolo died last year."

Vito nodded, and Lacey just looked at Nonna, wondering where this was going. What would Nonna think of next?

"I've been trying to decide what use to make of it. What can I do, at my age? I have a few plans, but the first one is I want to give you this." She reached into her handbag and pulled out a small, gift wrapped box. She handed it to Lacey. "Open it."

The box was featherlight, and inside, there was nothing but paper. "I think you forgot to put the gift in—"

"Nonna!" Vito had pulled out the papers and was scanning them. "You can't do this!"

"I can, and I've already done it. You're booked for a week at a villa in Tuscany, and then a week in Rome and Venice. You leave tomorrow." She crossed her arms and smiled with satisfaction.

"But…our reservations in South Carolina…"

"Canceled. That was the interfering part." Nonna looked only slightly abashed. "You'll still get a wonderful honeymoon. It's just the destination that'll be different."

Lacey stared at Nonna and then at Vito. "Italy?" she asked faintly. "I've never been out of the country."

"And that's why your brother had to check into whether you had a passport. You do. Some trip to Canada that didn't materialize?" Nonna waved her hand as if the details didn't matter.

Lacey looked at Vito. "Italy."

"Together." A smile spread across his face. "I've never been, either."

"And that's why you need two weeks," Nonna said firmly. "Everything's all arranged. The guesthouse, Charlie, reservations in *Italia*."

Lacey looked up to see Buck, Charlie, Susan and Sam all crowded together, looking at them, coming over to congratulate them on their changed honeymoon schedule and destination. It looked like everyone had been in on the surprise. Even Charlie knew that he and Wolfie would get to spend a little longer at the dog rescue farm with Xavier.

A regular clinking and ringing sound came, the traditional instruction to kiss. Vito pulled Lacey into his arms and kissed her tenderly, then held her against his chest.

"Is this what it's going to be like to be married to you?" he rumbled into her ear. "Surprises and adventures?"

"Enough to keep you on your toes." She laughed up at him as he pulled her closer, and then looked beyond, to the clear blue sky. Vito was amazing, and life with him and Charlie was going to be an adventure.

But she knew deep inside that none of this was a surprise to her heavenly father, who'd orchestrated all of it and would guide them through the rest of their days.

* * * * *

Kathryn Springer is a lifelong Wisconsin resident. Growing up in a "newspaper" family, she spent long hours as a child plunking out stories on her mother's typewriter and hasn't stopped writing since. She loves to write inspirational romance because it allows her to combine her faith in God with her love of a happy ending.

Books by Kathryn Springer

Love Inspired

Castle Falls

The Bachelor Next Door
The Bachelor's Twins
The Bachelor's Perfect Match
The Holiday Secret

Mirror Lake

A Place to Call Home
Love Finds a Home
The Prodigal Comes Home
Longing for Home
The Promise of Home
Making His Way Home

Visit the Author Profile page
at LoveInspired.com for more titles.

THE SOLDIER'S NEWFOUND FAMILY

Kathryn Springer

We ought always to thank God for you, brothers, and rightly so, because your faith is growing more and more, and the love every one of you has for each other is increasing.

—*2 Thessalonians* 1:3

This book is warmly dedicated to my continuity cohorts—Marty, Barbara, Arlene, Glynna and Jill.

For wisdom, grace, patience and a sense of humor while we linked the Texas Twins books together.

It was a blessing working with you!

Chapter One

"*And this one's Asteroid Man...*"

Another plastic action figure landed on Sergeant Carter Wallace's lap tray, adding to the growing number of soldiers that had formed a perimeter around the coffee cup the flight attendant had set down in front of him.

"I got him for my birthday." A pair of eyes the color of Texas bluebonnets regarded Carter solemnly, waiting for his opinion.

"Cool." Just like the coffee he hadn't taken a sip of yet.

A wide, gap-toothed grin rearranged the pattern of butterscotch freckles on the preschool boy's cheeks. "He can fly, too. And the bad guys can't see him coming because he's *inbisible* when he lands."

Across the narrow aisle, the boy's harassed grandmother caught Carter's eye and mouthed the words *I'm sorry* as she tried to calm the fussy toddler in her lap.

The frustrated looks the woman had been receiving from their fellow passengers had only compounded her stress. Which explained why she hadn't noticed her grandson unbuckle his seat belt and commandeer the empty seat beside Carter after the beverage cart rattled past.

Without an invitation, the kid had settled in next to him and announced that his name was Josh and that he was four years old.

"Are you a real soldier?" he'd whispered, staring at the patches on Carter's camo jacket in open fascination.

Carter wrestled back a smile. "Yes, I am."

"I like soldiers."

Those three simple words had derailed Carter's plan to get some shut-eye. Josh had plunged both hands into a backpack and proceeded to pull out his action figures, an eclectic blend of superheroes and guys in camouflage, all working together to save the world.

The kid might have prevented Carter from the luxury of a long-overdue nap, but he'd also kept the nightmares at bay.

At least for a few hours.

"This is Mike." Josh carefully placed another action figure behind a Lego bunker. "When he's in trouble, Asteroid Man does this—" The action figure came down right in front of Soldier Mike with a thump that rocked the lap tray and sent coffee sloshing over the side of the cup. "See? He saves him 'cause they're friends."

Carter felt beads of sweat pop out on his forehead as a memory slammed against the barricade he'd built around it. Josh's chatter was muffled by the deafening blast that sucked Carter back in time. He felt the sun-baked ground shudder beneath his feet. Saw a fireball bloom in the distance, reaching so high the flames licked the clouds. By the time he'd reached the scene, two trucks in the convoy had been reduced to smoking metal skeletons.

Along with the buzzing in his ears, Carter had heard shouts and the pop of gunfire from a sniper who'd moved in to finish what the roadside bomb had started.

You'll be nominated for a Silver Star, Wallace.

Carter didn't know why. Sure, he'd saved three men that day. But he'd lost Rob.

His closest friend.

He hadn't reached him in time. And God hadn't bothered to intervene....

Carter was almost relieved when the seat belt sign blinked on a few minutes later and the flight attendant told the passengers the plane would be landing soon. Josh's soldiers retreated to the backpack once again, and he scrambled back to his grandmother's side.

Carter stared out the window as the wheels came down and the plane began its descent. Sheets of gun-metal gray clouds began to unravel, offering a teasing glimpse of the city below. It had been over a year since he'd stepped on Texas soil.

A lifetime ago.

The plane rolled to a stop by the gate, and the child's grandmother smiled at Carter across the aisle. "I can't thank you enough for keeping Josh occupied."

A smile hooked the corner of Carter's lips. "Not a problem, ma'am. Marines are trained to handle all kinds of situations."

"Are you home for good?"

Carter hesitated, not knowing quite how to answer the question. He chose the safest response.

"For a little while."

The woman frowned. "But someone will be here to meet you?"

Carter nodded, touched by her concern. "My sister." In her last email, Maddie had promised to pick him up at the Dallas/Fort Worth airport, but that had been several weeks ago and he hadn't been in touch with her since then.

She'd hinted that she had something important to tell him, but insisted the news be shared in person. Carter couldn't imagine what it would be, but there were times he'd been grateful for the distance that separated him from family drama. Besides that, she had Grayson, their older brother, to confide in. The two had always been close, bound together by some invisible thread that Carter had never been able to grab hold of.

There was a flurry of movement around them as the passengers collected their bags. Josh grinned up at him. "Bye."

"Take care, bud," Carter said.

"I will." The boy's thin arms locked around Carter's leg and then he was gone, swallowed up in the line of passengers exiting the plane.

Carter slung the camouflage duffel bag over his shoulder and made his way toward the baggage claim. A businessman glanced up from his laptop and gave him a respectful nod. A woman on the escalator caught his eye and tapped the tiny yellow ribbon pinned to her collar.

Carter had learned that when he wore his uniform, he wasn't just a soldier named Carter Wallace. He was someone's dad. Brother. Son. Across three time zones, people had sought him out. Smiled at him. Thumped him on the back. By touching him, they were touching someone they loved.

It was strange. Humbling.

At the bottom of the escalator, he began to look for

Maddie. She was the kind of woman who stood out in a crowd. Stylish and sophisticated…

"Carter!"

Out of the corner of his eye, a blur of movement began to take shape.

Auburn hair. Big brown eyes…and cowboy boots?

Carter had only a split second to brace himself for impact before Maddie dived into his arms. His throat swelled shut when she clung to him. He couldn't remember his older sister ever being so demonstrative.

"I can't…breathe," he managed.

The choke hold around his neck loosened. A little. "Sorry. It's just—" Were those tears in her eyes? "I'm glad you're here." Sniffling, Maddie stepped back and clasped his shoulders. "Let me look at you."

Carter's lips quirked. "I haven't changed since the last time you saw me."

Not on the outside, anyway.

"You, on the other hand…" His gaze skimmed the Western-style plaid shirt and jeans and paused to linger on her feet. "Nice boots. Are you on some kind of undercover assignment for *Texas Today?*"

"I'll leave the undercover stuff to Gray—and I'm not working at the magazine anymore."

"Not working… I thought you loved your job."

Maddie flashed a wobbly smile. "I told you there have been a lot of changes."

"That's an understatement."

Carter's head whipped around at the sound of a familiar drawl. His brother, Grayson, sauntered up, hand in hand with a beautiful, dark-haired woman and a small boy sporting a cowboy hat and a Dallas Cowboys T-shirt.

Carter had come home on leave several times since he'd enlisted, but he'd never been greeted at the airport by both his siblings before.

"I didn't expect to see you here." He extended his hand but Gray ignored it and hugged him instead, adding a manly thump to his back for good measure.

The lump in Carter's throat doubled in size. Had the plane landed in Fort Worth or *The Twilight Zone?* Because things were getting weirder by the second.

"Carter, I'd like you to meet my fiancée, Elise Lopez, and her son, Cory." Gray smiled down at the woman, an expression on his face that Carter had never seen before. Identical to the one he'd seen on Rob's face whenever he'd talked about Savannah...

He thrust the memory aside.

"Congratulations." Carter glanced at Maddie. "I guess this must be the big news you had to tell me about in person."

A look passed between his siblings.

And that's when Carter felt it. The prickle of unease that skated up his spine and lifted the hairs on the back of his neck. He recognized the signs, similar to the ones he'd experienced trudging through the mountains of Afghanistan.

Suddenly, this no longer felt like a reunion. It felt more like an ambush.

"Let me get this straight. There are *two* of each of you?" Carter leaned forward, staring at his siblings in disbelief.

His *half* siblings, if what Gray had just told him was true.

"We thought it would be better if we waited until you got home to break the news," Maddie said softly.

It would have been better if they hadn't told him at all, Carter thought, still trying to wrap his mind around the fact that his mother, Sharla Wallace, hadn't given birth to Maddie and Gray. They'd spent the past hour explaining that a woman named Belle Colby was their biological mother and both Maddie and Gray had an identical twin.

Which meant their dad had never bothered to mention that he'd been married once before. Brian Wallace might be a distant father—more available to the missionary patients he served than his own family—but he wasn't the kind of man who would keep something like that a secret.

Unless there was a good reason.

Maddie reached for his hand across the kitchen table. At least they'd chosen the privacy of Gray's condo to drop this bomb on him. Gray had left Elise and Cory at Maddie's apartment, where they'd been staying now that his sister was living at the Colby Ranch near a small town named Grasslands.

Carter's older brother was apparently tying up loose ends in Fort Worth before starting his new job at the Grasslands Police Department. Gray and Elise planned on making a permanent move to Grasslands after they were married.

Carter had barely recovered from the news that his brother was engaged when Maddie spilled the rest of the story. Starting with how she'd recently reunited with Violet, her identical twin.

According to Maddie, Violet was the one who'd set things in motion. Her mother, Belle, had been badly injured after falling off a horse last July and she'd set out to find her biological father. A search that had led her to Maddie, instead.

"I know it sounds unbelievable—"

"Unbelievable?" Carter interrupted, shifting just out of Maddie's reach. "How about impossible? You both have an identical twin that you didn't know about. Dad was married before he met Mom. I think we've gone straight from unbelievable to a guest spot on the Dr. Phil show."

No one smiled. Probably because they knew it was true.

"We've been having a hard time accepting it, too," Gray said carefully. "Unfortunately, Belle can't answer our questions until she comes out of her coma. And… Dad." He stumbled over the word, which suddenly made the story more real than fantasy. Carter wasn't used to seeing his big brother, a tough undercover cop, lose a grip on his emotions. "I'm still trying to track him down."

Carter tried to put himself in Gray's position. While tracing their roots to an old address in Fort Worth, Maddie had met a woman named Patty Earl who'd cast doubts on the fact that Gray and his twin, Jack Colby, were even Brian Wallace's sons. Her late husband, Joe Earl, had claimed that *he'd* fathered the twin boys.

Carter had always felt like the odd man out in his family, but if the woman's claim was true, it meant that he was Brian's only son by blood.

He wanted to talk to his father, demand to know why he'd kept all this a secret. But according to Gray, their dad had disappeared while traveling near the Texas-

Mexico border and no one in the family had been able to reach him for several months.

Brian wasn't expected to return until Thanksgiving, but his wallet and cell phone had turned up recently and there was a growing concern that something had happened to him. Another piece of information that Gray and Maddie had waited to tell Carter until he was back in the States.

"I know it's going to take some time to sort all this out," Gray said. "We're still working on it. It's been just as hard on Violet and Jack."

The names meant nothing to Carter. He tried to picture another Maddie. Another Grayson. The "country" equivalents of his big-city sibs. Under different circumstances, the thought would have made him smile.

"I'd like you to meet Ty." Maddie touched the engagement ring on her finger. The last Carter knew, she'd been engaged to Landon Derringer, a Fort Worth CEO who'd been a close friend of the Wallace family for years. Carter was having a hard time keeping up. "And Violet and Jack have invited you to stay at the ranch until we hear from Dad."

"Why?" Frustration sharpened the word but it didn't faze Maddie.

She lifted her chin. "Because family should stick together."

Family? Is that what they were? Because Carter had no idea how to define this tangle of relationships.

"Come on, Carter." Gray met his eyes and Carter saw a glint of stubbornness there. Or maybe he was seeing his own reflection. "What would it hurt to hang out at the Colby Ranch for a week or two?"

"You'll love it there," Maddie said earnestly. "I promise."

I promise.

Carter's hand closed around the photograph in his pocket.

"Give me a few days."

Maddie's expression clouded. "Carter—"

"There's something I have to do first."

"Did you see the guy who just sat down at table four? Because he sure can't take his eyes off *you*."

"That's your section." Savannah Blackmore brushed aside her coworker's sly comment as she continued to restock the shelves behind the counter.

Libby hadn't been working at the diner very long, so all she knew was that Savannah was single, but not the reason why. Not that it mattered. The "cosmetology student by day—waitress by night" fancied herself a modern-day Emma, matching up people with the hope they would find their own "happily ever after" ending.

Over the past seven months, Savannah had learned there were endings, but they weren't always happy ones.

"He has broad shoulders, too." Libby fanned herself with the order pad.

Some girls noticed a man's smile or the color of his eyes. Libby judged a man by the width of his shoulders. Savannah doubted she could find a pair strong enough to carry her burdens. Guys avoided women with baggage and she had enough to fill up the cargo hold of a Boeing 747. The delicate flutter below her rib cage reminded Savannah there was someone else to consider. Someone *she* needed to be strong for.

That's why she wasn't even tempted to look at the guy at table number four.

"I'll be in the kitchen."

"You can run but you can't hide," her coworker teased.

"Watch me." Savannah made a beeline for the swinging doors that separated the kitchen from the dining area.

Come to think of it, the canned goods in the pantry could use a little organizing, too....

"Order up." Bruce, the diner's owner and self-appointed cook, pointed to a platter piled high with ribs, mashed potatoes drenched in butter and a generous helping of coleslaw.

It was Libby's order, but over the top of the doors, Savannah could see she'd been waylaid by a group of tourists wearing matching T-shirts with the words I Brake For Rodeos emblazoned on the front.

"I'll take it." Savannah grabbed the plate and caught Libby's eye as she rounded the counter. "Where does this one go?"

The impish light that danced in the younger girl's eyes answered Savannah's question even before she could say the words—

"Table four."

With a sigh, Savannah counted the scuffed tiles as she made her way to the back of the diner.

Part of her knew that Libby must have misunderstood the guy's interest. The past few months had taken their toll. She felt—and probably looked—as wrung out as the mop hanging in the utility closet.

Savannah summoned a polite smile as she approached the table.

Okay, so maybe Libby hadn't been exaggerating. The guy's close-cropped hair was the pale gold of winter wheat, a perfect setting for a pair of deep-set, cobalt-blue eyes. A gray T-shirt stretched across the broad shoulders Libby had gone on and on about....

Savannah's gaze locked on the familiar insignia and her mouth went dry.

A soldier.

He rose to his feet as she reached the table. "I'm Sergeant Carter Wallace, ma'am...."

Savannah felt a tingling numbness spread down her arms to her fingertips. The plate wobbled. As a river of barbecue sauce carried the ribs toward the edge, it was gently plucked from her hands and deposited on the table.

The soldier's gaze dropped to the apron tied around her waist, lingering there until Savannah felt the color rise in her cheeks.

What was his problem? Hadn't he seen a pregnant woman before?

"Your waitress will be back in a few minutes to see if you need anything else." Savannah whirled toward the kitchen.

"Savannah? *Wait*."

How did he know her name?

She slowly turned around, reluctant to face him again.

A muscle worked in the sergeant's jaw. "I know—*knew*—your husband. Rob."

Bitterness and sorrow clashed, splashing over the walls of Savannah's grief. She swallowed hard against the lump that rose in her throat and managed a smile.

"I'm glad one of us did."

Chapter Two

Carter watched Savannah disappear through the swinging doors that separated the kitchen from the dining area.

In his mind, this had played out differently.

Savannah had been happy to see him. Touched by the message that Rob had entrusted him to deliver. Instead, she'd looked at him as if he'd lobbed a grenade in her direction.

Maybe you did.

It occurred to Carter that he shouldn't have chosen a public place to introduce himself, but Rob had never given him their home address, only mentioned the name of the tiny diner in Dallas where Savannah worked.

Carter dropped into the chair again and pressed his fingers against his temples, an attempt to ward off the headache that had sunk its talons behind his eyes. When he'd stepped off the plane, he'd naively assumed that time would slowly begin to sand down the jagged edges of his memories and life would return to normal.

Normal, he remembered his nanny, Rachel, saying with a laugh, *is just a setting on the dryer.*

Carter finally understood what she'd meant. Because so far, nothing had gone the way he'd planned.

He'd spent a sleepless night at Gray's condo, fighting jet lag and the realization that everything he'd believed about his family had been based on a lie.

Breakfast with Maddie and Gray the next morning had been awkward; no one seemed to know how to fill the silence. Carter had politely declined their invitation to church. His brother took off shortly after breakfast to pick up Elise and Cory. After the service, Maddie planned to return to Grasslands so she could check on Belle Colby at the convalescent center.

Carter had welcomed the time alone to regroup. He'd decided to help Gray search for their father, the only person who could tell them the truth about the past. But first, he'd been honor bound to deliver a message.

If the woman the message was intended for decided to cooperate.

"How are those ribs tastin'?" Libby, the waitress who'd been so attentive when Carter had walked into the diner, bounded up to his table.

"Great." Once Carter tried them, he'd know for sure.

"Okaay." She glanced down at his plate and frowned. "Anything else I can getcha?"

How about an explanation for Savannah's parting words?

I'm glad one of us did.

The statement hadn't made sense. She was Rob's wife. Of course she knew him. Savannah's reaction—and her abrupt departure—didn't quite match up with the woman Rob had described. A woman with a sweet smile, a sense of humor and a strong faith.

Carter understood how grief could do a number on

someone, but wouldn't she want to talk to someone who'd spent time with Rob?

Been with him at the end?

His gaze shifted to the kitchen, where Savannah was hiding out. If he could outlast a sniper for ten hours, he could certainly wait out a pretty green-eyed waitress.

"I'll take a piece of pie and a cup of coffee."

Libby followed the direction of his eyes and grinned. "Coming right up."

A half hour ticked by and the dining room emptied as the lunch crowd dwindled. Carter finished off the pie and started on his third cup of coffee but there was still no sign of Savannah.

"Excuse me?" He motioned to Libby as she emerged from the kitchen, armed with two coffee pots. She changed direction, navigating through the maze of tables until she reached his side.

"Do you need a warm up on that coffee?"

He needed to talk to Savannah. "No, thanks. Just the bill." Carter reached for his wallet. "Is Savannah busy?" he tossed out casually.

"No." The smile dimmed. "She left a little while ago."

"Left?"

"She said she wasn't feeling well."

Savannah had slipped past him. Admiration and frustration battled for dominance. Frustration won.

Carter released a slow breath. "Will she be back tomorrow?"

"She's not scheduled to work again until Tuesday."

Great. Before she'd left, Maddie made him promise he would drive to Grasslands to meet the rest of the "family" as soon as possible.

"Would you mind giving me her home address?"

Libby looked uneasy with the request. "I don't know—"

"Her husband and I served together in Afghanistan. He introduced us." It was the truth. Sort of. He and Savannah might not have met until today, but Carter felt as if he knew her. He knew that she hummed when she was nervous and that her favorite color was blue. She liked yellow roses and coffee-flavored ice cream and black-and-white movies.

And she was more beautiful in person than she was in the photograph Rob had given him.

Carter set that thought firmly to the side.

"I didn't know Savannah was married to a soldier," Libby breathed. "She never talks about him."

"He talked about her." Twenty-four seven. "And he asked me to deliver a message."

"That's *so* romantic."

Only in the movies, Carter wanted to say. The reality hadn't been quite so warm and fuzzy.

He and Rob had been shoulder to shoulder in a shallow ditch, caught in the middle of a firefight. Under attack from both the ground and the air.

If anything happens to me, promise that you'll find Savannah and make sure she's okay. Tell her that I loved her.

But Rob hadn't told him that Savannah might not *want* to be found.

Or that she was pregnant.

"Going somewhere?"

Savannah whirled around at the sound of a deep male voice.

It was him. Carter Wallace. The soldier who'd shown

up at the diner that morning. He filled the doorway, arms folded across his chest in a casually deceptive stance. The set of his jaw warned Savannah that she wouldn't evade him as easily this time.

She didn't bother to ask how he'd found out where she lived. He must have sweet-talked Libby after she'd left the diner.

"Your landlady let me in." Those intense blue eyes scanned the living room and narrowed on the hedge of cardboard boxes that separated them.

"Look, Sergeant Wallace." Savannah heard a catch in her voice. "I don't know what you want—"

"That's because you didn't wait around long enough to find out." The corners of his lips kicked up in a rueful smile. "I'm sorry if I upset you when I showed up at the diner today. Rob told me where you worked but not your address."

Rob told him.

Savannah's throat tightened. She couldn't deal with this right now. Not when she'd spent the past few hours packing up her things, each box she taped shut one more reminder that she was closing the door on the past with no idea what the future would bring.

"Do you mind if I come in?"

Yes, she did.

"I'm really busy." To prove it, Savannah bent down and snatched up one of the boxes. A muscle in her lower back protested the suddenness of the movement and she winced in pain.

"Hey—take it easy." Carter Wallace was at her side in an instant and he plucked the box from her hands. "Should you be lifting stuff?"

Color flooded Savannah's cheeks when she saw his

gaze drop to her rounded stomach, something that even a loose-fitting sweatshirt couldn't hide.

"I'm not an invalid." She was just…tired. And not prepared for unexpected company. Especially a handsome, blue-eyed soldier who'd claimed to be friends with her late husband.

"Where do you want this?" Carter stared her down.

Good job, Savannah. Instead of convincing him to leave, she'd unwittingly given him a reason to stay.

"Really, you don't have to—" She saw his eyebrows dip together and realized there was no point in arguing. "By the door."

Without a word, Carter strode across the room and deposited it near the entryway. And then proceeded to do the same with the rest of the boxes.

As he set the last one down, Savannah didn't miss his swift but thorough assessment of the cramped upstairs apartment she'd briefly shared with Rob after their wedding.

"Thank you." Savannah glanced at her watch, hoping Carter would take the hint.

He did.

"I'll only take up a few minutes of your time," he said quietly. "It's important."

Savannah sighed. Maybe the best thing was to get this over with as quickly as possible and send Sergeant Wallace on his way.

"All right." She motioned toward a chair and sent up a swift, silent prayer for strength as Carter sat down. The flimsy wood creaked under the weight of his solid frame, the floral slipcover an almost comical backdrop for a guy who looked as if he could bench press the sofa.

It didn't matter that Carter Wallace wasn't in full uniform. His faded, loose-fitting jeans and a gray T-shirt with the marine insignia that stretched across his muscular chest proved to be just as intimidating. He looked as if he were born to be a soldier.

Savannah perched on the edge of the sofa and waited. But now that he had her attention, Carter didn't seem to know what to say.

"You mentioned that you knew Rob—" Savannah's voice cracked as grief sliced at the threads of her composure. She'd barely begun to accept the fact that her husband had walked out on their marriage when a military chaplain had knocked at the door and informed her that Rob had been killed in a roadside bombing.

Carter nodded. "He was assigned to my unit. We worked together. He talked about you."

Savannah's fingers knotted together in her lap. "He did?"

Carter looked surprised by the question. "All the time." He paused. "That's why I'm here. A few days before Rob… He asked me to give you a message."

Savannah heard a rushing sound in her ears. Spots began to dance in front of her eyes. "A message?"

This wasn't what she'd expected. She'd assumed that Carter had sought her out because Rob had owed him money. After the funeral, she'd received calls from some of his former buddies, asking if she would "make good" on the loans they'd given him.

Each one a reminder of how gullible she'd been.

"He was a good man. A good friend." Carter leaned forward. "And he…he loved you."

Savannah felt the color drain from her face. "You don't know what you're talking about."

Carter frowned. "That's the message that Rob asked me to deliver. He wanted me to tell you that he loved you."

Savannah's breath collected in her lungs, making it difficult to breathe.

"Sergeant Wallace, Rob *left* me."

Carter stared at Savannah, more shaken by the words than he let on. Rob hadn't mentioned that Savannah didn't support his decision to become a soldier.

"To serve his country, yes," he said carefully. "Rob thought he was doing the right thing, but he couldn't wait to finish his tour and come home to you. It was all he talked about."

Savannah vaulted from the chair and then swayed on her feet. For a split second, Carter was afraid she was going to pass out. Instinctively, he reached out to steady her but she spun away from him, one hand pressed protectively against her belly, the other one palm up, as if trying to keep him at a distance.

"Please. Just go."

Carter sucked in a breath, the flash of pain in those green eyes landing with the force of a physical blow. It was obvious that Savannah was still grieving. He fumbled for the right words, something that had never come easily. Unlike Rob, who'd entertained everyone on base with his anecdotes.

"Savannah, I know this must be difficult. Have you talked to someone—"

"I didn't mean that Rob left when he enlisted. I meant that he left *me*. A week after we were married," she choked out. "He sent one letter when he finished basic training saying that he'd made a…mistake. After that, I never heard from him again."

The words hit Carter broadside. "I don't understand."

"I think you do." Savannah's gaze didn't waver. "You just don't believe me."

Carter opened his mouth, ready to argue, and then realized she was right. What Savannah had just told him clashed with the man that Carter knew. The one who'd been devoted to his wife.

Rob had bragged about their plans for the future. Buying a piece of land. Building a home. Raising a family.

Why would—

Carter's heart plummeted to the soles of his boots, weighted down by a sudden, unwelcome suspicion. "The baby—"

Emerald sparks flashed in Savannah's eyes. "Is Rob's. But he…he never knew."

"You didn't tell him?" Carter regretted the question the moment Savannah started toward the door.

To see him out.

But Carter didn't move. Wasn't going to move until he got some answers. "Rob never mentioned that you were separated. In fact, all he talked about were the things the two of you were going to do when his tour ended."

"Then he lied to you, too."

Too?

The band around Carter's forehead tightened. "Rob and I were friends. Why would he do that?"

He had looked up to Rob. Admired him.

Envied him.

Carter had dodged serious relationships for years, never going out with the same woman more than once or twice. Knowing how hard it had been on him and his siblings every time their father left on a mission trip, he was determined not to subject someone he cared about to a relationship marked by uncertainty and goodbyes. Something the wife of a soldier had to accept. But listening to Rob talk about Savannah had made him question his decision to remain single. Made him wonder what it would be like to have a woman like her in his life.

Now she was trying to convince him that it had all been a lie?

Savannah opened the door, which didn't answer his question but guaranteed there wouldn't be an opportunity to ask any more.

Carter didn't know what—or who—to believe. Savannah? A woman he'd just met. Or Rob, the guy who'd laughed with him? Encouraged him to pray, even though every mile Carter had hiked through the rugged hills of Afghanistan had taken him that much farther from the faith he'd professed as a child?

The guy that Savannah claimed had abandoned her.

What he *did* know was that she wanted him to leave.

"I'm sorry," Carter muttered, although he wasn't quite sure why he was apologizing. Or even who he was apologizing *to.* "I won't take up any more of your time."

As he started to move past her, she touched his arm. A gesture that stopped Carter in his tracks.

"Sergeant Wallace? Thank you for keeping your promise," she whispered. "I am… I'm glad that Rob had a friend over there."

The words brought Carter up short. He had kept his promise—but not all of it.

Find Savannah and make sure she's okay.

For the first time, he noticed the lavender shadows below her eyes. Being the youngest in the family, Carter didn't have a lot of experience with kids, but he figured that working at a diner wouldn't be easy on a pregnant woman.

Savannah's grief might be coloring her perspective about Rob's feelings for her—maybe she'd somehow misinterpreted the reason he'd left—but Carter couldn't simply walk out the door until he knew that she wasn't alone.

"Are you moving back home?" he asked abruptly.

"Home?"

"Back to your family."

"I'm staying in Dallas." An emotion Carter couldn't identify flickered in Savannah's eyes. "But my landlady's nephew needed a place to stay so she asked me to find something else."

She was being *evicted?*

"Don't you have a lease?"

"Mrs. Cabera only agreed to let me stay here because Rob and her son had gone to high school together. It was a verbal agreement."

Carter didn't like the sound of that. "But you have somewhere to go, right?"

Savannah hesitated just long enough to make him suspicious. "Of course."

"Where?"

Her pink lips compressed. "This isn't your problem."

In a roundabout way, that answered his question. "What are your plans?"

Savannah was silent for so long that Carter didn't think she was going to answer the question.

"I'll check into a hotel for a few days. Until I find something else," she finally said.

"Isn't there a family member who can put you up for a while?"

"No."

Funny how one simple word could complicate a situation, Carter thought.

"Well, I happen to have picked up a few extras recently," he said lightly. "And one of them owns a ranch near Grasslands. My sister, Maddie, offered me one of the empty cottages on the property, but you can stay there—"

Savannah's eyes widened and Carter felt a slow burn crawl up his neck when he realized how that sounded. "—and I can bunk in the main house," he added quickly. "You'd have a place to rest up. Until you find something else."

Color swept into Savannah's cheeks, filling the faint hollows beneath her cheekbones.

"That's very nice of you." She regarded him warily, as if she wasn't sure it was nice of him at all. "But I can't just quit my job at the diner. And I'm sure that when your sister offered you a place to stay, she wasn't expecting you to pass it on to a random stranger."

Carter could have argued the point. Savannah wasn't a stranger. He'd carried her photograph around in his pocket for the past two months. Memorized the heart-shaped face and delicate features.

But how could he tell her that without coming across as some kind of stalker?

"I heard someone say that sometimes, a change of scenery can change your perspective."

Carter decided not to mention Rob was the one who'd told him that.

For a moment it looked as if Savannah was wavering. But then her chin came up and Carter saw the answer in her eyes.

"You don't have to worry about me. I know you were Rob's friend, but I'm not your responsibility."

Find Savannah and make sure she's okay.

Whether Carter wanted it to or not, that *made* her his responsibility.

"But it's not just you anymore, is it?" he reminded her. "You have your baby to think of, too."

Savannah flinched. "Goodbye, Sergeant Wallace."

Carter battled his rising frustration, not sure how to get through to her. "When I make a promise, I keep it."

"And you did. You delivered Rob's message—"

"Not that promise." Carter interrupted. "I'm a marine, ma'am. And we never leave a man—or a woman—behind."

Even though he was serious, Carter flashed a smile, letting her know that she could trust him.

A smile Savannah didn't return.

"You aren't leaving me behind, sergeant." The door began to close. "I'm *asking* you to go."

Chapter Three

"So, when will you be here?"

Carter sighed into the phone as he entered the post office. "Soon."

"How soon?" Maddie wanted to know.

"A few more days." Long enough to give Savannah time to change her mind.

Carter had jotted his cell phone number and the Colby Ranch's address on a piece of paper and tucked it under the windshield wiper of her car after she'd shut the door in his face the day before.

He hadn't been able to stop thinking about her. Wondering what had happened between her and Rob. None of the things Savannah had told him lined up with the claims his friend had made, but Carter couldn't shake the feeling that *she* was the one who'd been telling the truth. Unsettling, given the fact he'd trusted Rob with his life.

"Jack said he might be able to find some work for you around the ranch now that you're out of the service," Maddie continued. "You love being outdoors. You helped Dad build that playhouse in the backyard when we lived in Appleton, remember? Once it was finished, you told everyone that you wanted to live there. I had to lure you into the house with chocolate chip cookies when it was bedtime."

Maddie's low laugh flowed over him, stirring up memories from the past.

Carter remembered handing his dad the nails, one by one. It was one of the few times they'd actually worked on a project together. Once his dad had started medical school, he'd left Rachel, the full-time nanny he'd hired, in charge of the family. Carter had heard the words "don't bother your father" so often over the next few years, he'd eventually taken them to heart.

"I'll come to Grasslands and meet Violet and Jack—" Carter still couldn't think of them as family. "But I can't promise any more than that right now."

"I just want us to be together," Maddie whispered. "With Dad gone..."

Dad is always gone, Carter was tempted to say. He knew that Gray and Maddie were concerned that something bad might have happened to their father, but knowing Brian, he'd probably just got caught up in his work and assumed everything back home was fine. Thanksgiving, the day he'd promised he would be home, was still three weeks away.

Gray had explained they couldn't file a missing person's report because technically, Brian Wallace wasn't considered missing.

"I'll be there." Carter inserted the key into the post office box he'd kept in the city. "By the weekend—" A package tumbled out with an avalanche of junk mail. He winced as it hit the tiled floor. "I hope that wasn't something breakable," he muttered.

Maddie heard him. "Breakable? Where are you?"

"I'm at the post office and there's a package in here that didn't get forwarded for some reason."

"A package," Maddie repeated. "What does it look like?"

"Um…like a package?"

"Well, open it!"

Carter rolled his eyes. Bossy older sisters. But there was a tension in Maddie's voice that hadn't been there before. Not even when she'd been pestering him about coming to Grasslands. He dumped the letters onto a nearby counter and cut through the tape on the package with his pocketknife.

"Did you send this?" Carter stared at the small, leather-bound book swaddled in tissue paper. "Because I already have one."

Not that he'd cracked it open for a few years.

"What is it?" Maddie whispered.

"A Bible."

"Is there a note inside?"

Carter thumbed through the delicate, gold-tipped pages and found a piece of paper. "How did you know?"

"Because someone sent a Bible to me and Gray. And to Violet and Jack."

Carter quickly skimmed the contents of the letter and then read it out loud.

"'I'm sorry for what I did to you and your family. I hope you and your siblings can find it in your hearts to forgive me.'"

It wasn't signed.

"What is this about? Who sent it?"

"We don't know," Maddie admitted. "At first we assumed it was a mistake because whoever wrote the other letters specifically mentioned a twin. But Gray thinks it might have something to do with the reason we were separated."

"Maybe it has something to do with Dad's disappearance." Carter read through the words a second time, trying to make sense of the cryptic message. "Why didn't you mention this before?"

"We didn't think you'd—" Maddie stopped.

"Get one." Carter filled in the blanks.

Because at the moment, he was the only one in the Wallace-Colby puzzle who actually knew where he fit. Which, the irony wasn't lost on Carter, made him the odd man out. Again.

"I'm sorry, Carter." Maddie sounded on the verge of tears now. "Gray will want to see the letter and compare the handwriting, but it has to be from the same person. Maybe if we put all of them together, we'll find something that we missed."

Carter held back a sigh.

"I'm on my way."

"I have to admit I'm not happy with the numbers I'm seeing this morning."

Savannah felt a stab of fear as Dr. Yardley set the paperwork down on the desk and took a seat across from her in the examining room.

"Is there something wrong with the baby?"

"The baby seems to be fine. It's *you* I'm worried about," the doctor said bluntly. "Your blood pressure is elevated, and you've actually lost weight since your last appointment."

"I'm feeling fine," Savannah protested. "A little tired, that's all."

"Mmm." Dr. Yardley looked skeptical. "How many hours did you work at the diner last week?"

Savannah silently tallied them up. "Between twenty-five and thirty." Give or take a few. She'd volunteered to cover for one of the waitresses who was standing up in a friend's wedding so she would have money to cover the security deposit on a new apartment.

The apartment she still hadn't found.

After being on her feet all day, she just couldn't seem to summon the energy to search for a new place to live. Savannah assumed it was normal to feel this way but the concern in the doctor's eyes told her otherwise.

"That's what I thought." Dr. Yardley shook her head. "I want you to cut back to half that amount. Effective when you walk out of this office today."

"But I promised my boss that I could fill in on weekends and evenings when I wasn't working my regular shift." Savannah stared at her obstetrician in dismay. "It was the only reason he hired me."

"You've been under a tremendous amount of stress throughout this pregnancy, Savannah, and you still have three months to go. If you end up on complete bed rest, you won't be able to work at all." The doctor's stern words were tempered with a smile. "You need more rest and a little TLC. Two things that I'm afraid modern medicine hasn't figured out how to put in a pill yet."

Savannah laced her fingers together in her lap to stop them from shaking. "I'll talk to him." Although Bruce didn't exactly have a reputation for his easygoing disposition.

The doctor gave her a shrewd look. "Is there anything else going on that I should know about?"

"I've been looking for a new apartment," Savannah admitted. "But I'm sure that I'll find something in the next few days."

Dr. Yardley's pen tapped the clipboard. "Isn't there a family member you can stay with until the baby is born?"

"I don't have any family." One of the reasons she'd been so quick to fall for Rob's charm.

"All right, then. How about a friend?" the physician persisted.

Even as Savannah was shaking her head, an image of Carter Wallace's face flashed through her mind.

No. Way.

She didn't want to accept his help. Carter had been stunned when she'd told him that Rob had left her. Savannah hadn't really expected him to believe her word over Rob's—but still, it had hurt. Why, she wasn't sure.

She wasn't sure why Carter had offered her a place to stay on his sister's ranch near Grasslands, either. The sergeant had been Rob's friend. She, on the other hand, was simply an obligation. One he had probably been relieved to cross off his list. There was no way she was going to show up on his doorstep like an orphan puppy in search of a home.

She'd viewed Rob as a knight in shining armor, swooping in to rescue her, and look where she was now. A single mother on the verge of being homeless.

God, I know that I'm not alone. I know that You're with me. Show me what I'm supposed to do.

"I know things are difficult right now, but you have to do what's best for you and the baby," Dr. Yardley was saying. "If I could, I'd write you a prescription for a change of scenery. I think that's what you need more than anything right now."

A change of scenery can give you a change in perspective.

The words chased through her mind, stirring the memory of someone else who had said the same thing.

Savannah didn't know whether to laugh or cry. Because even though she'd just asked God to show her what to do, she wasn't ready to acknowledge that Carter Wallace just might be the answer to her prayer.

"Earth to Carter. Come in, Carter."

Maddie's teasing voice yanked Carter back to the present.

"Sorry." He cocked his head to one side. "Reception is still a little fuzzy between earth and *The Twilight Zone*."

Laughter rippled through the dining room and once again, Carter had to adjust to the sound. To the faces of the people gathered around the long plank table. Gray and Jack. Violet and Maddie. Identical but...not.

"What's *The Twilight Zone?*" Eight-year-old Darcy Garland's lively, brown-eyed gaze bounced back and forth between the adults.

"It's not real," Ty Garland, the little girl's father, explained. Carter saw him wink at Maddie across the table.

Yeah. That was another thing. His siblings hadn't only found each other, they'd found, in Maddie's words, "their soul mates." Carter was still trying to wrap his brain around that, too.

"That's what you think," Jack Colby muttered. "You

don't have to get used to a guy walking around with *your* face."

"Wearing a shirt and tie," Violet added, her eyes dancing with mischief.

"She's right." Jack flashed a wicked grin in Gray's direction. "When you start working for the Grasslands Police department in January, Sheriff Cole will have you trading in those fancy city duds for a pair of Levis and Tony Lamas in no time."

Their easy banter ricocheted around the table and Carter felt a stab of envy. Violet and Jack Colby had gone out of their way to make him feel welcome since his arrival, but Carter still felt as if his life had become a jigsaw puzzle in which the pieces no longer fit together.

But at least he *had* family. More than he was comfortable with, at the moment.

Carter's gaze drifted to the window. Again.

Almost a week had gone by since he'd left the city and he still couldn't stop thinking about Savannah.

He lay awake at night, scrolling through past conversations with his friend. Searching for scraps of information that verified what Savannah had told him. Rob had talked about her constantly...but had he ever talked *to* her? Sent an email or letter? Received one?

That's what Carter couldn't remember.

Lupita Ramirez, the ranch cook and housekeeper, bustled into the dining room. She rapped a wooden spoon against the palm of her hand to get everyone's attention.

"Who has room for chocolate cake?"

A collective groan followed the question.

"No one—" Jack started to say.

"But we'll take some anyway," Maddie and Violet sang out. At the same time. And then they laughed. In unison.

"Weird," Ty Garland muttered.

Carter had to agree.

"I'm going to have to start working out more." Gray sighed when the housekeeper left the dining room. "Lupita makes enough food to feed the entire county."

"That reminds me, Pastor Jeb wants the church to host a special harvest dinner the weekend before Thanksgiving," Violet said. "He's been calling around, asking members of the congregation to volunteer to help, but he wants to invite the whole community."

Unbidden, an image of Savannah's face swept into Carter's mind. Again. The flash of anger in those expressive green eyes when he'd asked about the baby. The vulnerable curve of her lower lip.

Did she have plans for Thanksgiving? Or would she be alone?

Carter shifted in the chair. In his mind's eye, he could see her standing by the door, arms wrapped protectively around her middle. Proud. *Scared.*

She made it pretty clear that she isn't your concern, he reminded himself.

But that didn't stop him from wondering how she was doing. Had she found an apartment yet? He hated to think of her staying in a hotel with a baby on the way, even for a few days.

Carter had made Rob two promises before his friend had died. He'd promised that he would always have Rob's back and he'd promised that he would make sure Savannah was okay. So far, he hadn't kept either one of them.

"I'll see if I can't round up a few of the boys from the teen center to help with setup or something," Landon Derringer was saying. "They're always complaining they don't have anything to do."

"Round up?" Violet grinned at her fiancé's choice of words. "You're starting to think like a cowboy already, sweetheart."

Gray shook his head in mock sorrow. "Another victim."

Across the table, Derringer smiled at Violet, confirmation that he'd been a willing one.

Carter had been stunned to find Landon, Maddie's former fiancé, at the ranch when he'd arrived. The guy had followed his sister to Grasslands and fallen in love with… Violet. And apparently no one but Carter thought that was strange. But in light of the other things the family had experienced lately, maybe it hadn't even made the list.

"I think a harvest dinner is a great idea." Violet handed a pitcher of cream to Maddie a second before she reached for it. "We have a lot to be thankful for."

Carter couldn't believe a murmur of agreement followed the statement. Maybe if they'd witnessed some of the things that he had over the past five years, they would have a different perspective. And given what they'd been through lately with Belle's accident and Brian's disappearance, Carter didn't think there was a whole lot to be thankful for, either.

Maddie's expression turned pensive but she smiled at Violet. "This is the first Thanksgiving we'll all be together."

"Mom loves holidays," Violet said wistfully. "She

pulls out all the stops.... I know she'll be home by then. She *has* to be."

"There are a lot of people praying for her," Maddie whispered.

But Carter noticed that everyone sidestepped the real question. Whether his father would be in attendance. Carter had managed to corner Gray for a few minutes and his brother had finally admitted how worried he was that something had happened to Brian. Their dad ministered to transient people in remote areas along the border, and the last person Gray had been in contact with had noticed that he seemed ill. Carter tried to convince himself that a physician would certainly know what to do—where to go—if he came down with something.

Unless he was alone and didn't have access to the medicine he needed to fight the illness. His dad's cell phone had been recovered a few weeks ago, but there were other ways he could have maintained contact with the rest of the family. Why hadn't he used them?

Carter felt the walls begin to close in and suddenly felt the need for some fresh air.

"No dessert for me." His chair scraped the floor as he rose to his feet. "I think I'll take a walk."

"Sure." Maddie frowned.

So did Violet.

Carter blinked but there were still two of them. Oh, yeah. He definitely needed some fresh air.

He could feel everyone watching as he walked out of the dining room. The second the door closed, he would be the next topic of conversation around the dinner table.

Carter wasn't used to that, either. His older siblings

valued and encouraged independence. Other than exchanging brief updates now and then, Maddie and Gray had pursued their own interests and left him alone. Carter wasn't quite sure what to do with the sudden interest they were showing now. Add Jack and Violet into the mix, and Carter was beginning to feel like it was four against one. Odds he didn't care for.

He stepped outside, back against the door as he made a swift but thorough sweep of the property. Searching for possible threats.

You're in Texas, remember?

It took a moment to let his soul adjust to the newness of his surroundings. The rustle of the wind through the pecan grove. The scent of the mesquite trees. Miles of blue sky. A place that Maddie and Gray were both ready to call home.

And yet Carter was tempted to reenlist after they located his dad. In the military, he knew exactly who he was. What he was supposed to do. Now, it felt as if he'd stripped of his identity along with his uniform.

Nipper, Jack's Australian shepherd, bounded up to him, and Carter reached down to scratch the dog's velvety ears.

"I suppose you want to go for a walk?" Roaming the property together had become a nightly ritual when Carter couldn't sleep.

The dog's tail slashed the air and he barked. Carter took that as a yes.

Restlessness drove him toward the creek where the cottages were located. In spite of Violet's generous offer, Carter had decided to stay in the main house and bunk in the guest room that Gray occupied when he visited the ranch, leaving one of the cottages empty in case Savannah changed her mind. A possibility that had begun to shrink over the past few days.

Savannah hadn't exactly welcomed him with open arms. What made him think she would accept his help?

Just as Carter reached the creek bank, his cell phone rang.

An unfamiliar number appeared on the screen and Carter's heart slammed against his rib cage. Had his father finally discovered they'd been trying to contact him?

"Hello?"

He heard a crackling sound. And then a tentative but familiar voice. "Hi."

"Savannah?"

"Yes." A long pause followed. "I hope I'm not interrupting anything."

"Not at all." Carter's hand tightened around the phone. "Is everything all right?"

"I'm sorry I didn't—" The line crackled, distorting her words. If they lost the connection, Carter was afraid she wouldn't call back.

"Savannah? You're breaking up. Where are you?"

"I'm…here."

"Here?" Carter repeated.

"At the gate."

Chapter Four

Savannah's heart performed a little Texas two-step as Carter Wallace approached.

In faded jeans and a long-sleeved black T-shirt that accentuated his athletic build, Carter was even more attractive than she remembered. His loose-limbed stride and the set of his broad shoulders conveyed the fierce confidence of a man who faced life head-on. A confidence Savannah couldn't help but envy.

Once again, she contemplated turning the car around. Something that had crossed her mind at least half a dozen times since she'd left Dallas.

Her boss hadn't exactly been thrilled when she'd stopped by the diner after her appointment with Dr. Yardley and told him that she had to reduce her hours. The next day, when Savannah checked the schedule, she saw that not only had Bruce honored her request, he'd given *all* her shifts to a new waitress he'd hired over the weekend.

Leaving her with no choice but to accept Carter's offer to stay at his sister's ranch for the time being.

But doubts began to creep in as Savannah parked

between the massive stone columns that stood like sentinels on either side of the driveway, guarding the property from outsiders. Like her. She wasn't sure what she'd expected, but the Colby Ranch was obviously a large, prosperous operation.

It only reminded Savannah how little she knew about Carter Wallace. Was she really welcome here? Maybe he was already regretting his impulsive invitation.

Rob had made a lot of promises, too, and he'd only kept one of them.

I'm leaving, Savannah.

Savannah's fingers closed around the shift stick but the passenger-side door opened before she could put the car in reverse. Carter hopped in beside her, his large frame folding almost in half to accommodate the passenger seat of her compact car.

Savannah took a deep breath. If he looked at her with pity, she'd turn the car around and head straight back to Dallas....

"It's about time." The crooked smile that Carter flashed in her direction coaxed a dimple out of hiding, an unexpected but charming contrast to the man's ruggedly handsome features. "If you didn't show up within the next twenty-four hours, I'd decided to round up a posse and find you."

He'd planned to return to Dallas? For her?

No, not for you. For Rob, she reminded herself sternly. An internal dash of cold water on the warmth his words stirred in her heart.

It would be a mistake to forget the reason she was here. To Carter, delivering Rob's message had been a duty. An obligation. But Savannah had an obligation, too. To do everything she could to protect the health of her unborn child. Even if it meant swallowing her pride and accepting help from a stranger.

"I hope this isn't a bad time," she stammered. "I probably should have called first."

Except that if she'd dialed Carter's number any earlier, Savannah knew she would have lost not only her voice, but her nerve. She'd packed her suitcase that morning and stowed it in the trunk of the car, giving God what she hoped was ample opportunity to send some kind of sign that He had another plan. One that *didn't* include Carter Wallace.

Yet here she was.

"I didn't call before I showed up at your door that day, either," Carter said easily. "So I guess that makes us even."

No, they weren't. Not until he understood that she didn't intend to be a charity case or outstay her welcome here. She'd scheduled another appointment with Dr. Yardley in two weeks. If the test results proved that she was obeying orders, Savannah planned to ask for an increase in her hours at the diner again and continue her search for another apartment.

"I can pay rent." Savannah didn't look at Carter as she put the car into gear and continued down the long gravel driveway. "I don't expect to live in the cottage for free. Or I can help out around the house or in the kitchen. I'm a pretty decent cook."

At one time, she'd dreamed of attending culinary school. Before she'd met Rob.

"Chicken and dumplings are your specialty, right?"

"How did you know…" Savannah's voice trailed off, leaving an awkward silence in its wake.

Rob must have told him.

The day they'd met, Carter had claimed that Rob talked about her all the time when they'd served together in Afghanistan. Savannah hadn't believed him—until now. The thought that Rob's friend knew more about her than she knew about him was a little unsettling.

And what else had Rob told him? The truth—or more lies? Less than twenty-four hours after they were married, Savannah had discovered that her new husband didn't seem to know the difference. She'd been so tired of being alone that she'd let Rob sweep her off her feet.

Believed everything he'd said…

"Don't worry about things like paying rent or washing dishes right now." Savannah could feel the weight of Carter's gaze, studying her profile. "How about I show you where you'll be staying first? You can unpack your things. Settle in and get a good night's sleep."

Which could only be, Savannah thought ruefully, a tactful way of saying that she must look as exhausted as she felt.

"All right." Self-consciously, she looped a wayward strand of hair behind her ear. She knew the past few days had taken a toll on both her health and her emotions. The stress of apartment hunting during the day. Wrestling with her fears at night. Savannah had been reading through the New Testament every morning, taking comfort in the fact that other believers had faced difficult situations, too, and God hadn't abandoned them.

She trusted Him. Men, not so much anymore.

"Keep going past the main house," Carter instructed.

The simple description didn't do the place justice.

Savannah tried not to gawk as they passed a magnificent two-story home fashioned from native stone and brick. The setting sun winked off the mullioned windows and painted the glass with a rosy, welcoming glow. Trumpet vine wove through the spindles of the wrought-iron fence that separated the landscaped lawn from the rest of the property.

Everything was neat and well cared for. The Colby Ranch could have easily been featured on the cover of *Texas Today* magazine.

"It's beautiful," Savannah murmured. "Did you grow up here?"

"No."

Savannah tried not to flinch at the sting of Carter's curt response. Although he seemed to know a lot about her, it was becoming clear that Carter wasn't going to be very forthcoming about his own life.

Carter saw Savannah's hands tighten around the steering wheel and realized the word had come out a little sharper than he'd intended. He tried again.

"No," he said more softly.

One-syllable words were okay on a military base, but if he wanted Savannah to stay at the ranch, it was clear to Carter that he would have to brush up on his people skills. He could coax a disabled vehicle back to life and make an engine purr like a kitten, but he'd never been much for small talk.

Especially when the woman sitting next to him took his breath away.

The photograph hadn't done her justice. Savannah's

honey-brown hair fell loose around her shoulders, a perfect frame for her delicate features and wide green eyes.

The only thing missing was the smile.

Carter still hadn't seen one of those.

When he'd heard her voice on the phone, he couldn't believe that Savannah had actually accepted his invitation. Not until he'd spotted her car parked at the gate. Both hands gripping the steering wheel, ready to turn around and exit his life as quickly as she'd entered it.

He wasn't sure why Savannah had changed her mind, but now that she was here at the Colby Ranch, Carter was going to make sure she stuck around for a while.

It's what Rob would have wanted.

Carter was certain about that, no matter what Savannah had said about their marriage. Why would Rob fake devotion to a wife that he'd abandoned? What would he have to gain?

Savannah might need a place to stay, but Carter needed some answers. And the woman sitting next to him was the only one who could provide them.

Another light winked on in the house. Carter hoped no one would glance out the window and see an unfamiliar vehicle nudging its way up the drive. Typically after Lupita served dessert, everyone pitched in and cleaned up from dinner and then gathered in the family room to watch a movie or play a game. Ty and Maddie would help Darcy with her homework. Jack and Gray would take part in what had become their favorite pastime—giving each other a hard time—while the women planned their upcoming nuptials with all the intensity of a military strategist.

And they insisted he join them.

Bonding, Maddie called it. Carter figured it was easier to bond with people who shared your DNA. He'd never had much in common with his siblings before, and now he was no longer sure he and Gray had *that* in common.

Carter would count the seconds until he could come up with a reasonable excuse to slip away. But now, for the first time, he hoped they followed standard protocol again and did not show up at the cottage to meet the newest visitor. It might overwhelm Savannah and give her a reason to bolt.

She didn't trust him, that much was clear.

But Rob had. Which meant that Carter was honor bound to shield her from potentially stressful situations.

Meeting his family definitely qualified.

Savannah fixed her eyes on the driveway.

The sudden drop in temperature inside the car made her wonder if there was some family dynamic going on between Carter and his sister that she should know about. The last thing she wanted was for her presence to add tension to an already strained relationship.

"You can take the first right behind the barn." Carter pointed to an enormous metal building with a green roof. Two chestnut horses stood shoulder to shoulder in a corner of the paddock, dozing under the branches of a cottonwood tree.

Savannah followed his instructions and saw a row of adorable little cottages scattered along a creek bed.

"I've been staying in the main house but the cottage on the end is empty. My sister had it all made up for me, but I never moved in. That means it's all yours," Carter said.

Yours.

In spite of her misgivings, the word flowed through Savannah, as sweet as a glass of tea on a hot summer day. Even knowing this was a temporary arrangement couldn't prevent the sense of wonder that swept over her.

The branches of two mature pecan trees formed a canopy over a cottage as whimsical as an illustration in a child's storybook. A sloping roof with patchwork shingles shaded an enclosed porch like the brim of a hat. Narrow wooden shutters trimmed the windows. Blue. Her favorite color. A hand-woven basket, overflowing with gourds and miniature pumpkins, sat on the top step like a welcome gift.

An Australian shepherd emerged from one of the outbuildings and ambled toward the car as Savannah pulled up in front of the cottage.

"That's Nipper. Jack Colby's dog." Carter shook his head. "Don't let the name fool you, though. The only thing that mutt might do is lick you to death."

"Is Jack part of your family?"

"That's the question of the day," he muttered.

Savannah frowned. "I don't understand."

But Carter didn't bother to enlighten her. Instead, he hopped out and jogged around the front of the car to open her door. His large hand gently cupped her elbow as he helped her out of the vehicle.

The warmth of his touch sparked something that sent Savannah's blood racing through her veins like a prairie fire.

She sucked in a breath, yanked her heart back in line.

It wasn't as if she were...*attracted*...to Carter Wallace. More than likely sleepless nights and low blood sugar had tipped her off balance.

Guard your heart, Savannah.

Savannah had forgotten her grandmother's advice when she'd met Rob. She wasn't about to make the same mistake again.

"Come on. I'll show you the inside."

Savannah balked. "You're sure that your sister won't mind an extra houseguest?"

Carter glanced in the direction of the main house. The flash of some emotion—*guilt?*—didn't exactly put her mind at ease.

"Sergeant Wallace?"

"It's Carter, remember?" That elusive dimple made an appearance again. A secret weapon designed to sneak through a woman's defenses and affect her ability to think straight.

Fortunately, Savannah had become immune to a charming smile.

"Now that we've got that cleared up...how about answering my question?"

Chapter Five

Carter realized he'd made a tactical error. He should have known that Savannah would see through his pitiful attempt to sidestep the question before she unpacked her suitcase from the car.

"No one will mind a bit that you're here." Carter hoped it was true.

According to Maddie, the Colby family had taken Keira Wolfe in after she'd been injured in a car accident and suffered short-term memory loss. The veterinarian was now Jack's fiancé and staying in a guest room down the hall until the couple exchanged their vows. Violet also made room for Landon Derringer and Elise and her son, Cory, during their frequent visits to the ranch. Even in the midst of their own problems, it seemed that Violet and Jack didn't mind lending a helping hand to someone in need. And Savannah definitely qualified.

He couldn't help feeling protective of her. It wasn't that she appeared weak and helpless. Just the opposite. It couldn't be easy to accept help from strangers, and yet Savannah had done the best thing for her and the baby. He respected that. He respected *her.*

Relief took some of the starch out of Savannah's slender shoulders. "That's good, because I don't want to take advantage of your sister's hospitality."

Carter decided this might be a good time to clarify a few minor details. After all, Savannah would find them out sooner or later. Although if he had his way, later—*much* later—would be better.

"Maddie doesn't actually own the ranch," he admitted. "She's a...guest...here, too."

Savannah, who'd started up the narrow sidewalk, froze midstep. Twisted around to look at him.

"A guest?" she repeated.

"Belle Colby actually owns the Colby Ranch. Maddie is spending some time with Belle's...daughter."

Violet. Maddie's identical twin sister. His long lost *half* sister. Carter could barely make sense of what had happened, let alone try to explain it to someone else. And something told him this wasn't the time to launch into a lengthy explanation about the Wallace family tree. The one that had sprouted a few branches since his last deployment.

"So Belle Colby gave you permission to invite me here?" Savannah asked slowly.

Carter drove a hand through his hair. "Belle is...recovering from a riding accident that happened last summer. She's in a long-term care facility in Grasslands right now, but the family is...hopeful that she'll recover."

Savannah's lips parted but no sound came out. She glanced down at the keys clutched in her hand and Carter realized she was only seconds away from getting in the car and driving back to Dallas if he didn't explain.

"It's complicated." Really complicated.

Savannah's eyes narrowed. "What exactly is going on, Sergeant?" she demanded. "Are you dispensing information on a need-to-know basis only? Because if that's the case, I need to know a whole lot more before I accept your invitation to stay here."

Carter suppressed a smile. Savannah was downright beautiful when she got riled up. She got some color in her cheeks and those eyes…as green as cottonwood leaves.

"Fine. I'll try to explain. But keep in mind that sometimes truth is stranger than fiction—"

"There you are!"

Carter slowly turned around. Great. Just great.

Walking toward them was the proof.

"Is that Maddie?" Savannah whispered.

Carter's eyes narrowed on the young woman striding toward them. Brown-and-gold-plaid shirt, complete with pearl buttons. A silver belt buckle roughly the size of a paperback novel.

And he still couldn't say for sure.

At some point over the past few months, Maddie had swapped her designer labels for Western wear. To make life even more interesting, the two women conspired together, taking an almost fiendish delight in making it difficult for people—like him—to figure out which one was which. Or who was who.

"Maybe."

"Maybe?" Savannah choked.

"I told you. It's—"

"Complicated?" A huff of frustration punctuated the sentence.

"Right."

"Darcy said she heard a car come up the driveway."

The flip of a long copper ponytail provided the clue that Carter had been looking for.

Violet.

Once Maddie's hair got longer and she could copy her twin sister's hairstyle, he was going to be in big trouble.

"Now I know why you ran off before dessert." Violet gave him an I'll-deal-with-you-later look but smiled warmly at Savannah. "Who do we have here?"

Carter caught the brunt of Savannah's accusing gaze.

Okay. He already *was* in big trouble.

Knowing that Carter hadn't been completely honest left a bitter taste in Savannah's mouth.

She was going to have a few choice words with the man. But at the moment, Savannah had no idea what to say to the woman standing in front of her. The one whose eyes were bright with curiosity—and who obviously had no idea that Carter had invited a pregnant stranger to stay with them.

"This is Savannah Blackmore." Carter came to her rescue.

Nice of him, since he was the reason she was in this awkward predicament to begin with!

Good manners forced Savannah to clasp the hand the woman offered when what she really wanted to do was hide. "Hello."

"Savannah, Violet Colby—" For some reason, Carter stopped.

"Carter's sister." The woman nudged him aside and finished the introduction.

Savannah felt Carter stiffen beside her.

"You're Carter's...sister?"

And why hadn't he mentioned that when he'd talked about Maddie?

"When he wants to claim me." Violet smiled sweetly at her brother.

Carter shifted his weight, almost as if he were uncomfortable with the direction the conversation was going.

Well, good, Savannah thought. Why should she be the only one?

Savannah's gaze bounced back and forth between Carter and Violet Colby but she failed to find even the slightest resemblance between them. Carter was blond and blue-eyed while Violet's hair, as bright as a new penny, framed an oval face dominated by a pair of eyes the color of dark chocolate.

"Savannah lost her apartment a few days ago," Carter explained. "I was hoping it would be okay if she bunked in one of the cottages for a while."

"I'd like to rent it," Savannah interjected. "If that's all right with you."

Violet was already shaking her head. And even though Savannah had been ready to drive away a few minutes ago, the thought of leaving the Colby Ranch left her with a sudden, inexplicable chill.

"Renting is out of the question," Violet Colby said firmly. "We always make room for friends. And you and Carter are friends, right?"

Savannah didn't dare look at Carter. They weren't friends. She wasn't quite sure what they were.

"Savannah's husband, Rob, and I were stationed together in Afghanistan," Carter said quietly. "I promised him that I'd check on her when I came back to the States. Make sure she was doing all right. There was a misunderstanding with her lease and she needed a place to stay."

"Just for a few days," Savannah choked out, feeling the sting of Rob's betrayal all over again.

He'd asked Carter to check up on her?

Every letter she'd sent to Rob had been returned, unopened. At any time, he could have picked up the phone and called to find out how she was doing. But he hadn't. And then suddenly, it had been too late.

Savannah hadn't known there'd been another part to the promise Rob had held Carter to other than the one he'd delivered, but it explained why he'd offered her a place to stay. Left his number so she could get in touch with him if she changed her mind.

Violet's gaze dropped to Savannah's midsection for a split second before lifting again.

"You're more than welcome to move in for as long as you'd like." The genuine sincerity in her voice convinced Savannah more than the actual words. "My mom is one of those people who believes in sharing the blessings we've been given. She would want you to stay here. And so do I."

Savannah's grandmother had been the same way. Edith Callahan reached out to those in need whether they needed a hot meal or a hug. Or a place to stay. Savannah had witnessed it countless times, she'd just never expected to be the one on the receiving end.

"Thank you." Savannah felt tears sting the back of her eyes. "I… I don't mind helping out, either—"

"We agreed to talk about that later, didn't we?" Carter cut in.

"Was that an agreement?" Savannah tipped her head. "Because it sounded like an order to me."

"Well, I am a sergeant. So technically, I outrank you." Carter had the audacity to *wink* at her.

Savannah knew she should have been irritated by the outrageous statement. So why did she have to fight a sudden, overwhelming urge to smile?

A polite cough pulled her attention back to Violet. There was a speculative gleam in the chocolate-brown eyes; her expression disturbingly similar to the look Savannah had seen on Libby's face the day Carter had walked into the diner.

"Carter's right. We'll have plenty of time to talk about that later." Violet linked arms with her. "I'll show you the cottage and rustle up some fresh linens for the bed. If you don't think you'll be comfortable here, we can probably squeeze you in somewhere at the main house. But I have to warn you, there's a lot of hustle and bustle going on around the place."

Savannah didn't mention that she would welcome a little hustle and bustle. She'd lived a solitary life after her grandmother had passed away the previous year. The loneliness had briefly subsided during her whirlwind courtship with Rob, only to return with a vengeance when he'd left her a week after they'd exchanged vows.

Long days had slipped into sleepless nights. Until she'd found out that she was pregnant. An unexpected blessing but one that had turned her world upside down. Especially after any hope of reconciliation had ended with Rob's death.

Violet flipped on the porch light and pushed open the front door. "It's not very big," she warned. "But it's cozy."

Savannah felt tears sting the back of her eyes as she took in her surroundings.

The inside of the cottage was as quaint as the exterior. A pocket-size kitchen. Colorful rag rugs. Corduroy furniture with oversize cushions, as deep and inviting as feather pillows.

She'd dreamed of a place like this.

"Not quite what you expected, huh?"

Carter was suddenly standing beside her and Savannah realized he'd mistaken silence for disappointment.

"I didn't expect it to be—" She fumbled for the right description.

"So small?" Carter supplied.

Savannah shook her head.

"So...perfect."

"Perfect?" Carter's husky laugh rumbled out, wrapping around Savannah like one of the quilts that Violet was pulling out of the antique armoire in the corner.

"I know what you mean. I love the cottages, too." Violet shot him a quelling look. "But I love them even more when they're being used, so please, make yourself at home."

Savannah already felt at home. That was a problem she hadn't anticipated. She would accept the Colby's hospitality for one or two weeks. No longer. She would be gone by Thanksgiving. Gone before she grew too attached to the sunsets and fresh air and a blue sky that stretched for miles, giving her space to breathe.

Gone before Carter's smile had a chance to work its way into her heart.

Carter took a restless lap around the living room as Violet took charge. Compared to the apartment Savannah had been living in, he had to agree the cottage was an improvement.

"You should be warm enough tonight with a few extra blankets but I'll ask Jack to drop off a load of wood for the fireplace tomorrow. The weather around here can be as contrary as his favorite bull."

"Is Jack your husband?"

Violet's eyes widened in response to Savannah's innocent question. Which made him feel guilty. Carter didn't have to be an identical twin to know what Violet was thinking. If he and Savannah were close enough friends to warrant an invitation to stay at the ranch, wouldn't he have filled her in on some of his complicated family history?

"Older brother," she replied evenly. "Jack runs the cattle part of the Colby Ranch. I manage the truck farm and produce stand in town."

"I see," Savannah murmured.

Carter had no doubt about that whatsoever. Just like Violet, Savannah could see that he'd left out a few pertinent details when he'd invited her to stay at the ranch.

"I'll make up the bed while you unpack your things." Violet frowned and looked around. "Where is your suitcase?"

"It's still in the trunk of my car."

Violet looked at him now, eyebrow lifted, and Carter shook his head. No *way* he was leaving them alone. He didn't want to take the chance that Violet might accidentally ask Savannah questions that would open old wounds.

She ignored him—just like Maddie would have.

"Carter? Will you be a sweetheart and get Savannah's things while I find some fresh sheets for the bed?"

Carter had enlisted in the military five years ago, the ink barely dry on his high school diploma. In spite of the sugarcoating on the words, he recognized a direct order when he heard one.

"Sure." He spun toward the door. It wasn't that he didn't trust Violet. He didn't *know* her.

But if she and Maddie were identical when it came to busybody tendencies, Carter figured he had better hurry.

Flecks of rust rained onto his boots when he lifted the trunk. Through a gaping hole in the metal, Carter could see the ground.

Rob had hinted that life had been good. He'd bragged about the house that he and Savannah planned to build, bordered by gardens because she loved flowers. Yellow roses, in particular.

So why was she driving an old beater with close to two-hundred-thousand miles on it?

There were a hundred questions Carter wanted to ask, but couldn't. Not yet. He'd seen the look on her face when Violet introduced herself. Savannah had assumed that he had lied to her. But the accusing look she'd tossed his way hadn't been the worst part. It was the look of resignation riding in its wake. As if she'd been *expecting* it.

Rob, what did you do?

And why had he thought that Carter could somehow make it right?

He grabbed Savannah's suitcase, a plaid relic as ancient as the car she drove, and made his way back to the cottage before Violet had a chance to interrogate Savannah about her personal life.

As his foot touched the top step, Violet's cheerful drawl stopped him in his tracks.

"So, how far along are you, Savannah?"

Carter winced.

Too late.

Chapter Six

"I'm back."

Carter lunged through the doorway and held up the suitcase, hoping to distract Violet.

She didn't so much as glance his way. Neither did Savannah.

Carter had been afraid this would happen. He dropped the suitcase with a thud. That didn't have the desired effect, either, although Violet did hold up one hand. Carter wasn't sure if she was acknowledging his presence or trying to shush him.

"You can put that in the bedroom, Carter."

Definitely the second one. Carter wondered if the bandana dangling from Violet's back pocket could be used as a muzzle.

Violet nodded at Savannah with a smile that encouraged her to continue.

"I'm six months along." The faintest hint of pink stained Savannah's cheeks.

Violet tipped her head. "So that means your baby is due sometime in February."

Savannah nodded. "The fourteenth."

"Really? Valentine's Day?" The woman who'd just tried to shush him released a piercing whistle, only several decibels lower than the one she used to summon her horse from the pasture. "That's awesome."

Carter silently did the math. Rob had been deployed the first week of June. The dates lined up with Savannah's claim that Rob had left her right before he enlisted.

The first time they'd met, his friend had bragged about his new wife. Her sweet personality. How beautiful she was.

But for some reason, Rob had neglected to mention that they'd been estranged before his death. Which meant that either his buddy's acting skills would have been worthy of an Academy Award—or Savannah was the one who wasn't being truthful about their relationship.

Neither possibility sat well with Carter.

"You must be pretty excited," Violet continued. "Do you know if you're having a boy or a girl?"

Carter cleared his throat. A less than subtle warning not to pry and one that Violet, of course, chose to ignore.

"I think—" Carter began. And then discovered that he couldn't. The simple ability to string several words together splintered under the impact of the smile that spread across Savannah's face.

Carter watched, mesmerized, as the woman in the photograph came to life right in front of his eyes. The sparkle in her eyes chased the shadows away until it looked as if she were lit from within.

"It's a girl," she said softly.

Violet reached down to plump one of the sofa cushions. "Do you have any names picked out?"

Carter opened his mouth. Closed it again. Not because he wanted to know if Savannah had any names picked out, but because she was *still* smiling. She didn't look uncomfortable or upset by Violet's questions. Questions that Carter hadn't thought to ask. Until this moment, he hadn't thought of the baby as being a separate person. A child who was going to grow up without knowing her father.

Because of him.

"Her name is Hope."

"Is that a family name?"

"No." Savannah settled one hand almost protectively on the rounded curve of her stomach. "It's a… reminder."

Something passed between her and Violet then. A look of understanding that told Carter the two women shared the same strong faith.

A few years ago, he wouldn't have felt like someone on the outside looking in. At the age of five, with Rachel's gentle guidance, Carter had knelt by his bed one night and prayed a child's simple prayer, asking Jesus to come into his heart. But somewhere along the way, life had become more complicated. Carter had witnessed people doing terrible things to each other—seen things that still haunted his dreams. He'd begun to think that God was as distant and unapproachable as his father.

Savannah had been through a lot the past few months and yet she hadn't turned her back on God. If she ever married again, it would be to a man whose faith was as solid as her own. A man who didn't have more questions than answers.

Married again?

Carter mentally slapped himself upside the head for even thinking along those lines. He'd provided Savannah with a place to stay. He planned to keep a discreet eye on her—from a distance. It was all he'd promised to do.

It was all he *could* do…

"I think Hope is a beautiful name. Don't you, Carter?"

Carter realized that Violet was talking to him now. He'd been distracted by the way the setting sun filtered through the curtains and picked out golden threads in Savannah's hair.

"Beautiful," he agreed absently.

Color flooded Savannah's cheeks and she averted her gaze.

Way to go, Wallace. Open mouth, insert combat boot.

Laughter danced in Violet's eyes. "I was talking about the name Savannah picked out for the baby. What were *you* talking about?"

"You and Maddie *are* alike," he muttered.

As if on cue, the front door swung open.

"Did someone say my name?"

Savannah's mouth dropped open as a young woman breezed into the cottage. A woman who, from the top of her shining copper hair to the silver tips on the toes of her cowboy boots, was the mirror image of Violet Colby.

"I thought I saw lights on over here. What's going on?" She parked her hands on her hips and looked around. Big brown eyes got even bigger when she spotted Savannah standing in the kitchen but she quickly recovered. "Hello."

Savannah glanced Carter's way, but he didn't seem inclined to rescue her this time. Call her crazy, but she got the distinct impression that *he* was the one who looked like he needed rescuing.

"Hi." Savannah scraped up a smile in response to the woman's cheerful greeting.

"This is Savannah," Violet interjected.

"Maddie Wallace."

So there really *was* a Maddie. Savannah supposed she should be grateful that Carter had told her the truth about that, even though he'd omitted a few other significant details about his family.

Like the fact that Maddie and Violet Colby were identical twins.

"Nice to meet you, Savannah." Maddie's smile grew and she turned to her sister. "I didn't realize we were expecting company this evening."

Carter didn't so much as blink, drat the man.

"That's all right." Savannah resisted the urge to cast a reproachful look in his direction. "Neither did Violet."

Maddie's forehead pleated, a sign of her confusion.

"Savannah is Carter's friend," Violet said helpfully. "She had some issues with her last apartment and needed a place to stay."

"Only for a few days." Savannah found herself repeating the words that were quickly becoming her theme song.

Violet pulled a set of bedsheets from another cabinet and the scent of lavender stirred the air. "I told her that we've got plenty of room."

"That's true enough." Maddie sauntered into the tiny living room. "Is there anything I can help with?"

"No, thanks. I think we're good," Violet told her twin.

Savannah cringed inwardly.

Although touched by their kindness, she didn't want Carter's sisters to feel like they had to fuss over her. Given the fact that Maddie and Violet hadn't known she was coming, they were handling her arrival with remarkable aplomb.

And neither one of them seemed to be in a hurry to leave.

Maddie reached for a stack of towels at the same time as Violet. They looked at each other and started to laugh.

In spite of her misgivings about Carter, Savannah couldn't help but be fascinated by the two women. She was an only child who had dreamed of having a large family someday, but to have an identical twin sister? She couldn't imagine what that would be like....

"Weird, isn't it?" Maddie grinned.

Savannah felt her cheeks heat up. "I'm sorry. I didn't mean to stare."

"That's okay." Violet gave Savannah's arm a friendly pat. "Most of the time, Carter can't tell us apart, either."

Shaking his head, Carter grumbled, "It might help if you didn't *dress* alike."

Maddie hooked her thumbs in the front pockets of her jeans and stuck out a foot. "Maybe it's the boots," she mused.

"Or the matching belt buckles?" Carter said under his breath.

"Well, it certainly can't be the Texas drawl." Maddie looked smug. "I've been practicing, *y'all*."

Carter rolled his eyes.

"That's right. You'll be speaking fluent cowgirl in no time," Violet teased.

Maddie turned to Savannah. "Where are you from?"

Carter shifted his stance, a movement that blocked Maddie from her view. Savannah got the distinct impression it wasn't an accident.

"I think we should leave Savannah alone so she can settle in. She's probably tired from the long drive." Carter's voice sounded strange. Almost as if he were gritting his teeth.

"You're right." Maddie peeked around his shoulder and smiled at Savannah. "How long of a drive *was* it?"

"I live in Dallas."

Carter cleared his throat.

"Catching a cold, little brother?" Maddie patted his arm.

"Lupita has a special remedy that will fix you up." Violet flashed an impish look. "But don't worry, it tastes better than it smells."

Maddie and Violet snickered. In harmony.

Savannah decided that she liked Carter's sisters already.

"Is that where you and Carter met? In Dallas?"

Savannah nodded, wondering why Carter seemed tense. It wasn't as if the questions she was being asked were difficult—

"How long have you two known each other?"

Except for that one.

Savannah swallowed hard, unsure of how to answer the question. What would Carter's sisters think of her if she told them that she'd met him less than a week ago? Would they think she was taking advantage of their hospitality?

"Not very long—"

"For a while."

Savannah's statement collided with Carter's in midair, leaving her momentarily speechless.

How could Carter stand there and tell his sisters something that wasn't true?

Two pairs of matching brown eyes bounced back and forth between her and Carter.

Now that the two women stood side by side, Savannah could see subtle differences between the two. Violet's complexion tinted bronze from the sun, evidence of hours spent outdoors. And Maddie's auburn hair was an inch or two shorter than her sister's....

Savannah groaned when she saw Maddie grin at her twin. "I'm doing it again, aren't I?"

"Don't worry. Violet and I are still getting used to it," Violet said.

"Getting used to what?" Savannah asked curiously.

"Seeing each other. I mean, we met five months ago, but it's weird to see your face on someone else."

Savannah tried to hide her confusion. And her rising frustration with the one person in the room who'd only said that his family situation was *complicated.*

Violet looked at Maddie. Who looked at her brother. They folded their arms.

"You didn't tell her."

Carter had never seen a simple mission go south quite the way this one had.

"I thought she might want to wait for the movie."

"Ignore my brother, Savannah," Maddie huffed. "He has a warped sense of humor."

Carter gave her a look. "It certainly helps in this family."

"Violet and I met for the first time last summer," Maddie explained. "She *accidentally* found me. After Landon found her, that is."

"We were pretty shocked," her sister added.

Shocked wasn't exactly the word Carter would have chosen.

"You didn't grow up together?" Savannah pressed her hand against her lips the moment the words slipped out.

"Neither of us knew the other one existed. I grew up on the ranch and she grew up in the city, but we're hoping it didn't cause irreversible damage."

Carter knew Violet was teasing, her own attempt to lighten the moment, but the words hit too close to home. Whatever the circumstances had been that caused Belle and his father to part ways, they wouldn't be able to undo the damage they'd inflicted on their children. Maddie and Violet. Gray and Jack. None of them could recover the years they'd lost.

Something must have shown in his expression, because Maddie looked at Violet and shook her head.

"It's a long story," she murmured. "I'm sure Carter will explain everything when he has some time."

Savannah glanced at him, and Carter saw the doubt shimmering in her eyes. He'd had the time, when she questioned him on the way to the cottage.

Savannah grasped the back of a chair with both hands, a weary gesture that brought him to her side in an instant.

"Are you all right?"

Savannah's teeth sank into her lower lip. "A little tired, I guess."

"That's it. We're out of here." Violet gave the afghan draped over the back of the sofa a final pat.

"Is there anything else you need before you turn in for the night?" Maddie asked.

"I'll be fine. Really."

Savannah's smile was convincing. Almost.

"We'll see you in the morning, then. Lupita is making her famous buttermilk pancakes." Violet tossed a smile over her shoulder as she walked with Maddie to the door. "If you need anything, just give a holler."

Finally.

Carter tried to conceal his relief. Once Maddie and Violet were out of the way, he could do damage control. Although he couldn't shake the sneaking suspicion that he'd been the one responsible for the damage in the first place.

His plan was thwarted when Maddie reached out and grabbed his hand.

"You're coming with us, Carter. Violet and I need your help with something, too."

Before Carter could protest, Violet had taken hold of his other hand.

"Two against one?" he muttered.

He thought he heard someone laugh. But when he looked over his shoulder, Savannah was already disappearing into the bedroom.

"You better get used to it." Maddie smiled sweetly.

Carter, who knew a dozen ways to extricate himself from a difficult situation, found himself being herded out of the cottage and up the driveway like one of Jack's stray calves.

Chapter Seven

Carter saw a light on in the kitchen and hoped it was Gray. His brother would recognize a hostage situation and intervene. After all, the guy *was* a professional.

Unfortunately, it was Keira, Jack's fiancée, who sat at the table, hands cradling a steaming cup of tea, a stethoscope still draped around her neck.

No help there. One of Maddie and Violet's allies, not his.

"Hey, ya'll." The veterinarian looked up as they shuffled past the doorway, Maddie and Violet attached to his side like a pair of amateur country line dancers. "Care to join me?"

"Sure," Violet sang out.

Maddie bobbed her head. "We'll be right back. We have to talk to Carter for a minute."

Talk?

Carter wasn't fooled by Maddie's bright smile. He was being hauled in for questioning.

"Aren't I entitled to a phone call?" he quipped.

"No."

Carter winced when the emphatic retort rang in both his ears at the exact same moment.

"My favorite meal?"

"Move it, soldier."

Violet kicked the door shut in some cowgirl-ninja move that left Carter inwardly shaking his head. Then he was free.

Sort of.

"Okay, let's hear it." They folded their arms, stared him down.

Carter felt like he was back in boot camp, under the gimlet eye of his commanding officer and resisted a crazy urge to salute.

"Everything," Violet said promptly.

"And don't even bother to waste our time with that name, rank and serial-number stuff," Maddie warned. "You know what she means."

Carter checked a smile. "You've been watching too many old movies."

"And you're stalling." Maddie's chin hiked up a notch. "Why didn't you tell us you invited Savannah to the ranch?"

"Because the first time I asked her, she turned me down." Flat. "I didn't think she would change her mind."

Maddie and Violet exchanged a look.

"That's why you moved into Gray's room instead of taking the cottage Violet offered," Maddie said slowly. "You were *hoping* that she would."

He couldn't argue with that, either. "Savannah didn't have anywhere else to go. She planned to stay in a hotel while she looked for another apartment."

Maddie continued to study him and Carter could almost see the wheels turning in her head.

"When we were at Gray's apartment the day you got back, you mentioned there was someone you had to see before you came to the ranch. Was it Savannah?"

Maybe Maddie should have been the detective in the family.

"Yes."

"You've never mentioned her before. How do you two know each other?"

Carter felt a hitch in his breathing.

"Her husband, Rob—" He managed to push the name out, past the lump that instantly formed in his throat. "He asked me to check on Savannah when I got back to the States."

"Then I'd say it's a good thing you did. Will he be home for Thanksgiving?"

Violet's innocent question landed like a punch to the gut. Pain radiated through his body, leaving Carter unable to do anything but shake his head.

He hadn't talked to his siblings about what happened to Rob. How did you put something like that in an email? Every time he said Rob's name, it was ripping the bandage from a fresh wound.

For the first time since he'd come home, Carter understood why Maddie and Gray had waited to share the news of their father's disappearance in person.

"You wrote that one of your friends was killed," Maddie whispered. "Were you talking about Savannah's husband?"

"He died in a roadside bombing two months ago." In Carter's arms.

The color drained from Violet's face. "Savannah must be devastated."

"And she's expecting." Maddie briefly closed her eyes. "I can't imagine what she's going through. Knowing that her husband will never have the chance to hold his child."

The child he hadn't known about.

The thought never made it past Carter's lips. Better to let them think that everything between Rob and Savannah had been fine. Until a week ago, it was what he'd believed, too.

Accepting the alternative was the equivalent of accepting Rob's death all over again…and he wasn't ready to do that. Not yet.

"Does she have any family?"

Carter had wondered the same thing. He'd tried to recall if Rob had mentioned anything about parents. Siblings. "I'm not sure. I don't think so."

"Well, she has us now," Violet said. "I meant what I said when I told Savannah that she is welcome to stay as long as she'd like."

"Thank you." Carter meant it, but suddenly it didn't seem like enough. "And I'm sorry I overstepped my bounds. I should have asked your permission to invite Savannah to the ranch."

Violet acknowledged the statement with a jerky nod, pivoting toward the door as if she couldn't get away from him fast enough now.

"Violet?"

She stopped and reluctantly turned to face him.

"Is something else bothering you?" Carter asked cautiously.

"Yes." Hurt flashed in Violet's eyes. "Your apology."

Apparently he'd somehow messed that up, too. "This is your home and I had no right to invite someone to stay here without asking your permission first—"

"Stop right there."

Carter stopped.

"You don't *have* to apologize at all."

"I don't?"

"I want you to think of the ranch as your home."

Violet's chin lifted and she looked him straight in the eye. "And do you know why?"

She didn't wait for him to answer.

"Because like it or not, Carter, *I'm* your sister, too."

The door closed softly behind her.

A peaceful silence settled into the corners of the room as Savannah started to unpack her things into a stout antique dresser next to the bed.

The faint scent of lavender from a sachet tucked in the corner stirred the air, soothed the raw edges of her emotions. Already she could feel her heart settling into the beauty of her surroundings.

Framed in the weathered window frame, a star winked against the indigo sky. A sky the same shade of blue as Carter's eyes....

Savannah yanked the unruly thought back in line.

She didn't want to think about Carter. And she certainly didn't want to notice the man's eyes.

Or the emotion she'd seen lingering there, one Savannah recognized all too well in spite of his attempt to hide it.

Pain.

The comment he'd made about his family situation

being complicated made sense in light of what she'd just found out.

Identical twins, separated. Why?

Savannah felt a delicate flutter below her rib cage and the rush of love that inevitably followed in its wake. She would do anything to protect her child.

Maybe Carter's parents had felt the same way. Had circumstances forced them to separate their daughters?

The deep affection between Violet and Maddie appeared genuine. Real. But judging from some of the comments Carter had made in the car, he didn't think of the Colby ranch as home. He'd claimed Maddie as his sister, but not Violet. And if Jack Colby was Violet's older brother, didn't that mean he was Carter's brother, too?

Savannah was beginning to believe that Carter hadn't been exaggerating when he'd described his family situation as "complicated."

But where did he fit in the equation…and in the family?

Not that it was any of her business. Carter had provided Savannah with a place to stay, not given her access to his personal life.

She had her own secrets to keep. Things that Carter wouldn't want to know, considering that he and Rob had been friends.

The less time she spent in his company, the better. Carter Wallace was too observant, attuned to the slightest change in her expression the way he would notice a shift in the wind. Savannah didn't need—or want—that kind of attention. It could only lead to trouble.

He was a soldier. Hardwired to defend. Protect. It

would be too easy to rest her head on that broad shoulder. Seek shelter and safety in his arms.

She'd trusted Rob and look what had happened. Now she was determined to make a new start for her and the baby.

Savannah smoothed out a wrinkle in the quilt and straightened one of the decorative pillows, a square of faded pink muslin with a verse from the Bible neatly embroidered inside the hedge of delicate ruffles.

Rejoice always. Pray without ceasing. In everything give thanks.

Her grandmother would have approved, especially the giving thanks part. She could still hear Edith Callahan's lilting voice.

Count to ten, Savannah. Count to ten.

As always, her grandmother had put her own unique spin on the familiar advice. It hadn't been a reminder to hold her tongue or her temper. Her grandmother encouraged Savannah to count her blessings—and not to stop until she got to ten.

Savannah had embraced the words. In elementary school, when she struggled to fit in at her new school after her parents had divorced and left her in the care of her elderly grandmother because neither of them wanted their daughter along the journey to find themselves. During her senior year of high school, when Edith's health started to decline following a stroke that put Savannah in charge of the tiny household. The last few months of Edith's life, when Savannah dropped out of college to take care of her.

There were times in Savannah's life when she'd flown past ten and kept right on going—and times when it took every ounce of strength to reach that particular number.

Like the day Rob had told her that their marriage had been a mistake. The day he'd walked out the door without looking back.

Savannah closed her eyes. Shut out the memories of the past that threatened to drag her down again. Focused on the present.

Tonight it wasn't difficult at all to find things to be thankful for. Her car hadn't broken down on the way to Grasslands. A place to stay. Space to think. Room to breathe. Violet. Maddie…

Savannah stopped, afraid to add the name that hovered at the edges of the prayer. It didn't matter. He appeared in her thoughts, anyway.

The man whose smile threatened to sneak through her defenses when she'd promised herself she would never let her guard down again.

Carter stood on the front porch of the cottage, wondering if he should take his own advice and let Savannah have the rest of the evening to settle in. Alone.

Except that he wanted to be sure her suitcase hadn't found its way back to the trunk of her car again. The way she'd grabbed on to the chair for support continued to bother him, too. Savannah had claimed she was tired—but Carter couldn't shake the feeling there was more to it than that.

He knocked once, lightly, just in case she'd already fallen asleep.

The light flicked on above Carter's head, dousing him with a spray of light. The door opened a crack and a pair of spring green eyes met his.

Carter lifted up the plate of leftovers he'd commandeered from the fridge.

"I thought you might be hungry."

The door opened a little wider and Savannah reached for the plate. A mouthwatering aroma drifted from the foil-covered dish.

"This smells wonderful."

A low rumble of appreciative agreement followed the statement and Savannah pressed one hand against her stomach, clearly mortified.

"I believe that's the typical response to Lupita's cooking." Carter couldn't help but grin. And he took full advantage of the moment and ducked inside the cottage, taking a brief but thorough inventory on his way to the kitchen.

Relief poured through him.

Not a suitcase in sight.

"You didn't have to do this, you know." Savannah followed, a look of consternation on her pretty face.

"I wasn't sure if you'd stopped for something to eat along the way."

The telltale color that bloomed in her cheeks told Carter his hunch had been right.

"I had some fruit," she murmured.

"If you write down a list of your favorite foods, I'm sure Lupita will add them to the cart the next time she goes shopping."

Savannah looked almost horrified by the suggestion. Not quite the reaction Carter had anticipated.

"I can drive to the grocery store in Grasslands," she protested. "I don't expect special treatment. Just...pretend I'm not here."

Somehow, Carter doubted that was possible. He

hadn't been able to stop thinking about Savannah since the day they'd met.

But she'd been wary of his motives then and judging from the expression on her face, those feelings hadn't changed.

Maddie and Violet were right.

He had some explaining to do.

"Thank you for bringing over dinner." Savannah set the plate down on the table and summoned a polite smile.

Carter's cue to leave. Which he ignored.

"Aren't you going to eat?"

"Yes." And then a cautious, "Are you going to stay?"

"Don't mind if I do."

Carter heard a faint but unmistakable chirp of alarm as he pulled a chair away from the table and guided Savannah into it.

He ignored that, too.

"Let's see what we've got here." Carter peeled the foil off the tray even though he already knew what was underneath it. "Baby red potatoes. Clover-leaf rolls. Sweet potato pie. Fried chicken. Ah, and my favorite Texas staple—barbecued ribs."

Savannah stared down at the variety of food mounded together on the platter. Carter didn't know what she liked, so he'd added a little of everything he'd discovered in the refrigerator. A veritable culinary relief map of texture and color.

"Is that a…waffle?" Savannah was pointing to something next to the green beans.

"Uh-huh. There are also bagels and cream cheese if you want to sleep in tomorrow morning and skip breakfast at the main house," Carter added casually.

Savannah's eyes narrowed.

"You wouldn't be trying to keep me away from your family, would you?"

Carter didn't miss a beat.

"Yes, ma'am."

Chapter Eight

"Carter—" Savannah's gurgle of laughter took them both by surprise.

They stared at each other across the table, a fragile silence humming between them, linking them together.

Carter pushed to his feet. The chair scraped against the floor and shattered the moment.

"Better dig in before it gets cold," he said, struggling to regain his equilibrium. "I'll see if there's anything to drink."

He retrieved a bottle of water from the fridge and shut the door just in time to see Savannah bow her head and close her eyes.

Carter felt a strange tightening in his chest as a silky tassel of toffee-colored hair slid forward, outlining the delicate curve of her jaw.

His fingers twitched with the urge to smooth it away from her face. To trace the half smile that touched her lips as her lips moved in silent petition.

A moment later Savannah's head lifted and she looked across the table at him, the smile still there, in her eyes.

"What did you pray for?" Carter couldn't prevent the words from slipping out.

"That I would continue to seek God's guidance," she said softly.

Something Carter had stopped asking long ago.

"And—" Savannah hesitated, stirring his curiosity in spite of the fact that talking about God left Carter feeling uncomfortable. Restless.

Envious.

"And—?" he prompted.

To Carter's absolute amazement, Savannah blushed.

And you.

Savannah wondered what Carter would say if she said the words out loud.

She hadn't meant to pray for him. By all rights, she should still be upset with him.

She *was* still upset with him.

He hadn't even bothered to tell his sisters that he'd offered her one of the cottages, making for an awkward first meeting....

"Yeah, I'm sorry about that."

Savannah blinked, wondering if she'd said the words out loud. Because it was unsettling to think that Carter could read her mind.

"I should have told Violet that I'd invited you to stay here."

Yes, he should have. He should have told her *a lot* of things. Savannah flattened a piece of potato with the back of her fork.

"Ouch."

Savannah glanced up and her heart got tangled in Carter's rueful smile.

"I'm glad you're taking out your frustration on those poor vegetables instead of me."

"I'm not—" Savannah started to deny it, but the proof was there, soaking in a pool of barbecue sauce.

A wave of fatigue swept in, eroding what remained of her energy.

"I don't know how to do this, either."

Savannah's gaze lifted to Carter. "Do what?"

"This." He leaned back in the chair and studied her. Serious. Intent. One hundred percent soldier. "Trying to figure out what to say. What not to say. How *much* to say."

For some reason, the candid admission moved Savannah more than the smile.

She traced a vine embroidered on the tablecloth. "Neither do I."

Savannah didn't know if she could trust him. Wasn't sure she could trust herself anymore.

"Did you ever play the game twenty questions when you were a kid?"

It was the last thing Savannah expected Carter to say.

"Yes," she said cautiously.

"Good. You start. We each get one question."

"I thought it was twenty questions."

"It's late—I'm fast-tracking this." Carter's lips curled at the edges. "You can ask another one tomorrow."

She would never have guessed that the man would have a whimsical bone in his body. His attempt to lighten the moment, put her at ease was charming… and terrifying.

Savannah speared a piece of chicken with her fork,

thinking hard. Afraid to delve too deeply into his personal life because he might expect her to do the same.

Some of the names Savannah heard mentioned scrolled through her mind.

Jack Colby. Landon.

Or did she ask about Maddie and Violet, who claimed to have met only five months ago?

Carter's fingers drummed against the edge of the table and he lifted an eyebrow.

Savannah took the hint.

"The woman you said was injured in a riding accident. Belle Colby? Who is she?"

Carter's expression darkened and Savannah immediately wished she could take it back.

"I'm sorry—"

"No, it's a fair question," he interrupted. "You just happened to pick the one question no one knows the answer to." The chair creaked as Carter shifted his weight. "We do know that Belle Colby is Maddie and Violet's biological mother."

But not Carter's, she guessed.

"Maddie and Gray—he's the oldest in my family—grew up thinking that Sharla Wallace was our mother. Our dad never said anything that led us to believe she hadn't given birth to all three of us. Not even after she died in a car accident when I was three."

"I'm so sorry." Savannah found herself mouthing the words that had brought little comfort when she'd learned of Rob's death.

"I don't remember her." The words were spoken matter-of-factly, but the flash of pain in Carter's eyes spoke of a wound that had never completely healed.

"A few months ago, after Belle's accident, Violet

went on a search for her biological father in Fort Worth. She found Maddie instead. It turns out that my dad had been married to Belle Colby. No one knows why they divorced."

The edge of bitterness in Carter's voice cut deep; his eyes flashed a silent warning to keep her distance. Savannah laced her fingers together in her lap because her first inclination was to reach for his hand.

To let him know that she understood what it was like to have your world turned upside down in the blink of an eye. To discover that all the things you'd thought were real had been based on secrets. Lies. But even more difficult to accept when they came from someone you loved.

"A few months ago, Violet's fiancé, Landon Derringer, hired a private investigator to do some digging into Belle's past. He hit a brick wall. There *is* no Belle Colby. Technically, the woman doesn't exist. At some point she took on a new identity. Gray's a cop and he's been using his connections to piece everything together, but so far, he's come up empty-handed."

Savannah tried to come up with reasons why a woman with young children would change her name. Cloak herself in secrecy. None of them were good.

"Even if your parents divorced, your dad must know something," she ventured.

"He might, but no one has been able to question him," Carter said tightly. "Dad's a medical missionary and he went off the grid near the Mexican border last summer. None of us has been able to get in touch with him. As far as I know, he doesn't even realize I'm back in the States. Not that it would have made a difference," he added. "It's not like he put aside his work the last time I was home on leave."

"It must have been difficult, to be so far away when you found out," Savannah said softly.

"I wasn't that far away," Carter said wryly. "Maddie and Gray decided it would be better to tell me in person. I found out about an hour after I stepped off the plane last Saturday."

The day before they'd met.

Savannah pulled in a breath so sharp it felt like a knife sliding between her ribs. Carter had been dealing with all of this and yet he'd sought her out at the diner, to deliver Rob's message.

It revealed the kind of man he was. A man who set aside his feelings to do the right thing.

"The police must be involved if your father is missing."

"He's not considered missing. That's part of the problem. If we had proof of foul play, the authorities would get involved, but unfortunately, this is Dad's MO. He gets completely focused on his work and forgets everything else."

Including his children, Savannah thought.

"He's supposed to be back for Thanksgiving," Carter continued. "That's why Maddie insisted that I stick around for a few weeks. Once he plugs into the outside world again, he'll know we're here, at the ranch, waiting."

"Praying," Savannah murmured.

"I'll leave that to the rest of the family." Bitterness edged into Carter's voice. "No matter what Dad says, nothing will be the same. I mean, maybe we'll finally understand why he and Belle split up, but nothing they say can ever make up for the damage they caused by splitting up two sets of twins."

There was no way—*no way*—Savannah had heard that correctly.

"You mean Violet and Maddie."

"And Gray and Jack Colby. They're identical twins, too."

Carter waited for the gasp of surprise. The expression of disbelief.

Instead, he was blindsided by Savannah's wistful smile.

"You're so lucky."

"Lucky?"

"No, not lucky," Savannah corrected. *Now* she was making some sense. Until she added, "Blessed. To have family. People who…want to be with you."

Carter hadn't considered that. Sure, Violet and Jack were okay but they were Maddie and Gray's identical twins. It was difficult to wrap his mind around the fact that they were his family, too, no matter what Violet had said in the den a little while ago.

"They're my *half* siblings. And Gray—" Carter couldn't even say it out loud. He still couldn't accept that a guy named Joe Earl could be Gray's father, not even if Joe's own wife believed it. Patty Earl had hinted that Belle Colby, at the age of sixteen, had been more attracted to the inheritance Brian Wallace would eventually receive from his grandmother than she was to Joe.

Violet was adamant that her mother wouldn't have married Carter's father for money. It was a touchy subject—one that Maddie had warned him not to bring up when Violet or Jack were around.

People in a small town talked and Belle's reputation had already come under suspicion when James Crawford, the original owner of the spread, had left the ranch to her after he died.

Belle had become a wealthy woman over the years, something that might have prompted Patty Earl's decision to get to know "her" boys.

The thought sickened Carter. It was one thing to maintain a polite distance from Jack Colby, but what would it do to his relationship with Gray if they discovered the only thing they had in common was the fact they'd been lied to all these years?

"What about Gray?"

Compassion shimmered in Savannah's eyes and Carter mentally took a step back. He hadn't meant to go into so much detail. He'd invited her to stay at the Colby Ranch in an attempt to ease her burden, not add to it.

"You only get one question, remember? You can ask another one tomorrow. Now it's my turn."

Savannah's fork clattered onto the plate.

It was clear she assumed that he was going to question her about Rob. What had gone wrong in their marriage? Why he'd left her?

Questions that Carter wanted the answers to—but not if they brought that wary look back into Savannah's eyes.

Maybe someday she would trust him.

Savannah's teeth sank into her lower lip but she lifted her chin to meet his gaze.

"What do you want to know?"

Carter leaned forward, elbows propped on the table. Smiled.

"Are you going to eat that waffle?"

Chapter Nine

"Got a minute?"

Carter took one look at his brother's serious expression and *knew* he should have gone straight to his room instead of taking a detour to the study to check his email.

The conversation with Savannah had left him feeling restless, the words she'd said continuing to play through his mind.

You're so blessed to have family.

Whenever Carter had thought through every scenario, he'd always thought of the outcome in terms of what he could lose, never what he might gain.

Carter shut down the computer so Gray wouldn't see what he'd been up to.

"I was just keeping up with traffic, officer."

"I'm off duty." Gray's lips twitched. "And from what I heard, you already got busted."

"Twice. Or—" Carter tipped his head thoughtfully "—maybe it only counts as once if the women who chewed you out are identical twins?"

"I'll have to look that one up in the statutes." Gray sauntered into the room and pulled up a chair.

Uh-oh.

"Are you sure I don't need a lawyer?"

Carter was only half joking.

"Maddie said you invited a friend to stay at the ranch for a while."

This was about *Savannah?*

Carter immediately bristled. "Is that a problem?"

Gray leaned forward and met his gaze.

"You tell me."

Carter wasn't fooled by the mild response.

"Let me guess. You want her full name and date of birth?"

"Do you know them?"

Carter ignored the question. "Savannah was being evicted from her apartment."

"And she didn't have anywhere else to go?"

The flash of skepticism in Gray's eyes turned up the heat under Carter's temper. "No."

"And you're sure… Savannah…isn't taking advantage of the situation?"

"Moving to the ranch was a last resort. She didn't want to come here." Not only that, Carter had a feeling that Savannah was already working on an exit plan. She'd made it clear she didn't want to be a burden.

"I'm surprised you never mentioned her, that's all."

"You're surprised," Carter repeated. "Really? Because we haven't exactly exchanged diaries over the past few years."

"You keep a diary?"

"You're worse than Maddie," Carter scoffed.

"And you're avoiding the question."

"I didn't realize you'd asked one."

Gray's bark of laughter echoed around the room, defusing the tension in the air. "Sorry. Elise says that sometimes I use that voice on her, too. I sounded like a cop just now, didn't I?"

He sounded like a big brother. Carter wasn't sure quite what to do with that. The changes in their family structure hadn't been the only ones he'd noticed in Gray since he'd arrived at the Colby Ranch. There'd been a few changes on the *inside,* too.

"Savannah isn't going to take advantage of Violet's hospitality. Or steal the silver," he added.

A heartbeat of silence followed.

"After dealing with Patty Earl, I admit I'm a little suspicious of people's motives," Gray finally admitted. "Jack and I suspect the only reason she's been trying to cozy up to us is because she found out the Colby Ranch is a lucrative operation."

Carter didn't want to be reminded of the woman who'd claimed that her husband was Jack and Gray's biological father.

Another secret. One that could have led to his father and Belle Colby's breakup. But if Gray and Jack weren't Brian's sons, why hadn't both boys stayed with Belle?

If these were the questions that Gray had been wrestling with the past few months, no wonder he was tense.

Carter released a slow breath, reminding himself to cut the guy some slack.

"I promised my friend Rob that I would check on Savannah. Make sure she was okay. I'm guessing that meant he didn't want her living on the street."

Instead of taking offense, Gray regarded him

thoughtfully, leaving Carter to wonder what else Maddie and Violet had told him.

"You remind me of Dad."

Carter stiffened. "Sorry."

"It was a compliment, Carter. Dad has devoted most of his life to taking care of people. Making sure they were okay."

Carter couldn't argue with that, but it would have been nice if their father had spent some time with his own family, too. Instead, he'd left them in Rachel's care.

Gray nodded, almost as if he'd read Carter's thoughts. "I always wondered why Dad seemed to think that his patients needed him, but it never seemed to cross his mind that we did, too."

Carter tried not to show how stunned he was by the quiet admission.

He had never considered the possibility that Gray might have felt the same way he did. Guilty for wanting their father's attention. But tossing a football in the backyard had seemed a frivolous thing compared to treating people who were injured. Sick. People who needed Brian Wallace more.

"Dad always told us to trust God—but it would have been nice if he would have trusted us, too." Carter couldn't keep the edge of bitterness from his voice.

"You're talking about Belle."

"Dad shouldn't have kept something like that a secret. Aren't you angry that he kept you from knowing your twin brother all these years?"

"We can't change the past," Gray said evenly. "All we can do, with God's help, is move forward."

"Easier said than done."

"It's occurred to me that Dad might have kept his distance from us for a reason," Gray went on. "No one knows why he and Belle split up—or why they split *us* up—but it must have been pretty big. Maybe his work is his way of trying to make up for something. Something he considered a…personal failure."

Carter wandered over to the window overlooking the courtyard to hide his expression.

He had more in common with his dad than Gray thought.

"For what it's worth, Violet and Maddie agreed that Savannah should stay here, too." His brother rose to his feet. "I guess the majority rules on this one."

"She needs some time."

"Meaning?"

"Meaning you don't get to interrogate her, Office Wallace."

A smile played at the corner of Gray's lips. "Got it. I'll see you in the morning. I'm sticking around until Sunday night."

"Thanks for the warning."

"It's better than a ticket," Gray quipped.

Carter's eyes narrowed. "I don't remember you having a sense of humor."

"You can thank Elise for that, too. The love of a good woman…" Gray began to whistle as he sauntered out the door.

Carter couldn't remember his brother ever whistling, either.

The love of a good woman…

Unbidden, an image of Savannah's face flashed through his mind.

No way. Not going there.

Carter wandered back to the desk and faced the computer again. Belle Colby smiled at him from inside a metal picture frame beside the monitor. Carter couldn't help but stare at the woman who didn't even know she'd turned his life—and several others—upside down. It was a candid shot, taken while Belle was sitting on a hay bale. Ribbons of sunlight winnowed through the cracks in the barn board, illuminating a face that was both familiar and strange at the same time.

Shoulder-length auburn hair. Wide, sparkling brown eyes. The strong resemblance between her and Maddie was almost eerie, but that wasn't what Carter found the most unsettling.

Who *was* she? Had his dad loved Belle? Had he married Sharla to provide his children with a mother or because he'd fallen in love with her?

Where are you, Dad? We need some answers.

Carter opened up his email account and skimmed through the messages in the in-box.

Nothing new.

Almost of their own volition, his fingers began tapping out a message.

Maddie and Violet said that every letter they'd sent to their father had been ignored, but something pushed Carter to try again.

Dear Dad,

When you get this message, please call me. I'm back from Afghanistan now and staying at the Colby Ranch in Grasslands with Gray and Maddie. We're all worried because we haven't heard from you in a while. Can you take a few min-

utes to let us know you're okay? There are some things going on that you should know about….

Things he needed to know.

Carter hesitated, unsure how to end it.

He released a slow breath. Wrote his name. Hit Send.

A few seconds later, a new message appeared. Carter's heart buckled.

Message returned. Unable to deliver.

He pushed to his feet, palms flat against the desk. Holding him upright because he didn't trust his knees to do their job.

What had he expected?

Without realizing it, Carter reached for the Bible that lay open on the desk, traced the embossed letters on the cover with the tip of his finger. While he was growing up, Rachel had encouraged him to read a passage every day.

It's a love letter from God, Carter.

A letter he hadn't read for a long time. And right now, God was silent. And as unreachable as his father.

Pressing a hand against the small of her back, Savannah eased into one of the chairs on the porch. In the distance she could see the boxy silhouettes of the Herefords grazing on a hill in the distance. Hear a low whicker from the horses in the corral and the rumble of a utility vehicle.

She hadn't seen anyone since Violet had delivered a basket of warm muffins and a container of fresh fruit right to her door that morning.

Savannah felt a stab of guilt that she'd let Carter's

sister think she'd missed breakfast because she'd slept in. The truth was, she'd been avoiding Carter.

It was only a matter of time before he asked the questions she had seen simmering in his eyes the night before.

Questions about Rob.

What was she supposed to say? That the man Carter obviously respected and admired had walked out a week after he'd promised to love and cherish her forever?

Carter hadn't been able to conceal his bitterness over the secrets his father had kept from the family. How would he react if he ever learned the whole truth about Rob?

A flurry of movement caught her eye and someone ducked behind one of the shrubs that formed a hedge between the two cottages.

A very small someone.

Savannah angled her head, trying to get a better look.

"Hello?"

A pair of big brown eyes peeked over the leaves. "Hi."

Savannah lifted one hand and motioned her over. "You can come over, if you'd like."

"I don't want to disturb you."

"You aren't disturbing me. I promise."

There was a rustling sound and a little girl about seven or eight years old inched into view. She wore a denim skirt with an embroidered ruffle around the bottom and a matching vest. Tiny cowboy boots completed the adorable ensemble.

Carter hadn't been kidding when he'd said there

were a lot of people coming and going at the ranch. Was she the daughter of the housekeeper? One of the ranch hands?

"I'm Savannah."

"I know that." The child giggled.

Savannah realized that word of her arrival must have gotten out. "And you are—"

"Darcy Garland."

"Do you live around here, Darcy?"

"The white house with the green door." Darcy pointed farther down the row of cottages. "My daddy is the foreman. That means he's the boss," she added proudly.

"I see." Savannah tucked away a smile. "I haven't had a chance to meet him yet. I just got here last night."

"I haven't lived here very long, either," Darcy said. "But you'll like it. I do. It's the best place in the world. I know where all the good hiding spots are." Her voice dropped to a whisper. "And where Lupita keeps the extra cookies."

"Lupita is the cook," Savannah remembered.

"Uh-huh. And she scolds people if they forget to take off their boots."

The cook and the housekeeper. Any ideas Savannah had entertained about helping out around the house died a quick death.

Savannah patted the wicker chair next to hers. "You're welcome to join me, if you'd like."

"Can't." Darcy wagged her head from side to side, setting the glossy brown ponytail swinging like a pendulum. "Uncle Carter said that no one's s'posed to bother you."

"Your *uncle* Carter said that?" Savannah didn't

know whether to be annoyed or grateful to discover that the man had been issuing orders behind her back.

"He's not really my uncle," the girl went on blithely. "He's Maddie's brother, but she said it's okay to call him that. She's going to marry my daddy, and then we'll be a real family."

Savannah had noticed the stunning diamond ring on Maddie's finger but hadn't realized Carter's sister was engaged to the ranch foreman.

"I'm going to be the flower girl and carry a basket of rose petals and wear a new dress and everything."

"That sounds like a very important job."

"Uh-huh. Pastor Jeb said it's the most important one."

Darcy's bright smile proved to be contagious.

"I wouldn't mind a little company if you're not busy right now," Savannah said. "It's been a little lonely around here this afternoon."

"Okay." Darcy was on the porch in an instant. She bounced into the chair and settled in. "Do you like animals?"

"As a matter of fact, I—"

"Good, 'cause there are *tons* of them around here. Goats and pigs and chickens—but you have to be careful because they'll peck your fingers if you try to pet them." Darcy examined the adhesive bandage wrapped around her finger, leaving no doubt in Savannah's mind that she was speaking from experience.

"I'll remember that."

"Daddy has been teaching me how to ride after school. Rambo is the sweetest horse *ever*."

Given the animal's name, Savannah would have to take her word for that.

"I'm going to get a pony for Christmas. It's white with brown spots so I'm going to call him Freckles." Darcy paused long enough to take a breath. "Everyone's going on a trail ride tomorrow morning and then we're going to have a picnic by the lake. Do you want to come with us?"

Savannah was touched by the invitation. "Not this time, I'm afraid. I'll have to wait until after my baby is born."

"When will that be?" Darcy stared at Savannah's belly with wide-eyed curiosity.

"February."

Darcy tapped the fingers on one hand, a look of concentration on her face as she silently added up the months. "That's not *too* far away."

To Savannah, it seemed aeons away…and much too close. Where would she be in three months? In three weeks? Not at the Colby Ranch, even though Savannah didn't have the heart to tell Darcy that. If everything went according to plan, she would be back in Dallas before Thanksgiving.

Spending another holiday alone.

The thought left a familiar ache in her chest.

Maybe staying here wasn't such a good idea. Although she hadn't met Carter's brothers, she'd liked Maddie and Violet immediately. What if being surrounded by Carter's family only made it more difficult to be alone again?

"Do you like kittens?"

"I've never had one." Savannah couldn't help but smile at the abrupt change in subject. Darcy reminded her of one of the songbirds she'd seen flitting from branch to branch outside the kitchen window while she'd brewed a cup of tea.

"Maddie and I found *five* of them living in a shed behind the barn. They get kind of lonely when I'm at school during the day. You can play with them if you want to."

"I just might do that." Savannah laughed.

Nanny to a litter of kittens. Well, she'd told Carter that she wanted to be useful!

"I've got a worksheet to do before supper. *Science.*" Darcy wrinkled her nose as she hopped down from the chair. "I better get home in case Uncle Carter comes back."

A masculine voice suddenly joined the conversation. "Uncle Carter *is* back."

Chapter Ten

Carter caught Darcy as she jumped down from the chair and launched herself into his arms.

"What are you doing here, young lady?"

"I'm not disturbing Savannah, Uncle Carter," she announced solemnly. "She *asked* me to come over 'cause she was lonely."

"We can't have that, now can we?" Carter glanced at Savannah, who quickly averted her eyes.

And blushed.

He *knew* she would blush.

With her toffee-colored hair falling loose around her shoulders and a bright yellow afghan draped over her lap, Savannah looked relaxed. Content.

Beautiful.

Carter had heard her laughing as he walked up to the cottage. The sound had spiraled through him, a melody he had a feeling would stick in a man's mind for a long time.

He'd spent the day following Ricardo, Lupita's husband, around the ranch in order to give Savannah the space he'd told his family she needed.

Who was he kidding? The space *he* needed.

Because knowing a handful of details about Savannah's likes and dislikes...carrying around her photograph...wasn't nearly as dangerous to his peace of mind as having her right there. Close enough to breathe in the delicate floral scent of her perfume. Close enough to see the flecks of emerald-green in her eyes.

Close enough to touch.

"Uncle Carter!" Darcy tugged on his sleeve. "You're not listening."

"Sorry, squirt. One more time?"

Darcy released a patient sigh. "Savannah's going to take care of the kittens while I'm at school."

"That sounds like a lot of responsibility."

Savannah must have sensed he was struggling to keep a straight face because she leveled a stern look in his direction.

"You can show her how, Uncle Carter. You took care of them yesterday."

Apparently, he was going to have to explain to Darcy what the term *classified information* meant.

"That's different," he muttered. "Savannah is a civilian. I'm a marine. We're trained to—"

"Handle all kinds of situations?" Savannah finished.

"Right."

Darcy bobbed her head. "He knows how to put barrettes in. One fell out yesterday right before I got on the bus," she told Savannah.

"Very impressive."

Carter stifled a groan when he saw the twinkle in Savannah's eyes.

He could also fix an armored vehicle, but Carter

decided that must not rank high in importance to an eight-year-old girl.

"And he—"

"Darcy?" Fortunately, Carter was spared from further embarrassment as Maddie's lilting voice drifted across the yard. "Where did you run off to, young lady? You've got some homework to finish before supper."

"Gotta go." With an engaging grin, Darcy scampered away. "I'll see you later, Savannah."

"Bye—"

The word hit the screen door as it slammed shut.

"It looks like you've already made a friend." Carter leaned against the door frame.

"So have you."

"Darcy's a sweet kid." Carter watched the little girl zigzag across the yard and dive into Maddie's waiting arms, proof of the close bond the two shared.

His sister had mentioned that Darcy hadn't always lived at the ranch. Ty Garland's ex-wife had died in a car accident and he'd become an instant father to a grief-stricken little girl he hadn't even known about before the tragedy. Ty had hired Maddie as a part-time nanny and Darcy had gradually come out of her shell, flourishing in the warmth of Maddie's love and attention.

Of the three of them, his sister's faith had always been the strongest, but she had always been focused on her career. So fiercely independent that Carter had never pictured her in the role of caregiver. But from what he'd seen so far, Maddie was a natural. Babysitting Darcy while Ty put in long hours at the ranch. Pitching in at the farm stand to help out Violet. Sitting by Belle Colby's bedside for hours.

Maddie was also quick to pull Carter into the family circle and ask his opinion on things, something she'd never done before.

You can't change the past. All you can do is move forward, with God's help.

Gray's words cycled through Carter's mind again, churning up the familiar restlessness that had plagued him since he'd arrived at the ranch. Carter seemed to be the only one having a difficult time leaving the past behind. And looking to God for strength.

"Darcy told me that Maddie's engaged to her dad."

Carter turned his attention back to Savannah. "Ty Garland. He hired Maddie to take care of her while he worked during the day. That's how they got to know each other."

Savannah tipped her head to one side. "But you don't approve?"

And here Carter thought he'd become adept at hiding his emotions.

"It's not that," he said slowly. "I hardly know the guy. He and Maddie have only been together a few months. The last I knew, she was supposed to marry Landon Derringer. You'll probably meet him within the next day or two. He travels back and forth between Grasslands and his office in Fort Worth."

"Meet him?" A frown creased Savannah's brow. "You just said that he and Maddie broke up."

"They did." He slid her a sideways glance to gauge her reaction. "Derringer's engaged to Violet now."

Maybe now she would understand why he'd done her a favor when he'd told everyone not to bother her. Savannah had enough on her mind without trying to figure out who was who. Especially with two sets of identical twins.

"*Another* brother." Savannah's wistful sigh stirred the air. "I'm trying really hard not to be envious."

"Future brother-in-law," Carter corrected. "And you're kidding me, right?"

"No." Savannah's eyes sparkled with sudden mischief. "And that, Sergeant Wallace, was *your* question for the day. Now it's my turn."

Carter stared at her in disbelief as she repeated his words from the night before. "The question of the day?"

"You said I could ask another one today, didn't you?"

Yes. Yes, he had.

"Fine." The word sounded grudging even to his own ears.

Savannah had a unique way of turning the tables on him. Making him see things from a different perspective. He just wasn't sure if he liked it or not.

"Don't look so grim," she chided. "I believe you just told Darcy that, and I quote, 'Marines can handle any situation.'"

True, but Carter was beginning to think it meant every situation that *didn't* involve a woman with sparkling green eyes and a smile that melted his defenses.

"What's the question?"

"When do I get to meet the rest of your family?"

Carter was beginning to regret starting this "game." Savannah had a gift for asking the questions he preferred not to answer.

"Tonight."

"Really?"

"Maddie and Violet issued a formal invitation for

you to join everyone for supper at the main house," Carter said reluctantly. "But are you sure you want—"

He stopped when Savannah's eyes lit up.

Well, that answered *his* question.

He'd been doing his best to avoid family gatherings for the past few days. The smile on Savannah's face told him that she couldn't wait.

"Are you sure I can't get you anything else, Miss Savannah?"

"I'm sure." Savannah smiled up at Lupita, who was hovering near her shoulder, a platter of homemade rolls balanced in one hand.

"All right." The gray-haired housekeeper looked a little disappointed as she moved to the next person seated at the table. "Elise?"

"No, thank you, Lupita." Elise Lopez had arrived just before dinner with her son Cory, who had peeked up at Savannah below the brim of a pint-size cowboy hat and offered a shy but adorable smile. "Everything was amazing, as usual, but I can't eat another bite."

"Good." With a satisfied smile, the housekeeper swept toward the door. "I will be back with coffee and dessert."

"Just to warn you, Savannah—" Jack Colby lowered his voice to a stage whisper. "When you tell Lupita that you can't eat another bite, she doesn't think dessert counts."

Savannah could smile at the handsome rancher now that the initial shock had begun to fade.

Carter had said that his older brother, Gray, had an identical twin, too, but when the two men had walked into the dining room, side by side, it had taken all the good manners her grandmother had taught her not to stare.

Jack Colby and Gray were the same height and roughly the same build. Both had brown eyes and chestnut hair, although the styles were different. Jack's was on the shaggy side and a day's growth of stubble shaded his jaw, which Savannah thought only added to the man's rugged appeal. Gray was clean shaven, his hair clipped almost military short, like Carter's. Although Gray wore jeans and a flannel shirt, it was easy to tell which twin had grown up on the ranch because Jack's skin was stained a deep bronze from working outdoors.

Savannah's eyes strayed to Maddie and Violet again.

Two sets of identical twins.

It was a little surreal, seeing all four of them together at the table.

No wonder she got the feeling that Carter, with his wheat-blond hair and deep blue eyes, felt like the odd man out when he was in their company. The bond that had formed was evident in every smile that passed between them.

"I agree with Lupita. I don't think dessert should count, either." Keira Wolfe, Jack's fiancée, winked at Savannah across the table.

The slender blonde had been the last one to arrive, dashing into the dining room with a breathless "sorry I'm late—colicky horse" right before Jack had said a blessing over the food. After the prayer, she'd bounded over to Savannah's side and said hello, the welcome in her vivid hazel eyes as warm as the one Savannah had received from Carter's sisters the day before.

She'd been a little worried that supper at the main

house would be a solemn affair, especially in light of what Carter had told her about Belle Colby's precarious condition and their mounting concern about Brian Wallace's whereabouts. Instead, conversation—and laughter—flowed as easily as the pitchers of mint tea that Lupita set at each corner of the mile-long table. Darcy and Cory Lopez sat next to each other, giggling as they tried to make words out of their pasta.

This, Savannah thought, was what a family was supposed to be like. Noisy and affectionate.

But she couldn't help but notice that Carter didn't join in. He didn't engage in the good-natured teasing or the laughter.

Savannah couldn't understand it. As an only child, she would have given anything to be part of a family like this. Before her parents divorced, she remembered silent dinners. And even though her grandmother's tiny home was filled with love, there had only been the two of them.

This was what Savannah had dreamed of.

What Rob had promised.

"Anytime you're ready to leave—" Carter's breath stirred her hair and Savannah suppressed a shiver as that unexpected jolt of electricity momentarily stopped her heart. It started thumping again, so loudly that Savannah was afraid everyone at the table would hear it.

"No." Her voice came out sounding a lot like the squeak in the screen door of the cottage.

"Okay, what are you two whispering about over there?" Maddie teased.

Savannah realized that everyone's attention was focused on them now.

"Is Carter telling stories about us?" Maddie's frown

belied the sparkle in her eyes. “Because if he is, Gray and I know a few we could share about *him.*”

“True.” Gray leaned back in the chair and crossed his arms behind his head. “Like the time Mr. Holbrook hired Carter to cut his grass.”

Maddie clapped a hand over her mouth. “I’d forgotten about that.”

“What happened?” Violet’s eyes glowed with anticipation.

“Here we go,” Carter muttered.

“I think he was about eleven—”

“Twelve,” Carter said under his breath.

Gray’s eyebrow lifted. “Do you want to tell the story?”

“No.”

“Then I will.” Gray didn’t seem the least bit intimidated by Carter’s scowl. “Mr. Holbrook hired Carter to do his yard work and then went out of town for the day. Carter was supposed to use his push mower—”

“Mr. Holbrook never actually *said* what I was supposed to use,” Carter interjected.

Gray ignored him. “All the kids hated to use it because it was one of those contraptions invented shortly after the wheel. And Mr. Holbrook had about two acres of lawn to cut.” He smirked. “Anyway, when he got home that afternoon, he followed a line of tools up the driveway to the garage. Instead of using the push mower, Carter had souped up—”

“Fixed.”

“—a riding lawn mower he had stored in his shed.”

“One of the neighbors heard the commotion and almost dialed 911,” Maddie added with a laugh.

She and Gray had everyone's attention now, even Darcy and Cory were listening.

"Why?" Keira asked. "Couldn't Carter put it back together?"

"Oh, my little brother got the thing running." Gray chuckled. "But he'd fixed the engine, not the brakes."

"In my defense, I did get around to it the next day."

It was the second time Savannah had seen that elusive dimple appear in Carter's cheek but the result was the same.

Instant tingles.

"*After* you took out his hedge," Gray pointed out.

"Did you get in trouble?" Cory's worried gaze swung back and forth between Carter and his brother.

"No way." Gray ruffled the boy's dark hair. "Carter was the neighborhood hero. Mr. Holbrook gave the push mower a one-way ticket to the salvage yard and everyone he hired to cut the grass after that got to use the riding mower instead."

"And people started to show up at our door, asking for Carter," Maddie said. "Dad couldn't even pull the car into the garage because it was filled with everything from lawn mowers to toasters."

"It became Carter's personal mission to fix anything that was broken."

Savannah fixed her eyes on her plate, unable to join in the laughter or meet Carter's eyes.

Was that what he saw when he looked at her?

Something that he'd promised to fix?

Chapter Eleven

"Is everybody awake?"

Darcy burst into the kitchen, almost colliding with Carter as he shuffled toward the coffeepot.

"They are now." Carter scooped the little girl up in his arms and gave her silky ponytail a playful tug. "You're up awfully early on a Saturday morning."

Darcy practically vibrated with excitement as he deposited her on one of the vinyl-covered stools at the end of the breakfast counter. "I couldn't keep my eyes shut anymore."

Funny. Carter had experienced the same problem—but for an entirely different reason. For once, it hadn't been nightmares that kept him awake most of the night.

He wasn't sure which was more dangerous to his peace of mind. The nightmares that continued to plague him...or thoughts of Savannah.

It hadn't escaped Carter's notice that she fit in with his family more than he did. After supper, she'd sat on the floor with a pillow propped behind her back and played a lively game of Chutes and Ladders with Cory and Darcy.

Watching her, Carter was convinced that Savannah was going to be a great mom. Her daughter would blossom the way that Darcy had under Maddie's loving care.

The difference was that Savannah's daughter wouldn't have a father like Ty to protect and cherish her. To slay invisible dragons underneath the bed and intimidate the teenage boys who would eventually ask her out…

The images that tumbled like dominoes through Carter's mind had brought him up short. The chances of Savannah giving him permission to be part of her baby's life were as slim as her letting him become part of *hers*.

Even if he wanted to be.

Carter had been relieved when his cell phone began to ring, providing the opportunity to escape for a few minutes. With everything that had been happening at the ranch the past few days, he hadn't returned his commanding officer's calls.

Sixty seconds later, he'd found himself wishing he hadn't taken that one, either. Carter had assumed the lieutenant would tempt him with another bonus if he agreed to reenlist. Instead, he'd been informed that his name had been officially submitted to receive a Silver Star.

Carter had said the right words and returned to the family room, wondering what he would say if Maddie asked him who had called. And why. The last thing he wanted was for Savannah to find out that he might receive a medal. A medal he might actually deserve if he'd saved her husband that day….

But Savannah had disappeared.

Maddie told him that she was tired and decided to call it a day. That she'd decided to leave before he could walk her home told Carter that she still wasn't completely comfortable in his presence.

Well, that made two of them....

"Are you going on the trail ride with us this morning?"

It took Carter a second to realize that Darcy was talking to him.

"I don't think so, squirt."

"But Lupita packed a lunch for us to take along and we're going to eat around a campfire like real cowboys." Darcy dug into the stack of pancakes Maddie slid on her plate. "It'll be fun."

"She's right, Carter." Violet sauntered into the kitchen, cowboy hat in hand, and made a beeline for the coffeepot. "It'll be good to get outside and clear our heads a little."

Carter was tempted to tell Violet that when he wanted to "clear his head" he chose to go alone, not travel with a herd.

Maddie must have read his mind, because her smile slipped a notch. "Everyone is going, Carter."

"S'vannah can't," Darcy said around a mouthful of sausage. "I asked her but she hasta wait 'til her baby is born."

"I think I'll stick around here this morning." Carter sat down next to Darcy. "I've got a few phone calls to make."

A quick but knowing look passed between Maddie and Violet.

"What?"

"It's just that you can keep Savannah company if you're staying at the ranch," Maddie said casually.

They didn't think…

Carter swallowed a groan. Because the smile Violet aimed at Maddie told him they did.

"You're way off track. Savannah is—"

"Your friend?"

Rob's wife.

"Someone who needs a quiet place to stay." Emphasis on the word *quiet*. "Not a bunch of people getting into her business."

"She's lonely," Darcy said matter-of-factly. "Last night she said that we make her smile."

Insert knife and turn, Carter thought.

Violet brightened. "I've got an idea—" She pretended not to hear Carter snort. "She might not be able to ride, but the two of you can drive out to the lake and join us for lunch."

Carter didn't know what was worse. Maddie and Violet's matchmaking or their sneaky tactics to get him to be part of the family.

"Double trouble. That's what you two are."

Darcy giggled. Maddie and Violet looked as if he'd just paid them a compliment.

"Savannah might have other plans." Plans that didn't include him.

"She seemed to enjoy herself at dinner last night," Violet said.

Enjoy herself? Savannah's expression had reminded Carter of a kid looking through the window of a candy store.

Someone squeezed his shoulder. He glanced up, expecting to see Maddie, but it was Violet who stood behind him.

"I'm glad you two met and that you brought her here," she said softly. "I'm sure it brings Savannah comfort that she can talk to someone who knew her husband."

That's what Carter had thought—*hoped*—until the first time they'd met. Now he knew better. Memories of Rob weren't going to be a connecting point between him and Savannah. If anything, they were a wedge keeping them apart.

Savannah opened her eyes and blinked at the old-fashioned light fixture on the ceiling until it came into focus.

For the first time in months, she'd slept through the night. No doors slamming. No sirens or horns blaring. No trains rattling down the tracks.

Just the low murmur of cattle and the faint but unmistakable sound of...laughter.

Wrapping herself in the quilt, Savannah padded over to the window and peeked through the curtain to see what was going on.

A group of people had gathered outside the barn and she remembered that Darcy had said something the day before about a trail ride.

Savannah recognized Violet and Maddie immediately, working in tandem as they brushed one of the horses. Gray, who traded his khaki slacks for faded jeans and a long-sleeved T-shirt, stood next to Elise. Darcy and Cory were perched on the top rail of the round pen watching Jack bridle an enormous gray horse. Keira knelt beside the animal, running efficient hands down its length, lifting up the enormous hoof.

Savannah's curiosity piqued as a man led a coal-black horse from the barn. He paused and flicked the brim of his hat back.

Ty Garland.

It looked as if the entire family had set aside their normal activities for the morning in order to spend time together.

Except Carter.

When Carter had left the room to take a phone call after dinner the night before, she'd seen Maddie glance at their older brother. The look of resignation and disappointment on Gray's face spoke volumes.

Savannah wasn't the only one who noticed that Carter held himself apart from the rest of the family. Gray and Maddie had told a humorous story from their childhood, but Savannah had read between the lines. Could see that the boy who'd kept his promises had grown up to be a soldier.

Carter was the kind of man people depended on. Looked up to. It was the reason he'd come to the ranch. He'd set his own feelings aside, his questions and confusion about the secrets his father had kept, because Maddie and Gray had asked him to.

And he'd invited her to stay at the ranch because she'd had nowhere else to go.

Carter's a good man, Lord. Help him see that his brothers and sisters are a gift from You. I pray that You'd bring his father home safely and that Belle recovers from her injuries. Bring healing to this family....

Darcy's squeal of delight brought Savannah's head up. She watched Ty swing his daughter onto the back of a buckskin horse that didn't so much as twitch with all the commotion going on around it.

Even from the distance that separated them, Savannah could see the camera in Lupita's hand as she herded everyone together for a picture. Violet planted a cowboy hat on Gray's head and Jack's shout of laughter scattered the chickens pecking the gravel. Ty's arm came around Maddie as they took their place by Darcy.

It was tempting to join them. Safer to hide behind the curtain.

This was a family it would be all too easy to fall in love with.

And not just the *family,* if Savannah were completely honest with herself.

She let the curtain swing shut and backed away from the window, afraid to let her thoughts continue down that road.

I'll take care of you, Savannah.

Rob had said the words and she believed him.

And even though she was beginning to realize that Carter was a man who could be trusted, she no longer trusted herself.

Carter watched Savannah brace one foot over the rail and lean across the fence to stroke Piper's nose. The mare whickered and nosed the pocket of her jacket, looking for a treat.

He took advantage of the fact she hadn't spotted him yet and took a moment to study her. The loose-fitting dress that was the exact shade of green as her eyes, her hair pulled back in a loose knot at the nape of her neck accentuating her delicate profile. And the pensive look on her face.

Guilt propelled him across the yard.

The group had set out half an hour ago, riding away in single file with Jack in the lead on an enormous gray horse.

Carter had checked his email. Twice. The house was quiet. Too quiet. He thought he would welcome the change, but the silence closed in around him instead. Along with the restless feeling that had become his constant companion since he'd returned to Texas.

"It looks like we're both temporarily sidelined, aren't we, girl?" he heard Savannah say. There was no resentment in her tone, only an undercurrent of laughter, bubbling below the surface like spring water.

"Her name is Piper."

Savannah's gaze lifted, and he saw a flash of disappointment in her eyes. "You didn't go on the trail ride?"

"I had a few things to take care of this morning."

"But what could be more—" Savannah stopped but the words dangled in the air between them, unspoken.

More important than family.

"You do have one question, remember?"

Carter tried to lighten the moment, but Savannah's eyes searched his face.

"That's not the one I want to ask," she said simply.

Carter felt a ripple of relief—and trepidation. It was his fault for bringing up that stupid game. The one *he'd* started.

Savannah seemed to have a gift for asking the one question that Carter didn't know how to answer.

Turning her attention back to the horse, Savannah combed her fingers through the tangled mane. Piper's liquid brown eyes drifted shut in absolute bliss. "I've never gone riding before."

Carter felt a stab of jealousy. For a horse.

No doubt about it, he was in trouble.

"Never?" He pushed the word out.

"City girl." Savannah shrugged. "My grandmother and I lived in an apartment that didn't even allow pets."

Carter filed that bit of information away. Rob had talked about Savannah, but never mentioned her family. Or his own, for that matter.

Why hadn't that occurred to him before?

"Does your grandmother still live in Dallas?"

Savannah shook her head. "She had a stroke two years ago and while she was in the hospital, she contracted pneumonia. The doctors couldn't get it under control with antibiotics and she…she passed away the next day."

"I'm sorry." Carter heard himself say the very words that had brought little comfort to him after Rob died.

"At least we had the opportunity to say goodbye. That made it easier."

Carter felt a strange tightening in his throat. The last time he'd been home on leave, over a year ago, his dad had asked him to hang out for an afternoon but he'd gotten a call just fifteen minutes after Carter had arrived. An emergency. Brian had been apologetic—told Carter that he'd make it up to him the next day—but Carter hadn't answered the phone. He'd grown tired of having his father's work schedule dictate their lives.

What if that had been the last time he'd spoken to his father? The email he'd written a few minutes ago remained in the in-box. Locked in the computer's memory like the emotions Carter didn't want to deal with.

"You must miss the city. It's pretty isolated out here." He steered the conversation to safer ground.

"No." Savannah shook her head. "I love the ranch. It's peaceful. There's room to breathe."

"I've heard Maddie say that, too. Five months ago, you wouldn't have thought she knew the front end of a horse from the back. The next thing I know, Gray will be bringing in cattle instead of criminals. He and Maddie both want to live here permanently."

Now why had he told her that?

Savannah tipped her head to look at him.

"Are *you* planning to stay?"

Chapter Twelve

One look at Carter's face and Savannah knew she should have chosen a different question.

"I'm sorry. It's none of my business." It really wasn't. But the more she got to know Carter Wallace, the more she *wanted* to know.

"You can ask me anything." Carter drove a hand through his hair. "I'm just not sure I'll always have an answer."

Which, Savannah decided, was an answer in itself.

Maddie and Gray were planning to make Grasslands their home and embracing the new members of their family while Carter prowled the perimeter, keeping a protective watch. Keeping his distance.

Well, there might be something she could do about that.

"When will they be back from the trail ride?"

"Not for a while. Maddie mentioned they'll be stopping at the lake for a picnic lunch and campfire. Like real cowboys, according to Darcy."

"She was pretty excited about the trail ride today."

"Darcy gets excited about everything." The affection in Carter's tone affirmed what Savannah already knew. In spite of his feelings for the Colbys, the little girl had won him over.

"How far is the lake from here?"

His cobalt eyes swung back to her. "About a mile or so. You aren't thinking of walking out there, are you?"

"No." Savannah tamped down a sigh. "I doubt my doctor would consider a mile-long hike 'staying off my feet.'"

Savannah regretted the words when Carter's eyes narrowed.

"What do you mean? Are you supposed to be on bed rest or something?"

"Not…exactly."

"Define *exactly*."

"Dr. Yardley suggested that I cut back on my hours at the diner, that's all."

Savannah could almost see him silently connecting the dots.

"Is there something wrong with the baby?"

"The baby is fine."

Another heartbeat of silence followed.

"Are *you* all right?"

Something in Carter's voice suddenly made it difficult for Savannah to breathe.

"I'm fine," she managed to say. "My blood pressure was a little high at my last appointment, that's all."

"That's why you came here, isn't it?" Carter said slowly. "It wasn't just because of the apartment."

Savannah nodded reluctantly. "When I asked my boss if he would reduce my hours, he gave all of them to one of the other waitresses. If my next checkup goes well, I can ask him to put me back on the schedule."

"But won't the same thing happen again?"

"I'll be careful." Savannah rested one hand protectively against her abdomen.

"What caused this? Stress?" Carter obviously wasn't ready to let it go.

"Dr. Yardley said the same thing you did." Savannah summoned a smile. "That a change of scenery would be a good thing right now."

She wished she hadn't brought it up. She didn't want Carter to feel sorry for her.

What do you want him to feel? an inner voice teased.

Savannah elbowed it aside. Those kind of questions only borrowed trouble. Trouble she didn't need. In a week or so, she would be returning to Dallas and Carter would stay at the Colby Ranch with his family to wait for his father's return on Thanksgiving.

What was important now was to somehow help Carter see that he needed his family as much as they needed him.

"A change of scenery," Carter murmured, squinting at the horizon. "I could take you out to the lake to join up with the others. If you want me to."

Savannah struggled to hide her astonishment. And then looked down to hide her smile.

Thank You, Lord.

"I'd love to."

Savannah's initial confidence that she'd done the right thing began to erode with every bump and jolt that brought her into direct contact with Carter.

"Doing all right?" Carter glanced at her as the utility vehicle rolled slowly through the gully.

Define "all right," Savannah wanted to say. Because

she was pretty sure that this time, the increase in her blood pressure didn't have anything to do with the fact that she was on her feet too long.

"That's where Jack lives." Carter pointed to an older, two-story home nestled between two mature pecan trees. "He moved in a few months ago and he's been fixing it up. Maddie said that he and Keira plan to live there after they're married."

Another couple who'd decided to make their home on the ranch.

"When will that be?"

"I'm not sure." Carter's expression clouded. "They're…waiting."

Savannah didn't have to ask, she knew what they were waiting for. For Brian Wallace to return. For Belle to wake up.

Carter slowed down as they passed the gate and Savannah saw the neat stack of lumber piled next to the stone foundation.

"It doesn't look like he's finished yet."

His jaw tightened. "From what I hear, Gray's been helping him on the weekends."

Savannah had guessed that he and his older brother had never been close, but that didn't mean it would be easy to accept Jack's presence in his life.

"Look." Carter aimed the vehicle at a wisp of smoke rising in the distance. "I think we found them."

The tiny man-made lake winked like a sapphire, a welcome oasis in the center of the windswept grazing land. Reins dangling, the horses stood, ground-tied shoulder to shoulder under a bouquet of cottonwood trees. A group of people circled a roaring campfire.

As they got closer, Savannah realized that everyone was looking at them, not the flames.

Violet rose to her feet and waved her cowboy hat as Carter stopped several yards away. "Look who's here! You're just in time for hot chocolate."

Savannah started to get down from the vehicle, but Carter was there before her foot touched the ground. His hand on the small of her back, guiding her forward over the uneven ground.

Savannah saw Maddie and Violet exchange a knowing look that she was afraid had nothing to do with some mysterious "twin" connection. It reminded her of the matchmaking gleam in Libby's eye the day Carter had walked into the diner.

Maybe this hadn't been such a good idea. She was glad when Gray immediately intercepted Carter and steered him toward the group of men standing around a portable grill.

"Sit down." Keira scooted down the blanket to make room for her. Elise already had the thermos open and was pouring another cup of hot chocolate.

"Yeah, now we can eat!" Cory pumped the air with one small fist as he and Darcy raced toward the adults.

Savannah glanced at Violet. "What were you waiting for?"

A smile played at the corner of her lips. "You and Carter."

"But...how did you know we'd be here?"

"Because we told Carter that he should bring you out here for lunch," Maddie said. "And no matter how he feels, my brother always does the right thing."

Savannah knew that, but for some reason, a knot

formed in her throat. He hadn't run into her at the corral by accident.

This was what you wanted, wasn't it? For Carter to spend time with his family?

What difference did it make what had prompted his change of heart?

Because Savannah didn't want to admit she wanted Carter to seek out her company because he *enjoyed* it, not because his family had suggested it.

Not because he felt sorry for her.

"Did I say something wrong?" Maddie was looking at her closely now.

"No," Savannah said quickly. "It's just that Carter might have had other plans. I didn't come here to be a...burden."

To her astonishment, Violet nodded. "I know what you mean. When Landon showed up at the ranch and tried to help, I didn't want to accept it. I wanted to prove to him that I was capable. Confident. The kind of woman who could stand on her own two feet, like my mom. But you know what I learned? God puts people in our lives for a reason."

"Even when you think you don't want them there," Maddie added with a smile.

That's how Savannah had felt. At first. She hadn't wanted to admit that Carter been part of God's plan. And now she was afraid that he *wasn't*.

Maddie squeezed her hand. "I'm really glad you're here. You're good for my brother, Savannah."

Savannah froze, not sure she'd heard her correctly. "I don't know what you mean."

"Carter has always been a lone wolf. He separated himself from the rest of the family years ago. Dad was gone a lot and all of us dealt with that in different ways." Maddie sighed. "I think that's why Carter joined the marines right out of high school. I see how protective he is around you. It's obvious that he really cares."

"He—" *Cared about Rob.* "He's a good man."

"He's great with the kids, too," Violet said casually.

Too casually.

Savannah couldn't look at them now. It seemed that Violet and Maddie had a plan, too. To get her and Carter to spend time together.

"Is there anything I can do to help with lunch?" she asked.

Fortunately, Violet took the hint. She reached into the picnic basket. "Let's see what Lupita packed to go with the hamburgers Ty is grilling. She had Ricardo drop the food off before we got here and then they were going to visit Mom at the Ranchland Manor for a few hours."

"How is she doing?" Savannah asked tentatively.

"No change," Violet whispered. "But we're waiting. And praying."

Savannah impulsively reached for her hand. "Sometimes that doesn't seem like enough…but it's everything."

Violet's eyes misted over but strangely enough, she smiled at Maddie.

"Would you like to go to church with us tomorrow morning, Savannah?" Maddie asked unexpectedly. "The service starts at ten."

"I'd like that."

"Great. There's so many of us, we carpool, so meet us in front of the house at eight-thirty."

Savannah's gaze drifted to Carter. He knelt on the

ground next to Cory, eye to eye, listening intently to something the little boy was telling him.

He would be a good dad, she thought.

She wanted to ask if Carter would be going with them to church. But Savannah was afraid she already knew the answer to that question.

"Thanks for your help, Carter." Ty wiped the beads of sweat from his brow with the back of his hand. "It's always good to have an extra set of hands."

"No problem." Even though Carter had a hunch that his sister's fiancé could manage just fine on his own. Ty Garland had pulled him aside when they'd returned from the trail ride and asked if he would take a look at one of the four-wheelers that was being, in Ty's words, "a little cranky." All part of a plot designed to make him feel useful.

Not that Carter cared. Because it also kept his thoughts focused on a project and not on Savannah. Kind of.

When she'd admitted that the doctor had some health concerns, Carter had gone cold, struck by a fear that hadn't gripped him since the day he'd run toward the smoking convoy. During lunch, Carter had found himself watching her closely, looking for telltale signs of fatigue.

He couldn't imagine her going back to Dallas alone. Who would watch out for her?

God, please keep Savannah and the baby safe.

The prayer slipped out before Carter even recognized it for what it was. Something that used to come as easily as taking his next breath.

"Here's the wrench you needed." Ty waved it in front of his face.

"Thanks." Carter reached for it and saw Savannah walking back to the cottage from the main house. The women had decided to watch a movie together in the family room, an announcement that sent the men scattering like someone had dropped a stick of dynamite in the chicken coop.

Carter was the first one out the door, although he was glad Maddie and Violet had taken Savannah under their wing. He'd heard the three of them laughing about something right before Ty had pulled him aside.

Ty rocked back on his heels. "I know you're the mechanic, but I think it might work better if you use the wrench to tighten the bolt instead of *staring* it on."

Carter tore his gaze away from Savannah. "I was thinking," he muttered.

"Yeah." Ty's lips twitched. "I could see that."

Carter used the wrench with a little more force than was necessary. "You're good to go."

"I have to go into town and pick up a few things before the feed store closes," Ty was saying. "Want to ride along?"

Carter shot him a wry look. "How much is Maddie paying you to babysit?"

Ty grinned, not even pretending he didn't know what Carter was talking about. "I'm doing it for free, although she might have said something about apple pie."

"That's what I thought. I'll see you later."

"Maddie worries about you."

Carter had started to walk away but Ty's comment stopped him in his tracks.

"I'm a big boy." *A marine,* Carter wanted to add.

"You're also her baby brother."

"*Half* brother." Carter regretted the words as soon as they slipped past his lips. Regretted even more the look of disappointment that flashed across Ty's face.

"Does that change the way you feel about her?" he said evenly.

If they were going to talk about feelings, Carter was out of here.

"I don't know what Maddie's told you about our father, but he raised us to be independent." A quality that had made Brian Wallace's life easier. "The four of us haven't exactly been what you'd call close over the past few years."

"Maddie wants that to change." The look in the ranch foreman's eyes warned Carter to make sure he was willing to do his part to make that happen.

"I'm not used to having her and Gray fuss over me."

"I get that," Ty said. "It took me a while to realize how important family is. I almost lost Darcy because of it."

"I know Maddie wants us to be one big happy family, but it's a little difficult under the circumstances, don't you think?"

"If this isn't the time when you need family, I don't know what is," Ty shot back as he hopped into the cab of his pickup. "I don't want you to make the same mistakes I did. When a man finds something precious, he holds on to it."

An image of Savannah's face rose in Carter's mind. But she wasn't his to hold on to.

"Where does this go?" Carter hoisted the old metal toolbox up in the air.

"Why don't you put it the shed?"

Carter thought he heard Ty laugh as the window rolled up. Strange, considering how serious the guy had been a minute ago.

What did they want from him?

Grabbing the toolbox, Carter headed toward the storage shed behind the barn.

And almost tripped over the woman sitting cross-legged on the floor.

Chapter Thirteen

Savannah had been so lost in thought she hadn't heard the door open. But light suddenly spilled in and there was Carter, looming above her.

"What are you doing here?"

Savannah could have asked him the same thing. The last she knew, he and Ty had been walking toward the barn.

"Darcy is helping Lupita make cookies so I volunteered to check on the kittens." On cue, a tiny gray-and-white kitten darted from the shadows and attacked the laces on Carter's boot.

"Are you going to adopt one?" He scooped up the ball of fluff, his large hand forming a safe cradle. A moment later, the tiny body began to vibrate with a loud, rumbling purr.

"I can't." Savannah picked up the kitten's littermate as it rubbed against her ankle. "My next apartment might not allow pets."

The reminder that her stay was temporary cast a shadow over Savannah's heart. A sign she was getting too comfortable at the Colby Ranch.

"There's no rush," Carter said quietly.

Maddie and Violet had said the same thing when Savannah had asked if she could use the computer in Belle's office to check for new apartment listings in Dallas.

Savannah didn't have the heart to tell Carter's sisters that the reason they wanted her to stay was the very reason why she had to leave.

"I saw Ty leave a few minutes ago." As soon as Savannah said the words, she hoped the dim light in the shed would conceal her blush. Nothing like telling the man she'd been keeping tabs on him!

"He had to run a few errands after I fixed the four-wheeler."

"Maybe I should talk to Ty," Savannah said darkly. "Your sisters won't let me set foot in the kitchen unless I want something to eat—and then they insist I sit at the table while they make it." Even something as simple as microwave popcorn.

"Mmm." Carter bent down and set the kitten on the floor, his innocent expression instantly setting off an internal alarm.

"Did you have something to do with that?"

"I *might* have said your doctor recommended that you take it easy."

And he didn't look the least bit apologetic.

"I'm not made out of glass."

"You're a guest here, remember?" he murmured.

"How can I forget? You keep reminding me—and now everyone else."

Carter's laughter rolled over her. "Someone has to look out for you."

Savannah felt tears scald the back of her eyes and

she buried her face in the kitten's downy fur before Carter could notice.

Rob had said the same thing. Savannah wanted to think she was a different person than she'd been seven months ago. That girl had been naive. Lonely. Susceptible to the charms of a man who'd used her vulnerability to his advantage.

Carter had never been anything other than straightforward with her from the first time they'd met. He'd told her the truth about what had prompted his invitation to stay at the ranch. She knew he was only following through on the promise he'd made to Rob.

She knew that every time Carter looked at her, he saw his best friend's widow.

The growing realization that she wanted him to see her as *more* than that left Savannah reeling. She leaned against the post before her knees gave way.

"It's okay to accept help, you know. You don't have to go through this alone." Carter reached out and tucked a strand of hair behind her ear. His fingertips paused to linger on the sensitive spot below Savannah's jaw, where her pulse had begun to jump in time with the erratic rhythm of her heart.

His cobalt-blue eyes searched her face and a frown settled between his brows, almost as if he were seeing her—really seeing her—for the first time.

"Savannah—"

A low, mournful wail erupted behind them.

Savannah was already following the sound to the back of the shed. "I think one of the kittens got tangled in something."

Carter caught her hand as she reached for the canvas tarp thrown over an old piece of farm equipment.

"What did I just say?" He pulled the cover off and knelt down. Savannah hovered in the wings, watching as he disappeared beneath the tire.

"Are you pulling rank again?"

"Yes," came the muffled response. Carter extracted the kitten and deposited it next to its brothers and sisters, perched like a row of knickknacks on a low wooden shelf to watch the show.

"I don't believe it," Savannah huffed.

"Neither do I." Carter let out a low whistle. "Do you know what this is?"

Savannah followed his gaze to the vehicle that, like the kitten, had been trapped under the dusty tarp.

"A truck?"

"Not just a truck." Carter prowled around the front, his palm following every curve and line. "It's a '67 Chevy."

"Um, that sounds like a truck to me."

Carter's husky laugh sent the kittens scrambling for cover. If Savannah were smart, she would follow their lead.

"It *is* a truck. A classic." His enthusiasm was so contagious, Savannah couldn't help but smile as she ventured closer for a better look. "Who put you out to pasture?" Carter gave the truck's chrome fender an affectionate pat.

"Someone who wanted to *drive* a truck instead of push it?"

Savannah couldn't believe she was actually teasing him.

Carter flashed a boyish grin and patted the door. "Let's take a look at her."

"How do you know it's a *her?*"

"Too pretty not to be."

Carter threw open the doors to let in more light and the wind snaked inside the shed. Savannah shivered. Without a word, he stripped off his sheepskin-lined coat and dropped it over her shoulders. The heat from his body wrapped around her like an embrace. She caught her breath, trapping the tangy scent of his cologne in her lungs.

Carter slid into the driver's seat. He took a quick inventory of the interior, checking the glove box and running his hand along the underside of the seats.

Savannah spotted a set of keys hanging from a nail near the door. "Here. Try one of these."

The truck shuddered to life. And promptly died.

Which did nothing to dim Carter's enthusiasm.

"What's wrong with it?"

"I'm not sure yet," he murmured.

"Is that easy to fix?"

Carter grinned. "Easy, no. Possible, yes."

"I thought I heard someone in here." Jack's shadow blocked the afternoon sunlight streaming into the shed. "Hey, Savannah…and Carter."

"He was helping Ty. And I was visiting Darcy's kittens," Savannah explained quickly. She didn't want anyone to get the impression that she was looking for anything more than a place to stay for a few weeks.

"Uh-huh." Jack sauntered into the shed to take a closer look at what had caught their attention. "I forgot that thing was here."

Carter twisted around, a look of patent disbelief on his handsome face. "You *forgot?*" he echoed.

"It belonged to James Crawford. I remember he drove it in the Fourth of July parade every summer.

It started to have issues so he must have put it out to pasture, so to speak."

"And you left it here."

Jack shrugged. "Ty and I have enough old junk to keep running around this place."

"Old junk?" Carter mouthed the words as if he couldn't bear to say them out loud.

"You're welcome to try—" Carter had the hood up before Jack completed the sentence. He winked at Savannah and dug a light bulb from a drawer in the storage cabinet. "The sun is going down. You might need this if you're out here all night."

Savannah noticed that Carter didn't contradict him.

"What's going on?" Maddie stood in the doorway. She'd changed out of her casual riding clothes into a long skirt, tall boots and a form-fitting suede jacket.

"Carter found a truck to play with," Jack quipped.

Maddie took a step forward, eyed the skeins of cobwebs hanging from the ceiling and stopped just inside the door.

"Violet and I are driving into town for a few hours to visit Belle. Pastor Jeb offered to meet us there so we can all pray for her. Do you want to come along?"

"Sure. 'Where two or more are gathered in my name,'" Jack quoted softly, a verse familiar to Savannah. "I'll meet you out front in a few minutes."

"Great. I'm going to track down Gray and ask him, too." Maddie lingered in the doorway. "Do you want to come with us, Carter?"

Carter's head snapped up. "No, thanks."

An awkward silence descended. Jack looked as if he wanted to say more, but the set of Carter's jaw must have discouraged him.

It discouraged Savannah, too.

Because even though Carter had claimed she didn't have to go through difficult times alone, it was clear he wasn't willing to take his own advice.

The sun had set by the time Carter returned to the house. He'd heard the slam of a car door signifying his siblings return over an hour ago. By now, the family would be through eating supper and lined up on the sofa in the family room, watching football.

He shrugged off his jacket and padded down the hall. An inner voice taunted that it was pointless to check his email again but Carter ignored it.

They needed answers, and with Belle not showing any signs of regaining consciousness, there was only one person who could answer them. His father.

Now if only he could make it to the office before Darcy spotted him…

Carter's hand froze on the knob as he pushed the door open. Because he hadn't bypassed game time in the family room, he'd stumbled into some kind of family summit.

Which explained why he hadn't been invited.

Guilt reared up to pinch his conscience. Maybe because they'd asked him to accompany them to Ranchland Manor only a few hours ago and he'd turned them down flat?

Maddie and Violet sat in the window seat overlooking the courtyard while Gray and Jack paced the length of the room like a pair of caged mountain lions.

Conversation skidded to a halt when they spotted him.

"Sorry." Carter started to back up. "I didn't mean to intrude."

Gray cast an impatient glance his way. "You aren't intruding. We were waiting for you."

Carter's emotions shifted into high alert, the same way they had in Afghanistan when there'd been an imminent threat to the soldiers on base.

"What's going on?"

"Maybe you should shut the door," Jack suggested, his voice tight.

Carter closed the door and looked at Gray.

"Landon got here about an hour ago. I'd asked him to stop by the apartment and pick up my mail before he left Fort Worth."

For the first time, Carter noticed the envelope in Gray's hand.

"Dad?" Carter felt his lips form the word but he wasn't sure if he'd said it out loud.

"No." Gray hesitated, glanced at Jack. "A few months ago, Jack and I decided to have our DNA tested, to see if Patty Earl was telling the truth about Joe being our biological father."

Something else no one had bothered to mention until now.

"Was it necessary for both of you to be tested?"

"No, that was our decision," Gray said.

Another indication that the men had not only accepted each other, but were forming the same strong bond that Maddie and Violet had since they'd discovered each other.

"What did you find out?"

The brackets on either side of Jack's mouth deepened. "We haven't opened the results yet."

Carter didn't have to ask why. At no time since his arrival had Jack and Gray looked more alike than they did at this moment, when they had the answer to a pivotal piece of their past literally at their fingertips.

"You should open them when you're ready," Violet finally said.

Maddie rose to her feet and took both men by the hand. "A piece of paper doesn't change anything. It's not going to erase the memories we have of growing up together. Or the ones we've made over the past few months."

Gray stared down at the envelope with the same intensity Carter had seen on a bomb tech's face. Wondering what kind of shape he'd be in if he made the wrong call.

"There's nothing saying you have to open it now," Carter heard himself say. "Why don't you give it a few days?"

"Carter is right," Maddie said, stunning him once again.

Gray looked at Jack. "What do you think?"

"Yeah." Jack plowed his fingers through his hair. "I wasn't expecting the results to come back this soon. I wouldn't mind some more time to think about it."

"And pray about it," Maddie added.

"Why don't we do that right now?" Violet stood up and stretched out a hand to Gray.

Carter felt that familiar tightening in his chest as both sets of twins clasped hands and formed a tight circle. It wasn't just the similarities in their looks that made him feel like an outsider.

For a split second, Gray's eyes met his and Carter saw the question there.

Carter responded with a shake of his head.

And this time when he backed toward the door, no one stopped him.

Chapter Fourteen

"You're going to love Grasslands Community Church!" Maddie linked her arm through Savannah's as they walked to the car. "It's small and everyone knows everyone's name, so don't be surprised if they ask you a million questions. It's not because they're nosy—"

"Sure it is." Ty winked at Savannah as he opened the door of the backseat and waited for her to buckle up next to Darcy.

Savannah glanced out the rear window as Ty's pickup cruised down the driveway, but there was no sign of Carter. When Lupita fussed about him missing breakfast, Maddie and Gray had exchanged a solemn look but didn't comment.

Savannah didn't know if it was because he hadn't accompanied the family to the convalescent center or if something else had happened.

Right before she'd gone to bed, she'd heard a door snap shut. When she'd peeked through the curtain, she'd seen a man sitting on the bench in the courtyard. Even in the dark, she'd recognized Carter's silhouette.

It had taken all Savannah's strength not to join him.

She'd prayed for him instead. Prayed that Carter would forgive his father for keeping secrets and let God heal whatever had caused the wounds in his soul.

The disappointment on Maddie's face when he'd refused to accompany the family to the convalescent center to visit Belle continued to weigh on Savannah's mind. While Gray and Maddie had made peace with the fact that Belle was their mother, to Carter she was a reminder that Brian Wallace had kept things from his family.

And Savannah knew firsthand just how painful secrets could be….

"That's the Colby farm stand." Maddie pointed to a one-story concrete building on Main Street. "I'm sure Violet would love to give you a tour. I've been helping out behind the counter once in a while."

"I wouldn't mind—"

"We're covered, Savannah." Maddie tossed a smile over her shoulder.

Savannah gave in. For now. But there had to be some way she could feel useful without breaking Dr. Yardley's orders—or Carter's.

They passed a small town green, and Savannah spotted the church up ahead. With its white clapboard siding and slender steeple, it looked like a picture on the front of a postcard. Ty stopped by the doors to let them out.

As Savannah slid out of the backseat, she saw Violet hurrying toward them. The man at her side had no trouble keeping up with her, and Savannah saw a few heads turn in their direction.

She wasn't surprised. Violet and Landon Derringer

made a striking couple. She'd met him briefly when he'd arrived the night before, just minutes before the rest of the family returned from visiting Belle Colby.

A reunion where, once again, Carter had been noticeably absent.

"Come on. We'll introduce you to Pastor Jeb." Violet tucked her arm through Savannah's as they reached the white paneled door.

People paused to greet her, and Savannah wondered what it would be like to live in a town like Grasslands. To have people know your name.

This was what she wanted for her child. A place to belong.

Violet waved at a tall, slender man standing just outside the doors leading into the sanctuary.

The minister was younger than Savannah expected, only in his late twenties or early thirties. A shock of russet hair matched the spray of freckles across his nose.

He smiled at Violet and navigated through the clusters of people until he reached their side.

"Pastor Jeb, this is Savannah Blackmore, my brother Carter's friend. She's staying at the ranch for a while."

Savannah hoped the pastor wouldn't read more into the "Carter's friend" description. She didn't want people to get the wrong impression about them.

Behind a pair of horn-rimmed glasses, the pastor's eyes were as welcoming as the church he served. "I'm glad you joined us for worship this morning, Savannah."

Two teen girls rushed over. "Did you bring something for the bake sale, Violet?"

"I brought one of Lupita's confections." Violet

grinned. "How are things going in the kitchen? Do you need some help?"

"Yes!"

"I'll meet you in the sanctuary in a few minutes." Laughing, Violet allowed the girls to tow her down the hallway.

"Violet and Landon are really involved in Teen Scene, our youth ministry," Maddie said. "Landon's foundation funded a remodeling project last summer and the number of kids showing up on the weekends has doubled since then."

"That's a good thing, because we're going to need their help for the harvest dinner next weekend." Jeb plucked at his tie in a halfhearted attempt to straighten it that wasn't quite successful.

Savannah glanced at Maddie. "Harvest dinner?"

"Grasslands Community is putting it on, but the whole town is invited. It's a chance to come together and publicly thank God for the blessings He's given us. The whole family will be volunteering in some capacity…." Maddie's smile slipped a notch. "Well, most of us."

With a sinking feeling, Savannah guessed she was talking about Carter. "I'd like to help, too, if you're looking for volunteers."

"Always." Jeb smiled. "I'll introduce you to Sadie Johnson, the church secretary. She knows more about what goes on around here than I—"

A petite woman wearing a shapeless green cardigan and ankle-length khaki skirt suddenly materialized beside them.

"Oh, good, there you are! Sadie, this is Savannah Blackmore." Jeb wrestled his tie into place again.

"She's staying at the Colby Ranch and would like to help with the harvest dinner."

A pair of bright green eyes blinked at Savannah behind oversize glasses. "It's nice to meet you," she murmured.

"Sadie's been handling most of the details so she can fill you in after the service," Jeb went on. "I don't know what I did without her."

Savannah was amazed to see twin swatches of color appear in the secretary's cheeks. Jeb Miller, however, seemed oblivious as he nodded at the usher who was waving a bulletin at them.

"I guess that's my cue." The pastor grinned, his tie flapping like a windsock as he loped away.

Savannah realized the prelude had started, beckoning the congregation inside the sanctuary. She followed Maddie down the center aisle to a pew near the front of the church where the rest of the family slid down to make room for them.

A feeling of peace swept over Savannah and she bowed her head.

God, thank You for bringing me here. Thank You for your presence. For the hospitality that Violet and Maddie have shown me…

The pew creaked as someone sat down beside her.

Savannah opened her eyes and slid a sideways glance at the latecomer. "Good morn—"

The whispered greeting died as she found herself staring into a pair of deep blue eyes.

The expression on Savannah's face told Carter that she hadn't expected to see him in church.

Well, he was a little shocked himself. He hadn't

planned to attend the service. The last time he'd attended church with his siblings was a Christmas Eve service shortly before he'd joined the marines. Their dad had promised to meet them there, but another emergency had come up and he'd missed it.

"Not everyone wants to be here this morning."

Carter's head jerked up as he heard someone voice his thoughts out loud.

The pastor, Jeb Miller, stood behind a wooden pulpit, Bible in hand.

"Some of you are worn out. Discouraged. Seeking. Maybe you've been running away from God. Maybe you're running to Him. But God brought you here—to this place—for a reason this morning. I trust that He'll reveal it to you."

Carter felt the words pierce his soul. He shifted in his seat, suddenly uncomfortable in a place he had once found comfort.

Savannah paged through the hymnal to the song listed in the bulletin. Her clear alto mingled with the other voices and Carter could tell she'd not only memorized the words, she believed them.

Maddie cleared her throat. The sparkle in her eyes told Carter she knew exactly where his thoughts had drifted.

He *knew* he should have stayed home.

When the song ended, Pastor Jeb tucked his glasses in the front pocket of his shirt and opened up the worn Bible.

"Praise the Lord. Praise God our Savior..." His gaze lifted. Swept over the congregation. "Some of you might be wondering how that's even possible. Maybe you've been experiencing health problems. Maybe

you've lost a loved one. Maybe you have to force yourself to get out of bed because even though the sun is shining, life seems…dark. You have doubts. Questions. Circumstances that make you wonder what there is to be thankful for.

"The rest of the verse gives us the answer." Jeb's smile encompassed the people around him. "*He saves us. He carries us.* No matter what we're going through, these are the things we can hold on to. God adopted us into His family—He saved us—and He'll never leave us alone…."

Carter felt beads of sweat pop out on his forehead.

Not here. Not now.

The flashbacks swept in without warning, like a flash flood. Something as ordinary as a word—or a sound—could release the images stored in his memory.

Carter's hands fisted at his sides. This was a part of *his* past he couldn't share with anyone. He swallowed the bile that rose in his throat, ready to bolt.

A hand covered his. Held him in place.

Anchored him.

His heartbeat began to even out and the haze lifted as Savannah's fingers twined with his.

Carter was dimly aware that the message was over and Pastor Jeb was closing in prayer.

He bowed his head, wondering how he'd drifted so far from his faith. Because it hadn't occurred to Carter that when he'd carried the wounded soldiers to safety, one by one, bullets striking the sand all around him, God had been carrying *him*.

Savannah rose to her feet, unable to look at Carter. What had she been thinking?

He had never given any indication that he wanted her sympathy. Or her friendship.

But something Pastor Jeb said must have struck a nerve. She'd heard the subtle change in his breathing, saw his hands clench at his sides. Sensed he was about to leave.

She hadn't thought—she'd simply…acted. And now that the moment had passed, Savannah was going to have to face Carter again, afraid he would question why she'd taken his hand.

Afraid of what her answer would be.

"Got a second, Carter?" she heard Gray say.

Savannah quickly made her escape. Sadie Johnson was waiting for her in the hallway.

"Do you need to think about it for a few days, or would you like to sign up to help with the harvest dinner now—"

"Now would be *great*."

Sadie gave her a curious look but nodded. "Okay. Follow me."

Savannah was relieved when the secretary bypassed the crowd of people milling in the hallway and turned down a narrow corridor to a small office tucked in the back of the church. Plants lined the windowsill and a large picture of Jesus, reaching for a lost lamb, hung on the wall.

"Is there a particular area where you'd like to serve?" Sadie handed her a clipboard and pen. "We need people on the setup crew and the hospitality team. I'm in charge of making the meal that night so I'll be doing a lot of the prep work that day."

"I worked at a diner, so I know my way around a kitchen. I'm not supposed to be on my feet for long periods of time, but if you give me a knife and a cutting board, I'm in."

Sadie paused to straighten a stack of papers on the desk. "This is Je—*Pastor Miller's*—way of filing things."

Savannah couldn't help but notice the secretary's tone sounded more affectionate than exasperated. She glanced at Sadie's left hand. No wedding or engagement ring.

"Do you have family in the area? Is that why you moved to Grasslands?"

Savannah had been making conversation, but Sadie shrank back as if she'd aimed a bright light in her eyes.

"Here's the sign-up sheet." She thrust a piece of paper at Savannah. "The youths are sponsoring a bake sale so I better make sure the kitchen is still in one piece."

"Sadie." Savannah took a deep breath. "I'm sorry—I didn't mean to be nosy when I asked about your family."

Sadie's shoulders hunched and her chin disappeared into the collar of her baggy sweater, reminding Savannah of a turtle pulling into its shell.

"It's okay," she murmured. "I don't like to talk about the past, is all. I'm in Grasslands because this is where God wants me to be."

Savannah felt an instant kinship with the woman.

"I understand." She really did. "I'm here to help. With...anything."

For a moment, Sadie didn't respond. And then her lips curved in a shy smile.

"I can give you a quick tour of the kitchen now, if you have a few extra minutes," she offered.

Savannah smiled back. "I'd like that."

A few extra minutes were *exactly* what she needed. To get to know Sadie better.

And to avoid Carter.

Even though something told her it would take a lot more time than that to sort through the feelings he stirred inside her.

Chapter Fifteen

Ten steps away from freedom.

Carter maneuvered around the obstacles in his path—a gray-haired lady holding a plate of brownies, a young mother pushing a stroller roughly the size of an SUV, a teenager holding up a coffee can filled with donations—and kept his gaze trained on the target.

The front door of the church.

"Carter Wallace." Pastor Jeb's lanky frame suddenly blocked his escape route. "I hoped I'd get an opportunity to talk to you after the service. You've been on my prayer list the past few weeks."

"Thank you, Pastor." Carter dug deep and scraped up a smile. The red-haired preacher reminded Carter of one of the young chaplains he'd met overseas. Compassionate. Wise.

Dangerous.

The pastor's message had stripped away Carter's emotional armor, left him feeling vulnerable and exposed. And running for cover.

He took a quick surveillance of his surroundings,

searching for the people he'd been trying to get away from five seconds ago. His family.

But now, when he could have used them as a buffer—or a shield—they were nowhere in sight.

"Everyone is checking out the bake sale in the youth wing." Pastor Jeb grinned, as if he'd read Carter's thoughts.

Dangerous, no doubt about it.

Carter weighed his options. Hang out with the preacher or join the people chatting in the fellowship hall.

"I'll wait here." Or outside. In the parking lot.

"Come with me." The pastor came up with another idea. "If you've got a few minutes, I'll show you what your sister's been up to."

"Knowing Maddie, it could be anything," Carter said as he fell into step with Jeb.

The pastor slid a sideways look at him. "I was talking about Violet. She and Landon have been working on Teen Scene, our youth program, for the last few months."

When was he going to start thinking of Violet as family?

It should have been easy, given the fact that she and Maddie were identical twins. There were similarities in their personalities, too. Jack Colby, on the other hand… The guy eyed him like he would a bronco trapped in a chute, as cautious about Carter as Carter was about him.

They turned down a narrow corridor that connected the sanctuary to another building.

"Landon funded the repairs so we could fix up this area for the teenagers after it was vandalized a few months ago. Every Friday and Saturday night, adult volunteers supervise the activities. Game nights. Pizza parties. You name it, we've had it." Jeb opened the door. "The kids congregate here after the Sunday morning services—"

The gym was empty.

"Well, they *usually* congregate here after the Sunday morning service," he said ruefully. "I guess it's a good sign they're all helping with the bake sale."

A door at the far end of the gym swung open and an adolescent boy with a shock of wheat-colored hair slipped inside.

"Tommy?" Jeb waved to get his attention. "Where is everyone?"

"The back parking lot. Jairo can't get his car started."

"Again?" Jeb chuckled. "I think he pushes that thing more than he drives it."

"I can take a look," Carter offered. "No one in my family seems to be in a big hurry to leave."

No one except him, anyway.

Tommy sidled closer. "You fix cars?"

"He can fix anything, kid." Gray had walked up behind them. "Cars. Armored trucks. Tanks."

Tommy's gaze swung back to Carter. *"Tanks?"*

"Sometimes."

"Sometimes." Gray cuffed Carter on the back of the head. "They give you a medal for modesty?" He lowered his voice to a conspiratorial whisper. "My kid brother can get a car without an engine to start."

"Cool!"

Carter rolled his eyes. "He's exaggerating."

"I hope you can fix it. Jairo is supposed to give me a ride home," Tommy added with a mischievous grin.

"You fix Jairo's car and you'll be a hero around these parts," Jeb said.

Carter flinched. There was that word again.

He followed Tommy to the parking lot, where a group of teenage boys circled a rusty pickup like mourners at a graveside service.

"This guy—Carter—he's going to take a look at the engine, Jairo," Tommy informed everyone breathlessly. "He fixes armored trucks. And tanks."

A lanky Hispanic boy stepped away from the vehicle, eyeing Carter with a mixture of skepticism and hope.

"I've got a few things to check on before I head over to Ranchland Manor," Jeb said. "Do you mind—"

"We're good." Carter was already bending down to take a look inside the engine. The boys crowded around him, blocking the light.

Ten minutes later, the engine coughed once and came back to life.

"That should do it." Carter wiped his greasy hands on a bandana one of the kids had tossed at him.

Savannah wouldn't want to hold his hand now....

Carter gritted his teeth in an attempt to channel his thoughts down a safer path.

A futile attempt, it seemed, because questions ricocheted inside his head.

Why *had* Savannah taken his hand? How had she known it was exactly what he'd needed?

"There you are."

Carter stiffened as a familiar face appeared in his

line of vision. A familiar face whose brown eyes were shaded by the brim of a cowboy hat.

Jack.

"Maddie and Violet are going to help Sadie clean up from the bake sale and then we decided to stop over to Ranchland Manor."

To see Belle. Fortunately, Jack didn't ask if he wanted to go along.

"Okay. No problem."

"Can you give Savannah a ride back to the ranch?"

The two of them. Alone in the car on the drive back to the ranch.

Now *that* was a problem.

Savannah crumpled up the empty wrapper and licked a smudge of chocolate frosting from her finger as she left the fellowship hall to look for Maddie and Ty.

She'd stopped by the bake sale for a few minutes and ended up buying a piece of cake from one of the teenagers. Violet had been scurrying around the kitchen, helping Sadie, and Savannah had caught a glimpse of Keira striding down the hall, but at some point she'd lost track of the couple she'd ridden with.

She saw an open door halfway down the hall and slipped inside to look for a wastebasket.

Music drifted from tiny speakers mounted in the corners of the ceiling. Checkered curtains trimmed the windows. A padded rocking chair was stationed at the foot of a rainbow stenciled on one bright yellow wall.

The church nursery.

On their own volition, Savannah's feet carried her forward. She traced a finger along the rail of a wooden crib.

"It's amazing, isn't it? The smaller they are, the more stuff they seem to need."

Savannah turned at the sound of the pastor's voice behind her.

"I guess so." Savannah was three months away from her due date and hadn't set up a nursery yet. She had to find an apartment. Soon. Had to paint the walls and buy a crib. No matter what Maddie and Violet said, she couldn't take advantage of their hospitality much longer.

"We've got a wonderful group of volunteers to staff the nursery," Jeb said. "Your baby will be in good hands."

It was too dangerous to imagine being part of Jeb's congregation. Part of the community.

"I'm not staying in Grasslands very long."

"Oh? Violet made it sound like—" Jeb shook his head. "Never mind."

Savannah could only guess what Violet had made it sound like!

"I don't want to be a burden on the family."

"I know the Colbys pretty well," Jeb said easily. "I doubt they see it that way."

Did Carter?

That's what Savannah wasn't sure about.

Jeb turned off the CD player and for the first time, Savannah noticed the ring of keys dangling from his fingers. It suddenly occurred to her that while she'd been lingering in the nursery, the pastor was ready to leave.

"I'm sorry," Savannah stammered. "I didn't mean to keep you from locking up." Not to mention that

Maddie and Ty were probably wondering what had happened to her.

"Don't apologize. I never want to miss out on a divine appointment." Jeb smiled. "God brings people together for a reason."

And hopefully, sometimes He kept them apart, Savannah thought as she made her way back to the foyer.

She pulled up short when she saw Carter prowling back and forth in front of the door as if he were waiting for someone.

The blue eyes drew a bead on her instead.

Heat swept into Savannah's cheeks even though she couldn't tell what he was thinking.

"Have you seen Maddie?"

"They decided to stop at Ranchland Manor and Jack asked if I'd take you back to the ranch. So I guess it's just you and me."

Savannah swallowed hard.

He'd been waiting for someone, all right.

Her.

Savannah kept her head down as Carter escorted her to the car.

It was clear he was going to have to have a little talk with Maddie and Violet. Because this arrangement had their matchmaking fingerprints all over it.

Carter opened the passenger-side door for Savannah and went around to the other side. When he got in, she was trying to wrangle the seat belt into place.

"Need some help?" Carter automatically reached for the buckle and ended up holding Savannah's hand instead.

"Sorry—"

"—Sorry."

The words bumped together and the interior of the vehicle seemed to shrink in size, narrowing his focus to a pair of stunning green eyes.

As far as casual touches went, Carter had had more contact with a woman in the checkout line at the grocery store, but suddenly he found it difficult to breathe.

"Let's try that again." His voice was as uneven as his pulse. "The buckle," he added, just for clarification.

Savannah ducked her head as Carter snapped the metal clip into place but even though she wasn't looking at him, a new awareness shimmered between them, as warm and real as the sunlight streaming through the windshield.

"Thank you." Savannah's sigh fractured the silence. "Some of the little things I've always done without a second thought are getting more complicated."

"I know what you mean." Carter spoke without thinking and then tried to cover the words with a laugh.

"Do they happen…often?" she asked softly.

Carter's gut clenched. No one in his family had questioned him about the flashbacks, although they probably wondered why he sometimes walked out of the room without a word of explanation.

"Often enough," he heard himself say.

"What—" Savannah hesitated "—helps you get through it?"

"If I can get away by myself for a while." Solitude didn't prevent a battering from the internal storm but at least when he was alone, his pride remained intact.

"Oh." Savannah's troubled gaze dropped to his hand and a hint of pink stole into her cheeks.

Carter suddenly had another flashback. Savannah

taking his hand during the worship service, holding the darkness at bay.

That wasn't the way it was supposed to work.

He was supposed to be there for her, not the other way around. Keeping the promise he'd made to Rob, not fighting a growing attraction to the woman his friend had left behind.

Maybe a few hours spent tinkering with the engine of the Chevy would put things back in perspective.

He understood the way an engine worked. Knew exactly what to do when it didn't.

It was too bad life wasn't that simple.

He was about to put the car in gear when his cell began to ring. He glanced at the tiny screen and saw Maddie's name and number pop up. Anchoring the phone between his shoulder and his ear, he adjusted the rearview mirror.

"What's up?"

"Are you still at the church?" Maddie said breathlessly.

"Just leaving."

"I left my bag in the sanctuary. Can you check—"

"Sure." Carter swallowed a sigh.

"—and bring it to the convalescent home? We're there now with Belle."

Carter's hands gripped the wheel.

"Carter? Are you still there?"

"Yes."

"Thanks." Maddie seemed to think his response covered all the questions. "Belle is in room one-fourteen. We'll see you in a few minutes. Bye."

Carter heard a click in his ear. "Maddie left her purse."

"I'll get it." Savannah reached for the buckle on her seat belt.

"Don't take this the wrong way—but I can move faster than you."

"Is there a *right* way to take that?" Savannah muttered.

Carter grinned, feeling some of the tension between them ease.

When he entered the church, he saw a slight young woman about Savannah's age sitting in the front pew, her head bowed. He would have tried to sneak in, locate the missing purse and sneak back out, but the floor creaked beneath his foot.

Her entire body jerked at the sound and she twisted around. The church secretary. Sarah? No. Sadie, that was it.

"Sorry." *Whoa.* Carter backed up when he saw the tears rolling down her cheeks. "I didn't mean to startle you. My sister left her purse in here."

"It's on the table."

Carter looked to his left and recognized Maddie's purse. Of course it had to be *pink.* If the guys in his unit saw him now, he'd never hear the end of it.

He stuffed it under his arm, took a step toward the door and hesitated.

"Is something wrong? Do you want me to get Pastor Jeb?"

"No!" The word ricocheted around the room. "I mean, thank you—but that's not necessary. I'm…fine."

Yeah. There seemed to be a lot of that going around, Carter thought grimly. But he sensed that pushing the issue would only make the woman more uncomfortable.

He retraced his steps back to the car. Fortunately,

Ranchland Manor was only a few blocks from the church.

"Maddie should be waiting by the door," Carter said as he pulled into the parking lot.

Except that she wasn't.

Five minutes ticked by and there was no sign of her or anyone else in the family.

Reluctantly, Carter parked the car and turned the key in the ignition, the engine dying along with the hope that Maddie was going to show up.

"I'll go inside and track her down."

To Carter's amazement, Savannah unbuckled her seat belt.

"I'm coming with you."

A nurse's assistant wearing bright yellow scrubs smiled at Savannah as she and Carter walked up to the desk.

"Can I help you?"

"We're waiting for my sister," Carter said.

"She might be in the family lounge. It's the second door on the left."

"Thank you." Carter was already on his way down the hall, obviously in a hurry to complete his mission.

"There's no one here." Frustration leached into his voice.

"Do you know what room they're in?"

He gave a reluctant nod. "One-fourteen."

Savannah didn't have to work to keep up with Carter as they walked down the hall.

"This is it." Carter made no move to go inside.

The door was open a crack but Savannah couldn't

hear the sound of voices. She knocked on the door and then gingerly pushed it open.

"They aren't here, either. Maybe they're getting a cup of coffee." Without waiting for permission, Savannah walked into the room.

A moment later, Carter followed. Fresh flowers bloomed in vases on the windowsill and someone had taken the time to fill the bulletin board on the wall with photographs of the family.

Savannah pressed her fingers over her lips when she saw Belle Colby for the first time.

Ribbons of copper hair spilled over the pillow, framing the woman's delicate porcelain features. Belle's eyes were closed, but Savannah just knew they would be the same shade of brown as Maddie's and Violet's.

Carter released a ragged breath. "Maddie… She looks just like her."

Savannah swallowed hard, trying to dislodge the lump that had formed in her throat.

What had Maddie thought the first time she'd seen her biological mother?

Belle moved restlessly and Savannah pulled the blanket up higher, tucking it around her shoulders. When she turned around, Carter was staring at the bulletin board. Someone had tacked a picture of Maddie and Gray alongside photographs of Violet and Jack.

"I don't understand why he did it," he said tightly.

Savannah knew Carter was talking about his father.

A soft moan from the woman in the bed brought both of them back to her side. Belle's forehead was furrowed and she tossed her head back and forth.

"Maybe I should get the nurse," Savannah whispered. "She seems agitated."

"Maddie said they talk to Belle like she can hear them," he said quietly.

Savannah's heart swelled as Carter reached out and took Belle's hand. An instinctive move meant to comfort the person who had turned his life upside down.

"It's going to be all right," he murmured.

The copper lashes fluttered in response to the husky timbre of Carter's voice. Belle's head rolled toward him. Her shallow breath took the shape of a word.

"Brian."

The color drained from Carter's face. "Did you hear that?" he said hoarsely.

"I…think so." Savannah pressed her fingers against her lips, certain her imagination had been playing tricks on her.

Carter stared up at her, his eyes dark with disbelief. "She said my dad's name."

Chapter Sixteen

"Mom *spoke?*"

Violet was suddenly there beside them, Maddie, Gray and Jack one step behind her as they rushed into the room.

Carter shook his head. "I'm not sure she—"

"Did she open her eyes?"

"What did she say?"

The questions tumbled over each other. Carter didn't know which one—or who—to answer first. But the commotion caught the attention of one of the nurses in the hallway. She poked her head in, her expression a mixture of concern and disapproval.

"Is everything all right?"

"Mom said something." Tears glistened in Violet's eyes. "Carter and Savannah heard her."

"Can you describe what happened?" The nurse moved toward the bed, her movements brisk and efficient as she began to take Belle's vitals.

Everyone was looking at Carter now, waiting.

"I'm not sure." Carter was already second-guessing what he'd heard.

Jack pinned Carter in place with a look. "What did she say?"

"It sounded like she said... Brian," he admitted.

Violet let out a startled cry and Maddie grabbed the back of the chair for support.

The nurse frowned. "Is that a name you recognize?"

"It's our dad," Violet whispered.

The room was silent as the nurse brought up Belle's chart and tapped something into the computer.

Jack finally voiced the question on everyone's mind. "Does this mean she's waking up?"

"I can't say that for certain," the nurse said cautiously. "But we'll keep a close eye on her today, and I'll bring it to the doctor's attention when he makes his rounds."

"I think I'll stay for a little while." Violet pulled a chair closer to the bed. "But the rest of you can go home if you'd like."

"I'm not going anywhere, either." Maddie brushed a strand of hair off Belle's cheek.

Gray pulled up a chair, and Jack propped a hip against the metal nightstand.

Apparently that meant they were staying, too.

Carter started for the door, prodded on by guilt.

"Are you leaving?" Maddie asked.

"It's pretty crowded in here already."

And he didn't belong. If—*when*—Belle Colby woke up, her family should be the ones at her bedside.

Carter forced himself to match his pace to Savannah's on the way to the parking lot. He opened the door for her and then slid in the driver's side. His fingers trembled as he stuck the key in the ignition.

"You didn't imagine it," Savannah said softly.

Carter's head whipped around. "Belle's own *children*—" he stumbled over the word "—have been talking to her for months. Praying for a sign that she'll come out of this and be all right. Why did it happen when *I* was there?"

"Maybe—" Savannah stopped.

He glanced at her sharply. "Maybe what?"

"You took her hand. Said her name. Maybe Belle heard your voice and thought *you* were Brian and she… responded."

"That's—" *Impossible,* Carter wanted to say. But then he remembered all the times that people had mistaken him for his father when he'd answered the telephone.

Could Savannah be right?

And had anyone else come to the same conclusion?

"She and Dad had been in their teens when they were together. They'd gone on with their lives. Why would Belle say his name?"

"Maybe there wasn't any closure," Savannah said after a moment. "She might…regret…the way things ended between them."

"Regrets." The word left a sour taste in Carter's mouth.

He had plenty of those. But did his dad have some, too? He'd married again. Had another child. Did he wish he'd stayed with Belle? Was that the reason he'd always seemed so distant? Buried himself in his work?

"You said no one knows why they split up. It could be that something forced them apart."

"Something like wondering whether Gray and Jack are really his sons?" The words slipped out before Carter could stop them.

Savannah stared at him. "What are you talking about?"

"Gray and Jack might not be my brothers."

"Of course they are. Look at Maddie and Violet."

"They resemble Belle—not my dad."

Savannah looked shaken. "That doesn't mean anything."

"Apparently Violet and Maddie met a woman in Fort Worth who claimed that her husband fathered the boys. Joe Earl and Belle went to high school together. So when it comes right down to it, they might not even be related to the girls by blood."

"I don't believe that. From everything Violet has said about her mother, Belle doesn't seem like the type of person who would have done something like that."

"It would explain why they split up," he ground out.

"Wouldn't a DNA test rule that out?"

"Gray and Jack took one while I was overseas. The results are back but they aren't ready to look at them yet. I guess they're not ready to deal with the ramifications of it."

"Or they already have," she murmured.

Carter parked the car in front of Savannah's cottage and turned to look at her. "What do you mean?"

"Maybe they decided it doesn't matter."

Savannah stared out the window.

The main house remained dark. Lights blazed from the window of the shed where Carter had discovered the truck.

It had been several hours since he'd dropped her off at the front door and she'd spent a lot of time in prayer.

There were things she might never understand about

the past, but she was determined to trust God's plan, for her and her unborn child. She thought she'd lost everything when her husband walked out, but the baby had been a gift from God. An unexpected blessing that had encouraged her to keep going. To keep trusting.

She prayed Carter would begin to trust Him, too. Understand how blessed he was to have a family who loved him.

But right now, he was alone.

Savannah grabbed her jacket and went outside.

The door was closed to hold the chill at bay but a country ballad rattled the walls, trying to escape.

Now that she was here, she was having second thoughts.

Carter hadn't sought out her company, which meant that he preferred to be alone.

Or it had become a habit.

The door opened and Carter stood there, effectively shutting off all thoughts of retreat.

"Come on in. It's cold outside."

"How did you know I was here?"

He raised an eyebrow.

"Marine. Right."

To Savannah's absolute amazement, Carter's elusive dimple surfaced, giving her the courage to venture inside.

"Did you get the truck running yet?"

"Are you familiar with the old saying 'good things come to those who wait'?"

"Uh-huh. So that means it's still broken."

"Not broken." Carter reached into the engine. "A work in progress."

Savannah reached out to pet one of the kittens,

who'd commandeered the jacket Carter had tossed on a chair.

"Did you eat supper at the main house?" Carter asked.

"No one's back yet."

Carter went still. "They're still at the convalescent home?"

"I think so."

Carter didn't say anything, but Savannah could see that he blamed himself for that.

"They're where they want to be, Carter."

And if she were completely honest, so was she.

"Can I help?"

Carter looked as surprised by Savannah's impulsive offer as she was to have made it.

"What do you know about trucks?"

"I know when you put the key in the ignition and step on the gas they're supposed to go."

"Then no, you can't help. But you *can* follow your doctor's orders." Carter yanked a chair into the light and swiped at the upholstered seat, an invitation to stay that Savannah didn't hesitate to accept.

For the next half hour, she watched him work, humming along with the radio or muttering under his breath, depending on what was going on underneath the hood.

A slow country song, as much a classic as the truck Carter was trying so hard to resuscitate, drifted from the speakers of the dusty radio parked in a corner of the shed.

The toe of Savannah's shoe tapped the dusty floor, and it caught Carter's attention.

"You're a fan?"

"Uh-huh, but I'm not sure how it happened. At the diner, Bruce either had a country music station blaring from the radio, or a football game. I tried to fight it—"

"And ended up liking both." Carter grinned.

"Exactly." Savannah couldn't resist grinning back.

"In that case—" Carter held out his hand "—would you care to dance, ma'am?"

"I can't...dance."

Savannah backed away from Carter as if he'd offered her a stick of dynamite.

"Everyone can dance." For his own sake, Carter hoped he was right.

"My balance is off. I can hardly walk a straight line anymore."

"Swaying...dancing...they're kind of the same thing, aren't they?" Carter had been teasing—until he saw the wary look return. Carter still didn't know what Rob had done to put that expression there but he wanted to do something to extinguish it. For good.

He drew Savannah into his arms and ignored her chirp of protest, surprised at how good—how right—it felt to have her there.

The top of her head grazed Carter's chin and the delicate floral scent of her shampoo reminded him of spring.

"See?" he murmured close to her ear.

She promptly stepped on his foot.

"I warned you that would happen."

Carter smiled. "What happened?"

"You'll know when the bruise shows up," she muttered. "I'm not exactly graceful anymore."

"You're beautiful." The words slipped out before Carter could stop them.

Savannah averted her gaze. "You don't have to do this, you know."

"Do what?"

"Tell me what you think I want to hear."

Is that what Rob had done? Just because they'd been good friends didn't mean that Carter was unaware of Rob's weaknesses. The guy could have sold fertilizer to a rancher.

Suddenly, Carter wanted her to see *him,* not Rob.

"I'm telling you the truth." He cupped the delicate curve of her jaw and lifted her face. Pressed a kiss against her forehead.

Savannah stared up at him, her eyes wide with shock. And something else; something that made his heart trip.

Carter's hands settled on Savannah's waist and he dipped his head, capturing her lips in a lingering kiss that she sweetly returned.

Something moved under his palm and Carter jerked back in surprise. *"What—"*

Color flooded Savannah's cheeks. "The baby is pretty active this time of the day. Sometimes I'm convinced that she's going to be a professional soccer player."

If Carter had ever questioned how Maddie and Gray could feel so...*connected*...to Belle, a woman they'd never met, he understood it now, when he felt another tiny flutter, as delicate as the brush of a butterfly's wing, against his palm.

Carter wanted to take care of *both* of them, and not because of the promise he'd made to a friend. Somewhere along the way, Savannah and the baby had become linked together in Carter's mind. And in his heart.

"Savannah—"

"Uh-oh." A teasing sparkle lit Savannah's eyes. "Why do I get the feeling that you're about to ask your question of the day?"

"What happened between you and Rob?"

Carter felt the tremor that ran through Savannah and she slipped out of his arms. He felt the chill of her retreat the moment she stepped away.

For a moment, he didn't think she was going to respond. And Carter was already regretting that he'd shattered the closeness of the moment by bringing up the past.

"I—I worked the closing shift at the diner and Rob came in one night. The other waitresses actually argued over who would get to wait on him because he was so good-looking.

"I was bussing tables that night, so I stayed out of it. Rob knocked a glass of water over and insisted that I let him help me clean it up. He told me later that he'd done it on purpose in order to meet me."

So far, that sounded like Rob, Carter thought wryly.

"He told me that he was in medical school and needed a quiet place to study."

That didn't. "Medical school?"

"To become a pediatric surgeon."

Carter frowned. "Rob never mentioned that he wanted to be a doctor."

"Because he didn't. He made it up to…impress me. Rob never even finished high school. When we met, he was working for a cleaning service. He stopped at the diner before his shift started and ordered a cup of coffee because it was all he could afford, not so he could stay awake all night studying."

"Why didn't he just tell you the truth?"

"Believe it or not, I asked Rob the same question. He didn't think I would be interested in a high school dropout so he made up all these stories to win me over." Her voice quivered with emotion. "I didn't ask for details, I just—"

"Trusted him."

Savannah nodded. "My grandmother was gone and I didn't have any family. It was easy to ignore the red flags and let Rob sweep me off my feet. He said if we loved each other, there was no reason to wait to get married." She swallowed hard. "Looking back, I think he was afraid I would find out the truth and leave—but he left *me,* a week after we got married. We had a huge argument. He said that marrying me had been a…mistake."

None of this lined up with the guy Carter had known.

"Is that why you didn't tell Rob about the baby?"

Savannah flinched. "I didn't know I was pregnant right away. I thought the symptoms, what I was feeling, was caused by…stress. When I finally went to the doctor, I was already four months along. I sent Rob an email, asking him to c-call me, but it was too late."

Carter did the math and released a ragged breath.

Would it have made a difference, if his friend had known about the baby? Would Rob have taken steps to reconcile with Savannah?

"I wanted to work things out," Savannah went on in a low voice. "I was hoping that when Rob found out

I was pregnant, it might make a difference. That he would give our marriage another chance."

Carter felt as if he'd just been sucker punched.

"You would have taken him back?"

"I may have rushed into getting married, but I took the vows seriously." Savannah searched his face. "You still don't believe me, do you?"

She pivoted away from him and walked out the door.

Carter let her go.

Because he was the one who should have died when the convoy was attacked.

Rob hadn't been given another chance.

But for some reason, *he* had.

If only Carter knew what he was supposed to do with it.

Chapter Seventeen

"Mail call." Violet breezed into the kitchen where Savannah sat at the breakfast counter, frosting a cake for the harvest dinner. With a little coaxing, Lupita had agreed to let her help out and this was the only job the housekeeper decided wouldn't be too taxing.

"The house is pretty quiet today. Where is everyone?" Violet hopped onto the stool next to Savannah and eyed the bowl of cream cheese frosting. "That looks yummy."

"Carrot cake. Lupita made three of them for tonight."

"I suppose Maddie isn't home from work yet, is she?"

"Not yet."

"This one goes to the bottom of the pile then." Violet sifted through the stack of envelopes. "Carter?"

The knife Savannah had been holding almost slipped out of her hand. "N-no."

"He must be helping Ty again today. I know he wants to feel useful, but I'm beginning to think we're taking advantage of him." She furrowed her brow. "I haven't seen much of him the past few days so he must have found something to keep himself busy."

Or else, Savannah thought, Carter was avoiding her. It was a little hard to tell, given the fact that she'd been avoiding *him*.

But keeping her distance hadn't stopped Savannah from thinking about the kiss they'd shared.

She ducked her head, hoping Violet wouldn't notice the color stealing into her cheeks.

Violet surreptitiously swiped her finger around the rim of the bowl. "Sadie stopped by the produce stand this morning and said you're planning to meet her at the church."

"She has some last-minute prep work for the harvest dinner." And Carter wasn't the only one who wanted to feel useful. "Making the stuffing. Getting the turkeys in the oven—"

"Peeling the hundred pounds of potatoes I donated." Violet grinned. "Keira and I signed on to set up the tables, so we'll swing by later this afternoon. Gray picked up Elise and Cory and they're on the way to Grasslands as we speak."

"What about Landon?" Savannah teased.

"He had a project to finish up, but he'll be here, too."

Savannah wasn't surprised to hear that everyone had adjusted their schedules so they could help with the dinner. Both the community and the congregation had rallied around the family over the past few months and the event provided a way for them to give back.

"Something smells good." Jack wandered into the kitchen, looking every inch the cowboy in a canvas work coat, faded jeans and leather boots.

"Carrot cake." Violet pushed the bowl of frosting toward him.

Jack reached for it, spotted the mail on the counter and flicked a questioning look at his sister.

"Nothing," Violet said gently. "Darcy got a card from her grandparents and there's a letter for Carter. Looks kind of official."

Jack nodded. "Gray mentioned something about him being nominated for a medal."

"A medal?"

Two pairs of brown eyes cut to Savannah and she realized she'd said it out loud.

"The Silver Star. Apparently Carter saved three men during an ambush a few months ago, one of them a high-ranking officer who was visiting the base. He risked his life to get them to safety."

"I can't believe he didn't tell us that," Violet murmured. "That's quite an honor."

"An honor Carter doesn't think he deserves, according to Gray."

"Why—"

Savannah saw Jack shake his head and Violet lapsed into silence.

That's when she knew.

The ambush they were talking about…it had to be the one that claimed Rob's life.

"Excuse me." Savannah slid off the stool and felt her knees wobble. "Sadie's waiting. I should probably go."

Violet caught her hand and squeezed it.

"I'm sorry, Savannah. I wasn't thinking." Violet bit her lip. "I didn't mean to remind you of something so painful."

"I know. And you *should* be proud of Carter. He's a hero."

He always does the right thing, Maddie had said.

Risking his life for a fellow soldier.

Or keeping a promise to the one he hadn't been able to save.

Sadie was already stationed at the sink when Savannah arrived at the church.

"You should have told me you'd be here early."

"I had some extra time so I thought I might as well get to work." Sadie nodded in the direction of an enormous plastic bucket.

Violet's potatoes.

Savannah grabbed an apron from the hook near the door and tied it around what remained of her waist.

The side door of the kitchen swung open and a teenage boy with shaggy black hair prowled in.

"What do you need, Jairo?" Sadie asked calmly.

"Is there anything to drink?"

"Lemonade in the fridge." Sadie gave him an indulgent smile. "And if you promise not to track in any more dirt, I'll throw in some of these cookies."

"Deal." Jairo flashed a boyish grin at odds with his tough exterior and tiptoed across the kitchen floor.

"How is it going out there?" Sadie began to pile cookies on a plate.

"We're working on the brakes right now. Carter has to order a part, but he thinks it will be here by the end of the week."

The potato Savannah had been peeling slipped out of her hand and landed in the sink with a thud. "Carter *Wallace?*"

"*Sí.* He's helping us." Jairo snagged a cookie from the plate, dodging Sadie's playful slap to the back of his hand. "Gotta go. They're waiting for me."

After Jairo left the kitchen with the refreshments, Savannah tried to wrap her mind around the fact that Carter was here. At the church.

Sadie didn't seem to notice how flustered she was. "Jeb…" The receptionist caught herself. "*Pastor* Jeb said that Carter Wallace donated an old truck to Teen Scene so the boys will have something to keep them busy after school."

"An old truck?"

"It's an antique, I guess. I can't remember what he said it was."

"A '67 Chevy."

Sadie's eyes widened. "That's right. Have you seen it?"

Savannah had not only seen it, she'd seen the look on Carter's face when he'd discovered it in the shed. And yet he'd donated it to the church. Volunteered to help the boys fix it up.

"You don't mind running a plate of sandwiches out there, do you? I've seen the way those boys eat and they're going to need more than a handful of cookies to tide them over until the dinner tonight." Sadie handed her a platter.

"I—" Savannah tried to come up with a reasonable excuse to decline.

"Go on." Sadie gave her a gentle nudge. "The setup crew will be here in a few minutes so I have to be here to tell them what to do."

Savannah somehow found herself on the other side of the door.

Her steps slowed as she spotted Carter, surrounded by a pack of boys who appeared to be listening intently to his instructions.

In a camouflage jacket and loose-fitting jeans the faded blue of an April sky, Carter looked confident and in control.

And way too appealing.

Carter handed Jairo a tool and the boy beamed as if he'd been given a medal.

A Silver Star...doesn't think he deserves it.

Jack's words cycled through Savannah's mind again and she suddenly realized why.

Carter blamed himself for Rob's death.

Savannah stumbled, wondering why it hadn't occurred to her before. But she knew without a doubt that Carter would have done everything possible to save Rob. The fact he'd put his own life at risk to save the other soldiers showed the kind of man he was.

The kind of man it would be all too easy to fall in love with.

"Food!"

Carter had just shimmied under the truck when he heard a muffled cheer and the clatter of tools hitting the ground around him.

It appeared he was going to have to lecture the kids on their priorities. Because they'd just abandoned an icon for an afternoon snack.

Sadie must have taken pity on them.

Out of the corner of his eye, he saw a dozen pairs of size eleven tennis shoes…and one pair of dainty blue ones.

Savannah.

Carter jerked. His forehead connected with the undercarriage and he growled.

"Are you all right?" Savannah was on her knees, peering under the vehicle.

"I'm fine." At least he would be. Once the spots in front of his eyes went away.

"I don't believe you. Your face is all scrunched up like you're in pain."

"Marines don't feel pain." He pulled in a breath. "And we don't...*scrunch*."

"You're bleeding."

That got the attention of the boys, who momentarily abandoned their snack and hustled over for a better look.

"Cool!" Tommy breathed.

Carter felt a trickle of *something* run down his cheek.

"I'll get the first-aid kit." Savannah was already pushing to her feet.

"Don't you dare." Carter rolled out from under the vehicle and pressed the hem of his shirt to his temple.

"You might have a concussion."

"I don't have a—" Carter's breath snagged in his throat as Savannah stood on her tiptoes to examine the tiny scratch on his forehead.

"It's not deep," she murmured.

Carter was close enough to see the lavender shadows beneath her eyes.

Close enough to kiss her again.

His gaze dropped to the full curve of her bow-shaped lips and he swayed a little.

Maybe he *did* have a concussion. Or maybe his subconscious was reminding him how right she'd felt in his arms.

Savannah's hands reached out to steady him and the contact sent another jolt of awareness rocketing through his veins.

He took a step backward to put some distance between them.

"You look tired," he said bluntly. "I think you should be on the sofa with your feet up, reading a book."

"Really?" Savannah crossed her arms. "And I think you should be at the clinic. This cut might need stitches."

The boys, who had drifted away, perked up their ears at that.

"I don't need—" Wait a second. "You're doing this on purpose."

"Doing what on purpose?"

"*Fussing* over me."

"Fussing?" Savannah blinked, as innocent as one of Darcy's kittens.

"Giving me a taste of my own medicine, so to speak." Carter's eyes narrowed. "You are under no obligation to worry about me. But I—" He stopped.

"Have an *obligation* to worry about me."

Carter tried not to let Savannah see how the words affected him.

How *she* affected him.

Over the past two weeks, the promise he'd made to Rob had undergone a subtle change. Now, instead of looking out for her, Carter looked forward to spending time *with* her.

Which was why he'd tried to put some distance between them the past few days. A plan that had backfired. Just because he hadn't seen much of Savannah didn't mean he'd stopped thinking about her.

Or the way she'd returned his kiss.

The one he'd had no business initiating. The one he had no business repeating.

"I told you before that I'm not your responsibility," Savannah said slowly. "But here's my promise to you—I'll be leaving soon, and you won't have to worry about me anymore."

Carter didn't miss the irony. The government wanted to give him an award for bravery but he was afraid to tell Savannah the truth.

He wanted her to stay.

Chapter Eighteen

The church kitchen was bustling with activity by the time Savannah returned.

Praise music played in the background, a sweet accompaniment to the chatter of conversation as everyone set to work. Maddie and Violet were working in tandem, chopping up fresh vegetables for the teenage girls who were making up the trays.

The phone began to ring and Elise reached for it. "Grasslands Community Church." She put her hand over the mouthpiece. "Does anyone know where Sadie went?"

Kiera glanced up. "I saw her a few minutes ago. She said she was going to look through the storage closet and round up the centerpieces for the tables."

"Sally has a question about the pies."

"I'll find her," Savannah offered. It would give her a few minutes to collect herself.

The unexpected encounter with Carter had left her shaken.

Savannah didn't like secrets—but realizing she'd fallen in love with a man who only saw her as his best friend's widow wasn't one she could share with the women gathered together in the kitchen.

Savannah heard voices down the hall as she rounded the corner.

Pastor Jeb and Sadie. They stood at the end of the hall and Savannah started in that direction. She saw Jeb touch Sadie's arm. With an anguished cry, Sadie jerked away from him and fled down the hall.

Right toward Savannah.

"Sadie! Wait!"

But the other woman streaked past her, tears streaming down her cheeks.

Jeb started after her but Savannah blocked his path. "What's going on?" In spite of what she'd just witnessed, Savannah couldn't believe that Jeb was capable of a harsh word.

"I didn't mean to upset her." Jeb winced when they heard a door slam. He looked discouraged. Defeated.

Two emotions that Savannah wouldn't have expected him to display, either.

"Was it bad news?" she asked cautiously. She didn't want to pry, but she was concerned about her new friend.

Jeb's lips twisted. "I guess so," he muttered.

Savannah didn't understand the cryptic comment. "I'll find Sadie and make sure she's all right."

Jeb scrubbed a hand across his jaw. "I guess that would be best, under the circumstances."

What circumstances? Savannah wanted to know. But she gave the pastor's arm a reassuring pat. "Can you let Maddie and Violet know I'll be back in a few minutes?"

"Sure." Jeb's gaze strayed to the door again. "Thanks, Savannah."

She had a hunch she knew where Sadie would go. Sure enough, she stepped out the back door of the church and spotted her sitting on a bench under one of the trees in the prayer garden.

"Sadie?"

Sadie's head jerked up and she rose to her feet, poised to flee again. The panic in her eyes subsided a little when she saw Savannah approaching.

"I'm sorry I ignored you." Sadie's voice wobbled. "I just needed…some air."

"No apology's necessary." Savannah drew her back down to the bench. "What did Pastor Jeb say to upset you?"

A sniffle followed the question. Sadie twisted her fingers together in her lap. "The dinner… Pastor Jeb asked me to go."

Savannah frowned. "The harvest dinner?"

Sadie bobbed her head.

"Of course you'll be there. Why would he ask you that?"

"He—" Another sniffle. "Asked me to go *with* him."

"Like a…date?"

"Yes!" Sadie wailed.

It was all Savannah could do to wrestle back a smile, but the anguished look on Sadie's face told her that this wasn't the time to tease.

"He likes you," she said cautiously. "Isn't that a good thing?"

"It's *terrible*." Sadie's shoulders wilted. "I didn't lead Jeb on. I have no idea why he would be—"

"Attracted to you?" Savannah pulled a clean tissue from her apron pocket and handed it to the other woman.

"Yes. I mean, just…*look* at me."

"I am." Savannah smiled now. "You care about people. You're pretty and smart and sweet and kind—"

"I'm none of those things." Sadie's voice barely broke a whisper but the hint of steel beneath the words told Savannah that she believed it. "I've been living a lie. I'm not who people think I am. I don't deserve a man like Jeb." She closed her eyes. "I don't deserve *any* of this."

"Sadie, that's not true. Didn't you tell me that God brought you to Grasslands for a reason?"

"Yes, but not *this* one." Sadie lurched to her feet. "I have to go. Do you mind handling the rest of the dinner preparations without me?"

"Not at all, but—" Savannah didn't have an opportunity to finish the sentence. Sadie was already running toward the parking lot and something told Savannah to let her go this time.

God, I have no idea what's going on with Sadie, but You do. Comfort her. Remind her that You love her.

Keira was just taking a pie out of the oven when Savannah returned. "Did you find Sadie?"

All she could do was nod.

"She left."

"Left?" Maddie echoed.

Savannah wasn't sure how much to say. "Pastor Jeb asked her to go the harvest dinner tonight—as his date."

A chorus of cheers rose from the women gathered around her.

Violet grinned. "It's about time! I knew they were perfect for each other."

"Did she leave early so she could get ready?" Elise asked.

"Maybe she's going to buy a new outfit." Maddie clapped her hands together.

"I think she turned him down," Savannah told them.

Everyone stopped talking and looked at her.

"I don't believe it." Violet smacked a palm against her forehead. "It's taken Jeb months to gather the courage to ask Sadie out."

"We all know she's crazy about him, too," Elise added. "Why would she do that?"

Savannah didn't want to break a confidence, but she was concerned about Sadie. Briefly, she relayed the conversation they'd had in the prayer garden.

"Why would she think that she doesn't deserve everyone's respect? Or Jeb's attention?" Kiera asked. "Sadie is amazing. Everyone loves her."

"We've been trying to get her to see that for months," Maddie said with a sigh.

Savannah knew it wasn't simply a case of low self-esteem. The pain in Sadie's eyes had been real. Deep. She had the feeling it wasn't that Sadie didn't care about Jeb. For some reason, she didn't want him to care about *her*.

"Did she go home?"

"I'm not sure—but she asked if we could handle the dinner preparations without her."

"That doesn't sound good." Violet reached for her purse. "Sadie has poured her heart and soul into this event the last few weeks. Maybe someone should make sure she's all right."

"I'll tell the kitchen crew to keep working." Maddie disappeared through the doorway.

"I'm coming with you." Violet started after her.

"I can stay here and supervise," Savannah offered. "I know what needs to be done."

Violet cast a grateful look over her shoulder. "We'll be back in a flash."

"With Sadie," Keira added.

Savannah, remembering the tortured expression on Sadie's face, could only pray she was right.

"You're pacing."

"I'm not—" Carter stopped, midpace. "I thought you said that Savannah was going to the harvest dinner. Where is she?"

"Maddie went to the cottage to check on her a few minutes ago." Violet slipped her coat on.

"She seemed quiet when she got back this afternoon." Carter was afraid that was his fault.

"She's probably worried about Sadie." A frown creased Violet's forehead. "We all are. It isn't like her to disappear like that. Especially with the dinner this evening."

Even though Carter didn't know the church secretary very well, from the positive comments he'd heard people make about her, he had to agree.

"Savannah—" Maddie rounded the corner and came up short when she saw Carter.

"What about Savannah?" he demanded when it became clear she wasn't going to finish the sentence.

His sister glanced at Violet. "It's just girl talk."

"But she's all right?" he pressed.

"She's fine."

Carter wasn't convinced. "I need more intel."

Maddie rolled her eyes. "She's fine...physically."

Okay. Carter released the breath he'd been holding. "What else is there?"

"Do we have to spell it out for him?" Violet looked at Maddie.

"It looks that way."

"She doesn't feel attractive," Violet said.

"And she only has one dress."

"Correct me if I'm wrong, but isn't that enough? I mean, you can only wear one at a time, right?"

"It's her little black dress," Maddie said, as if that should mean something.

It didn't. "So?"

"So, Savannah doesn't think she's...little...anymore."

"She doesn't feel like it's festive enough for the dinner tonight," Violet added. "None of us can lend her anything of ours because she's in maternity clothes."

Carter locked on a single word. "Festive?"

Maddie looked up at the ceiling, as if asking for divine help. "How to explain this in a way that a guy would understand?"

Violet nibbled on her thumbnail.

"I know." She brightened. "Chrome."

"Chrome?" Maddie burst out laughing.

"Chrome," Carter repeated thoughtfully.

"Uh-huh. And...detailing."

Now he got it.

"Give me five minutes."

Savannah heard the honk of a horn in the driveway. A final boarding call that she ignored, hoping that Maddie and Violet would give up and go to the harvest dinner without her.

The knock on the door a moment later told her that they hadn't.

She pushed to her feet and drew the crocheted afghan around her shoulders like a cape. It was the only thing that fit.

"You are in a mood," Savannah muttered on her way to the door.

It swung open before she reached it and Carter stood there, his broad shoulders blocking her view of the driveway. Just the sight of him sent her heart into a freefall.

"Ready to go?"

Maddie and Violet had obviously called for reinforcements.

"I...decided to stay here tonight."

Carter's gaze lit on the afghan and then traveled down the length of her black dress before pausing to linger on her bare feet.

"Are you feeling all right?"

The genuine concern Savannah saw in his eyes made her feel better. And worse.

He was checking up on her again. Performing the duty he'd been assigned.

Frustration surged through her. She wanted Carter to let her in, to share his thoughts and hopes and fears. To seek out her company and spend time with her, not out of obligation but out of...love.

Because she'd fallen in love with *him.*

How had it happened? *When* had it happened?

And what was she supposed to do now?

"Savannah?"

Carter's husky voice filtered through her panic.

"Sorry. I'm—" *Totally in love with you.* "—just a little tired, I guess."

It was the wrong thing to say.

"Fine. We'll put in a movie."

"What?" The word came out in a squeak.

"If you're not going, neither am I."

He wasn't playing fair, Savannah thought. Carter should be with his family tonight and she didn't want to be the reason he stayed behind.

"Fine. I'll go." The words rolled out on a sigh. "I'm shaped like a pumpkin, so at least I'll blend in with the harvest decorations."

Carter's low laugh rumbled through her.

"That's right—I have something for you." He dipped his hand into his jacket pocket and pulled out a long swatch of green silk.

"It's gorgeous." Savannah touched the shimmering fabric in wonder. Maddie had probably worn it to some fancy event when she'd worked at *Texas Today.* "But I can't—" Her voice cracked as Carter tugged the yellow afghan off her shoulders and replaced it with the scarf, his large hands surprisingly gentle as he looped it around her neck.

"It matches your eyes." He nudged her toward the antique oval mirror hanging on the wall by the door. "Look."

Savannah looked. Not at the scarf or even her own reflection—but at the man standing beside her. Tall. Strong. If she took a half step backward, her head would fit perfectly in the cradle of his shoulder….

Their eyes met in the mirror.

"Did you forget what I told you a few nights ago?" he asked quietly.

Savannah hadn't forgotten anything. Not the way he'd drawn her into his arms for a slow dance. Not the kiss they'd shared.

But she remained silent, afraid that her heart would speak out of turn.

"I said you were beautiful."

"You also said the truck was pretty."

Carter grinned and glanced down, settling his hand on the curve of her waist, in the exact spot where the baby had kicked a moment ago. "Your mama can be a stubborn woman, can't she?"

Carter realized what he'd done when he saw the stunned look in Savannah's eyes.

Great. Now he was blushing like one of the teenage boys who'd been helping him fix the truck. If the guys in his unit could see him now he'd never hear the end of it.

"Don't you ever talk to the baby?" He shoved his hands in his pockets. To keep them out of trouble.

"All the time, but—"

Savannah stopped but the word hung in the air between them. Reminding Carter that he didn't have the right to touch her. To hold her.

Reminding him that she—and her baby—didn't belong to him.

Chapter Nineteen

"This was a wonderful idea." An elderly gentleman smiled at Savannah as he reached for a glass of apple cider on the buffet table. "I hope the church puts on a dinner like this next year."

"I think we—*they*—will. I already heard people talking about it," Savannah said.

"Turn on the news in the morning and you feel like crawling right back in bed. We need to take some time and remember the good things that God has done." He punctuated the statement with a decisive tap of his walking cane against the floor.

"I love the scarf," Violet whispered as she picked up an empty tray.

"It was sweet of Maddie to let me borrow it tonight."

"It's not Maddie's scarf."

"Then who does it belong to?"

Violet grinned. "Maybe someone who thinks it matches your eyes?"

It matches your eyes.

Savannah sucked in a breath.

"Carter?" She was almost afraid to believe that Violet was telling her the truth—that the scarf had been a gift from him. Or what it meant.

"We might have mentioned that you were going to skip the harvest dinner tonight because you felt a little blue. Or orange, as the case may be. We weren't sure how to convince you, so Carter took matters into his own hands."

Of course he had. Because Carter *fixed* things.

Discouragement crept in, casting a shadow over the joy that had initially blossomed in her heart.

And it explained why he hadn't spoken to her since he'd arrived at the church. He'd convinced her to attend the dinner.

"I better start washing some of these dishes." Violet darted back into the kitchen.

"Savannah?" Maddie tapped her on the shoulder. "Can you tell Elise it's time to serve the pie?"

"Sure." She wiped her hands on her apron and ducked into the kitchen. Volunteers darted back and forth but there was still no sign of Sadie.

Savannah couldn't believe she hadn't shown up.

Neither, it seemed, could Pastor Jeb. He'd poked his head in the kitchen at least a dozen times in the last hour, his worried gaze scanning the faces of the volunteers.

Elise blew a spiral of dark hair off her forehead. "I heard! We're getting the trays ready now."

Savannah walked out of the kitchen, careful not to let her gaze drift in Carter's direction. He sat at a table with some of the boys who had helped him work on the truck that afternoon. They hadn't spoken, but several times over the course of the evening Savannah had felt him watching her.

"If I could have everyone's attention for a moment, please."

Conversation instantly subsided to a hushed whisper as Pastor Jeb rose to his feet and faced the people gathered in the fellowship hall.

"I would like to thank everyone for coming to the harvest dinner this evening. I didn't plan on preaching tonight, but with Thanksgiving less than a week away, I would like to take a minute to share some of the things we can be thankful for. I receive dozens of emails and telephone calls asking for prayer, and I think it's important that we take a moment to celebrate the way God answered them."

Savannah didn't recognize many of the names and situations that Jeb talked about, but she saw people nod at each other and smile.

"The entire congregation prayed that God would provide a secretary for the church and He brought Sadie Johnson here." A long pause followed and across the room, Savannah saw Violet look at Maddie and shake her head.

The pastor's gaze shifted to the long table where Jack and Gray had assumed responsibility for Darcy and Cory while the women helped in the kitchen.

"Belle Colby is alive after an accident last summer and is in the care of gifted physicians and her loving family. Ty Garland and his daughter, Darcy, were recently reunited. Keira Wolfe recovered from a car accident and her memory has come back.... Carter Wallace is safely back with us after his tour in Afghanistan.

"I'm sure that each of you can add something of your own to this list tonight." Jeb smiled. "And if you can't think of anything, well, all you have to do is look at the people around you. Will you bow your heads and join me in prayer?"

When Savannah opened her eyes, Carter was gone.

"Do you hear that?"

Savannah glanced up from the stack of thank-you cards she'd been helping Violet address. She tipped her head. "Darcy…singing?"

"Someone sounds happy to have a few days off from school." Violet sealed an envelope and added it to the growing pile.

Violet had asked for Savannah's help writing thank-you notes that afternoon. Belle not only received get-well cards on a regular basis, but the people in the community and surrounding area often sent flowers or small gifts to Ranchland Manor.

Everyone, Savannah thought wryly, was getting quite creative at finding things that she could do while sitting down!

"I'm hungry!" Darcy's announcement made its way to the kitchen a few seconds before she did.

"Lupita made molasses cookies. Help yourself, sweetie."

"I don't have school until next Monday." Darcy twirled her way to the plate of cookies cooling on a rack near the oven. "That means I can go riding and play with the kittens and feed the chickens every morning."

It also meant that Brian Wallace should be returning in less than forty-eight hours.

"Hi." Maddie trudged into the kitchen.

"What's wrong?" Violet, tuned in to her twin's mood, half rose to her feet.

"Pastor Jeb left another message on my voice mail."

Violet lowered her voice a notch. "Sadie still hasn't shown up for work?"

"No, and I drove by her house after I picked up Darcy from school. The lights were on, so I'm guessing that she's there, but she won't come to the door or answer the phone."

"I know that Gray suggested we give Sadie some space, but I'm worried about her," Violet murmured. "She hasn't left her house since the harvest dinner."

"That was four days ago." Maddie sank into a chair across the table from Savannah and set the mail down. "You two look busy."

"I got behind on the thank-you notes."

"That reminds me..." Maddie turned to Darcy. "What did you do with the mail, sweetheart?"

"It's in my backpack." Darcy wiggled out of the straps and handed it to Maddie.

"This one is for you, Savannah."

"Me?" Savannah glanced at the return address on the plain manila envelope and felt her heart drop to her toes. Something must have shown on her face because Maddie and Violet were at her side in an instant.

"Take a breath," Violet commanded. "Who is it from?"

Savannah pressed a hand against her stomach but that didn't stop it from churning.

"I'll be back in a few minutes."

"Are you sure?" Maddie's forehead creased. "You don't have a speck of color in your face, Savannah. Maybe you should stay here—"

"I'll be fine," Savannah whispered. She moved toward the door on autopilot. By the time she reached the cottage, her hands were shaking so badly, she could barely tear open the envelope.

Inside the larger envelope, a handwritten note was clipped to a smaller one.

Dear Mrs. Blackmore,
This letter was discovered after your husband's personal effects were shipped back to Dallas. Please forgive the delay, but it took some time to find out where you were living.

The signature was a name Savannah didn't recognize. But she did recognize the handwriting on the outside of the smaller envelope. It was Rob's.

Dear Savannah,
If you are reading this letter, it means I finally got up enough courage to send it. I want you to know how sorry I am for leaving the way I did. It wasn't that I couldn't live with you—it was because I couldn't live with myself. I'd lied to you and destroyed your trust. I was angry with myself and with God and I didn't think I deserved a second chance with either of you.

Dozens of times, I imagined coming home to you—praying that you would forgive me. But lately, I've started to wonder what would happen if I didn't come home. How would you know that I changed? That I recently gave my life to God? I think about you all the time and imagine what our life would look like if I had done things differently. I hope you find it in your heart to for-

give me. I've made a lot of mistakes, but asking you to marry me wasn't one of them.

I hope someday I can make up for the pain I caused.

Love,

Rob.

A tear slipped down Savannah's cheek and she dashed it away with the back of her hand as the words sank in.

Everything Rob had told Carter was the way he *wanted* things to be.

She left the letter on the table and went to find him.

Maddie had said he'd been tinkering with some of the farm equipment so she veered toward the barn.

She heard Jack's low familiar drawl through the open door.

"A Lieutenant Mitchell called a little while ago. He said he's been trying to get in touch with you."

"He's been encouraging me to enlist again."

Savannah's breath tangled in her lungs and she stopped just outside the door of the barn.

"I didn't realize it was something that you've been considering. Gray and Maddie never mentioned that you planned to make the military your career."

In the short silence that followed, Savannah realized she was holding her breath.

"I'm thinking about it," Carter said slowly.

"Have you told…the rest of the family?"

"I'm not used to checking in with anyone. But no, I haven't said anything yet. I'm waiting until I know that Dad's okay."

"Ever think of staying here?"

"In Grasslands?"

If Savannah had entertained a crazy notion that Carter was as taken with the area as she was, it died a sudden death when she heard the incredulous note in his voice.

"Hey, I know it's not Fort Worth, but you have to admit, we've got a lot to offer. If a man knows what he wants," Jack added.

"And a man can do a lot of damage if he doesn't," Carter finally said.

Savannah didn't wait to hear Jack's response. It didn't matter. What mattered was that Carter didn't want a ready-made family.

He didn't want *her.*

Carter couldn't believe he was spilling his guts to Jack Colby of all people.

"You're talking about Savannah."

"She's already been hurt enough. I don't have anything to offer her and the baby."

"I guess that depends on what she wants, doesn't it?"

"I want to protect her, not cause any more pain. She's been through enough the past few months."

"Convenient, isn't it?"

"What?"

"When a guy says he wants to protect someone, he's usually protecting himself."

Carter opened his mouth to deny it—

"Don't bother. Been there, done that and I was miserable." Jack tossed the reins at him. "Here."

"You want me to put your horse away?" Carter automatically reached out and caught hold of them.

"I want you to ride him. It'll clear your head."

"There's nothing wrong with my head." It was his heart that was causing the problems.

Jack folded his arms across his chest. "You've been headed for a showdown since you got here. This is probably as good a time as any."

"A showdown?" Carter frowned. "With Savannah?"

"With God," Jack said simply. "I think it's time you stopped avoiding Him and had a long talk. I had to do the same thing a few months ago. Let go of the guilt and the anger. It's like holding on to a hot iron. The longer you do it, the more it changes you."

Carter's gut rolled over. "Guilt?"

"It's eating you up. Believe me, I recognize the symptoms." Jack met his gaze evenly. "I blamed myself for Mom's accident for months. Until Keira made me see things differently. Go on now. I have a feeling that you and God have a lot to get straightened out."

Tiger nickered and Carter scowled at the animal. "You're only on his side because he's the one who gives you oats."

"He also knows I'm right."

Carter set his heel in the stirrup and swung over the stallion's broad back.

"You've got a home here at the Colby Ranch if you want one. As far as I'm concerned, we're family."

Carter's throat tightened and he nodded curtly.

"Come on, Tiger. Let's go for a ride."

The ranch was a speck in the distance when Tiger finally downshifted from a canter to a slow walk, but it wasn't as easy for Carter.

He'd been tied up in knots since he'd returned to Texas.

If he were completely honest with himself, he knew

it went farther back than a few weeks. He'd been angry with God…as long as he'd been angry with his father. It had burned deep, like that branding iron Jack had mentioned. Maybe it had already changed him.

I'm sorry, Lord. Sorry for trying to do all this on my own. For not seeking Your will and listening to Your voice. I have no idea what's going to happen in the future, but I know You're with me. I want to stick to Your path now.

And he wanted Savannah by his side.

Carter patted the horse's neck and tugged on the reins, feeling as if a weight had been lifted from his shoulders.

"Come on, Tiger, it's time to go home."

As he bent down to unlatch the gate, he saw Maddie standing by the corral, jumping up and down and waving both arms.

He waved back and loosened the reins, permission for Tiger to break into a canter as they reached the barn.

But one look at his sister's face chilled his blood.

"What's wrong?"

"You have to come to Grasslands Medical with me," Maddie choked out.

"Is Belle all right?" Carter gently took hold of her hands. "Did something happen?"

"It's not Mom." Tears filled Maddie's eyes. "It's Savannah."

Chapter Twenty

"What happened?"

Concern distilled to fear, causing Carter's blood to pump sluggishly through his veins. He was already unbuckling the girth but couldn't get his fingers to work properly.

Ty emerged from one of the outbuildings. "Go on, Carter. I'll take care of him."

Maddie struggled to match Carter's pace as he strode toward the car. "Savannah got a letter in the mail. Violet and I could tell she was upset, but she took it back to the cottage to read. I got worried when she didn't come back and went to check on her.

"She was lying on the sofa and at first I thought she was taking a nap, but she'd fainted or something. Jack and Violet drove her to the clinic to get checked out, but I thought you'd want to be with her."

"What was she doing today?" Gravel sprayed up from the tires as Carter put the truck in gear.

"Helping Violet. Savannah's been kind of quiet the past few days, but we just figured she had a lot on her mind."

Guilt burned its way through Carter. He should have bared his soul to her sooner.

When a guy says he wants to protect someone, he's usually protecting himself, Jack had said.

That's exactly what he'd been doing. He'd tried to convince himself that Savannah wouldn't be able to forgive him if she knew he hadn't been able to save Rob. That he had nothing to offer her…

"We love her, too, you know." Maddie's voice intruded on his thoughts. "She belongs here."

She belonged with him.

Carter nodded, unable to trust his voice.

The short trip into Grasslands seemed to take forever.

"Turn at the next stop sign," Maddie said.

Carter couldn't see anything that remotely resembled a hospital. When they arrived at the clinic, Carter turned to Maddie in disbelief.

"Jack brought her here?"

The clinic didn't resemble the ones he was used to seeing in the city. It looked like someone's home. But sure enough, a sign that said Grasslands Medical Clinic sprouted from the lawn.

"Don't let the outside fool you," Maddie said briskly. "Dr. Garth knows his stuff. He can treat everything from a bee sting to a fractured bone."

The receptionist looked a little surprised when they charged through the front door into the tiny waiting room.

"We're here to see Savannah Blackmore," Carter said without preamble. "My brother Jack brought her in about half an hour ago. Where is she? Is she all right?"

The receptionist frowned. "Under law, I can't release information about a patient. Are you immediate family?"

Carter sensed that the answer to the question would determine what happened next. He glanced at Maddie.

"Close friends," she said firmly. "Savannah lives with us."

"I'll check with Nurse Hamm." The receptionist slid the glass door shut and punched a number on her phone. A moment later, she turned back to Carter and Maddie. "The nurse is with another patient at the moment. You can take a seat in the waiting room."

Carter didn't budge.

"I want to see the doctor."

"He's also with another patient at the moment—"

"Another patient," Carter interrupted. "Shouldn't he be with Savannah?"

The receptionist gave him a patient look. "I believe they're waiting for some test results at the moment."

"Come on." Maddie tugged on his arm. "I'm sure it won't be long."

Sixty seconds would be too long, but Carter let her drag him to a chair in the waiting room.

"Do you want a cup of coffee?"

"I want you to cause a disturbance while I find Savannah's room."

In spite of her concern for Savannah, Maddie grinned. "I think *you're* the one causing a disturbance," she whispered. "Do you want to see Savannah or get arrested?"

"No one will arrest me." Carter crossed his arms. "Gray won't let them."

Maddie intercepted Jack as he strode into the room with Keira at his side.

"What did the doctor say?"

"They took Savannah away the minute we got here and no one will tell me anything." Jack raked a hand through his hair. "Clinic policy, I guess."

"That's what they told us, too. Family only."

"I'm open to suggestions," Carter said.

Violet and Maddie exchanged a smile and for the first time, it didn't strike fear in Carter's heart.

"Okay, what have you got?"

Savannah moved restlessly.

Someone should turn off the timer on the oven. It kept beeping....

She opened her eyes and blinked up at the fluorescent light fixture on the ceiling.

Where was she?

The sheets hissed as she struggled to sit up.

"Hey, take it easy."

Carter?

He loomed above her. Stubble shadowed his lower jaw and there were shadows under his eyes.

"You look terrible," Savannah said without thinking. "Are you all right?"

"Am I all right?" Carter tossed the words back. "I'm fine. But you sure gave us a scare."

Savannah pressed a palm against her stomach as the fog parted. The last thing she remembered was stumbling back to the cottage, feeling light-headed. "The baby—"

"Is doing fine." Carter pulled the chair closer to her bedside. "The doctor said that your blood pressure dropped and you had a dizzy spell. Maddie went to check on you and found you unconscious. Don't you remember?"

Savannah remembered reading Rob's letter.

And the conversation she'd overheard between Carter and Jack.

She looked away as a nurse came into the room.

"I'm Nurse Hamm. And you gave everyone quite a scare, young lady." She clucked her tongue. "Especially your fiancé."

Her fiancé?

Savannah looked at Carter and saw a red stain creep up his neck. She waited while Nurse Hamm took her vitals. When the woman bustled out of the room, she shot Carter a questioning look.

"It was Maddie and Violet's idea," Carter said gruffly. "Doctor Garth would only discuss your condition with a family member."

"Or a fiancé."

Carter nodded.

Savannah drew in a shaky breath. "And you picked the short straw?"

Her weak attempt at humor fell short at the expression on Carter's face. "Savannah—"

A rap on the door cut off the rest of what he'd been about to say. Doc Garth, a prematurely graying gentleman in jeans and cowboy boots, who looked as if he'd be more at home with a lariat in his hands than a stethoscope, ambled in. If the man hadn't been wearing a lab coat over his plaid, Western-style shirt, Savannah would have mistaken him for one of the cowboys that worked the Colby Ranch.

"How are you feeling, my dear?"

"A little better."

The doctor's eyes twinkled. "I'm glad to hear that, but I was asking your fiancé. He looked so pale a little while ago that Nurse Hamm considered assigning him his own room."

Savannah knew better than to take the man's words seriously. Carter was a soldier. Accustomed to remaining calm in stressful situations.

Dr. Garth flipped through the sheets of paper attached to his clipboard. "I spoke with Dr. Yardley, your primary physician, a few minutes ago. She said you're scheduled for an appointment on Monday and she wants to set up an ultrasound. A standard precaution, given the fact that it appears you had some trouble a few weeks ago. Have you been getting the rest she prescribed?"

"No, she hasn't," Carter butted in.

Savannah glared at him. "I get plenty of rest." When she wasn't thinking about Carter…

The doc looked back and forth between them and his lips twitched. "Your color seems to be coming back. That's a good sign."

"Does that mean I'm free to leave now?"

"I don't see why not." Doctor Garth scratched his signature on a piece of paper. "The nurse will be back in a few minutes to give you some instructions. And—" he leveled a finger at her "—I expect you to follow them."

"I will."

"If you're planning to stay in Grasslands, I'd like to see you in a week."

Savannah didn't look at Carter, afraid that he would see the answer in her eyes.

That was one appointment she didn't plan on keeping.

Chapter Twenty-One

Preparations for the family's Thanksgiving dinner were well under way when Carter wandered into the kitchen the following morning.

Maddie and Violet sat at the counter peeling apples while Elise, who'd arrived with Cory the evening before, was rolling out dough for a piecrust. Keira was at the table, chopping up celery and onions for the stuffing.

The room was filled with women. But none of them were the one Carter had been hoping to see.

Violet spotted him in the doorway and grinned. "Looking for someone in particular?"

He had been, but there was no way he was going to admit it. He wrestled down his frustration.

After Dr. Garth had signed the necessary paperwork and released Savannah the day before, Violet and Maddie had taken charge, clucking over her like hens with a brand-new chick.

When Maddie had finally returned to the main house, she'd pulled Carter aside and handed him an envelope.

"Savannah asked me to give this to you," Maddie had said.

Carter recognized Rob's handwriting immediately.

"If you need us, we're here, you know."

Carter had hugged his sister. "I know."

He'd gone into Belle's office and shut the door, almost afraid to read the contents of the letter that had upset Savannah.

But she'd asked Maddie to give it to him.

As Carter skimmed through the words, he understood why. Rob had asked for Savannah's forgiveness because he hadn't trusted her with the truth about his feelings.

Carter was determined not to make the same mistake.

"Hi, Uncle Carter!" Darcy ambled into the kitchen, one of the kittens nestled in the crook of her arm. She made a beeline for the cookie jar.

"I don't know, squirt." Carter shook his head. "Maddie used to scold me about eating cookies right before lunch."

Darcy stood on her tiptoes and reached into the jar. "They're not for me. I told Savannah I'd bring her some."

"You saw Savannah?"

The little girl nodded. "But I wasn't disturbing her. Promise."

Carter tried to keep a straight face. "I'm sure you weren't. Savannah likes your company and it's sweet of you to bring her some cookies. She likes those, too."

"Lupita says she's eating for two an' I don't want her to get hungry on the way home." Darcy carefully deposited several oatmeal raisin cookies in a plastic bag.

Home?

Carter's stomach clenched. "What do you mean?"

"Savannah said she hasta go back to Dallas. That's where she lives."

Everyone in the kitchen had stopped working and was staring at Darcy now.

"Did Savannah tell you that she was leaving?" Maddie shot him a quick look.

"No," Carter said tightly.

But then, he hadn't given her the opportunity. He'd planned to let Savannah rest a few more hours before showing up at her door to deliver the speech he'd been rehearsing all morning.

But if Darcy was right and Savannah *was* planning to leave, it was time to take action instead.

Carter squatted down until he and Darcy were eye to eye. "How about I deliver those cookies to Savannah?"

"You want to say goodbye before she goes home, too?"

"Nope." Carter winked at her. "I want to convince Savannah that she already *is* home."

Savannah zipped the suitcase shut and looked around the room to see if she'd forgotten anything.

The cottage felt so…empty.

But it was time to make a gracious exit. Release Carter from the promise he'd made to Rob once and for all. He needed to be with his family now—not distracted by her problems.

So why did it feel as if she were going to leave a huge chunk of her heart behind when she left?

Savannah shrugged on her jacket and grabbed the suitcase, careful not to let her gaze linger on the bouquet of yellow roses the florist had delivered to her door shortly after breakfast.

Carter's thoughtful gesture had only affirmed Savannah's decision.

Maybe it was cowardly of her to leave a note instead of saying goodbye, but she couldn't run the risk that he would see the truth in her eyes. She didn't *want* to leave.

But Savannah didn't want him to feel obligated to convince her to stay, either.

She left the key on the table and blinked back the tears that threatened to spill over as she pulled the door shut behind her.

"Going somewhere?"

Savannah's heart missed a beat when she saw Carter leaning against the side of her car.

"Dallas. I have an appointment with my doctor.... What's that?" Savannah was distracted as the sunlight glinted off the object Carter casually tossed into the air and caught again.

"A spark plug."

"I thought you got the truck running."

"I did." Carter looked smug. "This is *your* spark plug."

"My—" Savannah's mouth dropped open. "But my car won't run without that. Will it?" she added.

"No, ma'am."

Carter's lazy drawl—and his equally lazy smile—threatened to sever the last thread of her composure.

"You have to put it back. Right now." Her voice shook. "I have an appointment with Dr. Yardley—"

"Next week."

He wasn't making this any easier. "And I need to find a place to live."

"Why?"

The simple question lodged in her heart. "Tomorrow is Thanksgiving. You need to focus on your family." And she was a distraction that Carter didn't need right now. "Your dad—"

"Would love to meet you," Carter interrupted. "Everyone is expecting you to stay for Thanksgiving dinner. Why don't you stick around for a few days?"

Because it was getting harder and harder to keep her feelings to herself. Not that she could tell Carter that. If he knew how she felt about him, it would only be one more duty tying him down. Holding him back from the future God had planned for him.

"I can't," she stammered.

"Can't? Or won't?"

Savannah stiffened when Carter closed the distance between them.

"Why are you really leaving, sweetheart?"

The soft endearment broke through what was left of her defenses and the truth spilled out before Savannah could stop it.

"Because I don't want to be someone that you feel sorry for. The woman who always needs you to rescue her."

Carter didn't seem to hear her.

"I don't feel sorry for you, Savannah." He hooked a strand of hair behind her ear with a tenderness that made her heart ache. "And I *want* you to stay."

The suitcase hit the ground with a thud.

"Why?"

If Carter hadn't realized how serious the question was, he would have smiled.

"Because *you* rescued *me,*" he whispered.

"I don't understand.... I overheard you talking to Jack yesterday." Savannah's cheeks turned pink. "I didn't mean to eavesdrop. I was waiting outside the door for a chance to tell you about the letter I got... from Rob. You said you were thinking about enlisting again. That you didn't know what you...wanted."

Carter sifted through the conversation and tried not to wince.

"You should have stuck around a little longer. You would have heard the rest of the conversation."

"The rest of the conversation?"

"What you overheard...it was never about what I wanted, it was about what I thought *you* needed," Carter said quietly. "I told Jack that you've been through enough the past few months and I didn't want to cause you any more pain.

"I tried to convince myself that you and the baby deserved more than I could offer. That the best thing I could do was stand in the background and keep an eye on you. But the truth is, I'd rather be at your side." He swallowed hard. "I might not know what's going to happen down the road, but I trust that God does. He and I had a long talk and I realized something. The promise I made to Rob didn't bring us together, God did."

Tears shimmered in Savannah's eyes but there was something else there, too. Something that gave Carter the courage to continue.

"I love you, Savannah. That's why I want you to stay."

Carter *loved* her?

Maybe, Savannah thought, she should pinch herself to see if this was real. Or maybe...

She reached out and traced Carter's angular jaw

with her fingertips instead. She heard him catch his breath as he drew her into the circle of his arms.

It felt like coming home.

"I love you, too," she murmured. "But I never dreamed—" Her throat swelled shut, making it impossible to continue.

"I think both of us have been afraid to do that." Carter's arms tightened around her. "But you can trust me, Savannah. With today…and whatever happens tomorrow."

Tomorrow suddenly looked a whole lot brighter.

Carter's expression turned serious. "There is one thing we have to talk about, though."

Savannah's heart dipped. "All right."

"You have to let me teach Hope how to throw a football and change a flat tire." Mischief sparked in Carter's eyes.

She couldn't believe that God had brought this amazing man into her life.

"What if she wants to take ballet?" Savannah teased, responding in kind.

"Then I'll be sitting in the bleachers, right next to her beautiful mother, with a bouquet of roses."

Savannah felt as if her heart were going to burst.

"Agreed," she whispered.

Carter bent his head and his lips captured hers. When the kiss ended, Savannah could feel her heart racing in time with his.

"So I have a question," Carter murmured in her ear.

"I believe you only get one," Savannah said promptly.

"Will you go out with me?" Carter looked down at her, his smile a little unsteady. "On a real date?"

"That sounds…wonderful."

"I was thinking…dinner."

"When and where?"

"Tomorrow? Turkey with all the trimmings." Carter pointed to the main house. "Right over there."

"With your family?"

"Yes." Carter tipped his head. "Is that all right?"

"All right?" Savannah closed her eyes and felt the steady drum of Carter's heart against her cheek. "It sounds absolutely perfect to me."

Chapter Twenty-Two

"You were up early this morning."

Carter looked up and saw Maddie in the doorway, a cup of coffee in one hand.

"So are you."

"I had a hard time sleeping last night," she admitted. "Did you convince Savannah to spend Thanksgiving with us?"

Carter had a hard time keeping a smile from surfacing. "I think so. She'll be here in a few minutes."

"Good." Maddie released a heartfelt sigh. "We don't want any extra chairs at the table today."

She was still holding out hope their father would return.

They all were.

But now, Carter realized it was more important to see his dad's face again than to hear his explanations.

Lord, bring him back safely and we'll go from there.

Moving forward with God's help. Just the way Gray had said.

"Come on, you two." Violet shooed them toward

the dining room. "We've got a lot of last-minute things to do."

Things that kept him and Savannah apart.

Carter wanted to be alone with her, but decided he was willing to share her with his family for a few hours.

"Dinner is served!" Maddie called out.

Landon Derringer carried the turkey into the dining room and Violet lit two slim taper candles in the centerpiece.

Jack waited until everyone found a seat at the table. "Mom started a tradition when Violet and I were young. On Thanksgiving, she would choose a portion of scripture, reminding us how much we have to be thankful for. I took the liberty of carrying on the tradition this year."

Under the table, Carter felt Savannah squeeze his hand.

"'We ought always to thank God for you, brothers, and rightly so, because your faith is growing more and more, and the love every one of you has for each other is increasing.'"

Jack cleared his throat. "I think that's been happening the past five months. Our faith has grown—and so has our love for each other. Mom would say we have a lot to be thankful for today."

A murmured chorus of heartfelt *amens* followed.

"Amen," Cory chimed in. "Can we eat now?"

Gray laughed as Elise tried to shush her son. "We sure can."

Jack began to carve the turkey as the side dishes made their way around the table.

Above the hum of conversation, a car door slammed.

Maddie jumped to her feet and ran to the window, her lips forming a single word.

Dad.

A collective sigh circled the table as Maddie shook her head.

Savannah realized how desperately everyone wanted Brian Wallace to show up. To keep the promise he'd made to his family.

"Can I have another roll, Savannah?" Darcy pointed to the basket. "Before Uncle Carter eats them all?"

The comment brought a smile to everyone's face and broke through the shadow of silence that had fallen.

"Here you go." Savannah made a point to hold it out of Carter's reach as she passed it to the little girl.

Maddie smiled at her. "I'm glad that Carter talked you into staying, Savannah."

"They're gettin' married," Darcy said matter-of-factly.

Heads swiveled in their direction.

Savannah felt her cheeks begin to glow and she looked helplessly at Carter. "We aren't—"

"What makes you say that, Darcy?" Violet interrupted.

"I saw them kissing yesterday. Can I have some mashed potatoes, please?"

No one, Savannah noted, passed the mashed potatoes. She wanted to slide under the table—except that she wouldn't fit.

"If you marry Savannah, she'll be my aunt, won't she, Uncle Carter?" Darcy had obviously thought this through.

"And mine, right?" Cory wasn't going to be left out.

"That's right." Carter winked at her.

"Oh, don't blush, Savannah." Keira nudged her shoulder. "This family is getting so big, you may as well enjoy the attention while you can."

Carter took pity on her and cleared his throat. "Right now, I think the *turkey* needs some attention."

"Fine—but don't think you're off the hook, little brother," Maddie said. "We expect you to keep us in the loop."

"Whatever you say, sis," Carter muttered under his breath.

Savannah smiled despite herself.

"Not quite what you imagined when you prayed for a family, is it?" Carter murmured in her ear a few moments later.

"No," Savannah whispered back. "It's much, much better."

No one seemed in a hurry to leave the table, lingering over dessert.

Waiting.

Carter caught hold of Savannah's hand underneath the table.

"Would you like to go for a walk?"

There was a look in his eyes that made Savannah's heart skip a beat.

She nodded. "I'll help clear the table first."

"Oh, no, you won't," Violet said cheerfully. "We already assigned a cleanup crew and your name isn't on it."

Maddie made a shooing motion with her hand. "Go on. I'm sure you've got a lot to talk about. After we take care of the dishes, we're going to drive into Grasslands and visit Belle."

Savannah gave Carter a questioning look. She knew his feelings toward Violet and Jack had changed, but she wasn't sure how he felt about Belle.

"Do you mind if we delay our walk for a few hours?"

"I was thinking the same thing."

His smile took her breath away and he turned to Maddie.

"We'll come with you."

Carter followed Gray's car as it turned into the parking lot at Ranchland Manor.

The last time he'd been here, he'd heard Belle Colby say his father's name.

Savannah laid her hand on his arm. "We don't have to go inside."

"Yes, we do." Another step forward, with God's help.

Gray would be amazed to know Carter was following his advice.

The young woman at the reception desk, who looked barely out of her teens, greeted them with a bright smile. Her badge was the kind with the adhesive back and the name Taylor, embellished with several curlicues, had been neatly printed in blue marker.

"Can I help you?"

"Must be new here," Maddie murmured.

"I just started yesterday," came the cheerful response. "So far, it's going really well."

"I'm glad to hear that." Violet ducked her head to hide a smile. "We're here to see Belle Colby."

"Colby— *Oh.*" The girl's gaze swept over them and she lowered her voice a respectful notch. "You're Mrs. Colby's family?"

“That’s right.” Gray didn’t miss a beat.

For the first time, Carter didn’t feel any resentment that Gray considered Belle family.

“She’s our most popular patient today.”

Jack frowned. “Popular?”

The aide nodded. “She’s already had a visitor today.”

“Who was it?” Gray demanded. “A woman or a man?”

Taylor bit her lip. “Did I do something wrong?” she stammered. “I didn’t see a note that she couldn’t have visitors.”

“You didn’t do anything wrong,” Maddie intervened, her smile meant to temper Gray’s curt response. “It’s just that we’re not sure who it could have been, because everyone is…here.”

“Not everyone,” Jack muttered.

Carter looked at Gray. His dad knew where they were and what had happened to Belle. Was it possible he would have stopped by the convalescent home to see her first?

“Let me see.” Taylor checked the sign-in sheet. “I must have been on the phone at the time. She signed in a little after ten…. I can’t read the signature.”

She.

Carter released the breath he hadn’t realized he’d been holding.

“Can I see it?” Gray sounded more in control now but Taylor still looked nervous as she handed him the clipboard.

“I can’t make out the name, either.” He frowned. “You said it was a woman? What did she look like?”

Taylor took a step back.

“Cop voice,” Elise whispered.

"Sorry… Taylor." Gray flashed an apologetic smile. "Habit."

Taylor tipped her head. "She was short. Thin. Glasses."

"That sounds like Sadie," Savannah ventured.

"You know what a sweetheart she is," Violet said. "She was probably visiting some of the residents who don't have family and stopped in to see Mom."

Jack took Keira's hand. "Makes sense."

But it didn't erase the look of disappointment on the faces of the people gathered around the desk. Carter felt Savannah rest her head on his shoulder. Being on the receiving end of comfort was a new experience. One it would take some time to get used to.

A lifetime, if he was lucky.

Violet was peering at the clipboard. "I've seen Sadie's handwriting. It doesn't look anything like this."

"Maybe she was in a hurry," Maddie said.

"Maybe, but—"

"I was hoping to see you before my shift ended." A dark-haired nurse in lime-green scrubs and a colorful bandana emerged from the backroom.

Taylor retreated quickly. No doubt relieved to hand them over to someone else, Carter thought wryly.

"How is Mom doing?" Jack asked.

The nurse hesitated. "Belle seemed a little restless this morning," she admitted. "There've been a lot of people in and out of our facility visiting family over the past few days, so it's possible she's reacting to subtle changes in the environment. I made a note for the doctor to check on her tomorrow when he comes in, but I'm sure there's nothing to worry about."

Then why did she looked worried?

One glance at his siblings told Carter they had the same thought.

"We put out coffee and refreshments in the lounge for family members today in honor of Thanksgiving." The phone rang and the nurse reached for it. "Please help yourself."

The aroma of cinnamon scented the air as everyone made their way to Belle's room at the end of the hall. They could hear murmured conversations and laughter behind the doors.

"It's too gloomy in here." Maddie strode to the window and pulled open the drapes, flooding the room with afternoon sunlight.

"Someone fixed Mom's hair." Violet was staring down at her mother. "Do you think it was Sadie?"

Belle's thick copper hair lay in a neat braid over one shoulder. A vase of bright yellow daisies trimmed with delicate baby's breath graced the nightstand.

Jack bent down and kissed his mother on the forehead. "Hey, Mom. It's Jack. Keira and I stopped by to say hello."

"I'm here, Mom." Violet nudged her brother to the side and took Belle's hand. "Maddie and Ty and Gray and Carter are here, too."

Carter didn't feel awkward being included anymore. It felt…right.

"When you wake up, you're going to have a lot of weddings to help plan. Me and Landon are first, by the way." Violet cast a teasing glance at Maddie.

Belle's head rolled to the side and a soft moan escaped her lips.

"She seems different today," Violet murmured. "Do you think she's in pain?"

Carter put his arm around Violet's slender shoulders. "The nurse said it was normal, remember?"

She leaned against him. "That's right."

"I think we should pray for her." Jack took hold of Maddie's hand. She, in turn, took hold of Savannah's until the entire family was linked together in a circle around Belle's hospital bed.

"Lord, thank You for bringing us together. We can see that You are at work in our lives. We see Your hand in the things that have happened the past few months and because You love us, we trust You with the future. You've blessed us with so much—how can we doubt Your love?"

Carter didn't. Not anymore. Not in a million years would he have imagined that God would bring a woman like Savannah into his life.

Thank You, Father. I'm going to be the kind of husband Savannah deserves, and I'm going to raise Hope as if she were my own.

"We—" Jack's voice faltered. "Mom?"

Carter heard Savannah gasp and his eyes flew open. Maddie pressed her hand against her lips.

"What—" A second later, he understood why.

Belle's breathing had changed. The sudden silence more frightening than the soft moans they'd gotten used to hearing.

Gray turned to Elise. "Call the nurse, sweetheart," he said in a hoarse whisper.

"No." Jack's throat convulsed. "Wait."

"What's happening?" Maddie stared down at Belle, her eyes dark with rising panic. "What's wrong with her?"

"Mom?" Jack's hands closed around the metal rail,

his gaze riveted on Belle's face. "I think she's…waking up."

Maddie let out a strangled cry and Carter took a step closer to the bed.

Velvet brown eyes blinked at the faces above her.

Maddie and Violet clung to each other, unable to believe that after all these months, Belle was with them again.

"Thank You, God."

Carter wasn't sure who said the words, Gray or Jack, but it didn't matter.

He looked down at Savannah. Tears streamed down her face but she was smiling.

"Carter—"

"I know." He pulled Savannah into his arms.

No matter what happened next, they did have a lot to be thankful for.

* * * * *

SPECIAL EXCERPT FROM

Cowboy and veteran Yates Trudeau returns home to his family ranch bruised and battered and carrying a life-changing secret. When he bumps into Laurel Maxwell, the girl he left behind, she might just set him on the path to healing that his body—and his heart—so desperately needs...

Keep reading for a sneak peek at The Cowboy's Journey Home, *part of the Sundown Valley series by* New York Times *bestselling author Linda Goodnight.*

Had he really come to the woods before going to the ranch house? She had a feeling she was right and that he had. She wondered why—another habit of journalists. She needed to know everything, especially motives.

Yates's gaze seemed glued to her face, and she fought off a blush that would let him know he still affected her on some unwanted, visceral level. People say you always remember your first love. Yates had been her first and only.

She'd spent the better part of a year waiting to hear from him and another year getting over him.

Now here he was in the flesh, stirring up old memories. At least for her.

The annoying blush deepened. Laurel turned her attention toward the children and the dog. With a smiling

LIEXP0622

Justice in the center, they formed a circle of petting hands and eager chatter.

"Those aren't all your kids, are they?"

A small pain pinched inside her chest. "Sunday school class." To turn the focus away from her, she asked, "Was he really a military dog? Like a bomb or drug sniffer?"

"Explosives."

"Did something happen to him? Why'd he retire?"

Yates's face, already closed, tightened. "Stuff happens. Soldiers retire. Look, I should go. Enjoy your picnic."

With a snappy military about-face, he started to walk away.

"Yates, wait."

He paused, gazing back over his shoulder.

"After you get settled, come by the *Times* office. I'd love to interview you and the dog for the paper." She put her fingers up in air quotes. "'Hometown Hero Returns' would make a great feature."

"No interview. We're civilians now. Nothing heroic about that." Turning away, he gave a soft whistle. "Justice, come."

Before she could say more, Yates and his dog disappeared into the foliage.